I0779153

A Candle Is My Sun

By

Arthur W. Soderlund

J. S. Johnson

Publisher 2007

Soderlund, Authur William

A candle is my sun / Arthur W. Soderlund

p. cm.

ISBN 978-0-6151-5082-6

A Candle Is My Sun

By

Arthur W. Soderlund

Chapter 1

Raising his gray eyes, Anton with studied seriousness, surveyed a familiar scene; the red house and barn overlooking a cluster of out-buildings. Beyond these, snow-blanketed fields stretched in undulating waves to a hill where green spruce interposed a somber barrier against an overcast sky from whose murkiness ragged patches of spring-scurrying mist licked with dripping tendrils at the soughing trees.

For a fleeting moment his face lost the expression of determination that it had worn since his wife had agreed to his taking leave of the family in an effort to improve their circumstances. His eyes closed as an acute feeling of sadness possessed him.

While watching her husband, Marie became aware of a choking lump in her throat; and past this, she spoke in a voice holding a note of gentleness that belied the bitterness which she felt at his decision to leave, "Don't worry about us, Anton, surely we will be alright."

"Take him, mother, and keep him well; keep all of you well until I return," he instructed his wife as he gave the baby boy into her gentle hands.

Marie accepted the child from him and mechanically tucked its waving arms into the snug confines of the heavy wool shawl; then she gazed searchingly into her man's rugged face, as he squeezed them both roughly. Turning slightly, Anton whispered a word of cheer into the scarf-covered ears of his two small girls, who regarded him intently, their grave eyes expressing sadness that a limited vocabulary prevented them from voicing. Smiling, he pulled them to him making a compact group while the baby, whose arms were again uncovered, pulled strenuously at his father's mustache and accompanied the vigorous movements of its tiny hands with a babble of sounds resembling the tremulous voices of a waking brook.

"I'll carry the memory of you with me until I come back again," Anton promised as he folded his wife to him and raising her face, he clung for a time to her trembling lips.

The woman felt the warm nearness of his bulk. Her husband smelled like a combination of sweat, shaving soap, tobacco and much-worn clothing; subtly pervading her senses and stirring a multitude of memories. Her heartbeat quickened for a fleeting moment. She sighed and her eyes closed wearily, as though to shut out the finality of his leaving. When she at last opened her eyes to peer at him searchingly, a halting uncertainty brooded in their depths.

"I'll miss you so; we'll all miss you so," she whispered in a tight voice holding a suppressed note of rising hysteria. Her head bowed as a fit of trembling seized her, and she wept convulsively.

"Come now, little mother," he admonished as, smiling down on her, he placed a huge hand under her quivering chin and forced her to look at him; "you'll feel better after I send you more money than you have dreamed could be found outside of a bank. When I come home again," he promised cheerfully, "we can buy another home nearer to the city."

Marie smiled bravely, and encouraged he continued, "We may even save enough to send our children to the higher school. How would you like to see the day when your daughters are school teachers, and the boy, a doctor?"

"I don't know how I shall be able to live without you if you stay too long." Marie intoned disconsolately. "I'll count each day over and over again; nights I shall pray that God, in His infinite kindness, will watch over you wherever you may be. I'll pray that you may return to us unharmed."

"That is kind of you, my dear," Anton remarked; "I'll ..."

"Oh Anton," Marie broke in to exclaim, "I am afraid.... at night when the wind blows and a gray wolf cries for its mate, I, too, will cry for mind. Each time I see the 'lights' in the sky, I shall remember how we have stood close to each other, watching and wondering ..." She squeezed his arm fiercely. "Each night I will reach for your strong body, as I lay alone in a bed whose emptiness will mock me ..."

"Don't feel that way, Mother, I ..."

"Don't stop me, Anton; there is so much to say and such a little time in which to say it before you go." Anton looked at her pathetic face and gently shook his head.

"Why can't you stay here and share this simple life with us?" she asked plaintively.

"What will the children do when you no longer come back at the end of each month to visit them? How can they grow as they should without a father to encourage them when they falter, and properly discipline them for unruly behavior?"

"Come now, little mother," he chided, "it will not be bad as you think; you are here to love them and can make them mind as well as I. After all," he observed humorously, "there are plenty of birch branches growing in that grove behind the barn. I don't believe that with you, they will be wild," he said reassuringly; "they have good blood in them," he added in a voice brimming with pride.

While staring off over the frozen expanses of the lake with lusterless eyes, Marie shuddered at its lonely appearance and drew herself into her husband's arms. Anton's rough fingers squeezed her comfortingly.

"What good is a house to keep and children to look after, if there is no man around to smoke a pipe and talk in the evenings?" she muttered in a flat voice sounding strangely tired. After exhausting every argument in her own and the children's behalf, she had almost resigned herself to the inevitability of the circumstances. These past months of protesting had left her emotional reservoir strangely dry, as time and again, her objections had been overruled by this determined man seeking to disentangle himself from the web of frustration that hemmed him in. A bare subsistence had been his reward since the first child was born. Of what use, he had countered on numerous occasions when she had striven to change his mind; was it for him to tie himself down to a repetition of sowing, harvesting and the unremitting toil so necessary to clear the seemingly endless rocks from inhospitable ground? How could she expect him to meekly submit to an existence bordering on starvation; unless he were first given the opportunity to better himself in the land where so many of his friends had gone, and of which they had written in glowing terms? It was for the good of them all to allow his departure; there was the chance that he might find something better and he could always come back to her, after first having proved things to his own satisfaction. Then there might be peace for all of them.

"Marie, darling," Anton broke in on her musing to say.

"Yes, husband?"

"I would still like you to come and bring the children, but you have refused. We can borrow money on this farm for that purpose," he pointed out as a sweeping gesture embraced his acres. "Perhaps, after I am located over there, you may want to come," he suggested hopefully.

"Never, I insist, will I leave this country," she answered firmly; "I am too old to tear up my roots and leave my friends. Conduct such as that is for younger people who are single."

"Alright," he sighed, "I will return then; but I must hurry now," he said, "or I'll miss the train and boat. Say, I'll tell you what," he exclaimed in a voice betraying an underlying excitement, "I'll go for six-months, and if you can't stand being without me and money that I will earn, I'll return at that time. How does that sound to you?" He searched her face, and discerning her lack of interest in his proposal, his own face clouded; but he continued to cling grimly to his purpose. Grasping her by the shoulders, he stated, "Marie, if you refuse me this opportunity to better our way of living, there will never be any happiness in our home. I have wanted to go for so long that it is far too late to change my mind. When I send you money, you will feel better in regards to my absence," he added, "do you realize that I can earn enough money over there in one day to buy a pair of shoes? On the other hand, here I have to work for three days or more to gain the same amount." These words brought a smile to Marie's face, when others had failed.

"I suppose I can stand your absence for six months," she reluctantly conceded, "until then, may God bless you and keep you from all harm."

As she finished speaking and kissed him for the last time, the sun broke momentarily through the overcast sky. Anton hugged and kissed each child briefly, and picking up his valise, he turned away and walked down a path leading through the fog-enshrouded forest, where lake and trees merged in a distinct wavering line. He walked with celerity, his free arm swinging in unison with his pace-devouring strides. Hissing snow quickly obliterated all footsteps; while the group of forlorn individuals, whom he had left, stood with arms aloft in a gesture of farewell, until, whimpering hungrily, the baby recalled the woman's attention to more immediate needs.

"Come into the house," Marie commanded with undue brusqueness; "or you'll catch your death of cold in this wind." She blew her nose and wiped her eyes as she strode toward the house with the child jouncing on a hip. The girls followed in silence, pausing and turning occasionally to stare in the direction that their father had gone.

The huge front room seemed cloaked in a pall of gloom when the group entered. Cold wind blustered at the door as Marie forced it shut and held it with a restraining knee and slid the bolt into place with her free hand. The flames in the fireplace danced fitfully; the wind blasted with savagery at the solid log walls as though seeking entry; then it went on, growling its frustration in the suppliantly bowing evergreens.

Engrid accompanied her mother who laid the baby on a huge wolf-skin before the fireplace. The girl watched without interest as Marie unwrapped the boy and allowed the pleasant warmth to caress his sturdy body. The infant gurgled as it attempted to swallow a chubby fist.

Flames danced cheerily as the woman added several slabs of wood to the fire and a shower of sparks danced up the blackened chimney. A cheerful spluttering echoed through the room when the heat of glowing coals transmitted itself to the fuel.

When the infant's abortive attempts to swallow its moist fist led to a series of lusty cries, Marie promptly went to the pantry where she procured a cup of milk from an earthen crock. She spooned a generous portion of yellow cream and added it to the cup; then she carried it to the baby who, ceasing his crying, earnestly disposed of its contents in gurgling swallows. He nodded his head and wearily fell asleep.

Marie carried the baby to her bedroom where she laid him in his cradle. She looked down on him, brushed back a lock of curly hair hanging over his forehead, and wiped at tears welling from her reddened eyes; then withdrawing from the room, she seated herself at a wheel to spin clean wool into a heavy yarn.

Louise glanced at Engrid who sat staring into the fire. "Father," she observed, her expression one of extreme melancholy, although her tone betrayed the sense of superiority with which she looked down on her younger sister, "has gone to Amerika."

"How long will he be gone?" Engrid inquired in a listless voice.

"For six months, maybe a year." Louise said knowingly.

Engrid's eyes held a profound sadness as she asked, "How long is a year?"

She drew meaningless marks with one chubby finger in the dust, while reclining on the flat stones before the fireplace. She waited for an answer, although seemingly intent in her application to what she was doing, "Come on," she exclaimed impatiently and rather loudly, "How long is a year?"

"Children," Marie interrupted the conversation which, she sensed, was fast assuming the magnitude of a hair-pulling melee, "if you disturb Carl, you will have to go to bed without your supper." In a lower tone, she explained patiently, "A year is as long as from a person's birthday until the next one; or from Christmas until the following Christmas. If you insist on talking, please do not raise your voices."

Satisfied with her explanation and heeding the admonition, the girls found their dolls; seated themselves in tiny rocking chairs which their father had made for them and pretended to be women as they conversed in low voices regarding the imaginary ailments of their off-spring. Their subdued conversation, together with the whispering sound of the turning wheel, and the restless wind passing the house, all combined to envelop the room in an atmosphere bordering on contentment.

Upon tiring of their pretense, after a time, the girls stole on hesitant feet to watch in complete silence, seemingly spellbound as always, when the mass of wool fibers their mother was working with took on the appearance of yarn.

"I'm hungry." Louise spoke as she laid her head in her mother's lap. Marie turned from the wheel, and on an impulse, she drew both girls to her and kissed them.

"And what will my daughters eat?" she asked, as she drew herself erect. She contemplated each in turn with a speculative twinkle of her blue eyes.

"Potatoes," Engrid suggested hopefully, "and gravy!"

"With allspice pepper on them, please." Louise interjected. Jumping up and down she clasped her hands suggestively over her flat stomach.

"Potatoes and gravy, with allspice pepper it shall be. Perhaps we can find a mug of rye water to go with the butter and bread. If you will get the potatoes from the cellar, maybe we can have some smoked herring to go with the rest of the dinner. How does that sound, girls?"

When the girls danced away on nimble feet, Marie shrugged aside morbid feelings that sought to dominate her to the exclusion of all else. She lowered the oil lamp from its position in the center of the ceiling; after filling it, trimming the wick and polishing the chimney, she touched a burning sliver of wood to the wick and raised the lamp aloft.

With a studied glance of approval at the flame, she washed her hands in preparation for supper. All this she did in a painstaking and deliberate manner, forcing herself to think of each task, rather than allowing herself the luxury of giving in to her emotions.

The children returned from the cellar as Marie took three brown mugs from a shelf adjacent to the fireplace. She carried them with methodical steps to a pantry adjoining the huge room and filled them with slightly fermented rye water from a wooden barrel. She passed a mug to each of the girls and then carried the third into the living room for herself.

"Be careful lest you spill it," she cautioned them; "don't drink any before meal time or it will be gone and you'll have to drink milk or water."

The girls grudgingly lowered the mugs from their lips and moved reluctantly away from the table.

As Marie occupied her hands, her thoughts turned to her husband who must be, she decided, riding the train toward Helsingfors. She visualized him sitting in the tiny coach of the two-car train, listening to rumbling wheels crossing over bridges that formed so much of the road to the city, while he stared into the gathering darkness. Over lakes, marshes and on through heavily forested stretches of the bleak countryside her man was leaving her with every turn of the car's wheels; and for how long, she asked herself; while her mood answered, "Forever."

In two days, he would board a boat and soon be on his way from the Gulf of Finland, over the Baltic and North seas, finally to dock at the renowned port of London. A stop-over there for a change of vessels would precede his passage over the Atlantic to Amerika.

In a reminiscent mood, her thoughts bridged the years to the time when she had first known the lad who was later to become her husband. She recalled how they had ridden in the same community-owned church boat each Sunday morning, water and weather permitting, during the summer months before her father had moved to Jacobstad where he engaged in fishing. This girl and boy relationship had deepened with the passing years; so that it was quite natural for them to marry at maturity.

Anton's closest friend had come to the house, one autumn day, to act as an intermediary for her sweetheart. Her mother and father had served him brandy, followed by a sumptuous dinner. At the conclusion of the meal, the men and her mother had retired behind closed doors of the guest room to discuss Anton's request. After a lengthy conference, including much smoking of strong-smelling pipes, her father called through the open door, "Marie, come into the room. We have a matter of importance that we wish to discuss with you."

With her heart fluttering strangely, she had walked behind her bearded father who was surrounded with a heavy fog of acrid smoke. She seated herself in a chair by the guest table across from their visitor.

"Be seated, Marie," her father had belatedly commanded, meanwhile, dropping his gaze to the bowl of his massive pipe.

Marie remembered that she had glanced nervously across the table to find that her mother's face held a look of suppressed excitement as she flashed a reassuring smile. Her father had cleared his throat before saying, "Marie," he paused judiciously after speaking her name, "Clarence has come at the request of Anton to ask for your hand in marriage. Would you, perhaps, be interested in accepting Anton's proposal?"

Tenderly, Marie remembered that it had been her desire to shout aloud, "Yes, oh yes!" in response to the happiness threatening to overwhelm her at the question; however, she had waited in silence, eyes downcast, as though weighing the proposal. Custom, observed over the centuries, had dictated the necessity of remaining noncommittal, until the intermediary had pointed out advantages that would accrue from a match with such an upstanding man; so that all she could shyly say was, "I really don't know, although I have given the matter some consideration."

"Some consideration, indeed," Marie scoffed as she returned to the present where she was slicing potatoes and allowing them to drop into a pot of boiling water. She added a sprinkling of salt and stirred the fire; then her memory again leaped the years.

Ever since she had first known Anton, she had tenaciously clung to the thought of their eventual marriage. Her eyes had spoken volumes to the boy, the adolescent, and finally the man, as they sat in church each Sunday; Anton with the men and boys on one side and she on the opposite side with her own sex. Her most vivid recollections of happiness, during the services, were the times when the minister's sonorous voice, speaking of his Father's love for humanity, had become, in some ineluctable manner, confused with the love that she had felt for Anton when their eyes had chanced to meet across the room. On occasion when he had been detained at home by sickness, the service had seemed depressing indeed.

"Some consideration, I must say," she berated herself as she proceeded to set the table. What of the countless hours that they had spent in each other's company, though always in a group, as custom dictated? The very fact that they could not detach themselves from others, to wander, arm-in-arm, along the flowering paths, had made their longings for each other acute.

Clarence, meanwhile, had jumped into the gap that her seeming uncertainty had left to vociferously enumerate his friend's qualities. He went on to emphasize that the man in question came from a respectable, well-liked family of land owners who had never been involved in a crime of importance, nor was there any insanity inherent in the blood flowing through their healthy bodies, and drunkenness was ruled out completely. In fact, he hastened to correct himself when a look passed between her parents, the only times that Anton had ever been known to drink were on a few of the more prominent festive occasions, and on these he excused his friend's behavior, for almost everyone drank a little.

Anton would build a home for her on a piece of virgin ground. He would personally fell the trees and clear them by burning. In addition, he would have more than a hundred marks to bring with him as a present to his betrothed. And so the man had gone on for over an hour during which time he had been interrupted by only an occasional comment, or question from one or the other of her parents. Finally the visitor had fallen silent.

Emboldened by the warm smile that her mother had given her at the conclusion of the harangue, Marie had turned to her father; meanwhile, notifying Clarence by indirection, to say, "If it is agreeable to my parents, I shall marry Anton next spring. I must have time to prepare my bridal chest so it cannot possibly be any sooner. Tell Anton," she had directed Clarence, "that he may come to my home after church and dine with us next Sunday; and at that time, we can discuss things to our mutual satisfaction."

Rising from his chair, her father had poured a glass of brandy for each of them and they toasted the success of Clarence's visit. Marie smiled to herself as she recalled how their guest had walked a trifle unsteadily to his cart and turning the horse around, he had waved them all adieu; then had made haste to bear the glad tidings to Anton; who later confessed that he had been chewing his fingernails and smoking countless brown-paper cigarettes in the interim.

Marie had entertained Anton the following Sunday, and each weekend after that until spring. Such months of happiness she had known; what with her sewing, weaving, knitting and embroidering. She had, in addition, made a number of patchwork quilts.

Anton, meanwhile, had remained with his parents, working faithfully to complete this home in which he had left her with the children. Finally, the house had been completed and their marriage had taken place the following Mid-Summer dagen. Louise, the first child to be born, was alert, active and gay; whereas, Engrid the second born was of an introspective turn of mind. Then, filling a gap left by the rapidly growing girls, Carl had finally brightened their home.

In past years, after planting his crops, Anton had worked as a carpenter in the larger cities and he had returned to his home at the end of each month to deposit his pitifully small savings in the family chest. As time went on, their wants had increased and the money proved insufficient for their growing needs. Finally, he had asked her if she would care to go to the land across the water where so many of their countrymen were going to escape the poverty that the harsh land dealt them, as well as to get out from under the iron-heel of the huge nation to their east.

Because she had refused to tear up the roots binding her to a country that she loved with every fiber of her being, her man had grown increasingly morose with desire. Nothing that she had done, or said, could quite erase the constant and thoughtful frown over-shadowing his kindly features. Just a short time past, she had awakened to find her husband missing from the house. Out on the front porch she had found him; where he gazed at rivulets flowing toward the lake from melting snow.

Placing a hand on his shoulder, she had asked, "Are you going fishing?" Her husband, however, seemingly unaware of his wife, had failed to answer; he just stood there, his silence eloquently voicing the longings of his troubled heart.

"Anton, you may go." She had painfully said those words as had so many wives before her and many would yet say. She knew as long as lakes flow into rivers and rivers slip into the sea, their murmuring voices stirring the dreamer whose sleep is troubled until his questing spirit heeds their call to follow and find contentment.

Upon hearing her words, Anton had turned to her in amazement. "Oh, Marie," he had exclaimed, his eyes wide with incredulity, as he clasped her to him in a tremendous hug, "you come, too, and bring the children."

"No, Anton, I have thought things over," was her reply; "it is best that you go to see how things are over there. When you get settled someplace, perhaps we can follow. Right now, the things meaning the most to me are a roof over our heads, some ground to grow food and a bed at night. If we wait until you earn passage for us all, and enough to support us after we arrive there, you will have to wait for a lifetime. If you go alone, we can live comfortably until you send us some of your savings. We can live on so little here," she had pointed out.

Anton's face had shone in relief. "I have thought the same, but I haven't known how to say it, Marie. The situation that seemed hopeless, you have changed with a few kind words; you have made me so happy."

The woman smiled reminiscently as she recalled with what enthusiasm he had gone about preparations for his departure. He had enjoyed himself more than any of the envious relatives and friends who had come to the party in his honor to wish him "God speed!" That had been two days ago. Yesterday, taking care that five of his six pipes had been tucked away in his valise, she had packed his things. While glancing with loving eyes at the carved wooden pipe holder on the mantle, she stirred a mixture of flour, milk, molasses and spices into a kettle. This pudding would be served as a dessert after coming to a boil and being chilled. She procured a clean cloth and laid it on the table directly under the light; then set a plate for each of the children who came from the wash basin to show their mother their clean hands. Marie seated herself after placing potatoes smothered in gravy on each of their plates. She bowed her head and prayed, "Thank you for the food, O'Father," she whispered. "Amen," echoed the children.

Long after the girls had gone to sleep, Marie lay in bed thinking, with eyes wide. She tried desperately not to grieve as she watched where the girls lay, the firelight dancing on their pale faces. Although the boy snuggling on her arm compensated in a small measure for her husband's absence, with the thought that if her man was here, she would be lying on his arm; Marie dropped into a fitful sleep.

Chapter 2

Home was a plain structure of rough hewn logs, resting on a rock foundation, its inside and outside was covered with one-inch lumber. The floor made of heavy planks, assured usage for numerous generations. A steeply pitched, shingled roof gave testimony that the heavy snows would slide off before accumulating to a depth sufficient to endanger the structure. The top story, reached by a stairway from the living room, had been added to give the height needed for the pitch of the roof rather than for the resultant cramped room space.

The main room served as a dining room, bedroom for the girls, and a kitchen. In one corner of the fireplace sat a square bricked-in oven with an iron top and door. An assortment of copper kettles and iron pans were stored on shelves along the wall, off to one side of the fireplace. Other shelves held the necessary dishes. A drawer, fitted into the middle of a six-foot high row of shelves contained cutlery.

A long table, built in sections to facilitate moving, occupied the middle of the room under the oil lamp. A loom and spinning wheel rested in a position of prominence near a window with a southern exposure. Near each of these sat a sturdy chair. Others were placed at intervals around the walls for the accommodation of guests. Around the table, there were still more for the use of the family. In addition, a bench-like affair with arm and back rests, sat before the fireplace, long enough for the entire family to seat themselves during inclement weather.

Across from the fireplace, on the far side of the room, reposed two sturdy chests. Their detachable tops, when removed, exposed thick feather mattresses into which the girls sank with contentment after a busy day. Home-woven blankets and patchwork quilts made from discarded clothing, served to keep the girls warm in the small hours of cold mornings; when the logs in the fireplace became gray ash, sheltering a few glowing coals.

Almost every square foot of the floor, except for a cleared space around the hearth, was covered with rag rugs made from reconverted clothing. A huge wolf-skin, a constant reminder of the wilderness crowding the farm, also served as a rug. Anton had trapped the animal when it had repeatedly sought entry into the sheep fold in the dead of a winter night.

Of windows, there were four pairs, with six panes in the lower and upper frames alike. On the outside of these, with the advent of autumn each year, duplicates were inserted to form a dead-air space, adding immeasurably to the comfort of the room; when at mid-winter, frigid cold fastened itself with a relentless grip on the countryside. During that time, the sun would peer slyly over the southern horizon for a brief interval, its actions reminding one of a one-eyed alley cat venturing on hesitant feet into an unfamiliar thoroughfare. After describing a short arc, and giving the frozen land a perfunctory glance, cat-like, the sun would withdraw from the all encompassing night, leaving only the convolutions of the aurora borealis manifesting themselves to an ever-wondering populace.

In addition to the main room, there was a bedroom for Anton and Marie, another that the boy would occupy when he grew old enough to leave his cradle, and a tastefully decorated guest room where the woman kept all of her fineries.

A pantry was used for storing flour, bread, rolls, ginger cookies and sweetbread. On poles extending horizontally across the top of the room, hung several rows of knakabord; a thin, brown, wafer-like hard bread, having for its basic ingredient, rye flour. The age of the bread determined its value; the most highly prized being reserved for honored guests, such as Herbert Westerlund, the minister of their church.

In this small world of her own, for a period of nine years; while her husband was away, Marie raised her two girls and boy. The children grew healthy and strong as a consequence of her unselfish labor and endless patience.

She saw to it that each received their eight years of schooling in a one-room, barn-like structure located midway between their home and Jacobstad. This was six kilometers from the Isaacson residence by boat; although, three times the distance on foot. She was in attendance when the girls graduated from confirmation class and felt proud because they did. However, she grieved when the boy showed a lack of interest that prevented him from receiving a coveted bible as a gift, as his sisters did, at the conclusion of the class.

On winter days, Marie delivered the children to school in a horse-drawn droshky, picking them up on her return from the city, after having spent the day visiting with her mother, or a friend. If she wasn't outside of the school at closing time, the children reasoned that she had undoubtedly gone home; so they took to the ice on their skates, if the ice was free of snow; or else they rode home with some neighbor on a sleigh.

During their father's absence, life for the family was measured by the length of time separating one holiday from a succeeding one. With what eagerness did the children look forward to each May Day! This, they celebrated not clothed in sheer summer wear while dancing around a May Pole, but with a jaunt to a particular pole protruding above the surface of the ice-bound lake. There, each year, Nels Sundquist brought a huge wooden horse and fastened it to a plank with braces. This plank had a hole bored in the free end, and fitted down over a bolt that had been previously driven into the top of the pole. A generous amount of mutton tallow was swabbed on the bolt, and after drawing lots to ascertain in which order the couples were to ride, a pair would climb aboard the horse with the groans of their unlucky companions sounding loud in their ears. The losers would grasp the plank and push vigorously, until the horse attained a breathtaking momentum; then the boy would cast himself from the animal and pull his companion after him. On occasion, such squeals of joy resounded through the crisp air as to prompt Marie to enter her glassed-in porch and watch as a couple retrieved their stocking caps, and observe as the next pair climbed astride the handsomely carved animal.

A huge bonfire was kept blazing for warmth and a smaller one was used to brew "kahvia" in a copper kettle. This is what the Finnish children called coffee. When the children felt the pangs of hunger, they went to the fire and scraped out potatoes hidden in the ashes. After peeling the blackened outsides, they smeared them with butter and feasted. Those of the children who so wished, would bring smoked muikku, white fish, or perhaps a rib or two of mutton; which they roasted over hot coals to supplement their diet.

Through each short May Day, the children alternately feasted, rode or pushed the horse, while chanting a song that had come down from past generations. There in the bitter cold, standing over several feet of ice, their faces aflame with exercise and heat from the huge fire, they would hurl defiance at the departing winter:

> "Today is the first of May
>
> We can now go out to play
>
> The winter was long
>
> But now it is gone
>
> On this day, the first of May"

What mattered it they thought, with the resoluteness of youth, that the snow lay in deep drifts over the countryside; or that the lakes and rivers were frozen in deathly silence? Wasn't the sun rising higher each day and staying for a longer interval above the horizon? Wouldn't snow and ice disappear almost over night; when a warm wind would bring rain? In the meantime, the little people chanted their song, knowing profound joy because another winter had been endured. Soon, they knew, the first flowers would bravely peep from the ground, as the snow became water and the cries of birds coming from warmer climates, would take up their song of triumph when they tired of it.

Each spring, before the closing of school, the children were obliged to walk home when their mother was too busy to come after them. However, it was a walk that they thoroughly enjoyed; because the woods became a riot of growing flora bordering murmuring streams over which they crossed on rustic, moss-bearded bridges of logs. The road leading to the school was a winding path that could not, without exaggeration, be called a road. Nothing heavier than a two-wheeled cart ever traversed its length and, as a result, grass and brambles grew tall before the summer was over. There, indeed, was a primitive fairyland where it was easy to imagine that wee-folk abided among flowers carpeting the forest floor.

Each year when a warm wind dispersed the snow, Engrid and her sister walked a kilometer to a point overlooking the river that flowed from beyond the terminal moraine, a hill covered with heavy forest and running from the northwest to the southeast, it had been left at the southern-most point to which the most recent glacier and flowed during prehistoric times.

As saws screamed their strident challenge to the countryside emerging from its wintry silence, the girls habitually chose a place under a huge boulder where they would be sheltered from the blustering wind. From this vantage point, they observed with eager eyes as a river of logs floated down to the lake where they were brought to a halt by a boom adjacent to a sawmill. On numerous occasions, one of the girls directed her companion's attention to some log that appeared to be larger than the others. Together the eager youngsters would watch as it drifted from the placid waters of the upper lake, seemingly springing to life as white water bounced it along, and hurled it at up-thrusting rocks that ripped the torrent asunder.

At strategic points along the rapids, men sought to dislodge logs that tangled at times, against rocks in hopeless confusion. When such a jam proved too much for even a burly woodsman and his companions to break loose, a shaggy pony would deliver black powder to the location. This was placed at a chosen point where a key log rested. A fuse was then attached to a detonating cap and the cap thrust into a can of powder. After the fuse had been lit, the men would scurry away with the nimbleness of goats over the logs. After an interval, during which the sisters would stand with bated breath, a geyser of water belching skyward would lift huge logs and drop them with a smother of spray into the torrent which the blast had released. After a time, a muffled roar would cross the intervening distance between the eruption and the girls, and lose itself in the hush of the surrounding forest with hardly an echo. At this sound, the girls would expel their breath in long drawn, "Oh's" and "Ah's". The frenzied torrent would sweep the logs to the lake and screaming saws would again tear at the trees that the blast had released.

What child could resist such sights that quickened the heartbeat and forced one's attention outward and away from one's mysterious self, who, pygmy-like, moved in a giant world?

Engrid was profoundly influenced by her surroundings; so much so, that she inwardly rose to outside stimulus with surges of emotion, only to relapse into fits of brooding that the tremendous grandeur of the country served only to intensify.

At various times, the somber aspect of the girl's surroundings created forebodings that Engrid found herself unable to explain; and, as a consequence, more than once, when walking from school in the murk of the winter days, her footsteps quickened as she discerned light from the windows of her home. Taking leave of her brother and sister, she would plunge up the hill through the snow, to burst breathlessly in on her startled mother.

"Why do you hurry? Where are your brother and sister?" her mother asked in alarm on the first occasion that this occurred.

"Oh," Engrid answered evasively, "they're old pokies and couldn't keep up with me." As she spoke, she removed her outer garments; then sidled around the room, looking out of first one window, then another, while attempting to rid herself of her feeling of guilt because she had felt afraid.

"But why did you leave them to hurry on alone?" Marie asked in an infinitely patient voice.

The girl wandered aimlessly as though in some remote corner of the room or behind a piece of furniture, she might find an answer to her mother's query. Finally she confessed, "I don't like the way that the outside makes me feel sometimes. It is gloomy and I imagine that there is a wolf behind each tree, or a rock that I pass. I am happy only when I am in the light and warmth of the house. I hate this land in the winter and early spring."

Scowling through her tears, Engrid moved toward the fire where she sniffed at the usually tempting odor coming from the pot of stew that her mother stirred patiently. Somehow, the odor failed to appeal to the girl so she sat on the seat before the fireplace and stretched out her feet to feel the fire's warmth on her cold shoes. "I hate the fog, the wind and the snow. I hate anything that shuts out the sunlight." she added as an afterthought. Then she began to cry in earnest and her mother, who loved her country, climate and all, enough that she had refused to leave it to be with her husband, pulled the child to her and fondled her light braids.

"My dear child," she said in a kindly voice, "the things that you see are reflections of your innermost self. When you look at your surroundings and feel sad or fearful, it is your own fault and not the fault of whatever is outside of you. I love this country," she said emphatically, "and all of its changing moods."

The girl ceased crying and striving to add a semblance of coherency to her thoughts, she asked, "Are all places, oh, you know, heavy feeling?"

"Do you mean to ask if all countries are dark so much of the year?"

"That's it, mother!" The girl agreed brightly.

"No, my daughter, they are not." Marie answered reassuringly; "In Amerika and other lands far to the south, there is sunshine and darkness in intervals each day and not so much snow. Have patience, my daughter," she said as she stroked the girl's hair, "and later on you may read about it in your school books."

"When I grow big, I shall go to one of those places." Engrid confided with a hopeful look on her round face.

"That you may do at the proper time," Marie reassured her; "right now, however, I believe I know what you need before supper."

She took leave of the girl and motioned her to follow as she went to the pantry where she kept her meager store of remedies on the same shelf with her cardamom seeds, coffee and spices. From a brown jug, she poured out some of a concoction of her own blending and handed it to the expectant girl. Engrid accepted the liquid, swallowed it with a smacking of lips and seated herself at the fire again. Marie feeling confident that the next morning would find her child's disposition vastly improved; went about her preparations for the evening meal untroubled by her daughter's behavior. Such wisdom and calm reasoning helped the girl to go on her way; forgetting, as she did the following morning that the previous day had been gloomy, indeed.

Each summer, while waiting for the grain to ripen, the family found much to occupy their time. When the snow disappeared and the countryside throbbed to the urgency of returning warm winds, Marie drew on a pair of heavy boots and sank a shovel to the hilt in ground that their neighbor Nels had prepared for their garden. The children followed after their mother, dropping pieces of cut potato into the holes exposed by the up-tilted shovel. They also planted carrots, turnips, cabbage and onions, then watched them grow at an unbelievable rate when the sun shown almost constantly for a number of days during the midsummer. It was then that night was but a luminous twilight in which one could read with ease. After they finished with their planting, the family turned to other chores.

Wild fodder they gathered from the marshes bordering the lake and hauled on a wain to the drying shed; there fires on the dirt floor furnished curative heat so necessary in the damp climate where it rained for a time, daily. During the days when the children gathered wild grass, they received their reward in the form of rides from the shed to the marshes on the crude sled that Anton had made before leaving and which Nel kept in repair.

True, there were certain discomforts that Marie and her brood endured in common with their countrymen. Mosquitoes rose in unbelievable clouds to torture them and the cows were goaded to the brink of madness if they were not driven into a shed where a smudge was burned to disperse the pests during the brief twilight. Gnats too, pestered both man and animal alike; biting, probing and flying into their eyes and ears. At times the children cried in distress at their swollen features; but during the course of the summer, these pests with their voracious appetites, swarmed unnoticed becoming something acceptable in a spirit of resignation, along with the other discomforts of this country that the woman loved.

Marie found herself glad when there was much to do because the habit of work, forcibly nurtured by the rigors of the climate in which she struggled for an existence, made separation from her husband endurable. Days filled her with such weariness that nights were seldom lonely during the summer when she snatched a few hours of drugged sleep. She was grateful for work that wearied her mind and deadened her senses, until she moved in a half stupor, a day nearer to the time when her husband would return. In the meantime, she needed only to sleep, endure and wait; while satisfaction came at the sight of a full granary, a barn full of dry hay, and a cellar bursting with potatoes which the family shared with the cows. How nice it seemed to the woman to have ample wood, already cut in lengths and stacked in a shed rivaling her guest room in size. True, the number of trips that she had to make to the sawmill were seemingly endless; because the cart didn't hold a great deal of wood; but the trips had to be made. After she had filled the shed with tiers of wood, she needn't go outside in the cold to replenish the fuel as it was burned; she had only to open a connecting door to procure what she needed of the slabs.

But not all was labor for the family; there were visits to the neighbors, weekend trips to Jacobstad to call for the mail, and on occasion, to purchase supplies. There were sailboat rides on the lakes with the Sundquists to some inviting cove where they amused themselves angling for fish, or swimming in the nude; boys in one cove and girls in another closely supervised by elders of the same sex, who swam with them, also.

During those years, Carl lived a normal life for a boy temporarily without a father. With Walter Sundquist, from an adjoining farm, he passed his days when there was no work to be done. The boys sailed miniature ships that Nels had carved for them, or they fished, and on rare occasions, went hunting with guns Nels let them borrow. Tiring of those familiar pursuits, they explored by rowboat or rode horses to uninhabited parts of the woods; where it was impossible to penetrate on foot, because of the heavy growth of berry bushes. If they wearied of that, there was always egg-hunting and the trapping of wild ducks. Often they took to the lake shores when the ducks darkened the skies with the onset of spring. They erected cleverly fashioned cages that served as traps. Each of these cages had a door suspended in midair that could be dropped by releasing a string which one of the boys held while the pair of them crouched in a blind, watching with blue eyes agleam as they awaited the arrival of the fowl that some more fortunate, gun-carrying hunter, might drive their way.

On each occasion, shivering with excitement, they observed some hapless duck as it waddled ashore and fell to eating the grain. After consuming the scattered particles, the fowl would follow the trail of grain leading to the disguised trap, and others would rush greedily ashore to share in the feast. After a sufficient number had disappeared into the cage, the boy holding the string would release it. With shouts of triumph, the pair of watching boys would spring from ambush to dispatch the birds by a deft twist of each of the ducks' necks. On evenings when success rewarded their patient preparations, roast duck would grace the tables of their respective homes; a welcome change from the monotonous fish diet which formed the basis of most of their meals.

Louise, chipper and bright-eyed as a saucy sparrow, filled each day to the brim in play with Vinie Sundquist. At either of their homes, they set up housekeeping with tiny furniture that the ambidextrous Nels had made. If the weather was inclement, they remained inside; but on days when the sun shone from a blue sky, the horizon served as walls and the branches of silver birch their ceilings. Their jointed dolls, likewise made by the kindly Nels, were dressed and undressed in the short space of a summer, more than in the average individual during the course of a lifetime.

Engrid, too, played with them; but for her, on occasion, the lakes exerted an overpowering fascination. As a child of six, with the permission of her mother, she made her first memorable trip with Nels in his boat. While the man fished for bass, perch, pike and gwniad, Engrid, at times, leaned over the side of the boat to stare into the crystalline depths. She was moved to volubility when her companion pulled in the line, and a struggling fish flopped about for a time in the bottom of the boat; then followed an interval of silence as the man resumed his fishing, while puffing on his pipe. His clay pipe had an acrid odor; mingling with the fish smell, it became by some magical means, as incense to the nostrils of the girl. One fish followed another into the boat with amazing rapidity until the girl tired of counting their number. Whereupon, she turned to the water with observant eyes for a protracted period of time and saw in her imagination water nymphs splashing to the surface and not fish raising for a fly off to one side of the sun path that shimmered with a billion diamond-like flashes of light.

Finally, the girl turned over on her back and gazed with half-shut eyes at white clouds that tumbled overhead. She amused herself by discerning familiar figures in the ever-changing skies, as in the guise of animals, towering castles and huge mountains, the clouds formed and reformed overhead. While she squinted with fascinated intentness, one cloud, resembling a sailing vessel appeared in the sky off to one side of a group that she had been studying. "If it continues to sail," she mused, "it will one day go to where my father is living." With that exciting thought gripping her, she sank into a state between sleeping and waking as the boat, tossing gently, moved along the lake before a vagrant breeze. After a time, her opening eyes searched the expanse for the clouds that she had last seen. Was it a moment ago, or an hour ago? "What does it matter?" she thought to herself, "Time is always before us," was a quotation that her Finnish friends had taught her, and, "God created time, but said nothing about hurrying," was another that sprang to her mind. So it was with a feeling of contentment, Engrid drifted along in the boat while to her ears came the gentle whispering of tiny waves that laved its weathered sides. Through the girl's brown arms, on which lay her fair head, the blood coursed in a rhythmical surge, seeming one with the rise and fall of the water. She dropped asleep, her braids hanging over her arms like ropes of twisted silver; and the man smiled at his companion as he continued to drag in the fish.

As the sun dropped below the spruce forest at the south end of the lake, and the loon's eerie cry came like the cackle of a demented soul from the shadowless forest, Nels ran the boat aground and strung the fish on two lines. Slinging them over his shoulder, he gently shook the sleeping girl then started up the hill toward the road which led to his home. Pausing at the foot of the pathway leading to the house where the girl lived, he said, "I believe I have caught too many fish today; perhaps I should throw some away." His blue eyes in his weather-beaten wrinkled face twinkled merrily as he spoke through teeth clamped over the stem of his clay pipe. It was in his mouth so much of the time, that it appeared to be permanently rooted and made Engrid ponder if he removed it upon retiring. Nels dangled the fish from hands as gnarled and weathered as the sides of the boat. "What do you say, little one?" he asked with a shrewd smile.

"Mother says that food must not be wasted," Engrid replied seriously. "Some day we may all starve if we waste food."

"Here you are," the man stated as he passed the girl one of the strings of fish; "you can have fresh fish for supper."

Engrid accepted the string and her thanks was dismissed with a curt, "No thanks." from the man as he moved along the road towards his home. Engrid picked up the string and attempted to carry it over her shoulder; but as it was awkward, she finally trailed it in the grass behind her. Observing her daughter from the house, Marie walked down to meet her and relieved her of the welcome burden. She smiled and gave the girl her attention as the little one, her voice bursting with excitement, told of the day's experiences.

"Nels is a kindly man." Marie said, "We can salt away all we don't eat for supper."

It was as the girl had said; nothing in the line of food was ever wasted. If a child failed to eat a whole slice of dark bread with its generous coating of butter, Marie saved the remainder of the slice until the next meal when she placed it on the owner's plate before allowing another. In the woman's mind was the fearsome memory of her own childhood, when many of her neighbors had attempted to substitute birch bark for cereal after a frost had killed the crop of grain. As a result, many of them had been very ill with fierce cramps in their stomachs and others had perished.

On an average of once each month, Marie received a letter from her husband while he was absent. Each letter contained a commentary of events transpiring from day to day. Also, in each, she found money and with what satisfaction did she stow away a portion in a copper box that she kept hidden in the cellar away from prying eyes.

Each letter, written to while away an idle hour before retiring, presented to the family a history of nine years of wanderings through the land called Amerika. Finally, letters came regularly from Michigan where he engaged in carpentering as a contractor. Although his profits after deducting living expenses, was not to be considered enormous, he succeeded in sending home to his wife, many times more than he could have saved had he remained at home with her. He asked her, on many occasions, to sell the farm and come to Amerika but the woman remained adamant. However, it turned out as Anton predicted; the money that he sent home compensated in a great measure for his absence. But in spite of her savings, she came from a race of people who matured late in life, and after reading and rereading her husband's letters; sometimes, her nights and days were filled with profound loneliness and longings that, at times, bordered on desperation.

Chapter 3

The years crept along on snail-like feet for the little family; while that for which they waited, the return of Anton, made them seem endless. Short summers followed hurried springs, and furtive autumns ushered in lengthy winters. During cold weather, much of the family's time was passed indoors, either at their own or at a neighbor's home. However, as long as winters proved to be, there were always holidays on which the family kept their thoughts. Days such as Christmas served as a milestone along the weary road of waiting for Anton's return.

Each year in preparation for the event, the group made numerous delicate, spider-web-like decorations of brightly colored straw. These were suspended from the ceiling of the front room and swayed constantly in the currents of air circulating through its confines. They were a delight to the eyes of visiting guests as well as the family.

The little group went to the woods beyond the hillside and brought back the indispensable Yule log as well as an evergreen. Marie supervised the making of numerous candles from mutton-tallow that she had saved for the purpose so that for once, in the days of darkness folding the house in its toils, the house was brightly lighted when a candle gleamed cheerily in each window and cast a yellow glow on the deeply piled banks of snow.

Of course, before the holiday could be called complete, Marie was required to bake numerous goots-gooba, miniature figures resembling tiny, spraddle-leg men. Each of the children received several, and in the event that other children came to inspect the children's toys, there was always one to be found for each of them.

On Christmas Eve the children placed hay in their shoes so that Saint Nickolas might have something to feed his reindeer, over which the Laplanders kept watch for the remainder of the year. If the children had been obedient during each successive year, they received gifts for which they had longed; but if their conduct had not been exemplary, the good Saint left a birch branch in each of their shoes with instructions to the mother to put them to use. That had actually been the case on one occasion; but before the day had dragged by, Marie had repented and brought forth the gifts that Anton had thoughtfully sent from Amerika.

During the summers, weekdays were workdays; but Sunday? Ah, Sundays… Only routine chores were done, and after the family had dressed in their best, they went down to a wharf at the side of the lake to await the arrival of one of the community-owned church boats. These were huge craft approximately forty-feet in length and manned by stalwart rowers who were also in their dress clothes. At numerous wharves along the way, the boat would stop briefly to take on other passengers and then continue on its way again. Because the number of boats converging on the city was numerous, many were the impromptu races in which the children participated. When Carl grew big enough to row, he proudly replaced another man and as a result, the boy developed a powerful physique.

The sermon generally lasted at least two hours, as the minister capitalized on the willingness of his audience to remain silent for protracted periods of time, when he had the floor. Early in their lives, the youngsters erroneously came to the conclusion that the minister had some supernatural power enabling him to restrict the passage of the white sand from the top of the hour-glass, to its bottom; while he preached at great length of a heaven made desirable and attainable only after great effort on the individual's part and of a hell that was easily reached without much striving.

During the course of one such sermon, the substance of which Engrid never forgot, he assured his audience that, "If a man is guilty of moving the stakes designating the limits of his own and adjoining property, in order to profit at his neighbor's expense, then," he emphasized, meanwhile slamming a clenched fist into the palm of his other hand and running his stern glance over the audience, some of whom failed to meet his direct look, "you will have to remove the stakes from the ground with your bare hands; while they burn with fierce flames, and each hole shall have to be dug again in its true position. The rocks," he pointed out with an emphatic pounding at the top of his pulpit, "shall be hotter in hell than the rocks in your bathhouse; so that with charred hands, you shall make amends for your greed in the present. Unlike your bathhouse, however, there will be no water to cool the stones."

At the conclusion of that sermon, the audience had sung a song to raise their spirits from the gloom into which many of them had sunk; and the minister had stood at the door to shake a hand of each of the departing flock, meanwhile, inviting them to attend the next service.

On some Sundays, by arrangement with Nels to care for her livestock, Marie and her brood remained at her mother's house overnight and as a result, the children enjoyed on numerous occasions, the ever-welcome novelty of sleeping away from home in someone else's guest room. Sometimes, friends joined the group thereby assuring the children of an opportunity to listen in on an evening's conversation on a variety of subjects and much to their delight, generally terminating in a discussion of folklore gleaned from the Finns and Laplanders, and of the supernatural.

"Spirits…pshaw… there are no such things," an unbeliever might exclaim and from that moment on, a feverish discussion generally occupied the gathering for many hours, broken only by the oft repeated cry of, "Kahvia is served." After stuffing themselves on fresh rolls and drinking several cups of coffee apiece, they would again resume their interrupted discussion. Because the non-believers were generally in the minority, they would sit with cynical grins on their faces as tales were repeated by popular request. The fire was generally allowed to die down until it became glowing coals, and if the wind added to the desired atmosphere by snuffling at the chimney, so much the better!

Out of the mouths of fisherman came tales of ghostly barks that had been seen on various occasions, manned by vanished sailors with whom many of the men had worked on numerous fishing trips before they had been drowned. These ghostly apparitions were generally seen on calm nights; when the clouds splotched the skies but dimly lit by a crescent moon and the helmsmen had grown weary at the wheel.

A storyteller accomplished and versed in the lore, could almost cause the children to crawl on their hands and knees into the fireplace. The children used to drink in these tales in the same manner that a confirmed drinker swallows his liquor and they would feel a fearsome fascination when the scruffs of their necks tightened at some particular point in one of numerous narratives. Proud indeed was a storyteller who succeeded in bringing tears into the eyes of his youthful admirers.

At gatherings during the long winter evenings, the youngsters learned of the wee-folk haunting the woods; that could be counted on to guide lost children to the safety of their homes. Before entering a strange house, they were taught that they must first knock at the door which usually hung askew, or was non-existent. After knocking, they cautioned that they must say, "Good day to you all here," and if this admonition was heeded, they could spend the night there without harm and feel the comforting presence of the friendly spirit who most assuredly was there. And, if, as it happened, Marie one morning found that one of her sheep or cows had died, of a certainty someone, who disliked the fact that Anton was sending money from Amerika, had taken a few grains of sand from a newly dug grave, and entered the barn at night to sprinkle some into the bran, thereby causing the animal's demise.

When some individual died in the locality, a night watch was kept by several men who were strongly fortified with a cheery fire, brandy and kahvia; so that the evil one might not slip in and whisk the departed one's spirit away. Engrid, suspected after reaching maturity, that the men used the death of their friend as an excuse to do some friendly imbibing and card playing; because on numerous occasions, when she attended funerals, the corpse reclining in its pine box, could easily have been replaced by some wan-faced individual who had shared in the wake. And did the deceased pass on in a delirium, unable to leave word as to the whereabouts of the buried copper chest that contained his savings? The surviving relatives needed only to gather on the front porch during the first evening following his burial; and one of these relations of the recluse would undoubtedly observe a ghostly flame rising briefly from the ground where the treasure was buried. Now, whether the survivors were greedy, or subject to hallucinations prompted by over active imaginations, remained a question open for discussion; because, Engrid observed, the ground from the floor of the departed one's cellar to the surface of the dooryard was generally turned over by overzealous treasure hunters.

And, dreams? Ah, dreams… Low in spirit was the individual having none to relate over the first cup of kahvia, each morning. All members of the Isaacson family would discuss, bisect, divide, add-on-to, and analyze each one until it appeared as plain as the nose on one's face, what the spirits were trying to convey to the dreamer. Dreams weren't something for them to discard with an "It's something you ate" expression on one's face, no indeed! Dreams were for Marie to interpret as an authority on the subject, which she undoubtedly was, and attach a certain importance to along traditional lines. If she added embellishments that only proved to her youngsters what an uncanny person she was; she, who could understand the dream world into which the children ventured nightly.

Of the weddings that the family attended, at none were the brides left waiting at the doorsteps. Everyone from the locality, and distant relatives of the couple to be joined in wedlock, would congregate for the event. A trip to the church by boat was usually followed by three days and nights of drinking, eating and lecturing the bride. First of all, the father would advise the bride while the dinner was in progress. Then the girl's mother would have her say before retiring to the seclusion of her guest room, to be followed after a respectful interval, by her sympathetic lady friends. There she would relate the history of her daughter's life, from the time when she had been spanked into her first tearful wail by the attending midwife, until her marriage. Meanwhile, the men would give the bride advice, until tears would flow down her cheeks, and her husband was made to appear as pure as the fallen snow; even though, like the proverbial sailor, he had bundled with every fallen woman in the country. In this way, the unfortunate maiden was led to publicly acknowledge that she was undoubtedly unworthy of her spouse. After succeeding in that purpose, the men would allow the newlyweds to depart to their new home; but here they would keep the couple in such an uproar for the first week of their honeymoon, that the couple generally doubted the wisdom of having made public an elicit affair that they had, in all probability carried on for a protracted time; so said the folks who had been married for a long time, or hinted with sly jokes and knowing winks to a flustered groom, and an even more flustered bride. However, the newlyweds liked it!

In past years, during the last few days before the grain had ripened, anguished fears had frequently clutched at Marie's heart if heavy clouds had shut out the sun for a period of a week or so, and if the wind had come from the north. If clear skies had followed rain, there had been the ever present danger of frost. At night, Marie never closed her eyes without first rekindling the flame of faith by resorting to prayer. But this year, things were different, although she still prayed. Clear skies prevailed when Marie received a letter from Anton. Her husband informed her that he was satisfied with their savings and was definitely coming home during the coming November. So almost gaily the woman accepted the judgment of the Sundquists who came over the hill to walk through the fields, testing the grain with their fingers and observant eyes. After a walk around the farm, Nels stood with pipe in mouth to smilingly pass judgment.

"The grain is ripe," he said emphatically, thus confirming Marie's eager wishes. "If you will but wait until I finish harvesting my own, I will come to help you."

Marie thanked them and stood for a time, looking over her fields of gold. Without waiting for her neighbors to help, she called to her children and started down a field, she scythe cutting wide swaths in the standing stalks. In certain places, along the boulder-strewn field, she shortened her strokes, lest she dull the blade on the partially concealed rocks. Should this happen, she knew, it would require a protracted period of time at the grind-stone and she had plenty of work to do already without asking for more.

The children followed after her while she cut the grain, binding the sheaves and piling them high on the cart then hauled them to the curing shed. In its top, Carl crouched over and reached for the bundles that one of the girls passed up to him. He stacked them to the eaves and left a runway open along the center leading to a small door at its end. A fire was burning on the dirt floor. The degree of heat was regulated by the addition of fuel to the fire and opening and closing of the door.

When the grain was judged to be dry, it was moved to the threshing floor in the same building. Here the children and their mother beat the outspread stalks with flails, a tool for separating the bulk of the grain from the straw. Sweat poured down their faces in endless trickling drops and cut through the grime to expose the oily skin beneath.

After the bulk of the straw was removed with wooden rakes, the grain was poured on shaker boards a portion at a time. Two members of the family grasped the board and shook it up and down, while a third fanned it with a piece of cloth, and more of the chaff and straw was removed. After this treatment, the grain was passed into another room and thrown against a far wall with a sweeping motion of a wooden shovel. The straw fell short, and grain struck the wall, and dropped with a slithering sound on the growing pile.

Oh what busy days! Long before the sun brushed with faint saffron strokes at the sky, and made form out of the vast formlessness of the lakes, the children wakened to the odor of boiling kahvia, and the sound of their mother's cheerful humming. They slipped into their clothing and hurried to the blazing fire that caused dancing waves of light to scurry after indolent shadows across the breadth of the room. After dining on coffee and rolls, they worked in the shed for two hours of each morning; then back they went to the house; where they ate huge bowls of clabbered milk and rye bread sweetened with molasses. After having satisfied their appetites; they again plied their flails with renewed vigor until the self-assigned task was completed. With the conclusion of the harvest, Marie gazed happily at the precious grain; the children, meanwhile, experienced the contented feeling coming to people whose feet are deeply rooted in the soil and who have steadily labored with a definite goal in mind. Removing the dirty mask from her face, Marie looked at the grain with a gleam of avarice in her eyes.

"This is so wonderful," she remarked in a pride-filled voice. She slowly turned from the pile, thereby betraying with her movements, the weariness that she felt. She looked down on her children who lay on their backs in the straw. She observed that they were chewing rhythmically on mouthfuls of grain that had turned to gum between their firm white teeth.

"Look my children," she said in a voice reflecting a faith as firm as the heart of a mighty spruce which reaches its branches toward an every-changing sky, "God has seen fit to give us a bounteous harvest. Because that is so, we shall have mush and flour to give us strength to endure the icy knife-thrusts of the coming winter when your father will again be with us..." Her voice broke as emotion overcame her and she turned to the door overlooking the lake that glistened restlessly in the late afternoon sun. Golden bars of light probed through the dust about her; a gentle breeze entering the door, swirling the dust and rustled dryly and with whispering sounds through straw that lay here and there where it had fallen from the shovels.

"Let us give thanks to Him who has sent us warm sunlight from a clear sky; thereby enabling us to grow enough for next year's planting as well as for our own needs."

The children obediently closed their eyes and rose to their knees, their heads bowed as the woman spoke, "Oh, Father, Thou hast withheld the frost that could have blackened our growing grain and also hail that could have beat it into the ground and caused us to hunger. Perhaps, we have lived properly, with thanks in our hearts for our healthy bodies and minds which Thou hast seen fit to bestow upon us. We thank Thee for the goodness of our neighbors who have been at our call whenever we have been in need of help during our father and husband's absence, Amen."

Engrid listened with cold fear gnawing at her. To be dependent on a God who rewarded or punished at will; sometimes for no understandable reason, gave her a feeling of helplessness and impotency. In addition, she felt weariness in the whole of her body. Water ran from her nose in a persistent burning drip. Her nights of late had been filled with resentment against the slavery that life had forced upon them all by the mere reason of their existence in this harsh land. But, as quickly as her mood appeared, it passed away and an eager desire pointed to the day when all of the neighbors in the county would gather to feast, drink, dance, trade and make merry in the final celebration of the passing summer at the Harvest Festival.

"Have you the rocks sufficiently heated for the sauna?" Marie asked of Carl as he started to his feet and stepped outside of the door where he brushed at his clothes with a folded hat.

"That I have mother," he responded.

"You may then go to the house and do as you wish; we shall have our turn today. Tomorrow, if you feel so inclined you and Walter may take a steam bath together."

"That will be excellent, mother," the lad replied as he followed after her to the house where he procured a bar of homemade yellow soap and a rough rag. Throwing a towel and a change of clothing over a shoulder, he disappeared behind some trees to swim in the lake and rid himself of at least the top layers of the day's accumulation of grime.

Down at the bath house, after she and her daughters were undressed, Marie transferred a number of hot rocks from a fire into a pit in the center of the floor. She poured water on the rocks from a dipper. She followed the girls' example by grasping a birch branch and flailing herself as vapor rose from the stones; but taking care, nevertheless, that she did not strike her breasts, and warning the girls against the practice. The exertion and the vapor combined made them all perspire, and when they were covered with beads of water, they scrubbed themselves with rough towels and yellow soap; then they climbed to the highest of a number of seats that rose, bleacher-like, to the top of the house; where the girls made fun of each other as perspiration, moving down from their shoulders and faces, dropped from the rosy red of their shapely breasts which were beginning to show the vigor of their womanhood. Here, in satisfactory indolence, they sat or sprawled for a time, and occasionally, one of them would pour some more water onto the pile of stones and the air was again saturated with warmth.

Gradually the soreness left their tired bodies; then at a gesture from their mother, the girls followed her out of the door into the sunlight, And with squeals of joy and gasps of shock and excitement, the girls dove into the lake. After swimming about for a time, they swam ashore and rubbed themselves with rough towels. Of course, the water was cold but not a fraction as cold as was the snow into which they plunged their naked bodies following a similar steam bath in the wintertime. Following a half-hour of sunbathing, they clothed themselves and gathering up their dirty garments went into the house.

Autumns were always colored with warm expectancy, climaxing in the Harvest Festival. It was to this gala affair that the inhabitants of the farms and deep woods came, emerging caterpillar-like from their cocoons of loneliness. From the somber forests came handsome Finns whose bodies spoke of the indefatigable endurance so necessary to men who work in the logging camps the year around. During the course of the day's merry-making, rival woodsmen would jump on a log floating in the water of the lake and each of the two men would attempt to cause the other to lose his footing by spinning the log with his spiked, boot-soles. When one of the men succeeded, the other plunged with a splash into wet, ignominious defeat. The victor would accept the plaudits of the spectators and challenge any of the men from a rival logging camp to emerge a victor in another attempt. The favorite challenger would step out on a log and begin to spin it as had the other man who now stood on the bank, shouting encouragement to the second challenger, heedless of his own sodden clothing.

The two men would warily eye each other as they began to spin the long log and one or the other of the pair would suddenly brake its momentum by pushing backward against the log's direction of spin. After a few stops, starts and reversals, one of the two naturally lost his balance to plunge into the water; while the crowd shouted its distain at the loser, it loudly cheered the champion. Each year, for many years, all men met defeat at the feet of a giant of a man called Elmer Engstrom.

Because the Finns, whose gray eyes coupled with dusky complexions and irascible dispositions, were predisposed to violent and active flirtations with lighter-featured girls of Swedish extraction, each festival contained the elements necessary for the promotion of numerous fights in and around Jacobstad. If a jealous Swedish suitor resented the attentions that one of the woodsmen showered on his inamorata, action was promptly forthcoming. The men would hurl themselves at each other like raging bulls, and before long, one of them would arise with broken features to stare down at his unconscious rival with a grin of triumph. The man would then calmly walk away with the girl who was the cause of the brawl; with all the girls loving it.

When several festive days had flitted satisfyingly by, during which time the woodsmen had dissipated their energies and dispersed their hard-earned money with profligate hands, they wearied of their celebrating and retired to their familiar haunts. Meanwhile, Marie and her daughters had seized an opportunity to display some of their handiwork in competition with other women, and if one of the family chanced to win a ribbon for something that they had woven, knitted, or grown, their rejoicing was great indeed.

Life would again settle into a routine, broken at satisfactory intervals by visiting or being visited for several hours of each day. During these gatherings, knitting, drinking coffee and discussing the contents of letters that many families regularly received from some point in far-off America, were the chief diversions. As a consequence, most of the neighborhood children grew up with a chronic disease that their parents laughingly referred to as "Amerika fever". If the disease grew progressively worse with the passing years, there was only one known cure; go to Amerika. But this cure presented a problem. If they were fortunate, they could borrow money for the passage, and if not, they had to save for many years and in the meantime, feel their desire to leave the country dim then wane according to the amount that they were able to hoard.

After one member of a particular family had borrowed from others, he or she could buy a passage and as quickly as possible, refund the money so that another could follow. In time, only the aging parents were left and at their death, their farm and house generally fell into decay and nothing indicated that people had lived and loved there except crumbling logs and a pile of stones where once had stood a chimney. There mournful winds swept through the desolation and wolves passed without even a furtive glance at what had once been a home humming with purposeful industry.

Chapter 4

On a November morning during a weekly visit to Jacobstad, Marie received an expected and long awaited letter. She tore at it with eager fingers, while her children waited expectantly for their mother to speak. It proved to be a short note and Marie finished it to say, "Oh, children, your father is coming home tomorrow but he didn't say whether by boat to this place or cross-country on the train. I suppose," she added happily as she passed the letter to the eager children, "all we can do is go home, clean the house and have plenty of food waiting for him when he arrives."

Oh, the joy of it! Oh, the suspense! What house cleaning, baking and cooking to be done through the day; the pots to polish until they shine on the inside and outside like new. Oh, the scouring to be done with a bit of flannel and sour cream, until the copper coffee pot shines with a luster rivaling the setting sun. There were rolls to twist and bowls of fresh milk to clabber. They had to gather fresh branches of spruce to replace those used as brooms during the past week. A veritable frenzy of house cleaning took place that day and everyone seemed to be in everyone else's way. That, however, caused little of the usual bickering. Personal animosities were forgotten while the family waited the coming of their lord and master.

The following morning found Carl stalking around the house, his demeanor that of a vain roaster. His blonde hair, parted on the side, was slicked down with a generous application of fresh lard. New boots showed a rich brown where they encircled his tucked-in trousers. A woolen scarf, snuggly fastening the collar of his brilliant green and red-plaid flannel shirt was tied in a bow with tassels of white hanging jauntily at each end.

The mother and girls were fresh appearing in their linen shirtwaists and skirts of checkered red and white billowing over their petticoats. Marie had scolded, bossed, scrubbed and rubbed finally completing the girls' and her own toilet with a facial of sweet cream.

"Keep clean now, all of you," she admonished as she adjusted the white stiffly starched bonnets on her daughters' heads, "or your father will think that I have raised a family of swine."

Interminable hours dragged by; the day slowly waned without a sign of Anton walking or riding from the trees; so the children became restless at the enforced idleness. At length, when it seemed that Marie's nerves must snap because of the refractory attitude of her brood, she spied a sail, a pinpoint of white where it rounded a point in the direction of town. "Your father comes there!" she exclaimed, pointing a trembling arm toward the dot. "He's probably riding with the Sundquists who went to town today to get Walter's tooth pulled."

With excited shouts, the children ran to climb a huge rock for a clearer view of the boat coasting swiftly toward them. It's main sail straining like a big bosomed woman in the rising wind. Shining eyes saw at the same instant a flutter of white at the stern where someone waved repeatedly. Immediately four handkerchiefs returned the salute.

A surge of conflicting emotions swept over Engrid; finally crystallizing in resentment against her father as she watched her mother reach toward the boat as though her gesture might hasten its landing. The girl placed a hand comfortingly around her mother's waist squeezing it gently; but the woman seemed unaware of Engrid's presence. Her eyes glued on the approaching craft and her hands trembling in a mute appeal until the boat bumped against the dock.

Anton sprang forward and pinioned his wife's arms to her sides when he swept her from her feet in a bear-like hug. Marie held helpless in his embrace, gladly surrendered herself as he smothered her with kisses. Finally the man desisted although he continued to hold her until her eyes fluttered open then closed again when he pressed each lid with his lips.

"Oh, Marie, my love, I've missed you so much, open your eyes, let me see them," he pleaded. She complied then turning her head with a nervous trill of laughter as Anton lowered her to the ground.

"The children … these are your children," the woman said through her tears; "look at them and tell me what you think of them."

Anton looked at his youngsters who had hesitantly moved forward while the tall stranger embraced their mother. The man said, "Come to me and let me hold you."

The girls came forward. Louise impulsively eager, Engrid with a quaint shyness enhancing her charm. Carl grinned boyishly, as he stared at this father with a feeling of pride. Anton held his daughters for a long moment.

Releasing his daughters, Anton blew with a tremendous honking sound into a square of linen; then he directed his attention to the boy who stood, eyes alight, but disturbed with conflicting feelings. Anton extended a huge hand. "Come here, my son," he exclaimed jubilantly.

Carl looked at his father with clear-eyed intensity and seemingly satisfied with the results of his appraisal, he thrust out a hand to grasp this stranger's. He squeezed it firmly as his father drew him close and subjected him to a bone-crushing hug. The lad buried his face in clothing that smelled strongly of tobacco while for the first time in his life, he felt as though he had an ally in this feminine world through which he had moved so lonely at times without an elder of his sex in whom he could confide.

"You look just like your picture, father," the boy ejaculated as he stepped back a pace and peered into the older man's features. "You're so much taller and heavier than I imagined, though." Anton laughed heartily as he thumped the boy on the back.

"I am glad that I exceed your expectations," he responded warmly.

"Will you help me to build an ice boat with real sails?" the boy asked hopefully. "If you do, I can then race Walter, instead of riding with him all the time." Carl turned to his youthful companion who displayed a missing tooth when he grinned his approval of the boy's question.

"Did it hurt?" Carl asked.

"No," answered Walter.

After promising that he would not only help him to construct an ice boat with sails, as well as skies and snowshoes, Anton turned his attention from the boy to observe that Nels was busily engaged in unloading the craft.

"Here," he admonished, "let me help you with those things. I did not mean for you to unload the boat; I forgot in the excitement attendant on my arrival."

Together the men unloaded the boat while Carl eyed the growing pile of boxes with incredulity written on his features. Finally he turned to the house saying, "I'll get the cart." He strode up the slope away from the lake with Walter in tow.

"What is in that large box?" Marie inquired, referring to a long crate that required the combined efforts of the men to carry from the wharf.

"Ah, mother," Anton said, "that is a secret I must not divulge, or it will detract from the enjoyment of opening it." He looked aside at Nels who was mooring the boat in a manner more to his satisfaction, after looking at a sky that was fast becoming hazy.

"Would you and your wife stop in for a time?" Anton asked, "I have some special brandy from across the water, something to make my homecoming lively."

Nel nodded in agreement and until Carl appeared with the cart and pony, the group entered into a spirited discussion regarding the contents of the numerous boxes. Anton listened to each query with a smile and a sly shake of his head. His only answer was, "Just you wait and see."

"The same old Brownie," Anton observed as he walked to where Carl turned the cart around with a tug of a rein. "How are you, Brownie?" he asked, while placing a hand into a pocket of his mackinaw, he extracted a piece of hardtack candy and placed it between the teeth of the ancient horse. He rubbed his hand over its coat, already growing heavy in preparation for the coming cold. "I suppose he doesn't remember me," he remarked as he turned from the horse and helped to pile the baggage into the cart. It required three trips to remove the collection of boxes and bundles to the house. When the last box was loaded, the group followed the cart up the hill, chattering and gesticulating as everyone tried to out talk the others in their enthusiasm. After the cart was emptied of its contents, Carl drove the animal to the barn, accompanied by Walter who proudly displayed an enormous cavity for his friend's closer inspection.

As the group carried the assortment of packages and boxes into the house, Louise kept up a barrage of questions that Anton found hard-put to answer. "Tell us about Amerika, father, how would you like it if we lived there? How are the people different from us who live here? Did you enjoy the trip back on the big steam ship? What are the boys like over there? Do they dance like they ..."

"Wait a minute, wait a minute, daughter, I can't answer all questions in the first few minutes of my homecoming," he objected. However, he added an understanding smile to his rebuke so that the girl felt not in the least put out, but squeezed his waist companionably. On an impulse, she drew him down and delivered a kiss on his rough cheek, with its beginning of a red beard pricking her lips; an altogether novel sensation for the girl.

"Your face is so rough, father," she marveled as she placed the back of a hand to her mouth, "I do believe you need a shave."

Anton laughed heartily. "Am I the first bearded male that you have kissed?" he chided her. The girl blushed as the crowd burst into laughter.

"You're the first man I ever kissed," she admitted shyly.

"You are right, daughter, I do need a shave." He rubbed a rough hand over his chin and observed, "I shaved yesterday in the city, but I have always had a fast-growing beard." He said that with a hint of pride in his heavy voice. "I will shave this evening, just to please you."

After the long box had been carried inside of the house, Anton ventured into the open and the others trailed after. Placing his hands in the pockets of his mackinaw, he stepped down into the yard and rested his eyes on the weather-beaten house; after casually surveying the rest of his property.

"I do believe that the house needs a coat of paint, little mother," he observed with a rueful smile.

Marie went to stand at her husband's side, and saw patches here and there where weathering through the years had caused the yellow boards to show forth.

"Yes, it does," she conceded, "but I have never bothered to have it done because as we have already discussed in our letters, we still intend to sell. We shall build a nice one on the outskirts of Jacobstad, overlooking the bay. I have already placed a retainer on a piece of ground and I also have a sale for this house and the ground."

"Who is the interested party?" Anton asked in surprise.

"You need only to look around you," Marie answered happily. Anton allowed his eyes to survey the group until he saw Nels, who had the biggest smile of any assembled there, give him a knowing wink.

"Well, have you heard?" Anton ejaculated; "I can't think of anyone I would rather sell to," as he promptly gestured toward the house, "let us go in and drink to the changing life of all of us. You are certainly getting a fine piece of ground, Nels; I hope you will be well satisfied."

"You're telling me? I have helped to farm this land for nine years; that is the reason I decided that I would like it for my own. I can certainly put these fields and stands of timber to good use. I am building boats now," he pointed out with pride.

"Good for you, my friend," Anton observed as he again clapped Nels on the back, "let us go and do as I suggested and get that drink."

"Leave it to you to think of that," Marie said as she started through the door after her guests. Anton stopped her, however, by grasping her in his arms and sweeping her from her feet. "I'm going to carry my bride through the door for the second time and I hope for the last in this house. You'll never know how I have longed for this opportunity," he said as he looked down into her smiling face. She pretended to feel angry and struggled in vain as he made good his remarks, then kissed her soundly before allowing her to regain her feet.

The guests took their places at Marie's invitation and Anton asked in a casual voice, "How do you know that I will like my future home's location?"

Marie detected the concern hidden in his voice but she decided to say what she had on her mind regarding the matter. "Listen, my husband, for a period of nine years, I have scraped, saved and done without while you enjoyed your independence with nothing to stop you but the fact that you had to work for the money that you sent home. I have been tied down raising these children during those nine years," she emphasized, "now I am going to have the say about the location of our new home."

"There, there," Anton said in a placating voice, "I know that it has been long and hard for you but that is over now. If you have decided that we shall build in Lapland and herd reindeer, it will be alright with me. Wouldn't we look fine," he added with a whimsical smile, "living in tents, drinking deer milk, and gnawing bones as we follow our straying herds over the tundra? Come," he invited as he made for his valise, "I am about to succumb to the sad implications that the thought holds, a drink of brandy we must have."

From a valise he drew a box of candy and opening it, placed it on the table and told the children to help themselves. "Will you have a drink, Marie?"

"Oh, to be sure; but only one, though. This occasion must not be marred by any lack of gayety on my part; although I feel happy already. I wish time would stop and things would never change. Here are you, the children and our good friends to share in the joy of your homecoming. These alone have filled me with sufficient happiness without recourse to drink." She accepted the preferred drink and remarked, "You will never know how much Nels helped us on a thousand occasions. He has done more to earn the miserable pay that I have given him, than you can imagine."

"What do you mean miserable pay?" Nels broke in gruffly, "You have paid me at the prevailing rate when you could have hired more competent men to help you than I, but you wanted to give me the extra work. I know how you have been toward us, when we stood in need of help. Who else could we turn to when there was sickness in the family?" Aside to Anton he said warmly, "You have a fine wife."

"That you have," Hilda Sundquist broke in to say as she placed her empty goblet on the table and wiped her mouth with the back of one brown hand. "I have considered myself fortunate to have such a neighbor all these years. At child birth, she has been indispensable. She is better than any midwife that I have ever known. Before she shows on the scene, I lie there wishing that I were dead, while father," she remarked with an amused glance aside at her grinning husband, "runs around with a worried look in his eyes as though he thought the world was coming to an end, and he hadn't time to repent of his sins. When he sends one of the children for your wife, I know that the worst is over, and I want to live again. Such is the comfort and help that she has bestowed on us through the years."

"I have done only what you would do, under similar circumstances," Marie objected, her face blushing furiously; "let us forget the whole matter."

As the men settled down to serious drinking, Carl burst into the room followed by Walter. "There is a storm coming from over the lake," he gasped. His eyes fell on the open box of candy and motioning to Walter he helped himself to a generous handful of an almost unheard of luxury, hard-tack candy.

Anton walked leisurely to the door, throwing it wide to find that the boy was correct in his observations. Across the water, a tumbling mass of black clouds with trailing torrents of rain drew near with unbelievable rapidity. Gusts of violent wind were even now whipping the surface of the water into a white seething mass.

"The boy speaks the truth," Anton remarked; "it looks as though we are in for a real blow. I am glad we got ashore when we did or we would have to spend the night elsewhere."

Nels nodded his agreement, meanwhile, looking at the boat fastened snugly at the wharf. "I think that the boat will be alright where it is; there isn't much that can hurt it. It's a good boat if I do say so myself."

Hilda rose to button her great coat around her portly form. She walked to the door through which the rising wind was coming in and causing an American flag to flutter to and fro on the wall. "I think that we should go home before the storm strikes, or the family will be worried. Vinie is there with the baby; she might think that we are at the bottom of the lake with a capsized boat over us." She grasped Nels by the arm saying, "Come on, father."

Nodding his head at the wisdom inherent in his wife's words, Nels grasped a sack in which he carried a few sundries. Together the couple started up the path leading over the hill to their home. Walter sprang ahead and quickly disappeared from their view. Anton thought quickly as the couple moved away. He called to Nels, hurried inside to reappear in a moment and make his way quickly to where the couple waited in the wind, their great coats waving wildly about them; their bodies turned to the side in an effort to minimize the force of the gale.

"Here," Anton remarked, thrusting a bottle of brandy into a hand of his neighbor, "take this bottle so that together you may share in the happiness that I feel at my return." He waved Nels objections aside and insisted he take the bottle. "I refuse to take 'no' for an answer," he said firmly as he backed away from the protesting man. "And you take this to your children," he added as he thrust a box of candy into Hilda's hands.

"Thank you, Anton, thank you," the woman exclaimed.

"Thank you a thousand times, thank you, Anton," Nels said warmly. "This is a special brand from Amerika?" he gasped, his mouth hanging open in awe. "My, my," he breathed prayerfully, and placing his hand over the top of the sealed bottle to prevent it from jouncing out of his pocket. As he turned to leave, he said, "I will nip at it, and think of you when the mellow glow starts moving around in me."

"After you milk the cows, my husband," his wife reminded him firmly, her voice barely distinguishable to Anton's ears.

"After I milk the cows," Nels agreed; then with his wife clutching at the great coat whipping wildly about his legs, he redoubled his efforts to surmount the hill, his steps a trifle unsteady.

Grinning, Anton slammed the door and strode to the fireplace where he removed his coat. He threw it carelessly over the table and the girls promptly pulled him down on the bench before the fire. Carl leaned with assumed nonchalance against the side of the fireplace, and Marie beamed down on her husband, a she patted a tawny cat until it purred with contentment.

"Where is Wolf?" Anton asked curiously, "I haven't seen him around."

"The poor dog died of old age." Marie informed him. "It was a good thing though, because for a long time he had been unable to hear and could hardly get around. We had to keep him in the house each winter for a long time. It only happened a month ago."

"I buried him by the side of the path under that biggest spruce on the road to Sundquist's place," Carl said sadly.

"Tell us about Michigan," Engrid said, thereby changing a subject that was distressing to hear. She rubbed her face against his gray flannel shirt, while Louise played with his tie.

"I suppose you know where we can get another dog?" Anton suggested, completely disregarding his daughter's outburst.

"Sundquist's bitch will have a litter sometime in December," Carl exclaimed hopefully. "They have good dogs, big enough to pull a sleigh in harness."

"That is fine, son; we'll see if we can bargain for one when they come. Home isn't home without a dog," he said thoughtfully.

"Father …" Engrid pleaded reproachfully, "you didn't even answer me when I spoke to you."

"Oh, I'm sorry, daughter, what was it you asked?"

"About Michigan," Louise burst in to say.

Well, there isn't much to tell and yet; there is much to tell," Anton added as he removed a pipe from a pocket of his shirt. He tamped a generous quantity of tobacco into its bowl; then with calloused fingers, he plucked a live coal from the fire and pressed it against the tobacco until a drifting cloud of smoke rose in obedience to his puffing. "Where I spent most of my time, the country is similar in many respects to this one. There are trees, lakes, growing things, rivers and much farming and fishing. There aren't the thousands of lakes such as we have here; but on the other hand, the lakes there are enormous. The lakes are so enormous that you can't see across them in many places."

"Are the lakes beautiful?" Louise inquired, moving to seat herself with a lively rustle of crisply starched petticoats on the arm of the bench so she could see her father better.

"They are when calm; but when the wind blows, the waves come up on the land with such violence that one doesn't have any desire to watch them. These lakes here, small as they are, are beautiful beyond description," he said in a pride-filled voice.

With her half-closed eyes peering into the fire, Engrid said dreamily, "Sometimes they resemble strings of jewels held together with silver wire."

"Most aptly put, my little girl; or should I say my big daughter? By the way, how old are you?"

"I am thirteen on the sixteenth of July," Engrid answered importantly.

"My, how time does fly." he exclaimed in amazement. Turning to Louise he asked, "And you?"

Louise twisted his tie around her finger as she answered, "Fifteen on the ninth of June."

"And you, Carl?"

The boy chewed vigorously on a piece of candy before answering, "Ten years on the tenth of May."

"And big for his age, I might add," Marie said proudly as she placed on arm around her stalwart son's shoulders; then at her children's insistence, she prepared a meal which surpassed anything that the family had ever eaten.

Anton broke open boxes containing nuts, and more candy at the conclusion of supper. For a time, hearth stones resounded excitingly to the cracking of nuts. Anton, his tongue loosened by brandy consumed in leisurely sips, answered their every question, smiling occasionally with smug satisfaction because he held the stage that he had relinquished so long ago.

Finally, he began removing boards from the remaining boxes. As he opened one, the family thronged around and the girls' delighted squeals echoed and re-echoed throughout the room when he handed them each a new black silk parasol with fringed edges.

"Oh, father!" Carl exclaimed when Anton placed a heavy package wrapped in butcher's paper into eagerly reaching hands. The youth tore the paper open with trembling fingers and pursed his lips in an admiring whistle as he spied the shining skates with adjustable clamps.

Dashing into the bedroom and jerking off his dress shoes, he slipped his feet into his high-top boots and fastened the skates to their soles; clomping back to join the family where he strutted importantly. His sisters admiring the shinning miracle of new skates; while they strolled here and there with parasols opened wide, disregarding their mother's admonition that they would assuredly bring bad luck to the household.

"How can we have bad luck?" Louise chirruped brightly. "We have had our bad and now it is time for the good!"

"How did you get the correct size of skates, father?" Carl wanted to know.

"It was nothing at all," Anton explained modestly; "all I had to do was take the outline of your shoe soles that your mother traced for me; then find skates that would fit the pattern."

"It was smart of you to think of that, mother!" Carl regarded the skates jubilantly for a moment. "Look," he pointed out, "they have an Amerikan name on them." Again

Carl fell silent for a time only to erupt once more, "So that is why you wouldn't let me buy a pair in the city."

"That is so," Marie agreed.

Each of the sisters as well as the mother received two pairs of silk stockings.

"That is the kind that both young girls and women wear in the new country," Anton informed them.

With an unspoken query at her mother in her glance, Engrid stroked her stockings.

"Oh, those?" Marie asked. "I also sent your father a pair of each of your stockings to measure by."

"And what have you brought for mother?" Carl asked as he moved to stand beside his father who was breaking the top off the largest crate with the aid of a nail bar from his tool chest. The girls crowded expectantly around the box that was all of nine feet long.

While Anton removed wad after wad of paper from the top of the object that lay mummy-like in the crate, the children's curiosity reached a pitch of intensity that glued each to a spot from whence they craned their necks over and around their father's moving hands and shifting bulk to try and see what it was. Finally with the removal of one last piece of brown paper, the face of a grandfather clock was exposed.

A chorus of, "Oh's," and "Ah's," rose from those assembled as to cause Anton to feel humble indeed that he was acting the role of Saint Nickolas in a manner that would have pleased the latter, had he been there to witness the man's kindness.

"It is for you to have placed where you will, Marie," he remarked; then turning from his work, he tossed the bar on the floor and looked at his wife with questioning eyes.

Marie didn't know whether to laugh or cry; so she did a little of both and wiped at her brimming eyes. "You shouldn't have done this," she said. "How much did it cost?"

"Never mind the cost," Anton replied. "I thought it would be nice for you to be able to stand any place in the room without walking to see the time; besides, someone will not be forever asking, 'What time is it?'"

Marie searched the room and in a corner receiving the most light from the rain-drenched windows, she directed that the clock be placed. With cautious deliberate steps, the man and boy carried the clock to the designated spot. After a little twisting and turning, under Marie's critical direction, Anton finally placed the object to his wife's satisfaction.

When the children had sufficiently admired the ornate carvings covering the bottom where hung the counter balances and chains by which they were suspended, Anton remarked, "Instead of spending my allowance as did many of the men, on a drunk each month, I saved mine, getting something to remember the new country by."

"Make it run," Carl suggested, breaking a silence which held the admiring group in its spell. Anton obligingly adjusted the weights, then reached into the pocket of his vest and observed the correct time on his pocket watch. He adjusted the hands of the big clock to correspond; then gave the pendulum a gentle swing. Immediately a rhythmical tick-tock; tick-tock marched forth into the room.

"Will it sound the hour?" Marie asked expectantly, her eyes on the clock.

As if in answer, the clock spoke in a mellow cadence; six notes rang out simulating the pealing of the church bell whose solemn chimes drifted over the waters of the lake on windless nights. The group stood in a hushed silence, feeling as though their kindly minister had pronounced a benediction on their home. Unbelievably monotonous was the life that these people lived; so few were the opportunities for social intercourse and variety; that the clock sounding a new note of life in the great room held them momentarily in a state of spirit bordering on ecstasy. The last note trembled into a whisper, then into silence, however, the clock continued its ticking seemingly determined to regulate the lives of the group; but what a comfortable supervision Marie thought to herself.

Anton tore his eyes away from the ticking timepiece to partake of another drink. He gulped it down then moving to another box, he tore the top off and exposed several rolls of wool, silk and cotton prints.

"These pieces of cloth will eliminate a large share of the weaving that you have been doing," he remarked. "In Amerika they pay women to do the weaving with machinery. One woman can turn out more cloth in an hour's time than you can in a year at your loom. What do you think of the cloth?"

Marie's course fingers felt of the materials and her happiness was indescribable. With care, she knew that she had enough material to clothe herself and the girls for several years.

"They are beautiful!" she exclaimed, "and their designs are such as I have never dreamed of working into a piece of goods. Why did you do this for me?"

"So that you can have time to do with as you see fit, rather than what you feel you must do. I don't think because a woman is raising a family, that she should spend every moment of her time doing something for them."

"Oh, Anton…"

"But you haven't seen anything yet," he assured her with a mysterious smile as he picked up another wooden box and placed it on the table. "Pass me the bar, again, Carl," he commanded. Again the others crowded around him with a hushed expectancy.

"What is it, father?" the children chorused as he removed the object.

"Do you know, mother?" Anton asked with a superior smile.

"I… don't… believe… I do," Marie said haltingly.

"Watch me," Anton directed as, from a box, he procured a spool of thread which he placed on the spool holder. With several deft twists of his fingers, he strung the thread from this mysterious gadget to that mysterious gadget until he adjusted a needle above the machine's flat surface. After a great deal of fumbling, he succeeded in placing the end of the thread through the eye of the needle. As the watchers saw the needle and thread an inkling of what was in store for them began to penetrate their minds. He showed them another spool of thread that was already firmly placed on its holder inside the machine. He explained as clearly as he could, how the thread formed the stitch. After asking for and receiving a piece of cloth, he grasped the handle of the machine and turned it. Before the startled eyes of his audience, he ran the cloth through, broke the thread and showed them how he had fastened the two edges of the cloth together.

"It's called a sewing machine," he said, trying to sound casual while in reality he was inwardly boiling with excitement.

Marie stood in a daze, unable to fully comprehend that she would have time for idleness. Her life had been devoted to work, with additional labor staring her in the face when she had rested; as a consequence; her periods of relaxation had been made uncomfortable with the thoughts of what she yet had to do. She seemed unable to grasp the fact that her husband had given her precious hours to do with as she saw fit, and merely because some machine duplicated what she had spent a lifetime in learning and practicing. "But … that is … I … I mean … what shall I do with my spare time? That machine stitches cloth that I won't have to first make myself and afterward sew by hand; and so neatly, too."

Anton laughed boisterously, his cheerful voice sounding strange in the room which had for so long echoed only to the hum of the spinning wheel, Marie's quaint songs, and the voice of the boy rising in heated argument with his sisters. At last he paused for breath and at the same time he held his stomach. "There'll be books to read after we move nearer to the city. You can visit more often and join a lodge; get interested in something besides your own family."

"This pipe needs cleaning," he remarked as he tapped the bowl on his hand and tossed the used tobacco into the fire. "You can do sewing for women who like that kind of work but who are too lazy or too wealthy to be bothered themselves. Now ask me what you are to do with your leisure time, if you have any, after helping with the cows. I still intend to supply many of the city folks with good milk."

"Everything is too, too beautiful and wonderful for words." Marie ran her glance as well as a hand over the machine and the cloth. "The cloth is far too nice for me to use for myself, although, 'twill look wonderful on the girls."

"To hear you talk," Anton laughed scornfully, "you would have me believe that you are eighty-eight years old."

"I am thirty-eight, look, my hair is turning gray."

"Perhaps that is from worrying what Amerikan girl I went to bed with," Anton suggested dryly.

The children shrieked gleefully at this coarse jest; then Engrid lapsed into a nervous titter as she clasped Louise by an arm, and Louise added a note of throaty laughter, meanwhile flashing her mother a speculative look to observe how she might receive the remark. Carl stopped laughing and stared at the lamp with a thoughtful expression on his face as though he hadn't really seen it before. Marie's eyes flashed and her words exploded in the silence hanging over the room.

"That is no way to talk around the children. I won't stand for it; there has never been anything like that said around this house since you went away. I loathe the words that drip from your tongue, you … you boardinghouse-tramp!"

"Oh, mother, my poor little mother," Anton murmured apologetically. He moved to his wife, drawing her into his arms as she burst into endless sobbing. He patted her on the back, while murmuring soothingly into the distraught woman's ears. "Don't cry, little one; I only meant it for a joke. It is true that I am a boardinghouse tramp, and I have not been around women and children much. I have just got in the habit of talking as do the rest of the men who do not have to watch their words; because they are around men most of the time. Forgive me, say you will," he pleaded.

I do," Marie stopped her weeping to reply. "I am sorry that I called you what I did; but I couldn't help flaring up like that. You will never know what it has meant to take the place of both mother and father during your long absence. I'm afraid that it has affected my mind. Besides that, the children bickered and quarreled when you failed to show up sooner today. I made them desist from normal play for fear that they would soil their clothing. I am sorry, Anton," she said humbly, "I told myself a thousand times, if once, that I would never quarrel with you again, and now, the first evening we are together, I have broken by vow. I am so weak," she said piteously as she clung to his broad shoulders.

"There, there," he comforted her while he stroked her hair and pressed a kiss on it; "perhaps this will make you feel better." He reached into his coat pocket and gave his wife a green, plush-covered box. Marie stared at it hesitantly and made no move to open it.

"Look inside." Anton said persuasively.

Marie moved a hand toward the lid as if reluctant to lift the top. "I was merely trying to guess what is in it, before I open it," she replied; disregarding the clamor raising from the children whose curiosity was more compelling than her own. She turned it over. "It is your picture!" she exclaimed happily, "But it is tiny!"

"Look inside, now," he urged, as he pointed to the delicately engraved yellow-gold case hanging from a chain whose links were infinitely smaller than any the woman had ever seen. He showed her a tiny catch and also a stem as he directed her to push the former.

"It's a watch!" she exclaimed as the lid with his picture on flipped open and exposed the timepiece. She lowered her hands and showed it to the curious youngsters who crowed around her in a frenzy of excitement; while they alternately kissed and hugged each of their parents in turn.

"You shouldn't have done this for me," she exclaimed.

"Think nothing of it," he said as he took the object and set the hands to the correct time. Then he placed the delicate chain around her throat and closed the clasp. "There," he remarked in a gay voice, "you look just like one of the higher-up women in the new country. They wear them all the time when they dress."

"You are too good to me." she stated softly.

"Nonsense," he protested, "I am only trying to repay you in a small way for the job that you have performed during my absence these long years." He placed an affectionate arm around his wife, noting as he did, with a feeling of compassion, how years of toil had broadened her figure and also removed the grace that had once been his delight. Love, stranger than he had ever known, welled up to his eyes and tears shown briefly. His thoughts were humble indeed, as he thought of what she had accomplished during his absence.

"I have brought these to you girls," Anton said, as from his pocket came two heart-shaped lockets and two pairs of earrings. "And for you, Carl, a signet ring," he added.

After the children's enthusiasm had cooled to a semblance of normalcy, Marie looked at the clock and remarked, "Now that everyone is happy, I propose that you children retire. You girls sleep in my bed until father and I get ready to go to sleep. I would like to sit here before the fire and talk; it has been so long."

Reluctantly accepting their mother's suggestion, the children retired, after first kissing their mother and also their benefactor.

"I'll just sit here awhile and smoke a pipe," Anton remarked as he sighed luxuriously and removed his shoes and flannel shirt. He then stretched his feet toward the fire. "I want to watch the coals before I put on the night log."

Marie sank beside him, after dousing the light. She stirred the fire and added a stick of wood, then leaned back to watch her husband pluck an ember from the bed of glowing coals. As Anton puffed at his pipe, the wood ignited in the fire. The couple sat in contented silence, listening to rain beating at the front door. Wind snuffled at the chimney; Marie crowded closer to Anton, recollection that this sound was supposedly made by people who had become lost souls at death, and were hovering around the heat rising from the chimney, in the vain hope that they might somehow enter into the cheery interior of the house. Leaning her head against her man, "It has been so long, so long," she said.

Breaking a silence of several minutes duration which seemed inexplicably precious to the pair, Anton suggested, "I'll give you a kiss for your thoughts."

"Oh, I was just thinking of ghosts, the wind and rain, and how wonderful it is to have you home again."

"And what else?" Anton asked.

"Anton, there were no women in Amerika ..."

"Oh, yes, thousands, even millions of beautiful women."

"Oh, I mean ... that is ..." Marie stammered in confusion while attempting to explain her doubts to this man who was a stranger, and yet, not a stranger. "Did you sleep with any of them?" she blurted out, then turned her head to conceal her embarrassment.

Turning to face her, Anton clasped her chin in a huge hand as he forced her to look into his eyes. "There were none that I went to bed with, or had anything to do with in the manner that you think. I danced with them and that was all. What little drinking I did was about once each month, and sometimes less; but I always drank with other men. No, Marie, there were no women to take your place."

She looked into his eyes; satisfied with what she saw and heard, she again laid her head on his shoulder with a sigh of profound, deeply-felt contentment. Anton rose to place his pipe on the mantel in his beloved holder, then placed his arms around her, kissing her fiercely as he did. Marie, at length, was forced to push him away. Rising to her feet, she whispered breathlessly, "Remember that the children are grownups now; let us go to bed."

The wind continued to sob about the house; while the man and woman echoed its restless moaning for a time. Off in the woods sounded the mournful cry of a wolf, then a faintly-heard answering call. Marie shivered, although not in fear. This time, hers was a shiver from ecstasy as she listened to her husband's quiet breathing.

Chapter 5

Anton utilized the following winter in cutting pine from the grove standing on ground that his wife had chosen near Jacobstad. Laboring industriously, he felled trees and hauled them to the site of his contemplated home. Mornings he rode one of his team of horses bareback, the other trailing behind, with harness chains jingling as the team plowed through deep snow. Evenings, he returned to his old home again, sometimes picking up his boy who still attended school.

Anton kept his promise in regards to the dog. Nels gave him one for the asking and the boy proudly started the dog's training by hitching it to a tiny harness and sleigh to match; so that the dog might become useful as it grew in size.

For two hours each evening, Anton worked on an ice-boat with sails, and then accompanied his son on frequent occasions when he taught him the finer points of speeding over the ice behind a billowing sail, after the ice-boat was completed.

He made skis for both the girls and boy, and taught them how to handle them behind a running horse.

Before the winter had run its course, Louise and Engrid had moved to their grandmother's house in town and the former found employment in a tobacco factory where she hand-rolled cigar and Engrid, for less money, went to work as a cook and maid for a Jacobstad lawyer.

The following spring, after plowing, harrowing and seeding the ground, most of which had already been cleared by the former owner, Anton notified several of his friends who helped him to raise the walls and rafter. He installed the fireplace, making it out of cobblestones. In the window frames, he placed single panes and at the same time, left room for others which colder weather would necessitate. This house was similar to the one that he had moved from, except that the boy and the girls had bedrooms of their own. The girls shared one room between them.

After the house was completed, the family moved in and for a week, the Isaacson's held open house for all who wished to become acquainted. When that week passed by, Anton went to work on his outbuildings and cellar. One-by-one, he purchased cows and calves until he built up a dairy herd from which he supplied butter, milk and cottage cheese to the town's inhabitants.

Cementing the bonds of friendship of past years, the Sundquist family visited each week when they came to Jacobstad to trade.

The girl's wages were small; but living at home as they did, after their parents moved into their new home, enabled the girls to save most of their money. For amusement during the warm months, they went boat riding and on dancing parties into the woods about the town.

Winters, they took to skiing and ice skating and became proficient in the use of both. On occasion, they went boat riding with their brother on his ice boat when the bay became frozen over.

In the meantime, Louise passed her leisure hours with a clear-eyed, strapping giant of a man by the name of Emil Flink. If one wished to know where the girl was of an evening, the answer was invariably, "She is with Emil." This relationship continued until Emil served his necessary term in the armed forces; during which time, Louise refused to accompany other men on trips and dancing parties.

Engrid proved to be unpredictable in her relationships with those of the opposite sex, going from one to the other, and never allowing herself more than an occasional infatuation as she had been in the habit of doing since she was a small girl. Of course, there was at one time, a youth whom she would have married in the first feverish rush of mature blood through her veins, but he had succumbed to Amerika fever, while she was still trying to make up her mind as to whether she should marry or not.

It is on Mid-Summer dagen of each year that the natives of the Finnish archipelago mingle, but without trading and bartering characterizing the Harvest Festival later in the summer. In every gathering, there appeared accordionists and fiddlers to set the spark lighting the fires of merriment which culminates in dancing, love-making and feasting.

In the vicinity of Jacobstad, such a colorful sight it is as boats, decorated with branches of silver birch, ply the waters of interlinking lakes; while the passengers, all in their very best, sing and play music when making their way to the city. Over crystal-clear waters dancing under a hot sun, chanting singers bending their oars, time their strokes to the notes of accordions and fiddles.

Along roads and pathways from the surrounding countryside, come natives in carts drawn by sturdy ponies. On the wheels of the vehicles are bound branches of silver birch and occupants wave other branches of silver birch in time with their joyous singing. There are those who have neither horse, nor boat; but such trifles cannot prevent their arrival in the city to which they walk with spirited strides; for who is there among them that cares to miss the greatest social event of the year?

There, on green slopes running from the side of the lake to the tops of low, rolling hills, children chase each other like colts turning out to pasture. There, too, older people move about from one group to another, renewing acquaintances, drinking mead, and the more fortunate of the men folk, surreptitiously sharing a bottle of imported vodka or brandy. There too, maidens hiding coyly under peaked linen bonnets, tossing their braids as they laugh and chatter feverishly, or pretend to listen to another's conversation; when in reality they are waiting, eyes sparkling, for some freshly shaven lad to invite them into his group for the day's festivities.

Some carefree boy and girl travel through their crowd acquiring other couples along the way until a large party has been gathered. This chattering, singing group moves to a level spot and forms the nucleus of a dancing party. The musicians play until they can play no more, and the dancers dance until they can dance no more. When the elders observe this, they issue a call to kahvia and the tired dancers seat themselves to feast. After an interval of rest, the dancing begins again; continuing until the sun dips briefly below the southern horizon causing the countryside to glow with an unreal, half-dark half-light radiance. Then dancing and chattering ceases when spent couples sink to the ground sharing surreptitious kisses as boats move from the shore, towing dark blobs that close scrutiny reveals to be rafts, piled high with dry wood thoroughly soaked with tar. The blobs of darkness are lighted, and orange tongues of flame rising high in the air, trace shimmering rays from the rafts to the shore.

As the sun again surmounts the southern horizon, after a brief interlude of dusk, boats moving homeward, create ripples that douse burning rafts into hissing oblivion. Giant woodsmen trudge their lonely ways into the forests and weary farmers allow their ponies to pick their own ways to familiar barns; because they are too weary to drive.

It was mid-summer day, and while apparently pausing for a time, the sun flooded the archipelago with its glorious rays. The earth responded to its lover's ardent caress with a burst of fecund activity common only to that particular clime. Once around the clock, grass could be seen to grow an inch or more. Pine and spruce seemed bursting in fragrance as they added clusters of lighter colored needles to their branches. Daisies spread an undulating cloth over the forest floor for the annual feast of summer; and adding their cheerful silver to the wealth of color over all, birch trees unfolded new leaves. Blackberries weighted their branches to the breaking point. Below the birch, in places, were lovely bachelor buttons. Canterbury bells opened seductively to bees that nuzzled buttercups, until their legs became incased with armors of pollen; while their contented droning fell with mesmeric indolence on the ears of the girls who gathered birch branches to decorate their home.

Engrid mechanically added to her armful of branches while giving her senses full rein to the passionate smell of summer that fairly smothered the countryside. She thrilled to the piping of chickadees swarming in trees about her, and pondered at the dexterity of the tiny feathered wanderers which enabled them to hang from the branches while dining on the eggs of insects. The diminutive birds paused frequently in their search for food, to utter their plaintive, "Dee- dee-dee," which, though cheerful sounding in a way, held a note of ineffable sadness suggesting the loneliness of somber woods.

Louise laid her branches down then threw herself in the grass with one arm curled under her head; thereby preventing the brown leaves of yester-year from contacting her neatly braided hair. Her mature breasts rose and fell under her blouse; while she chewed meditatively on twig and watched her comely sister through half-closed eyes. "I'll certainly be glad to see Emil when he comes," she observed.

"Oh," Engrid said in a noncommittal voice as she eyed the results of their efforts with a speculative glance. Satisfied that what the two of them had gathered would be sufficient to trim the doors and windows of their home, she sank indolently into the grass beside her sister, where she lay on her side, her head resting on an open palm and her elbow propped on the ground. With her free hand, she gathered humus and compressed it, then idly watched as it dropped from her opening fingers. Tiring of the awkward position in which she held herself, she stretched out; turning over on her back to peer through the branches, and pondering on the bond between Louise and Emil.

"When are you going to be married?" Engrid asked curiously.

"I don't know," Louise answered.

"Do you want to get married?"

"Yes; but Emil definitely has the Amerika fever as father did at one time. He says there is big money to be made in that country. He says a man should choose the kind of work he wants to do. He doesn't want to waste his life milking a cow or plowing a few acres of ground with no end to the number of rocks that the plow turns up."

Engrid turned her head a trifle to gaze in a detached manner to the long walls of rock constituting the boundaries of her father's farm. These increased in size from year to year so, to the casual observer, it was apparent that there could be no time for idleness during the short summer months. From her contemplation of the rocks, her thoughts went to Emil, a tall, broad-shouldered giant of a man, who expended his energy in a hard day's work and who sought relaxation in dancing. The man's vitality seemed without limit; because a two hour rest after supper found him eager to do something to rid himself of restlessness. He possessed a rugged, not unhandsome face beaming with friendliness, but a temper that got no opposition when he started going steady with Louise; not that Louise wanted another suitor, she was content to wait for Emil indefinitely; or so she had told her sister on numerous occasions.

When couples joined in wedlock, Engrid often found herself wondering, as many people are prone to do, what the couples could see in each other. But it was not so with Louise and Emil, she thought; on the contrary, if these two didn't wed, the world could stop revolving in so far as Louise was concerned. The sun and moon could halt and stars glow like so many useless fragments of chipped ice where they traversed their orderly pathways through the infinite void above the pondering girl.

"If Louise doesn't get married to Emil, before long, it will…" She faced a blank wall in her pondering. "Will what?" she questioned herself. "It just can't happen any other way," she wisely concluded. "They must marry; or Louise will die of a broken heart."

Heaving a pent-up sigh, Engrid stood erect and brushed the leaves from her clothing. However, Louise remained at full length in the leaves, her petticoats peeping immodestly in their lacy fullness around her shapely ankles and bare feet. As Engrid looked down on her sister, she found herself wondering why it was that someone like herself couldn't be just like Louise. Louise was so certain and assured of her future and of the means to attain her goal. Hers was no problem of what she should do, but a life seemingly filled with answers to her every question.

On the other hand, Engrid mused, she herself seemed to drift from day to day around an aimless circle, not knowing what she wanted and not knowing how to attain it. Opportunities for interesting work were definitely limited and housework, for many years now, had been her only means of earning a livelihood. Her only alternative other than drudging for others was to marry someone; but that, in it's self, presented a problem. So many of the country's available young men had gone to Amerika at the first opportunity; that the women, finding themselves in the majority, were also leaving at every hand.

To the girl's mind came an incident which had occurred shortly after her father had returned home after years of absence. She had walked by their bedroom one night after spending an evening with Vinie Sundquist, to hear her mother and father discussing the possibilities of the children attending the university; and while listening out of curiosity, she had heard her father state that things appeared in a new perspective. Now that he had spent so many years away from home, he had definitely decided to invest the balance of his savings in a herd of dairy cows, thereby providing for his wife's and his own future after the children had moved from home.

Bitterly the girl remembered how she had gone to sleep after crying to herself for a long time. How sad she had been, after being forced to discard the hope of attending an advanced school to become a teacher. It wouldn't have been so hard had her mother not held the thought before her for so many years. Afterward, she and her sister had both decided to work and save their money with the intention of eventually leaving the country in favor of Amerika.

Of late, especially when one of her friends told her of a letter that they had received from a friend in Amerika, Engrid had felt as if life in the community was stifling her. The schooners' masts rising like a forest of trees whose trunks had been swept bare by fire, no longer suggested an out for her. Even the sailors traveling to and from Sweden and England, offered only the promise of a conversation that invariably began or ended with, "When I was in Amerika," or, "When I get to Amerika," and, as a consequence, an evening with them only added unrest entirely out of proportion to the number of coins in her copper chest.

Now, standing on the hill top, overlooking the bay, Engrid knew that she wanted to leave the country of her birth, and this desire to be off was all consuming. But where to go in Amerika? She couldn't just take an atlas and place a finger on the vast country with eyes closed and move her finger haphazardly until it came to a halt just any place and then say, "I shall go there." She had tried that and one time her finger landed on what represented the Pacific Ocean. Her father had laughed heartily, then told her to be patient until she had saved the necessary fare, and surely a way would open for her to some particular place.

"If I were a man," she mused, "I could pack a valise, buy a fare to New York City, and after landing there, find someone who has already preceded me from either Sweden or Finland; then I would go to work as father did."

Standing there in the hot sunshine, Engrid became increasingly aware of the turmoil inside of her; so at variance with the calm rhythm of nature. From high overhead a bird effortlessly followed its mate on a rising current of air. Without conscious direction of her thoughts, Engrid dropped her head to look down on herself. She felt her strong heart beating in regular pulsations beneath her blouse and her breasts tightening where they pushed against the white cloth. She flushed guiltily at what she found herself thinking; her breathing quickened and she stole a glance in her sister's direction lest Louise be watching her and read her thoughts, as she was in the habit of doing at times.

The two of them had discussed men on numerous occasions, and of late, most of their discussions had been factual, tempered with intrigue. Her dreams, too, had often been warmed with the thoughts of men. This beating, throbbing, tumultuous clamoring inside of her, strongly felt when the sun hung almost constantly over the horizon, had become unbearable at times. She sighed, knowing that when her thoughts moved in this particular channel for long, she would end up in a fit of blues caused by frustration. Only one thing to do, she thought; turn her mind to other things.

"Let's go, Louise, we must get the branches hung before we go to the city, remember?"

Louise stifled a yawn as she raised herself and gathered a portion of the branches from the pile. Together, the girls started homeward, pausing occasionally to grasp a handful of berries as they carefully picked their way between rocks heated to an uncomfortable degree. Here and there they also stopped at beds of wild strawberries nestling in hollows where the snow had been not long before. They ate of the fruit, seemingly never getting their fill of their crisp, mouth-watering flavor.

When the sisters threw the branches on the floor of the living room, their mother met them with exclamations of pleasure as she came from the kitchen that she had insisted on Anton building. The odor of coffee cake baking followed her in a tenuous cloud.

"My, they are lovely this year," Marie exclaimed with enthusiasm as she placed the mortar bowl on the table. She grasped one of the branches and held it aloft for closer inspection. "Do find father and let him tie them to the doors and windows. If company should drop in, we want things to be just right."

Engrid found her father and Carl busily engaged in sawing a dry spruce into proper lengths for the fireplace. Anton was laboring industriously, the odor of his pipe discouraging the swarms of gnats dancing madly over the perspiring workers.

"By golly, that I will do," he said in English; thereby causing his daughter to smile. She had grown used to occasional phrases which he spoke in that intriguing tongue; although she failed miserably to understand what he was saying. However, she knew by the tone of his voice that he had said, "Ya!"

Carl was only too glad to abandon the back-breaking work, and on hurried feet, he raced to the house where he groomed for the festivities.

While Anton hung the branches, a chore that he insisted only he knew how to do correctly, the girls busied themselves with the packing of lunch baskets. Into these went cold mutton sandwiches, herring dipped in crumbs and fried to a rich brown in parsley and butter and tasty coffee cake. At long last, the family deemed themselves prepared to leave the house, after Anton had closed the doors to discourage stray dogs; then they started the short walk toward town.

As Engrid tripped blithely along, her steps proclaimed her inner buoyancy, and well they might! Many young men from inland attended the yearly festival, affording by their presence, opportunities for flirtations with others than city youths who felt themselves important because they were so few in comparison to their feminine admirers.

When the family drew into the main road, they became one with a ragged line of gaily singing revelers, and the girls added their voices to that of the multitude. Finally, at the city center, where vendors called out their wares in sing-song voices and the divergent streams of people swelled into a colorful flood, Engrid followed Louise in her search for Emil. Kanteles sounded their plaintively haunting notes, and accordions and fiddles heightened the spirits of an already enthusiastic crowd. Carl went in search of Walter Sundquist; so that the two might get their heads together over a glass of mead; and afterward, find some fair companions with which to while away the hours. Anton and Marie strolled about, stopping here and there to converse with friends and relatives whom they hadn't seen for many months.

These people had gathered in attire similar to that which their ancestors had worn when Eric the Ninth, at the beginning of the twelfth century, had led the first group of Swedes to accompany the Bishop Henry of Upsala, when he had brought the Lutheran religion to the heathen Finns.

Women in the crowds through which the sisters moved, were clothed in practically the same manner; although in differently colored and patterned clothes according to the wearer's preference. On their heads were affixed white bonnets of linen, freshly laundered in a solution of soda and run through wooden rollers when slightly damp. These bonnets were roughly pyramid-like in shape, and under them, hair had been gathered in coils or braids tied with gaily-colored bits of ribbon. These swung free as the women walked to and fro, or joined one of the many swirling groups of dancers.

White blouses had long sleeves fitting tightly at the lace-crocheted cuffs. Large collars embroidered with red and pink roses that seemingly grew green stems and even greener leaves cheerfully contrasted with the backgrounds. The blouses fit well down in the high-waist skirts, the tops of which were laced tightly over the three cotton or linen petticoats. The skirts were models of originality as no two families used the same pattern in weaving cloth; and, as a consequence, each woman passing furnished a contrast that was pleasing to the observer's eye. High-buttoned shoes over long stockings of various colors completed their attire.

The men's hats, for the most part, were dark and around each was a gaily-colored band of ribbon detracting from their drabness. White linen shirts were fastened at their throats by scarves tied in bows. Each man wore a vest, coat and trousers; the latter fastened above the knees and hanging over in a fold covering the tops of their long stockings. Their feet were clad in slippers held in place by straps pulled tightly over the insteps.

Here and there, standing in small groups, the girls distinguished Lapps, a wealthy race of people in their own right; their wealth being measured by the number of reindeer that each family possessed. Engrid found herself staring in fascination at these squat people with their mongoloid features and dark hair. Her curiosity seemed insatiable as she regarded their Hats-of-the-Four-Winds, as the owners called their broad, four-cornered headgear, trimmed with red piping. The diminutive people, even though the weather was exceedingly warm, wore their long, dark-blue tunics embroidered with red and yellow braids. Their feet were incased in well-tanned deerskin boots of incredible, moccasin-like softness.

"There is Emil!" Louise exclaimed gleefully.

Engrid withdrew from her absorption of the dwarf-like visitors to ask, "Where?" However, she was unable, for the moment, to pick out one figure from another of those who sat in the green grass munching on sandwiches, or as some were doing, dancing to the gayest, liveliest music that accordionists and fiddlers could evoke from their instruments.

"There under that tree. He is with someone that I don't recognize." Louise answered. Louise raised an arm and waved eagerly as she quickened her pace toward her lover.

Evidently Emil saw Louise at the same moment; because he stood up and ran hurriedly down the slope to catch her in his arms. Raising her aloft, he kissed her as he murmured tenderly, "My love, my love." He set her down and said to Engrid, "Hello, sister."

"Hello, yourself, soldier boy."

"We had to gather birch bows or we would have been here sooner," Louise hastened to explain. "Why didn't you come up to the house?"

"I have a friend along who served in my company, and he didn't exactly feel right about intruding on you, without advance notice. We had no way of knowing whether or not Engrid would have a companion for the day; consequently, I decided to stay here in town with him. Did I do wrong?"

"Maybe, and maybe not," Engrid chimed in. "What does he look like?"

"Oh," Emil replied hesitantly, "he's tall, has a beautiful mustache and light complexion; come see for yourself. I'll bet he is just the kind of man you would like to bundle with on a crisp night."

"Interesting, if true," Engrid chirped; "lead me to him!"

With a girl hanging on each crooked arm, Emil moved up the grassy slope toward the trees where he stopped at the foot of a spruce and the trio looked down on a recumbent figure with one arm covering his eyes. He was snoring contentedly and a strapped accordion lay within arm's reach in the grass.

"Is he drunk?" Engrid asked apprehensively.

"No, he hasn't had a drink. He's tired out and bored with living." Emil replied with a grin as he stooped over, plucked a blade of grass and began to run it over the lips of the sleeping stranger. The man brushed irritably at whatever he felt pestering him, then turned over with a sigh and buried his face in his arms. His snoring continued regularly, after but a small break in its continuity.

The girls giggled. Emil burst into a bellow of good-natured laughter. "Hey, Elmer, wake up and see what papa has brought you!" he called.

Turning over with a groan, Elmer opened his eyes and darted a quick glance from one to the other of the girls. "It isn't a dream," the man argued in a deep bass voice, "because you are in it," he went on with a meaningful look at the grinning Emil, "and no matter how hard up I get for a change of companions, I never see you in my dreams." As he finished speaking, he rose to a full six feet and brushed off his clothes.

"This is Elmer Lund, he of the big mouth and witty tongue. This girl here is my betrothed, Louise; and this fair-haired daughter of a fortunate farmer whose name is Isaacson, we shall call Engrid. They are sisters."

"My mother tried to teach me to believe in wood sprites, fairies and angels; but she seemingly failed until now." Elmer gallantly responded.

"My goodness," Engrid gasped admiringly, "I do believe that I am going to like you."

"And I, you," the man crowed. "It had to happen to us. What is the first thing on the program? Shall we eat, drink, dance or make love?"

"Let's find mother and father and tell them that we are going to take father's boat and ride out to some island and eat." Louise suggested. "Afterward, we can return to the city and dance."

"Agreed," replied her companions in unison. Before long they were skimming over the clear waters of interlinking lakes, the boat's red sail breasting ahead under the impetus of a fresh breeze blowing steadily from over the ocean. Their gay songs and laughter caught them up in a spirit of excitement and, as a result, the hours and kilometers fairly flew behind.

"And what did you heroes do during your two years of training to be soldiers?" Engrid asked during a lull in their singing.

"Heroes, indeed!" grunted Emil from his position at the tiller, as he steered the boat in and out of rocks protruding above the surface of a channel leading to a cove that Louise had pointed out. "Soldiers, Bah!" Elmer exclaimed. "We signed up for our allotted time and what did we get? I'll tell you what, a hundred-thousand trees to fell when we made a road all the way across the land to the south of here for the Russians to use when they decide to take the country over in earnest. All of this under a Russian-born commander, mind you! We spent endless days filling swamps in water up to our necks and nights polishing filthy boots so that we could dirty them the following day. In between times, we fed smudges to blood-thirsty mosquitoes that grow as large as woodpeckers in the swamps. We endured two winters crawling on our bellies and posing as snowmen. The weather was so cold that trees popped like cannon and our guns wouldn't shoot. We couldn't get enough heat out of our fires to warm rocks for our steam baths; but that wasn't bad enough," he rambled on in disgruntled tones, "a lousy, dirty Finn who had never seen a bar of soap, started lice in our barracks; and I scratched myself bald before I got rid of them."

Engrid glanced at his heavy head of blonde hair; then she blushed as Elmer caught her look and promptly burst forth in laughter that infected them all as the boat ground to a halt.

On shore, the sisters unpacked their lunch baskets and procured water for their coffee. The men disappeared inland in search of dry wood as Louise spread a cloth and began to set the table.

"Do me a favor, Engrid."

"If it's within reason; what is it?"

"Emil has informed me that he is leaving for Amerika tomorrow. He already has train tickets to Helsingfors where he is going to withdraw his savings and purchase a passage on a steam ship. He has thought things over and come to the conclusion that he doesn't want to remain here and get married. You go for a ride with Elmer and allow me an hour or so alone with Emil. It'll be the last chance I will have," she said with a hurried glance toward the trees as she removed sandwiches from the basket and placed them on the cloth; then covered them with another.

Engrid's brow wrinkled into a puzzled frown as she asked, "Last chance for what?"

"Oh, blockhead," Louise said with disgust, "the last chance I shall have to be alone with him before he leaves. I am going to see if I can get him to propose to me. I don't want to let him run away and leave me here. I'll never see him again if he does that," she explained, her eyes agleam with excitement.

"And how do you intend to accomplish your ends if he doesn't want to?" The youngest asked naively.

"I have it all planned out; but we have to be alone … shhh…here they come now."

"Mother won't …"

"Be still," Louise hissed, "mother isn't me and I am old enough to know what I want. Don't you dare say a word about us separating into two parties, or we'll never be allowed to forget it; and on top of that, I'll never forgive you, you goose."

"Listen, sister," Engrid muttered heatedly, "if you think for one moment that you're going to turn me loose with a soldier who has been away from decent women for two years, and, as a consequence, has probably forgotten how to conduct himself, you are loony … I'll not do it!"

"Be still!" Louise warned frantically. To the approaching men she called quite unnecessarily, "I see that you found some dry wood!" She gave her sister a long look fraught with meaning that Engrid found not at all difficult to interpret.

"That we did," Emil said brightly; "as fathers of all woodcutters, we know where every dry piece is between here and Russia; don't we, Elmer?"

"And as soldiers, where to find the most comely maidens," Elmer added with a wink at his companion as he carelessly let fall an armload of wood and prepared to light the fire.

Emil took charge of the coffee making and Elmer favored them all with compositions of his own on the accordion. Engrid acted her gay self as she drank her coffee and ate her lunch; although she felt ill at ease under her sister's questioning glances. Finally, when she realized that it was useless to thrust the problem into the background for a longer period of time, and as the sun set briefly, she turned to Elmer and asked, "Will you take me for a boat ride?"

Elmer sprang to his feet, "No sooner said than done; where shall we go?"

"Oh, just out on the lake for a time. I enjoy the feel of water under me at this time of the day."

"Are you coming along?" Elmer asked of Emil and his companion.

"I'd sooner not," Louise replied with a quick squeeze of Emil's hand clasped in her own. "The only reason I ride a boat at all, is to save myself the trouble of walking; you see," she explained, "I'm not a water-dog like my sister."

"But I thought … that is …" Emil began to object; Louise cut him off, however, saying, "Oh, let them have a ride. We can still chaperone them if they'll stay in sight."

"But your mother …"

"Shan't know anything about it, when and if she asks", Louise hastened to reply to Emil. "I'll tell her that I never let my little baby sister out of my sight," she added; too gaily, Engrid decided.

Against her better judgment, she seated herself in the craft and Elmer pushed it from shore; then he jumped in and raised the sails while Engrid held firmly to the tiller. Soon they were heading at a brisk rate toward the far side of the lake. From where Louise sat, the boat and its occupants presented dark silhouettes against a paling sky.

Engrid's troubles began almost immediately when Elmer sought to demonstrate that he was as proficient in love-making as he was at playing his accordion. However, when the man found that Engrid considered sex as something to enhance marital relations, he desisted, and thenceforth conducted himself most honorably until the boat grounded at the same place from whence it had taken its leave.

As Engrid jumped ashore, she looked to where Louise sat with her back to a spruce and her legs folded under and off to one side. Emil lay with his head in her lap, contentedly smoking a brown-paper cigarette whose tip winked cheerfully in the gloom. Engrid searched her sister's face and found it blank. Louise seemed to be her usual self, as she began to chatter gaily when the couple came to where she sat.

After partaking of another cup of coffee and a sandwich, the quartet embarked for the city, arriving there just as the sun rose again. There the men took their leave; Emil meanwhile excused himself and Elmer; saying that they just had time to catch the train. Elmer and Engrid stood in an awkward silence as Emil kissed Louise.

"I'll either return for you, sweetheart, or else, if you'll still have me, I'll send you money to come over and marry me. Will you do it then?"

Louise nodded her head despondently; then after kissing him hungrily, she turned and watched as Elmer took leave of her sister and walked hurriedly toward town. "Don't look back when you leave me," Louise begged tearfully, "or I'll never see you again."

"I love you, believe me, sweetheart." Emil whispered as he turned away leaving behind him a heart-broken slip of a girl.

Long after lowered blinds plunged the room into an artificial darkness, Engrid was awakened by the muffled sobbing of her sister.

"What is the matter, Louise?" she asked feeling afraid of what the answer might be.

Louise's bitter crying diminished and finally she whispered, "I've lost Emil, I know it as surely as I am lying here."

"Explain yourself," Engrid encouraged. She waited tensely for an answer, while it seemed to her that the darkness of the room was crowding in on her, smothering her. Her voice seemed strangely detached from her body.

"When you left us to go for the boat ride," Louise continued in a lifeless tone, "I had my mind made up as to what I intended to do. We started kissing and I threw myself at him, offered myself to him; he knew that I wanted him ..." She ceased speaking as the palpable darkness descended on her waiting companion.

"And then?" Engrid asked as she felt her way to the window and raised the blind.

"He … he left me," Louise agonized through her sobs which began anew, "to … to walk on …on the b-b-beach by himself for a time."

"Then he didn't …?"

"No."

"Oh," Engrid said, the word sounding like a profound sigh of relief as with her blue cotton robe gathered about her, she seated herself on her sister's bed and asked softly, "Why did you do it?" She stroked Louise's hair, noting, a she did, the swollen eyes and bitter lines around a tense mouth. "Was it because you wanted him so much that your feelings temporarily got the best of you?"

"That was the reason, but not the only one," Louise replied in a calmer voice. She reached for her handkerchief, wiped her nose and replaced it under her pillow.

"What other reason could there be?" Engrid asked. "That, I can understand."

Obviously seeking for words to frame an answer, Louise gazed out of the window. After a time, she dropped her eyes to the quilt on which she lay and plucked aimlessly at a tied piece of yarn. "I planned to force him to marry me; then he would have to take me with him rather than leave me here, alone."

"You did that?" Engrid sounded shocked.

"Yes," Louise muttered, "but you wouldn't understand and won't until you live for someone else besides yourself."

"And what happened after you got together with him, after he had taken the walk?"

"He… he came back," Louise answered, seeming to sink lower into the quilt in her sorrow.

"Go on," Engrid encouraged soothingly.

"I… I explained to him why I acted as I did; but he said that he didn't want to marry me, leave me here with a child, something might happen to keep us from ever getting together again, and he didn't want to place a burden on my shoulders. What a noble man!" She burst out vindictively, "I despise his insides." She balled her hands into fists, pushing as she did so, one against the other in her distraction.

Engrid thoughtfully regarded her sister's empty fingers void of a ring as Louise lapsed into a brooding silence.

"Why didn't you just ask him to marry you and take you with him?" Engrid broke the silence.

"I did just that; but he said he doesn't know where he is going to look for work; or what kind of work he can find. However, he did promise that after settling down somewhere, he intends to send for me. He even said that he would send passage money," she said hopefully.

"I would certainly consider that fair."

"If he meant it, and I doubt that he did," Louise objected.

"Why do you say that, knowing the man as you do?" Engrid flared.

"I… I think that he considers me a cheap trollop because of the way I acted. I hate him!"

"You do no such thing, you loon," Engrid remarked springing to Emil's defense; "you actually hate yourself and your foolish pride." A furious note crept into her voice. "You've spent years picturing to yourself how it would be when you settled down on a piece of ground that he had cleared with his own hands. You also have imagined yourself at a spinning wheel and children toddling around the floor. You actually seem to think you are the only one that would matter if you married him. Emil knows what your motives were, as well as I ... the Lord only knows that he has known you long enough to be able to judge your character. You tried and I can't say that I blame you; but things didn't work out as you planned. Why; because you didn't consider his desires as well as your own. You can't plan his life, Louise, at least not until after marriage; and even then, you'll have to continually compromise with him. You couldn't get him on your own terms; so it will have to be on his, if at all. You'll have to face that fact, whether you like it or not."

"I... I'll m-marry someone else." Louise sobbed despairingly.

"You poor, deluded fool," Engrid said bitterly; "you must wait for your man as mother did and you shall reap happiness as she has. Marry another and you'll regret it for the remainder of your life. For that matter, so will Emil. If you marry another for spite, you'll make life a living hell for some man who really loves you; when you don't love him. Giving your body to him would be sheer mockery. You'll succeed in breaking three hearts. Won't that be something to gloat over in your old age?"

She fell silent and with unseeing eyes, stared thoughtfully out of the window. Her preoccupied glance, after brushing over her father's rippling fields of ripening grain, rested on the dancing surface of the lake.

"If I had Emil to wait for," she said softly, and a far away look shone from her eyes, "I would wait forever; even if I died as a lonely old woman. It is a woman's place to wait, once a man has promised."

Rising, she pulled at the blind and after kissing her sister on the forehead, she threw herself on the top of her bed with a tired sigh.

Chapter 6

Engrid gasped in awe as she stared wide-eyed out of the window viewing the mountains rising to dizzying heights above the tracks over which the train thundered at an unbelievable rate. The screech of the train whistle reverberated from the canyon walls; sounding like a tortured demon must sound in the hell which her mother had spoken of with such trepidation.

"Why did we come here?" she thought to herself; knowing full well that this had been planned for quite some time. Emil had finally sent for Louise and Engrid had always known that she would come to Amerika.

"For heaven's sake, Louise," Engrid remarked irritably, "if you must look, kindly take your elbow out of my stomach and move to the window; I will gladly trade places with you." She stepped into the aisle and Louise promptly took her seat then glued her nose against the pane to watch, as coming swiftly on, night dropped a mottled cloak of purple and black on the pine-covered lower slopes and tinted the snow above with a banner of exquisite pink.

"Oh, sister," Louise exclaimed breathlessly, "had I but known there was so much beauty in this country, I wouldn't have wasted these twenty-two years back home."

"How could you know what this would be like before coming here?" Engrid countered; "You can have your train and mountains; as for me, give me a boat on a lake." Her voice sounded disgruntled and the experience of being above the sea at such a height, for the first time, gave her a feeling of giddiness which was intensified when she glanced out of the window. In addition, her ears felt as though they were stuffed with cotton. "I feel as though I had just taken a drink of liquor," she murmured in a faint voice.

"What do you mean?" Louise asked, as turning from her contemplation of the scenery, she eyed her sister questioningly.

"I'm dizzy, and worse still, I can't hear as well as I should."

Louise stretched her arms upward to relieve a cramped feeling, and abruptly, a startled look came into her eyes. "Engrid," she exclaimed, dropping her hand to her sister's arm; "when I yawned, my ears popped and I can hear as well as ever, you try it," she encouraged.

"How can I yawn when I don't have to; don't be foolish?" Engrid grumbled. Nevertheless, she tried. The action left her with a feeling of futility.

"Did it help?" Louise asked in a voice that was all but inaudible to her ears.

Engrid shook her head with a look of boredom showing on her features. She pulled out a handkerchief and violently blew her nose in an attempt to rid her head of congestion. As she prepared to tuck the accessory away, she noticed with amazement that a splotch of crimson was on the delicate square. She stared in surprise as, intermittently, a series of drops fell into the confines of the cloth.

Louise quickly sized the situation up. "For goodness sake, take this towel and I'll get some water and soak it for you; just don't let any fall on your blouse or skirt or it will ruin them." She hurried down the aisle to the tap, and in a moment, with one end of the towel dampened, she applied it alternately to the back of her sister's neck and the bridge of her nose.

"I feel much better, now," Engrid remarked as she dabbed tentatively at her nose; "the stuffiness has gone and I can hear." She grinned ruefully saying, "That's the first time that I remember ever having had a nose bleed."

After a time, the girls fell into a fitful sleep. As the night grew colder, they pulled on their great coats and leaned against each other in the manner of tired children, their light and auburn heads together. Through their attempts to slumber, came the rhythmical clicking of the wheels on joints, the stopping and starting of the train, and the arrival and departure of passengers. These sounds were heard all through the night. At times, Engrid opened weary eyes and glanced disinterestedly at other passengers who were in various states of sleeping and waking. Some peering through the windows, vainly attempting to glimpse the country through which they traveled, and others too weary to care where they were bound, huddled in their seats. As the girl leaned there, head lolling backward against the seat, she idly compared herself to a detached fragment of a meteorite being whirled through space, without desire or interest in its ultimate destination. It appeared to her that she had been traveling all of her life. She was traveling from a past to a future that would never be any different. At other times, when she awakened after slumbering, she felt as one with the motion of the train and mused to herself that it would be nice to go on like she was doing forever and ever; never having to work, eat, converse with people, or to even have to think again; just to feel the sensation of the riding without any conscious effort of her own, into eternity.

At times she shifted her head's position on Louise's shoulder; then she fell asleep again, her mind filled with the vision of wheels that rumbled forever onward, as the drivers chopped off the miles. Indulging in such harmless forms of escapism, the girl managed the night.

The following morning, the girls broke their fast on apples and rolls peddled by a hawker who passed from car to car, crying his wares.

Finally, at a stop when the train changed engines, a woman and her two children left a vacancy across the aisle from the girls and later, a fastidiously dressed man boarded the train when it was about to depart. He seated himself across from the sisters. After placing a valise on the seat beside him, he passed Engrid a newspaper and made some observation in English.

"What did he say?" Engrid whispered a trifle self-consciously to her sister.

"How should I know? Anyone in their right mind would interpret his gesture as an invitation to look through the paper," Louise answered irritably.

Engrid accepted the paper, even though Anton had warned them both not to become friendly with any men until after arriving at their destination. For a time, the sisters whiled away the miles looking at advertisements and comparing styles in men's and women's clothing with those of the country that they had abandoned a short three weeks ago. While they "Oh'd" and "Ah'd," over the fashions displayed in the paper, they compared cuts of dresses with those that fellow travelers wore.

Into Engrid's line of vision came a sack extended by the man across the aisle. The girl dared a peep inside and her eyes fell on several strands of string, with what appeared to be cut-glass beads adhering to them. Hesitantly, she thrust a hand into the sack and grasped a strand, then pulled it from the sack. She nodded her thanks with a quick smile and turned to her sister as she placed the strand to her throat.

"Pretty," Louise observed, "but you can't very well accept beads from a stranger. He must merely mean for you to admire them, I suppose, then give them back again."

Engrid turned to follow her sister's advice and what she saw the man doing to a strand similar to the one she was holding, caused her jaw to hang slack in amazement. She nudged her sister with her elbow and in a falsetto voice, exclaimed, "The man is eating some beads!"

Louise looked, and so he was. With head tilted backward against the seat, he lowered a strand, oh, ever so slowly into his open mouth and with evident relish, he munched on it.

"Good heavens!" Louise exclaimed, "He can't be; but he is." For a moment, amazement heightened her pretty features. "Say, let me see that," she remarked and placing one end of the crystalline covered string into her mouth, she bit gently. "Candy," she decided; whereupon, she giggled and at last, unable to excuse her own and Engrid's ignorance, she burst into merry laughter in which her sister joined.

"Now, what?" the man across the aisle asked as he deftly retrieved the soggy string from his mouth and reached into the sack for another strand. He appeared puzzled as he stared at the sisters. Because they could not set him right in regards to the cause of their merriment, their storm of mirth was prolonged, until others turned to look their way with vacant grins on their features. Their expressions induced the girls to laugh harder still, until with hands clasping their sore abdominal muscles, they fell silent, except for an occasional titter.

"That laugh was worth a fortune," Louise commented as she wiped at her eyes

"And did you see the expressions on the faces of the other travelers as they turned to stare at us?" Engrid added with a giggle.

At the next station, the stranger gathered up his overcoat and valise, and with a smile and tipped hat, he left the girls to themselves. Although the man had not been able to engage them in conversation, he had given them a hearty laugh; and that was more than the girls had been able to enjoy previous to this day since leaving their homeland.

"I thought that I was going to die from laughter," Louise remarked as the man made his departure.

Engrid giggled nervously, then said, "Father told us to beware of tall, dark strangers who wished to become familiar; but we can be excused; this man was light and had blue eyes." She fell silent to watch as mountains thrust excursive feet into the variegated green of a valley along which the train was speeding. On each side of the car, green fields extended invitingly.

"Springville, Springville!" the conductor called as he followed his ample stomach down the aisle and stopped at the sisters' seat. Reaching for their valises and beckoning them with a cheerful smile toward the door, he said, "Here's where you get off, ladies." Understanding his gesture but not necessarily his words; Louise stated, "It appears as though we are about to change trains again." The sisters gathered their coats and walked down the length of the car watching with anxious eyes to see if their trunk would be unloaded at they exited the train. It was, and landed with a bang on the gravel; then the baggage man stood in the door and waved at the girls as the train pulled away.

As the girls moved away from the train, the station agent came forward and looked at their tickets. He removed a watch from his vest pocket and pointed to the time which was 11:32 a.m.; then he spun the hands with a deft motion until they pointed to 4:30 p.m. "Savvy?" he asked as he swept the hand along the length of the track.

"Ya," the girls said in unison.

After the grinning agent placed the trunk and valises inside the station for safekeeping, Louise grasped him by the arm; and removed a pencil from his vest pocket. Louise went through the motions of writing. Raising her hand aloft, she pointed to the wires strung from pole to pole; as far as her eye could see.

"Come on," the agent ordered, then moved into the station where he handed the girl a sheet of paper and laboriously, lest the man be unable to read her writing, Louise printed out a message in Swedish, signed her name and passed it to the agent. From her purse, she extracted a five-dollar bill and paid for the service. The agent gave her change, smiled and turned from the girls to tap out the telegram.

Louise and Engrid walking to the end of the station platform looked about them. Engrid noted with satisfaction that a lake lay to the west. "This is more like it," she remarked; "I was just beginning to think that I would find myself parked on some hillside and forced to grow one leg longer than the other to keep from falling down. There are some fairly level places hereabouts, after all. Say, what do you say we find something to eat?"

Seeming not to hear her sister's question, Louise stood, lost in contemplation of the grandeur of her surroundings. Far to the west and across the silver mirrored lake, a string of deceptively low-appearing hills met the clear blue of the sky in a wavering line.

To the north, these hills joined with massive mountains running from the east of the girl. To these latter giants, the girl's eyes clung.

"Oh, Engrid, did you ever think anything could be so high? Look how tiny those trees appear to be on the slope of that mountain. I feel as though I could reach from here to that forest and brush it flat with my palm and sprinkle the trees across the valley. The air just does something wonderful to me." Louise's cheeks flushed with excitement and her lovely eyes danced with emotions that the sight of the up-thrust, towering peaks caused her to feel.

"You are twirly," Engrid protested crossly while staring at the, to her, forbidden bulk where it had been pushed by some stupendous force in layers of upright rock that had at one time, lain in a horizontal position. Now these same layers writhed heavenward, folding back on themselves again and again in twisted, tortuous convolutions of gray rock. These, in one place had been torn asunder, and a mass, forming a mountain in its own right, seemed as though it had fallen aside, and struck another mountain, thereby causing the layers of rock to bend to the south so that they seemed as so many tightly drawn bows. Where the huge mass had detached itself, a deep canyon had resulted. Down this a torrent of water, in appearance like a stream of silver, flowed toward the valley floor where it disappeared behind a long line of poplar trees. One particular crag resembling a tall church spire, weathering of softer lime had left a cliff gleaming white in the sun, and detached from the parent cliff. In the hollows of the mountain, patches of snow radiated with a brilliance that dazzled the eye when contrasted to the trees and brush surrounding the banks. However, a cap of clouds concealed portions of the summit at the northern-most point, giving the eager Louise an impression of a retreat from the vigor of the sun which was beginning to be felt with warmth that she was quite unused to, so early in the year. Beyond this first and closest mountain that was almost denuded of tall trees, rose another covered with a heavy growth of mahogany, scrub-oak and some species of pine.

While Louise waxed enthusiastic, Engrid voiced the revulsion possessing her saying, "I wish I were home with nothing higher than a rock at the edge of the lake to look at. I would be in a boat, peering into the water and watching fish swimming below. These mountains fill me with dread; I am terribly disappointed to find that this country isn't like what father said Michigan is."

"White-rabbit," Louise chided, "you are not up there; you are down here; so stop your brooding." Laying an arm on her sister's shoulder, she hugged her close for a moment saying, "Why do you have to have such an accursed imagination?" She tugged at Engrid's arm. "Let us take a walk and we might possibly find a place to eat; that will cause you to feel like a new person again."

Falling in line with Louise's suggestion, Engrid moved up the road staring curiously at the houses which she passed; and remarking in amazement at the adobe brick of which many of them were constructed. Here and there she passed handsome teams of horses pulling black surreys with red wheels. Curiously attired men with huge Stetson hats, colorful bandanas and high-heeled boots walked with loud clumping sounds away from horses that carried enormous saddles. Huge hay racks with four wheels instead of the two that served for the tiny carts back home; moved through the roads and were pulled by horses that dwarfed the ones in the vicinity of Jacobstad.

Even more curious was the attire of women from surrounding farms who wore faded sunbonnets that were wide enough to hide their features.

"I'm hot," Engrid complained as she removed her heavy coat. "Take yours off and you will also feel better. The trouble with us is we are wearing winter clothing in a summer climate."

Louise complied, remarking, "Here it is the twenty-third of March and unbearably warm. There is probably three feet of snow or more on the ground back home. I believe I am going to like this climate." Recalling the bleak ocean and heavy fog that they had left behind in England, she gave an involuntary shiver. So heavy had been the mist that she had experienced difficulty in breathing and she had coughed almost constantly during the passage.

The two girls paused at the corner of an intersection with what appeared to be the main street of town, for here traffic was heaviest and they perceived a line of business establishments. Passing wagons rolled dust from their wheels and a gentle breeze deposited it along the store fronts in layers of gray. The sisters glanced questioningly at each other, then by mutual assent, they turned to the north and continued with their stroll until the intriguing odors emanating from a country store, caused them to pause and look questioningly at each other.

As they entered, a bald storekeeper came forward with a big smile and inquired of their wants. Louise gave him a nod; then said to her sister, "How ridiculous not to be able to make our wants known. What would you like to eat, Engrid?"

"What I would like and what there is to choose from, are two different things," she replied.

After wandering about for a time, the oldest sister's eyes chanced to fall on an open barrel of crackers. She dipped her hands into it and pulled out what she thought should be sufficient for herself and told Engrid to do likewise.

"What are they?" Engrid asked curiously.

"They look like knakabord, like we had at home, although they are white," Louise replied with a studied expression as she made for the counter and laid her purchase down.

Engrid pulled out a dollar bill. She passed it to the man and the look in her eyes plainly asked, "Is this sufficient?" Evidently it was for the man gave her several coins in return and out of the store the shoppers went their merry way, munching on the crackers and exclaiming at the flavor imparted by the tiny crystals of salt with which they were sprinkled.

Followed by the appreciative eyes of the Morman men who stopped their discussions to stare at the comely maidens, up one side of the business section and down the other side the sisters strolled.

"The men are looking at us, Louise."

"To be sure," she replied jauntily, "it isn't every day that they get to look at a pair of pretty sisters from the old country." She gave each of the men that she passed a shamelessly bold smile as she ambled along, chewing the wafers with undeniable relish.

At a well by a livery stable, the girls eyed a wooden bucket hanging from a well-worn rope. They peered into the depth and promptly decided that they were thirsty. As Engrid was about to pull a bucketful of water from the cool depths, a stockman standing nearby stepped forward and swept off his hat, saying something that the girls could not, of course, understand. His actions however, seemed determined as he grasped the rope and pulled quickly with hardened hands. He hoisted water from the well and poised the bucket on the edge of the platform; while the girls helped themselves from its goodness with the aid of a tin cup.

"My, that is wonderful," Louise exclaimed as she finished drinking and passed the dipper to Engrid.

Engrid, too, drank her fill, then thanked the man in Swedish and rewarded him, in addition, with a warm smile showing strong, white teeth and ripe lips parted in an unconscious invitation. The tall man dumped the remainder of the water into a moss-line drinking trough; then with the interest common to men of virility when in the presence of mature beauty showing in his eyes, he watched them walk away.

"Jake," he exclaimed as he replaced his hat and leaned indolently against the door of the shop where his horse was being shod, "I certainly don't blame the territory of Deseret for giving defiance to the government. If I had a pair of well-built heifers like that to bunk up with, I'd hold an army off, if need be, to keep them for myself!"

The smithy gave a grunt as he worked on the hoof that he held between his knees.

"What do you think? The rancher persisted.

"I'm too old to be thinking that I can care for a couple of females as well-build as they and work at my trade too," the smithy growled.

"Shucks," the stockman snorted, "the older a man gets, the more wives he should have to keep his youth alive. There's nothing like a change to make a man feel his oats in the spring."

The departing girls were young; it was spring; their appetites, for the time being, were appeased and before long, they were to meet Louise's fiancé; and in the meantime, other men's eyes made clear their interest. Laughing and chattering, they gazed into the numerous store windows and eagerly contemplated what they would buy were they but in possession of sufficient money and the ability to translate their wishes into terms understandable to the store owners.

Seemingly repenting of its hurried, carefree pace after the girls arrived at the station again, the day finally slowed itself to a crawl. It dragged interminably, and it seemed to the sisters that their once cheerful surroundings were becoming boring. The sun hid itself behind a patch of hurrying, inky clouds that opened, as it were, and dropped a deluge of rain while the girls clung to the station windows, their moods echoing the running water that puddle the fields and caused a patient farmer to withdraw with his team from his labors. But with the change of weather; when the ground began to steam, the man again made his appearance. Graceful gulls followed his plow in the field directly across the tracks, and rising on symmetrically curved wings, they circled to land again directly behind the plow as it cut a wide furrow in earth made black by the water. At each end of the field where the farmer turned his team, the birds, eating until the last moment in their greed to gorge themselves with worms, rose aloft just as the laboring horses seemed about to stomp them underfoot.

The movements of the farmer and the birds soon lost their appeal to the girls whose thoughts now turned to the town of Tintic, while they gave themselves up to an idle speculation of the nature of the place. Regarding their destination, Engrid's indifference proved to be almost apathetic; but Louise longed to be gone on the last leg of her journey with a fierce desire that was almost unbearable. Several times when trains paused to discharge passengers, she was tempted to board one that would have taken her to the wrong city had she allowed herself, because of her expectancy, to doubt the wisdom of the station agent's instructions.

On each occasion, Engrid restrained her saying, "The man knows better than you, where we are to go, because his pay comes from that knowledge; stop being so foolish."

Louise, feeling deflated after each rebuke, sat beside her sister on a bench adjoining the station wall; while soaking in the sun and waiting interminably for the proper train. Much to her surprise and Engrid's satisfaction; which the latter expressed in a gloating, "I told you so!" their means of transportation puffed into the station on time. The agent directed them to go aboard, and after making certain that their trunk was placed in the baggage car, the girls settled themselves in a seat with contented sighs.

Chapter 7

They rode first to the south, then through a declivity in a low line of naked hills skirting the lake. The train quickly abandoned the fertile farming country and the travelers found themselves climbing a long stretch of ground covered with sage, last summer's tumbleweeds bloated with foot loose pomposity, and a lone cedar tree standing in dreary seclusion as though pondering on the quirk of fate that had placed it miles apart from others that frequented the hills to the west.

A glimpse of this countryside caused Engrid to feel a sense of profound dejection for a time, as the arid appearance of the plains subtly changed her mood. Unpredictable, irrepressible Louise, however, paid small heed to her surroundings; her thoughts were projected far ahead of the rolling wheels, and the anticipation of meeting her sweetheart after these long years.

Here and there, a little removed from drab, canvas-covered wagons, Engrid discerned sheep that were as gray in color as the sage through which they forged. Once she observed a man seated astride a horse; his upraised arm directing a brown and white dog which streaked around the herd, bunching strays into a compact group. Now that evening was drawing near, the herder evidently wished to bed his charges down and protect them from predatory animals.

All along the tracks where the ground was fairly level, numerous mounds of earth could be plainly seen; and Engrid saw what appeared to be stumps standing erect at each. Her amazement was great as many of the 'stumps' disappeared into the mounds of earth. This incident of the moving stumps would later furnish her with laughter when she had it made known to her that the 'stumps' were prairie dogs. They were squirrel-like animals.

As the perspiring fireman poured coal into the firebox, and the train moving steadily forward, trailed smoke smelling strangely sweet to the girls' nostrils, huge, gray jackrabbits flashed away from the tracks to pause and sit with long ears pointed upward.

A flock of monstrous crows flew away from the track, abandoning, in their flight, the almost clean-picked remains of a sheep that had met its demise probably from the attack of some sneaking coyote.

Over a curving bridge of wood appearing altogether too fragile to support its weight, the train pounded; the timbers of the structure groaned in fierce protest. The wheels of the cars shrieked as they rubbed the sides of the rails. For a few breath-taking moments, Engrid experienced vertigo as she allowed herself to imagine that the train might conceivably cause the structure to collapse and hurl them all into the wash below in a twisted, helter-skelter mess of broken cars and bent rails.

Running under the bridge was a road, and at intervals along its gray surface, Engrid perceived wagons with canvas tops moving at a snail's pace up the barren countryside in the same direction as the train. On either side of the track, yellow masses of porphyry blending with dolomite, give a striped appearance to otherwise smooth hillsides. The girl who had been used to the colorless sameness of low rubble hills at home, these presented an appearance of beauty that again influenced her emotions in an antithesis of her recent dejection.

Crawling, ever on-and-on; up-and-up, the track laid shining ribbons for the wheels to follow. Over several bridges the gleaming steel unrolled invitingly as here and there, cotton-tail rabbits sought hasty concealment in rocks and brush of the hillside. In places, the girl found herself carried above track that she had recently traversed as the train, rounding horseshoe curves, crossed over bridges at a higher elevation. Patches of Indian red shawls flashed alluring scarlet greetings to the observant girl's eyes, and tiny lizards, moving with lightening-like rapidity, disappeared from sight under the friendly branches of sage whose odor, blending with the engine's smoke, subtly lulled the girl into a dreamlike trance. On past conical coking-ovens of red brick, and a scattering of houses which a sign on a station designated as Hommansville, the engine chugged its laborious way. A stamping mill, busily rendering ore into tailings for further processing in far-off Wales, covered the train with a pall of dust as the steaming engine continued methodically onward, after pausing momentarily to allow the discharge of several cans of milk and two male passengers from its ubiquitous, trailing cars.

After another mile had been marked off; during which time Louise glanced again and again at a letter that Emil had written her, to tell her of the places through which she would go after leaving Springville, the engine slowed its labored breathing and came to a panting halt.

"All off for Summit," the conductor bellowed, and two bearded individuals carrying bed-rolls tied with rope, staggered unsteadily on crooked legs down the aisle. Upon reaching the ground, they lowered their packs and filled their pipes, conversing in the meantime, with several other lounging miners who had gathered to witness the arrival of this link with civilization. Then, as the train again renewed its movement, Engrid stared curiously at the hills on either side of the town which they were entering from the east. From a distance, the hills dotted with mine dumps, seemed, in appearance, like great blobs of hasty pudding that, after swelling enormously, had given vent to bubbles that had broken and run down the pudding's sides. The girl dropped her eyes to survey frame shacks interspersed with crude log shelters. The former were in various stages of completion, and would presumably house the inhabitants of tents scattered here and there in the sage-covered fields sloping gently toward the hills that were approximately a half-mile from the track on either side. Anticipating the arrival of the evening train, children scurried forth to stand waving in an eager manner as do youngsters to whom the passage of a locomotive has not become commonplace.

"How ugly and depressing this town appears," Engrid remarked; "what in heaven's name can the people live on in a place like this? I see no plowed fields, and surely those gray bushes and trees can not produce food?"

"Don't be silly," Louise rebuked her as she squeezed an arm; "Emil said that the hills were covered by a gray bush called 'sage', and it appears to me that this is the place; because he also told me that after we came to a station spelled, S-u-m-m-i-t, it's right there in the letter, the next stop would be Tintic." Louise's eyes were alight with expectancy, and she fairly bubbled over with eagerness while pointing out the sentence to her sister.

With the peculiar inconsistency characterizing local trains, when one longs to arrive at a particular destination, the conveyance came to a stop beside a redwood water tank a short distance below the Summit.

"Damn!" Louise exploded in an unladylike manner, "if it isn't one thing, it is another!"

"Oh, calm yourself," Engrid said wryly; "you've waited a lifetime and a few more minutes shouldn't matter."

A door clanked on the tender, and an iron spout dropping down, allowed the engine to drink greedily and belch its contentment in light spirals of smoke. After a time, the fireman elevated the pipe with a resounding bump of the counterbalance; then, sliding from sight over a greatly diminished pile of coal, he disappeared into the cab as the train gathered speed.

Louise was engaged in an expectant contemplation of the village; when she felt huge hands cover her eyes, and she cried out in a startled voice, "Who is that?" As she vainly strove to pull them away with her tiny hands, a joyful, masculine voice sounded in her ears. At that, she ceased struggling and gasped, "Is that you, Emil?"

Stirring poignant memories, a familiar, although almost forgotten voice, replied, "Nobody else but!"

What a surge of rapture rose in the eager girl as she started to turn her head, Emil grabbed her and kissed her soundly.

"It's been so long, Emil, three endless years of waiting and it is actually you." She stepped back from the grinning man and regarded him through tears. "I'm so glad to see you that I hardly know how to conduct myself." Looking closely at him Louise went on, "Emil, you have changed; your face is pale. Have you been sick and failed to tell me?"

"Hell, no," he boomed cheerfully; "it is just that I am working in a mine." Then Emil's eyes strayed to Engrid. "Who is with you?" he stated with a wave of his hand.

"A surprise, but don't tell me you have forgotten Engrid."

"She has gone on quite a growing spree since I last saw her," Emil admitted observing the fullness of her breasts and the beauty of her fair skin. "Say, after looking you both over, I believe that I had better join the Morman church and marry the both of you. Boy! What a honeymoon that would be!"

Engrid dropped her eyes and blushed in confusion. Stooping, he asked coyly, "Have you a kiss for your future brother?"

Engrid surveyed him with an appraising look, then said, "Thank you for the nice compliments; but then you have always had a way of saying the kindest things." She then allowed him a quick kiss.

"Well," he said, running a hand down his jaw, and giving her a rueful smile, "I can't say that it was much of a kiss; but it will have to do."

Leaving his face, Engrid's gaze moved beyond Emil and paused on a stranger who was leaning with an air of ease against an arm of a seat. He sported a full, brown mustache, neatly waxed and pointed, she noted, as he met her glance from eyes of a clear gray that held a note of direct appraisal; and some unfathomable emotion resembling a shock, passed through the girl when their eyes locked briefly. Moving quickly to an overall survey of the man, she noted his light-brown hair with evidence of a not to recent trip to the barber. It was heavy, with the main part combed to the right side, and backward a trifle. He wore a linen shirt with alternating blue and white lines, a stiff, celluloid collar and black bow tie. A coat hung loosely in the crook of one arm, and both cuffs of his shirt, gleaming with gold studs, were held well up on the wrists by armbands of blue. His suit, including the opened vest, was of wool, and the color, indefinite; somewhere between a deep purple and blue. Thin lines of gray alternated with diamond-shaped checks of a lighter shade than the body of the cloth. His black shoes shone with newness or else a recent application of polish and vigorous brushing. A gold chain with large, twisted links, trailed from one vest pocket, over through a buttonhole, thence to another vest pocket on the opposite side where reposed a huge watch; to judge by the bulge. A cap of light gray, its faint blue lines forming large squares on the material, rotated occasionally on a strong-appearing forefinger. Inside of a pocket, his other hand moving restlessly, repeatedly grasped a handful of coins and then dribbling them through his fingers with a series of pleasantly related, tinkling sounds.

"Oh, girls," Emil said, following Engrid's prolonged glance, and turning to his companion with a jovial gush of good humor, "I want you to meet John Semell. He had nothing to do at this particular moment, after taking a walk with me to discuss a matter of business, so he has now been retained to help with the trunks and things ... you have trunks?"

"Two valises," Engrid replied as she acknowledged the introduction with a quick handshake and a smile. "You see...," cutting her explanation short and causing the girls to exclaim in alarm, there sounded a series of deafening reports. The sisters stared out of the window to observe the fireman hurling imprecations at a band of urchins who stood with thumbs to dirty noses and outstretched fingers wriggling in his direction. Withdrawing his head from the cab window, the irate man appeared on the steps, and leaned out as though preparing to jump off the train and pursue the children. Evidently the youngsters seemed to think so, for they ran like so many frightened rabbits into the sage, disappeared momentarily in a wash, and reappeared on top of a knoll where they continued to ridicule the angry man.

"What... why...?" Louise stuttered.

"It's only some of the kids who have picked up unexploded dynamite caps from the mine dumps. They place them on the track to irritate the engine crew. Kids are kids the world over," Emil said. "What a reception you are getting," he remarked with a grin. "It may be that they will turn out the town band!"

"Heaven forbid!" Louise exclaimed.

"Tintic! All out for Tintic!" The conductor called into the door of the car.

As Engrid stood erect to accompany Louise and Emil, brake shoes grabbing at the wheels, caused a lurching motion of the car, and the girl found herself propelled into the restraining arms of Emil's friend. She emitted a frightened gasp as she felt her forward motion halt. Queer tremors coursed through her at the man's proximity and the feel of his strong hands helping to restore her equilibrium. For an instant, Engrid's eyes looked briefly into his face wreathed in a smile whose warmth was unmistakable.

"Throwing yourself right at me, you are," he chided; "and that, before we are no more than casual acquaintances."

Engrid laughed nervously. "Excuse me; I fear that I wouldn't make much of a trainman."

"Think nothing of it, Miss," John replied warmly, "I wouldn't like you to be a man, there are already too many of them hereabouts. What we need in this town is a flock of women as pretty as you are." He released her and allowed her to pass, then he called, "Wait a moment; you forgot your coat. Here, you carry it and I'll take the valise."

Turning in confusion, Engrid allowed him to relieve her of the valise; then preceded him down the aisle. Through the door she stepped from the relative silence of the car into a bedlam of shouting voices and excitement attending the arrival of an evening train in the booming mining camp. As she pushed her way through a jostling, eagerly moving and surging crowd, newsboys shouting their wares forced themselves on her attention, and other youths, in search of a dime, called, "Smash-your-baggage-and-show-your-hotel?" All of which meant nothing to the girl. And providing an added note of animation, a pair of dogs fell on each other in a snarling, writhing mass at her feet. Around the furiously battling mongrels she threaded her way, until she found herself in a cleared spot at the outskirt of the crowd.

"You wait here until I get the trunk," Emil cautioned as he grasped her baggage check and he and John disappeared into the swirling tide; then, in a short time and sweeping protesting individuals before them, in his eagerness to rejoin the girls, Emil burst through the throng with the trunk and John in tow.

"There!" Emil exclaimed, "Let's see what kind of an arrangement we can make to carry these things to the boarding house."

Raising her voice so that she might be heard above the clamor, Louise suggested, "You men carry the trunk and lead the way; we'll follow with our valises."

"Good enough." Emile answered, then with the girls following, up the track the men moved. They struggled awkwardly over the ties, sometimes stepping from one to the next with hurried steps. At other times, covering three or four in a stride while the trunk dangling heavily between them, bounced repeatedly off their legs and caused them to stumble.

"Just a second, Emil," John protested; pausing he set his end down and stared back at the girls who were struggling slowly over the uneven surface of the track. "None of us seem to be getting any place in much of a hurry."

"You men present a picture of how not to carry a trunk," Engrid said with a laugh after catching her breath.

"I can't understand what the matter with me is; I don't seem to have any wind and my heart is pounding out of my chest." Louise admitted as she wiped at her brow with the sleeve of her coat.

"I feel as though my valise weighs ten times more than it did when I left home, and I am so out of breath," Engrid added.

"I believe that is because you are not used to the altitude." John suggested with a look from one to the other of the girls. "You'll be alright in a couple of weeks when your bodies adjust themselves to the change. Everybody feels the same way, more or less, after coming to this height."

The quartet looked at each other and then at their luggage.

"We should have hired a rig," John observed with a frown as he sought a solution.

"What we should have done and what we have actually done, are two different things," Emil answered. "But I have it, John help me get the trunk on my back, just so," he remarked as John grasped one end of the trunk and eased it onto the broad form of his companion. Emil balanced the trunk over the back of his neck with lowered head.

"But it is far too heavy for one man to carry," Louise protested to John as he picked up both valises.

John laughed reassuringly, "He can carry both of you in addition to your valises if you would care to get on the trunk." And thus they went on until they reached a red-colored, wooden-framed building.

"What manner of place is this?" Engrid asked.

"This is home, our boardinghouse, and the best this side of Jacobstad," Emil proclaimed proudly, as he opened the door and the sisters glanced curiously inside; then they moved into a long hallway where a number of door knobs indicated numerous rooms on each side. "You'll like the cook," Emil continued. "I'll bet she is in for a surprise," he said in a lowered voice. "Leave your valises here and see if she can guess that you are from the old country."

They entered the dining room which held a clean, scrubbed look. The western sun shone cheerily through yellow curtains, and a magnificent oleander, in a large wooden pail, stood proudly erect, its deep green foliage supported pink blossoms. Several ferns and geraniums grew in wooden boxes resting on shelves before the window sills. Spittoons partly filled with clean sand and placed at intervals along the walls added their note of gleaming decorum.

"Hello, Alena," Emil boomed and during the interval following his call, the girls heard clanking stove lids and the scraping sounds of pans being moved about.

Occasionally, the cause of the disturbance showed itself to be a portly-appearing woman who passed a door leading to the kitchen.

"What is it that you want now?" came the worker's disgruntled voice.

"I have a surprise for you!" Turning, he winked at the girls. "Drop what you are doing and see for yourself."

"So I should splatter stew from hell to breakfast, just to please you. What have you now?" she growled. "I suppose it is another bohunk looking for an easy meal," she conjectured not too cheerfully. She failed to make an appearance rather, sounds of scraping at the insides of the stove, coupled with a few choice expletives, directed at soft coal that she was forced to burn instead of good spruce reached the group's ears. However, the woman eventually put her head through the door followed by her corpulent figure. She chattered away in English; then started with surprise upon seeing the girls. Engrid appeared disheveled, weary and lacking in spirit; while Louise's face held a radiant smile as she linked an arm through a huge one of Emil's.

"God–in-Heaven, what have you here? A pair of those harpies from Kitty's Palace, I presume," the woman exploded as she stared with visible hostility at the grinning Emil. "Get out of here with those floosies; I'll not have my respectable place cluttered with the likes of them!" As she spoke, she advanced with menacing, deliberate steps, brandishing a scraper in one hand.

Emil reached the point in his attempted self-control, where he could no longer restrain himself; laughter rolled forth from his chest. He put out a restraining hand, wiped at his eyes, and glanced to the side at Engrid who had concluded that she was going to beat a retreat while still capable of doing so. True, she had failed to understand the flooding tirade; nevertheless, there was no question as to the advancing figures intent, garbed as the Alena was in a dark dress with billowing, mutton-leg sleeves, and her features covered with streaks of soot giving her a ferocious appearance in addition to a black mustache which the woman inadvertently created with a swipe of a sooty finger.

"Calm yourself, Alena," Emil chuckled. "You have made a grave mistake." Again he broke into laughter directed at the puzzled expression clouding the cook's usually amiable appearing countenance.

Alena hesitated and wiped her hands on the grimy apron. Emil pressed the advantage gained by the woman's confusion.

"Mrs. Kosky," he stated in precise Swedish, "you have the pleasure of being the first woman to meet my future wife, Louise, who comes from Jacobstad, Finland; and this is her sister, Engrid."

Alena's features underwent a lighting-like transformation. Her face which had been white under the stress of anger, now blushed as embarrassment struggled with a growing sense of pleasure and the words of the grinning boarder gave clarity to replacing confusion.

"They just arrived on the evening train," Emil informed her importantly.

"Oh, forgive me, my dears, forgive me. Perhaps it is just as well that I spoke in English; or I would never live down what I said about you; thinking what I did and all. Oh, how could I ever misjudge you so?" she asked. Catching up her grimy apron with one hand, she again attempted to wipe off the accumulation of soot. "I was just cleaning out the stove; it chokes up and once a week I have to burn the soot out… it is that coal… did you ever use coal? Of course not; there is wood and only wood in the old country, and there it is so cheap. Excuse me while I remove this filth; then I can welcome you properly. Sit down, take off your coats." Alena said as she walked hurriedly into the kitchen to cover her embarrassment and gain her composure.

The girls seated themselves and in due time, Alena returned, saying as she walked into the room, "Yes, girls, I am glad that you can't speak English… or can you?" she gasped placing a hand over her mouth.

"No, indeed," Louise hastened to assure her; "but whatever you said forget it. I do admit that we look as if we had spent a night in an ash pile; however, that is a discomfort one has to endure when traveling."

"Thank you, my dear, it is so easy for one to make mistakes; and I am more than willing to atone for mine. I believe that best thing that can happen to you girls is a good bath, followed by a cup of coffee and a bite to eat. When did you eat last?" She went to the girls and shook each of their hands.

"This morning," Engrid informed her; "we had some white wafers with salt on them and water to wash them down."

"Oh, you poor dears," the woman remarked sympathetically while eyeing the sisters' bedraggled appearance. "Emil," she turned to the man who seemed to be enjoying the furor he had created by his failure to prepare the woman for the girls expected arrival, "I could beat you with a poker for your pig-headedness! The biggest thing that has happened to me in years finds me looking like a hog. I would have a special dinner ready for them right now, poor dears, if you but knew how to use what few brains the devil gave you. There you stand, shameless as the day you were born, and meaner than Satan. You ought to be ashamed of yourself for conniving against all of us, bah!" she spat in disgust, "Move your lazy hulk and bring two tubs of warm water into the washroom. There is hot water in the reservoir and cold water aplenty in the well. Now go," she commanded, "and quit smirking at me."

Emil's grin vanished as he said apologetically, "I was merely trying to surprise you; I thought it would be fun to have them pop in on you."

"Surprise me?" she gasped, "don't' let it happen again, unless …"

"What?" Emil prompted.

"…unless it is more pretty girls coming to tell me all of the news of the old country. You see," she informed the girls, "I came from Uleaborg; but that was all of twenty-five years ago this spring." Her eyes reddened for an instance and she dabbed at them with a clean apron.

Louise placed an arm about the woman's shoulder, "I know how you feel about us dropping in like this, and garbed as you were; but Engrid and I are far dirtier," she murmured sympathetically. "We would appreciate a bath and a change of clothes." Louise turned to Emil and said, "Emil, do as Mrs. Kosky says, or I swear I will not even sit at the same table with you for a cup of coffee as much as I need one."

"It seems that the women have the situation well in hand," Emil observed in a mocking voice; "so here I go to obey your orders." He swept his cap around and bowed gravely; then he winked at John who appeared to be ill at ease. Finally, with laughter following after him, Emil left to do the women's bidding.

"Such a man," Alena remarked; however, she combined her words with a warm smile showing deep-seated affection. "Come girls, I will show you to a room where you can unpack your things and prepare to bathe. I have some flatirons that I will use to press your skirts. I guarantee that you will feel fresh as a daisy before long." Moving down the hallway as she spoke, she produced a key and turned a lock; then crossing the room she raised a blind flooding the room with the light of the setting sun.

Waving a hand to indicate the room that had for furniture, two chairs, and bureau and a double bed appearing immaculate in its white cotton cover, Mrs. Kosky said, "It isn't much, however it is clean and there are no bedbugs. I'll have the men bring in the valises and trunk; and when you are ready, you may go to the washroom. There is a bolt on the washroom door that you can lock to keep out any of the men who might come from town."

The sisters thanked the kindly lady and removed clean garments from their truck; then they retired to the washroom.

Chapter 8

"You've really gone overboard for that girl, Emil." John said.

Eyes alight with the first real happiness that he had known since his arrival from Finland, Emil answered, "You bet your boots; I haven't been able to get her off my mind since I left home. I have saved, dreamed and slaved for just this. What a glorious thing to love someone and not have doubts as to whether or not they feel the same way about you. Is that the way with you and Rika?"

Giving a noncommittal grunt, John spat deftly into a spittoon, then watched disinterestedly as Emil dealt himself a game of solitaire.

After half an hour or so, the door to the washroom opened and the sisters emerged appearing as fresh as the flowers embroidered on their clean blouses. Louise strolled over to where Emil was engrossed in his game. "How do I look?" she asked with a delightful smile.

Emil stopped an arm in midair as he was about to slam down a card on another. "Gosh-oh-golly!" He breathed prayerfully, staring wide-eyed at the vision. He pushed his chair back then sprang erect to grasp it in his arms should it attempt to disappear. "You're something out of a storybook! Oh, little girl, let's get married!"

The observing John watched his friend with an ironical smile playing over his features.

Engrid tripped over to occupy a chair three removed from the one in which John sprawled. Her hair had been taken down, brushed and combed; then carefully braided and tied at the ends with a bit of blue ribbon. Her face shone with the polishing that she had given it while bathing. Her blouse fitted snugly over the fullness of her breasts, and

John couldn't help himself when he remarked that she appeared to have stepped out of a storybook, also.

"I must say that the transformation is both pleasing and amazing," said Mrs. Kosky as she came from the kitchen where she had cooked a pot of fresh kavia. "Would either of you girls care for a bowl of clabbered milk, covered with heavy cream?"

Up jumped Engrid, feeling relieved to remove herself from the scrutiny of the man who was, as yet, a stranger. "Have you actually got some of that here?" she asked while following the woman to the kitchen.

"To be sure! We eat all the things that we found tasty at home, and in addition, the best of everything that we find in the stores and peddler wagons. One thing that we never do around this place is to go hungry. Stay around for a few days, and you shall find out for yourself."

Engrid was amazed at the proportions of the huge stove covering one side of the kitchen; while the woman prepared roast beef sandwiches, Engrid set places for all five of them at the table.

"Be seated, everyone," the woman said, "you are my guests," she told the sisters, "and as such, you must eat of what there is until the 'morrow when you may dine with the rest of the boarders. As it is Sunday, we generally have an early dinner and I have the remainder of the day to myself. If any of the men get hungry before going to bed, they will have to help themselves."

The gracious lady poured coffee; then picking up a cube of sugar, she put it in her mouth and poured some of the black coffee into a saucer. Holding it deftly aloft on a thumb and three fingers, she blew on the coffee, inhaled some past the lump of sugar as she savored of the flavor. After the saucer was empty, she replaced the cup on it saying, "Help yourself to what there is." She glanced at Engrid and remarked, "Don't sit there stirring your coffee as though your thoughts were a thousand miles away, sink your teeth into a nice roast-beef sandwich and you will feel better."

"I'm more tired than hungry," Engrid stated apologetically, "I'll have a sandwich, though." She grasped one and began to munch on it and before long, she ate another.

"Help yourself to the cream, Louise," Alena said as she poured another saucer of coffee, "you look to me as though you could stand to put on a little fat, here and there."

Louise laughingly accepted the pitcher that John passed her. "I was never meant to be fat; I run it off as quickly as I eat; however, I need no coaxing." She plunged her white teeth into a thick sandwich, and sighed in contentment.

"Do tell us about the trip over on the boat," Mrs. Kosky prompted; "did you get sick during the passage? I didn't have a well day until I set foot on dry land. I would never make that trip again if all the money in the world were waiting for me on my arrival in Helsingfors."

"You would if a certain bachelor were waiting there, though," Emil commented with a wink aside at John.

Blushing furiously, Alena poured coffee.

Observing her confusion, Engrid came to her rescue. "Oh, the trip wasn't bad; we were only sick for two days. We were alright the third day as soon as I got a little salty meat into me and a pot of coffee. Louise didn't want anything but cold coffee. When we reached the town of Springville to catch the train back to here, I was hungry indeed. All we had this morning were some thin white breads sprinkled with salt."

"You mean crackers." Alena prompted.

"Did you girls find a coffee house?" Emil asked between huge bites at a fourth sandwich.

"Heavens no," Louise replied; "we looked all over the main street for something remotely resembling a coffee house; but we failed to find one. We ended up drinking water from a well beside a blacksmith shop."

"I would have given my right arm for a cup of coffee." Engrid said.

John chuckled and pulled at his mustache. "You won't find any coffee in that town," he informed her, "or any other town down the valley way. The people around there are mostly Mormons and they are not supposed to drink liquor, tea, or coffee. They aren't supposed to smoke either."

At this startling information, Engrid gasped her incredulity and Louise asked, "Mormons? What are Mormons, a nationality?"

"Ha, ha, ha," Emil laughed until he choked on the coffee he was swallowing. Pushing back his chair, he rushed for the front door coughing spasmodically. He wiped at his mustache that caught a spurt of coffee coming through his nose. His laughter was resumed as he walked back into the room; tears rolling down his cheeks. He doubled over with his huge hands clasped to his stomach; while his booming voice caused the others to laugh, also.

Mrs. Kosky's laughter started in a series of short, "He, he, he's," that increased in volume and frequency until a veritable flood of high-pitched cackles tearing through the top of her mouth, squeezed past her tongue with a force that put John in mind of the whistle at the Little Chief mine when the steam was high.

Louise found herself laughing, although she knew not why, unless it was because of the ludicrous expressions on the faces of others. John vented a weak snicker; then he, too, burst into a full-throated roar. Engrid laughed long and joyously, feeling the weariness depart from her spirit; until her vivacity and gayety rivaled that of her eager sister's. Finally, the group subsided into an exhausted silence, broken by an occasional titter of amusement from one of the women, or a chuckle from a man to remind them of the storm of mirth that they had weathered together until stomach muscles felt sore with each breath. Fidgeting nervously, John pulled at his chain and glanced at his watch as he compared its time to that of the huge clock at the end of the dining room.

"Restrain yourself, big boy; she'll be here any minute now, John." Emil stated, and then turning from John, Emil addressed Louise to say, "Excuse me for so rudely receiving your question; but I couldn't help it. If there is anything I like, it is a good laugh and that remark sure gave me cause to enjoy one. If I hadn't given vent to my feelings, I'd have exploded like a stick of dynamite for sure." He grinned as he repeated the question that had given birth to his merriment. "Are Mormons a nationality?" Again he laughed, although with not so much gusto. This laughter, more reserved as it was, moved through his mouth in such a slow volume, that one would believe he were sampling the sound as one savors the flavor of a rare wine in an appreciative and deliberate manner.

Louise glanced at Engrid with a look of inquiry; Engrid turned to Alena with uplifted brow to ask, "Would you explain what is so funny about Louise's remark? I quite fail to catch the point. Are they trying to joke with us because we are newly arrived?"

Mrs. Kosky wiped at her eyes and obligingly complied. "Mormons are ordinary people of a certain religious faith. They crossed over to this portion of this vast county on foot, for the most part; and they pushed their worldly belongings in hand carts. You girls found it weary traveling for days on end in the comfortable train. Imagine what the Mormons endured in their efforts to migrate to this place. When they came to this territory of Deseret, as they named it… by the way, they have finally succeeded in getting permission from the central government to be admitted into the union of states, and this place where you now live, will, from that time on, be known as Utah. As I was saying, when they traveled here, they found a country entirely covered by sage, as this valley is. They established irrigation systems, plowed the land, and after nearly starving to death, they finally became almost self-sufficient. It is a noble work that they have done. As you have been told, they deplore the use of intoxicants, and so forth."

"Of course they deny themselves of certain pleasures." Emil broke in on Alena's dissertation to say with a mocking grin spread widely over his features.

"And what do you mean by that remark?" Louise asked in a perplexed voice.

"Well…" Emil ventured with a wink at John as he placed his hands into his pockets and tilted backward on the legs of the chair, "there was a time when the leader of the church claimed to have a divine revelation, and in this, he was supposed to have been notified that it was God's will that the men take several wives and follow his admonition to multiply and replenish the earth…"

"No!" Engrid gasped and her lips remained in a circular state as she seemingly clung to the second letter in her astonishment.

"Yes!" Emil said emphatically as his chair dropped forward; he slapped one leg with a big hand to emphasize his statement, and with a forefinger pointed at Engrid, he punctuated his statement as he exclaimed, "And, sister, they have done just that!"

"Incredible!" Louise ventured.

"Not at all," Emil replied smugly; "for many years this custom, or, should I say practice, had been followed to the gratification of the men and, I imagine the discomfort of the women. The government of these United States sent out an army to enforce an edict against this adulterous practice, and the Mormons actually took up arms in preparation to fight the troops for what they considered their rights. Their leader served a jail sentence; and finally, he made a speech in which he stated that the populace would henceforth refrain from the practice of polygamy. This territory, because of that, has had a devil's own time gaining admission to the Union."

"This practice of polygamy, does it still exist?" Engrid asked with a look of interest brightening her blue eyes and tracing itself in eager dimples around her mouth.

"Oh, yes; but without the sanction of the church." Emil remarked. "Occasionally a group of people will band together and practice it until the law catches up with them and gives them a term in jail. The term, however, is a farce because they are notoriously lenient with the offenders. They sentence them for so many years; then release them after a time in jail, on probation. The sentence is ineffectual because one cannot stop a man from sneaking about in the dark to spend a night with one of his many wives, if he so chooses. To prevent such an occurrence they would have to have an officer of the law camped on the trail of each man day and night; and that is impossible because, as it has been variously estimated, there are in the neighborhood of fifteen-hundred such marriages at the present time. Added to that, the damage has already been done."

"What damage?" Engrid asked innocently.

"There are several thousand children who have to grow up under the stigma that attaches itself to them, because the parents preferred to conduct themselves in such a manner."

"I am certainly glad that we do not live that way," Engrid commented with a visible shudder.

"How many wives do the men have; those who can afford them?" Louise asked.

"Some of the old bucks have more than a dozen." Emil said with an amused grin. "Their leader has had a total of nineteen."

"These are assuredly tales," Engrid protested with a glance at Alena. The evening promised a novel discussion, she told herself. Here was a subject that one could get ones teeth into and chew all over the place. Home and weariness alike, were forgotten as her eyes filled with eagerness, and she searched the faces of those about her. Alena appeared placid; John's, impassive; Louise's perplexed, and seemingly Emil had discussed the matter about all that he cared to for the present, as a look passed between the man and Louise.

"Louise and I are going to go out and look at the moon; excuse us, please and thank you for the coffee and food, Mrs. Kosky. I suppose that there are chairs on the porch? I have so much to say to her."

"Go ahead, my children."

"But here is no moon, as yet," Louise observed with a glance out into the gathering darkness.

"So much the better for me," Emil said as he smirked knowingly, and then followed Louise from the room.

"It is this way, Engrid," John explained as his eyes met the girl's with an appraising look. Her glance fell to the table, and she began rolling cake-crumbs into a pile with her spoon as he continued, "missionaries go out and preach to people who have a desire to live in this country, and they flock over here. It is my guess that women from England and the Scandinavian countries who could never have been married, due to a preponderance of women over men, came here to share in the life of polygamy, if need be, thinking to themselves that half a loaf is better than none."

"Merciful heavens," Engrid ejaculated, "I don't see how a woman could stand to share a man with other women. It smacks too strongly of brute animals. It isn't human or civilized at all."

Further discussion was cut short by the return of the couple and a third person who accompanied them into the room. She was of average height and wore her auburn hair in an up-do with a figure of a dark hat fastened to her hair with a hat pin. Her cloak was of black taffeta with leg-of-mutton sleeves fastened snugly at the wrist. The front of her cloak was loose, other than around the waist where it was held by a belt tied at the side.

John rose to welcome the girl into the room, and Engrid knew beyond a doubt that these two had something in common by his face which lighted perceptible at the girl's appearance. He helped her to remove her wrap and she thanked him in a husky, appealing contralto voice.

Emil and Louise seated themselves as the newcomer and John found chairs and the girl asked cheerfully, "And how is the coffee this nice spring evening?" Her words addressed to Alena, were spoken in English.

"Ah, Rika, the kahvia was never finer. Do have a cup; but first, I want you to meet the girls who just came from Finland. This one," pointing to Louise, "is Louise, so Emil informed me; and this one," she paused with warm eyes to Engrid, "is her sister, Engrid Isaacson. She accompanied her sister who is to marry Emil as soon as they can get their head and hearts together; isn't that right, Emil?"

"That is right, Mrs. Kosky; it would be tomorrow, or now, if she would only say the word."

"Oh, I forgot," Mrs. Kosky said hastily in Swedish, "the sisters understand little or no English, so we must speak Swedish in their presence."

At the oldest woman's words, Engrid's face lost the cloud of perplexity which it had worn since the newcomer's entry into the room, and the ensuing conversation.

"I am Rika Westerland from Park City, and you, I have been informed, are Engrid Isascson. I am very glad to make your acquaintance," Rika said brightly as she extended a hand which Engrid accepted with a spontaneous smile.

"How lovely your cloak is!" Engrid said in a rapt voice as she glanced in the object's direction. "I never knew such beautiful garments were made."

"And your shirtwaist is adorable," Rika, not to be outdone in courtesy, exclaimed. "Did you make it yourself?"

"Yes, and the linen cloth, also. You see, we do our own weaving at home. Up until the time father came from this country with some material already made, mother had to do all of the knitting, making of cloth, as well as sewing. Incidentally, she taught us how to do all of those things, also. Perhaps all of our learning is for naught, now that we are here. Mrs. Kosky has informed me that we can buy anything ready-made! Just imagine," she breathed raptly, and her eyes filed with excitement at the vision which her words invoked.

Rika favored the eager girl with a warm smile of understanding, and then turned her attention to Emil. "So you two are going to be married! I must say that you have extremely good taste, and also a wonderful memory to live in this country for three years and not even give another girl a tumble. No wonder I have never been able to make an impression on you, though Lord only knows I have tried." She made this statement with a bold twinkle in her eyes that caused Emil to chuckle. Engrid glanced at John and found his face expressionless.

"What kind of work do you do?" Engrid asked of Rika. "You see; if I am to stay here, I shall have to find employment of some kind, and all I know is housework and cooking. Perhaps you would know of something suitable?"

"Oh," Rika said, a look of concentration causing tiny wrinkles to appear above her slender nose, and replacing the smile of coquetry which she had beamed at Emil, "I don't believe I know of anything, offhand; but I will certainly keep my eyes and ears open. It really shouldn't be too hard to get work, as this town is growing by leaps and bounds."

And, at this time, having poured coffee into Rika's cup, Mrs. Kosky inquired, "Anyone else care for some?" When the others declined, the woman placed the pot in front of Rika and sat down with arms folded over her ample bosom.

Engrid unobtrusively scrutinized Rika who sipped coffee and made conversation. She observed a nice face with a well-molded nose impishly turned up at the tip. Her skin appeared flawless, and when Rika smiled... "That's it!" Engrid told herself comfortingly... instead of being a smile formed by full lips which would enhance any beautiful woman's charms, her smile seemed tinged by cynicism because her lips were a trifle thin. At first glance, the girl's beauty had appeared to be flawless when she removed the cloak to expose a shirt-waist of silk, beautifully embroidered with pink lace at the throat and cuffs. Engrid felt herself relax, knowing that she was at least an equal of the lovely creature sitting across from her, and the feeling added to her self-confidence.

John and Emil excused themselves, saying that they were going outside for a cigarette. As they left the room, Engrid ventured; "What big men they are!" in an attempt to break the silence when she perceived that Rika noticed she was studying her covertly.

Rika placed her cup upside down on the saucer, forestalling any attempt the genial landlady might make to fill it again. It was then that Engrid perceived the diamond.

"What a beautiful ring you have!" she exclaimed; quite forgetting herself.

"Do you like it? It is an engagement ring from John."

"When are you to be married?" Louise asked.

"There is nothing definite about the matter," Rika explained with an airy wave of a hand, "we decided to become engaged and not go out with any other, is all. John wants to have a June wedding; however, there are so many things to be considered."

"Oh," Engrid said, not knowing what else to say, "I see;" however, she didn't see at all. "Things to consider," were none of her business, she decided, and if they were to be, she would probably find out in due time, from this girl or others.

As Rika stifled a yawn with a polite gesture of a white hand, Engrid decided that evidently this girl was of importance, for only the wealthy people in Finland wore diamonds before and after marriage. Others had to be satisfied with a plain gold band given by their husband at the marriage ceremony; or else a family heirloom borrowed for the occasion.

Alena sat placidly in her chair enjoying the spectacle of these two, obviously beautiful girls making awkward attempts to carry on a conversation, and seemingly meeting with failure. Indeed, she pondered, there seemed to be a definite antipathy between them. She looked at Louise and found her busily polishing her nails on her skirt, as though that were the most important matter in the world. The air of ease that had pervaded the group prior to Rika's arrival, had vanished like a puff of smoke on a windy day. Rika, too, seemed to sense restraint. She glanced uneasily at the clock while she concealed a yawn of boredom behind a gracefully moving hand.

"We have a choir in our church," she informed her listeners; "we would certainly like you girls to join us. We practice each Sunday night after church. We have a minister who talks both Swedish and English; you will feel right at home." She glanced uneasily at the clock again. The girls thanked her and vaguely promised to look into the matter.

"Do you girls think that you shall like this country?" Rika ventured, after another glance toward the door.

"Right now," Engrid replied with a wary sigh stretching her arms to their full length above her head, "I am so tired of traveling, and the lack of sleep, that were I to commit myself, I would probably tell you that I wish I were back in my own bed and had never left home. That wouldn't be fair, after the kindness that Alena has shown us. After a rest and a chance to orient myself to the climate and surroundings, I shall be in a far better position to make a fair appraisal of things; until then…"

"Of course," Rika answered, and turning to the men who entered the room, she gave them a quick smile. "Take me home, now, will you, John? I am tired after singing. I really shouldn't have stayed after church. I rather expected you there, John," she added with a pout.

"I talked him into helping me with the girls' baggage," Emil said apologetically.

Rika accepted the explanation with a smile; then stood while John helped her with her wrap. She adjusted her hat at its most becoming angle; then pulled on a pair of white silk gloves. Turning to Alena, she thanked her for the coffee and bade the sisters and Emil goodnight; promising to see them again. When she departed, silence found her vacant chair, and an illusive scent lingered as a reminder of her femininity.

"What do you think of John's fiancée?" Emil asked of no one in particular.

"I think she is about the prettiest thing I have seen in this country," Louise admitted; "but then, she is the first I have become acquainted with since my arrival."

"I presume that there are others just as nice looking?" Engrid suggested, trying to conceal something suggestive of envy in her voice.

"Oh, yes, yes there are others as pretty; but none prettier. She wears the latest in women's fashions, each season. I like the perfume she uses and on top of that, she is well-educated. She went to college in Salt Lake City."

"Was she born in the old country?" Louise ventured.

"No, of Swedish parents in this country; however, she talks just like a native-born Swede because she has been interested enough to learn how." Emil stared thoughtfully at the wall; then went on, "I thought you girls would be able to tell that she wasn't born in the old country."

"And why should we?" Engrid queried.

"After you are better acquainted with native-born people of old-country parentage, you will see that they are much different than you and I."

"In what way is that?" Louise asked.

Well," Emil drawled, "when an Amerikan-born girl comes into a room, she acts as though she were bestowing a favor on the person who owns the abode. Maybe it is a good thing to be that way, but I never shall. Perhaps my children, if I ever have any, will take on those self-assured characteristics."

"And what causes Amerikans to be that way?" Engrid asked curiously.

"They are born in the greatest, youngest, most independent nation in the world," Emil said in a pride-filled voice. "This country has never had to bow its head, or humble itself to any other, and God-willing shall never do so as long as people cherish freedom."

Silence embraced the room for a time as the group pondered Emil's words. Finally, he pushed back his chair. "Would you like to take a walk, Louise?"

"Where would we walk to? I'd get lost," she objected.

"Not with me, you won't," he urged.

"Alright," she replied and the pair took leave of Engrid and Alena who promptly engaged each other in a warm discussion.

Chapter 9

The sky was clear and the temperature mild enough to make strolling pleasant. Linking Louise's arm to guide her along the road, "When are we to be married?" Emil asked.

"Why Emil," Louise mocked, "we're not even engaged."

"But I asked you to marry me in my last letter." He looked aside at the girl, barely able to see the oval of her attractive face in the starlight, as strolling along they passed houses through whose windows oil lamps cast friendly beams into the growing darkness. "Didn't… didn't you come over here to marry me?" he asked in a halting voice.

He didn't seem to be self-assured, Louise decided, and at that thought she felt mounting excitement. After all, it was he who had run out on her, as though she didn't particularly count. Again she recalled that long ago day when she had stood watching his retreating form; he had chosen to go into the future without her and for a brief moment his seeming uncertainty left her feeling self-assured.

"Not necessarily," she responded in a composed voice; "you see; my sister had her mind made up since she was a child that some day she would come to this country. She saved enough money over a number of years to pay her way over, and having nothing else to do, I just followed her along."

"And I suppose that it was quite by accident that you happened to pick the place where I last wrote you from," he said with a hint of sarcasm woven though his words.

"If you must act childish, I don't have to be the object of your ill-humor," Louise said heatedly and disengaging her arm, she turned toward the boardinghouse.

"Wait a minute; you can't do this to me!" Emil protested. Hurrying after the retreating girl he caught her with both hands by the shoulders, stopping her in her stride.

"Oh can't I, though?" she exclaimed vehemently as she attempted to continue.

"No… you can't," Emil said firmly.

"And why not?"

"Because…" he floundered, "because…I won't let you."

"Look Emil," she snapped, "this is a big country. I never knew how big until I rode across it on a train. I am my own boss, and I shall do as I please. I have lived without you for a lifetime not to mention these last three years when you have been wandering around in this country and making love to heaven only knows how many women. I, too, have a perfect right to choose my friends." She backed up, seeking to walk away for him but Emil stopped her.

"Sweetheart… for heaven's sake… don't act like this," he pleaded; "don't make trouble with me the first evening that I have had a chance to be with you since leaving home… look at me," he insisted as he grasped her tightly and turned her so that she was forced to face him. "Louise," he pleaded, "a long time ago I sent you money and asked you to use it to come and marry me; you sent it back without any explanation for your action. Why did you do that? Why didn't you take the money and buy passage? We could have been married for two years if you hadn't been so stubborn."

"Stubborn?" she gasped, "you call me stubborn?" Her laughter held a trace of hysteria. "Mr. Flink, you took too much for granted when you left me over home as you did. I came here to work, not to marry you."

"Do you mean that, sweetheart?" His question was run through with a melancholy reflecting the inherent gravity of his race. His shoulders sagged, and his hands dropped as though they had suddenly become leaden weights.

As Louise searched his features, her determination wilted. Moving closer, she rested her head against his broad chest. "Of course I didn't, dear; I was trying to take the hurt I have felt over these past years out on you… a getting even, as it were. Somehow, I am not up to the task; because I love you, Emil?" she stated simply. Then raising her face aloft, she displayed the starry-eyed loveliness reposing there, and Emil hugged her yearningly.

"Let's take that walk," he breathed, after clinging to her lips for a long unbelievably precious kiss. "I have a place picked out overlooking the schoolhouse where we can watch the moon come up. I believe you will like that… just the two of us; the world at our feet."

"Is it far" she asked; trembling a little from expectancy and uncertainty.

"You're not afraid of me, are you?" Emil chided her.

"I'm afraid of myself," she whispered squeezing his hand. "It's so dark that I can hardly see where I am going."

"You just hang on my arm. I've been up there so many times that I can find my way blindfolded." Emil assured her. Restraining her momentarily he guided her around a rock all but indistinguishable in the murk.

"And with what girl did you go there?"

"None…me alone, and occasionally with John. When I wearied of hanging around the boardinghouse, or the saloons, I used to go in warm weather and look out over the town, thinking of you and wishing that you were beside me… you can't imagine how many times I've done just that. I used to see the sunsets, and as it drew darker, lights came on all over the town; one-by-one. Finally, with the first star, I would always make a wish."

"And what was your wish?"

"That you would someday climb to the top of this mountain with me; and there we would be, just the two of us, forgetting all others."

After crossing the town, they climbed in silence, conserving their breath because the way was abrupt. When at last they came to the top of the hill after several pauses, Emil led the girl to the side for a short distance and sank into a cushion of leaves under the interlacing branches of two maple trees.

"Oh," Louise gasped as she settled herself beside him, "what a task it is to climb this high. I thought my heart would pound through my breast."

Emil placed one arm about her shoulders and drew her close. Here and there, in the surrounding darkness, sounded the muted twitter of birds calling sleepily. The voice of the town, reminiscent of a stream running at a distance, came to them in a subdued murmur. Occasionally they heard the voice of some woman calling a straggling child, and the reluctant answer. From above, with a startling suddenness, came a sound resembling the tearing of a gigantic piece of cloth, and Louise, with a startled cry, frantically embraced her companion.

"What was that?" she gasped as the same disturbance, repeated from different directions caused her to flinch involuntarily.

Emil chuckled. "They are night hawks who dive for insects. The noise is their wing-beats as they level off. There are hundreds of them hereabouts at this time of night. Although they also fly above town where the insects are attracted to the lights, it is generally to noisy down there to hear them."

Louise tittered; "I suppose I am overtired from the trip; because, ordinarily I am afraid of nothing."

"Not even me?" he murmured.

"Least of all, you." she replied in a low voice and grasping one of his hands she pressed a kiss on it.

Emil's left arm encircled the girl's neck, and his other moved inside of her coat. Languidly, Louise let herself recline on the cushion of leaves. With open eyes, she perceived the pale features of her lover interposed against the bare arms of trees whose naked fingers traced dark lines against a clear sky. She felt Emil's hand gathered under her neck, supporting it, and the other moving restlessly, hurriedly in search of the wonderful mystery that is woman. Progressive waves of trembling marshaled themselves into a need to pull the man to her, and encircle him with her strong arms. All of the accumulated loneliness, self-denial, and wistful dreams of past years of separation, called from the depths of her tremulous being. An intense yearning, eclipsing for a time over everything else, began at her lips, moved through her breasts and centered in her middle. Emil's heart beat like a huge drum, and hers responded with rapidity comparable to its activity when she had climbed the mountain. Emil shook as with the ague. Now, it was not enough that she pulled him to her; she must engulf him with the warmth of her young body. She must meet and overcome the force of the river that rushed toward the depths of a tumultuous ocean storming within, and whose waves heaving madly, rose higher and higher through her senses. For a time that seemed an eternity, the full tide and the insistent river locked in a moaning, breathtaking, storming frenzy of opposition; then with a faltering sigh, they merged, and the full tide retreated from the spent river…

"Did you hear that?" Louise asked. Sitting erect she turned and stared into darkness of the valley at her back.

"What?"

"There it is again… a sound like a small dog howling. Listen… there are several of them."

Emil chuckled. "They are called coyotes; and how they can sing! Just wait until the moon rises; then you will hear something."

Louis spellbound, listened for the first time to a plaint which has lulled westerners to sleep since man came to this continent.

Silence, except for the night sounds reaching the pair enclosed them in a dream-like spell. Finally, Emil tilted Louise's chin and asked softly, "Will you marry me tomorrow, sweetheart?"

"Tomorrow?" she gasped; "why, Emil, I haven't any clothes. There is a trousseau to pick out, invitations to be sent, and to top it all off; I don't know anybody around here to invite to a wedding!"

"But I do!" Emil ejaculated and folding her in his arms, he kissed her on the forehead, eyes, cheeks and neck until she gasped in ecstasy as his lips perceived the quickening pulse in her throat. "Let's forget this business of a formal wedding and go to Salt Lake City tomorrow and get married there. The money you refused to accept for the boat and train fare will pay for a honeymoon," he pleaded.

A restless breeze, redolent with the odor of sage and cedar, stole up the hill causing the woman to shiver so she drew herself close to Emil. Emil in turn, pulled her down on his lap and folding her in his arms kissed her again and again. Louise responded hungrily and for a time, they were conscious of nothing except each other's lips and arms as they clasped each other in an eager embrace. Emil's kisses became more insistent, his breathing labored and he pleaded, "Love me, sweetheart… please love me… oh, Louise, if you only knew how much I have needed you…"

Dimly, Louise remembered how she had thrown herself at him, on that day so far in the remote past. Now his lips burned with a consuming desire and his hands began a restless quest. "Take me, Emil," she whispered. Through open eyes she saw his features blot out the stars, and she signed with incredible happiness.

"There…" Louise gasped at length as she moved from Emil's arms, "does that satisfy?"

"Oh Louise, darling, you don't know how lonesome I have been for you," he answered mournfully. "I have been lost for so long that I believe if you hadn't come over here to me, I would have gone to you."

"It was hard not to come." She said softly as she lay back on his lap and ran her fingers through his heavy hair. "Life was dull after you left and I never met anyone with whom I wanted to go... I had to come here." She went on in a voice devoid of guile.

"Sit up, you!" he said suddenly; "I have something to show you." He reached into his coat pocket and, Louise recalled, just as her father had done upon his arrival from Amerika, he brought out a plush-covered box. From it he extracted a ring and placed it on a finger which she extended at his command.

"It's so dark; I can't see what it looks like."

"That is easily remedied; I'll light a cigarette." The match flared and the cigarette glowed as Louise held the ring up for inspection.

"Oh, it is lovely, Emil," she gasped before the light vanished.

"John is not the only one who can buy rings. Do you like it? Does it fit?"

"It's adorable and it does fit," she exclaimed.

"I'm glad you like it; I have saved it for the first night I would be with you. Just when I despaired of your coming, I received the telegram; and even if it hadn't been my day of rest, I would have laid off work. God, I am so happy!"

"I too," she whispered as she pulled his face down and looked for a moment into his eyes, then closed her own. "Even now it seems a dream that a few weeks ago I was on the other side of the world in the cold, and here tonight I am where it is warm and beautiful. I would like to lie here forever on your lap and look at the stars. See where the moon is rising over the mountain?"

Emil looked to where she gestured and together they watched the moon rise up in the heaven.

"I will marry you," she said happily, "after I buy some clothes; and when you find us a house."

They remained there for another hour as the huge moon rose higher into the sky seemingly diminished in size. From their position, in two directions she could see valleys each of which was drenched in a hazy glow. Across the town, a peak revealed silver ridges and black ravines where the beams failed to reach.

The Emil lifted Louise to him and kissed her until she felt his lips grow urgent and then she pushed him away. "Keep kisses like that until after we are married," she protested. Standing erect she drew her coat about her. "Let us go back; Engrid is probably worried about her sister who even now is in danger from your amorous designs." Her laughter was charged with light-headed buoyancy and optimism of youth.

Going down the hill was much easier than coming up had been, and before long they arrived at the bottom; where they stopped to share another kiss. When the couple entered the dining room of the boarding house, Engrid threw aside a paper whose contents she understood not at all.

"Oh, I am happy for you both!" she told them, throwing her arms about Louise and holding her close upon seeing the ring.

"Now, you had better find you a man," Emil chided Engrid; "you are about to lose your bed partner, and I to gain one."

"No man for this woman; I am going to work"

"Where."

"In someone's house, or on a farm."

"The only farm work hereabouts," Emil pondered, while thoughtfully rubbing his chin, "is down in the valley and it's only seasonal. Maybe there is someone in need of a housemaid or cook."

Footsteps sounded heavily on the front porch, accompanied by the rumble of masculine voices.

"Here are the boarders," Emil observed.

As the men filed into the room, they paused in amazement upon catching sight of the girls in their native skirts and blouses. Incredulity showed on their faces and exclaiming warmly, they crowded forward to be introduced. After the sisters had made the acquaintance of the six newcomers, one of them disappeared into his room, to reappear immediately with two bottles of brandy.

"I had no idea what I have been saving these for; however, this is just as good an excuse as I will ever find to have a drink!" remarked Norman Erickson as he joyfully opened one of the bottles and another man, at his request, brought forth tumblers from Alena's kitchen cupboard. A third man went to the kitchen and procured several cups and a pot of coffee, while still another brought spoons and sugar, and in a laughing, chattering circle, the men blended coffee with the brandy; although the women drank a plain cup of coffee. The barrage of questions was answered as the sisters were able to do so; most of the questions dealt on relatives and friends that three of the men had in the immediate vicinity of Jacobstad. Such rounds of toasting there were that night! Such reminiscing and jollity, tempered by fierce waves of nostalgia that ended in maudlin singing of old folk songs that the men had not sung for years.

At long last, Engrid grew weary of stifling yawns and looked at the clock. "I believe that I shall retire; I want a good night's sleep if I never have another," she told Alena.

The woman accompanied her to her door saying, "I believe you will find the bed a little hard after sleeping on feather mattresses all of your life; but you are young and will get used to it. There are no bedbugs, my dear."

"Thank you, you have been so kind; it's like coming home." Engrid said gratefully as Alena withdrew.

Engrid fell asleep almost as soon as her head touched the pillow. She failed to hear Louise, who entered much later. Louise raised the window and stood for a time peering across the moon-drenched town to look at the hills in their garments of sage. She dimly perceived the trees under which she had been with Emil a short time ago and it made her shiver as she relived precious moments of indescribable happiness.

Chapter 10

"Hey, wake up, sleepy head!" Louise called, shaking her sister who yawned and lazily opened her eyes.

"What is all the excitement?" Engrid snuggled down into the quilts that Louise had partially pulled from her body.

"Excitement enough," Louise replied, "Mrs. Kosky is taking you down to see a woman who she believes might have a job for you!"

"Alright," Engrid grumbled; "but I certainly could sleep for another ten hours. I believe this vacation has spoiled me; I don't have the slightest desire to work at all; but here goes, though. Close the door, and up I come."

She jumped from bed and in a few moments, her hair was brushed, braided; after coiling it on the back of her head and fastening with hairpins. She washed from a dish that Louise brought to her. Then, rubbing her face with a rough towel until she had a healthy glow on her skin, she got dressed and going into the kitchen she greeted Alena who cheerfully returned the salutation while rubbing polish on the massive cook stove.

"And what will you eat this morning?" the lady beamed with good humor lighting her eyes. "Here… have a cup of kahvia; one should always start the day with it." She poured the sisters a cup each and placed the pot off to one side of the stove and spat expertly on the black rag, then rubbed at a spot of batter adhering to a front lid. From the warming oven she drew a frying pan, after first washing her hands.

"How many eggs will you have, my girls?"

"Eggs, did you say Eggs?" The sisters gasped as one.

"Certainly," the woman replied in a matter-of-fact voice, "haven't you ever eaten eggs?"

"Once that I recall," Engrid said dreamily, "and it was delicious."

"I'll throw two in the pan for each of you, along with a slice of ham."

"Ham, did you say, 'ham'?" Louise gasped, "Oh, my lord."

"Amen!" Engrid signed as Mrs. Kosky, walking to a shelf covered by a curtain, withdrew a large pail full of brown eggs. She cracked four of them into a bowl; then poured them into a smoking pan which had a generous coating of ham-fat to float the eggs away from the cast iron. The girls observed her actions with expressions of rapture. With her mouth watering, Louise asked, "Where do you get eggs?"

"I buy them from Frank Holmes down Warm Creek way. He brings then to me each weekend when he comes up with his wagon to peddle. He has over fifteen hundred hens besides ground on which he raises vegetables and such."

"Do they cost much?" Engrid asked.

"Twenty-cents a dozen."

"Oh," said Louise vaguely; then let the matter ride as she watched a white plain grow around golden hills, and even now; she wondered what the eggs would taste like. All she could remember about them was that she, too, had eaten one in the remote past, and had liked it very much.

From the warming oven, Alena drew a platter on which reposed two slices of ham done to a golden-brown.

"Sit here at the kitchen table and I won't have to bother with serving you in the dining room," she said as she cut slices from a loaf of home-baked white bread and stacked them high on a saucer. She poured a second cup of coffee for each of the girls.

"Aren't you going to eat?" Engrid inquired as she pulled up a chair and glanced in Alena's direction.

"I only eat when I get hungry," Mrs. Kosky replied. "I shall have a cup of kahvia, however." So saying, she poured herself one and placing a square of sugar into her mouth, she contentedly sucked the liquid in.

"My, I never imagined that bread could be so delicious," Engrid exclaimed. "I do believe I like white bread better than I do the brown. What I have missed all of these years!"

"For the first time in my life I have had all of the eggs I can hold," Louise said patting a stomach that felt comfortably full.

"Forget the dishes for now," Alena admonished as the girls began to stack them. "I'll wash and clean up a little; then we shall see this woman about a job for Engrid."

Outside the sun shone benignly. A spring-like freshness lay over all causing both girls to remark at the pleasure of seeing a sky that was cloud and fog free... in contrast to the weather prevalent at home.

A scattering of buds were unfolding on the maple trees off to the side of the house where a flock of gross chattered as they walked clumsily about picking at shriveled seeds that had lain buried under last winter's snow. Water ran past the house in a dirty stream, and before disappearing under the railroad track through a wooden flume, it left a cap of yellow foam circling in its wake.

Mrs. Kosky, followed by the girls, walked the three blocks to the main street roughly separating the north and south sides of the town. The trio picked their way carefully over a street deeply rutted with the tracks of wagon tires; then they proceeded down the boardwalk before the business houses whose false fronts descended step-by-step in conformity with the terrain. They passed the Vienna bakery and a livery stable run by Lucas; so a sign proclaimed. Next there was a saloon whose windows set back a foot in the thick brick walls, and protected by iron bars, hinted of permanence. They ambled along the walk, meeting and disregarding the stares of lounging miners. Engrid made the observation that every other establishment was a saloon. Turning a corner by the Tintic Mercantile store, the travelers headed at a right angle to the main street along a tree-shaded road leading to a gap between two hills, thence under a bridge of a railroad track clinging precariously to the porphyry hillside. Picket fences enclosed the yards of frame houses that they passed and up to these came a motley assortment of curs who angrily challenged the visitors.

Engrid clutched at Alena's arm, noting with a touch of envy that the woman seemed indifferent to the clamoring brutes. "They frighten me," she admitted, moving away from the dogs.

"They won't bother you," the woman assured her, "as long as you don't go inside of the fences." She looked at one particularly bold animal that reared up barking and placed its front paws on the fence. "Scat! you whelp of Satan," she said, and with an unbelievable quick movement, she thrust the point of her umbrella into its chest. The startled animal bowled over backward, then turned tail and raced around the corner of its master's house with a series of anguished yelps.

The trio plodded along a little further and then Alena opened a gate and moved up a boardwalk. At its end, she puffed up four steps and rapped on the door.

"Well… good morning, Mrs. Kosky," a slender woman said as she recognized her visitor; "it is indeed a surprise to see you. Do come in."

"It is a surprise that I came this far," Alena said in English, "what with my work and all of my weight, I hardly get farther than to town. I long ago passed the stage where walking was a pleasure; now rocking is a pleasure," she added with a humorous smile as she motioned to her companions and entered.

"Sit down, while I prepare a pot of tea."

As the woman disappeared into a back room the visitors seated themselves in the luxurious front room noting, as they did, the flowered walls, the dining room set, the china closet with its glass windowed doors and a cozy fireplace. Finally their hostess reappeared with a pot of tea which she placed on the table; then she set a cup and saucer for each of them, and poured the tea.

"I want you to meet two girls who arrived yesterday from Finland. This one is Louise Isaacson, and the light one is Engrid, her sister. They speak only Swedish, so I will interpret."

"Oh, I see," Mrs. Wilken responded with a nod and smile to the sisters.

"The darker one came over here to marry one of my boarders, Emil Flink. They used to be sweet on each other in the old country. You know Emil, I suppose?"

"Oh, to be sure; everyone knows Emil."

"Well, it is for the lighter-haired one that I came to speak. She wants work. She has excellent references from a lawyer and his wife for whom she kept house and cooked over a period of years. Of course, you can't read the letter; nevertheless, it recommends her highly for housework and cooking."

"Will you tell the girls to pull up a chair?" Mrs. Wilken asked. Alena obliged, saying a few quick words to the sisters who immediately followed the others to the table.

"Your husband remarked that you were looking for a girl when I was in the store about a week back. I was wondering if you still needed one."

"I do, although it poses a problem; I can't speak her tongue and she can't speak mine." Mrs. Wilken objected.

"Oh, I do not believe that it will be too hard to get along with her." Alena pointed out as she glanced aside at the girl. "Take her around for a day or two; show her what you want cooked, and how you want it flavored. Repeat names of things, and I guarantee that within two weeks you will find her indispensable."

"I do need a girl badly, still ..." Mrs. Wilken paused and turning to the girl; she subjected her to a searching look. She saw the firm breasts, sturdy arms, and strong appearing fingers. She noticed the friendly mouth that at times, drew itself into a serious line as Engrid vainly tried to gather an inkling of the women's conversation. The girl met the woman's scrutiny with a direct look; then dropped her glance feeling self-conscious. She fell to tracing obscure designs with one finger on the armrest of her chair. Evidently Mrs. Wilken was satisfied with what she saw, or was tired of doing her own work, for she nodded her head, remarking, "I'll give her a trial; when can she start?"

Mrs.Kosky conversed rapidly with the girl. "She says she can start tomorrow; she wants to know about wages and also the hours that she is to have off each week. She wants time after lunch for a rest and to take care of her own needs."

"I believe I can arrange things to her satisfaction," the woman answered; "tell her the hours will be from six in the morning until six at night, with two hours off from one until three. She can have Sundays off after ten a.m. provided she is finished with bed making, dishwashing and mopping the kitchen."

Alena relayed the gist of conversation to the girl who sat poised on the edge of her chair.

"And wages?" Mrs. Kosky asked.

"Oh, yes, how will two and a half dollars a week suit her?"

"She said everything is satisfactory and that she will come in the morning."

"Before you go, I shall show her to her room, this way please."

The party climbed a long flight of stairs and Alena grunted and signed until she stepped into a room which possessed the characteristic of any unoccupied room. An ordinary, wooden four-poster bed and cheap pine bureau stained a dark color took up almost all of the space. On the windows, which were badly in need of washing, yellow curtains hung dispiritedly, harboring an accumulation of dust. Cobwebs, also dust covered, hung here and there from the ceiling.

"It hasn't been cleaned since the last maid left to get married. A bucket of water, a bar of soap with a little fresh air and sunlight, will do wonders in here. Tell Engrid she can clean it to suite herself when she comes tomorrow."

Mrs. Wilken paused at the door while the trio passed through. She thanked Alena for bringing the girl; then stood watching as they descended the steps and turned down the road where the dogs once again picked up the threads of their vituperative threats where they had previously dropped them.

"How does it feel to be going to work?" Louise asked.

"Why, I can hardly believe my good fortune," Engrid exclaimed. "At home, I had to search for several months before finding a job in the city. I don't know how I shall manage without knowing her language, however. I wish father had taken time to teach us something... he was always too busy."

"Do you think you will like the lady?" Louise asked a she bobbed her head to avoid striking a low-hanging branch.

"That remains to be seen; I'm afraid to commit myself until I work for her."

Upon their arrival in town, as everyone called the business section, Alena placed her order for the day, while the girls strolled about, admiring shelves full of groceries and gaping at the glass fronts of drawers which enabled one to view the contents.

"I would like to buy some clothes; but I will wait until I have earned some money," Engrid remarked with a look of longing at the ready-made women's apparel. For a short time, the sisters moved in a seventh-heaven, exclaiming at the silken coats that were the rage this spring of 1897, and Engrid peered even more eagerly at hats bedecked with feathers that made a far cry from the linen bonnets of her native country. It was with reluctance that she departed in the company of her companions after having laid out a ten-cent piece in return for some horehound candy.

"When are you getting married?" Engrid asked as her firm teeth shattered the candy.

"Anytime now, Emil asked me last night to name the day."

"What did you tell him?"

"That I would as soon as he finds a house for us to move into."

"Will that be hard?"

"I hardly think so; he says there are new houses going up everyday. The man who runs the biggest mine in the area is building homes as an investment, and to encourage family men to move into town."

"And why is that,"

"Well, he says family men are better workers, and show more interest in their work as a general rule. They don't dissipate as much as the single men do on their days off; therefore, they can do more work... simple, isn't it?"

At the boarding house, Engrid turned down an invitation to coffee, and after helping with the dishes and sweeping; then she sat down at her bureau to compose a letter to her parents. She wrote the heading, "23 March 1897" after which she sat in silence for a time, trying to compose her thoughts. On an impulse, she went to the window and raising it breathed deeply of the warm air. One of the boarders was playing a game of horseshoes with a companion invited her to join them. She declined the invitation with a warm smile and returning to the letter she seated herself and began to write. A feeling of nostalgia gripped her. Louise was happy, because her problems of adjustment to this strange land and its alien people would be gradual; she would have Emil to help her. Emil… who even now spoke English as did a native… to aid her. All she would have to do was please her husband, the girl pondered, while she herself would have to satisfy a strange woman and if she failed to do so, things would wind themselves into a mess. She would have to fit into an unfamiliar household, unable to understand a spoken word. She would do work that the woman would refuse to do herself, and if first appearances counted, Mrs. Wilken would expect much of her hired help.

"I have one thing in my favor," she pondered ruefully, "If she criticizes or scolds me, I will be unable to understand her."

She settled herself to write in a cheerful vein, in spite of forebodings that she forced herself to disregard. Louise came in after a time, and Engrid inquired whether she might want to write a few lines.

"I am in such a dither that I wouldn't make sense," Louise replied. "You just tell them that I am to be married and that Emil is just as fine as he was when he left home. Have mother to tell Vinie 'hello' for me, and also that she ought to come over here because the country is simply wonderful!"

"I suppose you will sing another chorus to your song after you have been married for awhile and the thrill of marriage is gone; then you shall be another household drudge."

"Be that as it may," Louise answered happily, "I am looking forward to a honeymoon in the city and I'm really going to love that man!" Her face was transfigured with a memory of the past evening. Once more, in her imagination, she was on the hill overlooking the town and a faint breeze, heavy with the cloying fragrance of sage brushing her face as Emil leaned over her to blot out the light of the stars. Again she closed her eyes and the light of the glimmering stars became notes of heavenly music, interwoven with memories of pleasure so intense, that she shivered with delight. During this time, Engrid's fingers were busy with the pen.

"Is there anything else?" She asked of her motionless sister.

"As if there could be anything else…" Louise pondered dreamily.

"I hope that when I love someone, it won't make me go around like a walking dream," Engrid remonstrated in biting words. "Do you want to read it before I seal it?"

"No," Louise answered as she opened the trunk and removed her garments. She chattered gaily while unpacking. "Don't you think Alena is a dear? She is so motherly and self-sufficient. She lost her husband to a cave-in at the mine; after that, she opened this place and substituted grub for love, and I do believe she is happy on a one-side diet. They… she and her husband…had one child who died of small pox when but nine years old. It was a pretty girl, so Alena said. The father was killed a year later. Mrs. Kosky thinks the world and all of Emil because he is so kind to her. He calls her 'mother' and takes her to the Finn hall occasionally. Emil says she doesn't make much profit on this place, because she sets too nice of a table and allows the men to piece when they want to."

"It would be nice if she could fill her rooms. She could accommodate several times as many men as she already has," Engrid mused. "Maybe she could then hire some help. I feel sorry for her; she is too heavy to get around as much as she should." She watched her sister spread the contents of the trunk on the bed.

Louise pulled out two pictures and placed them on the dresser, saying, "Hello, mother and father, I wish you were here and having a wonderful time, also."

"You are," Engrid remarked cynically. "They have already had their good time; so here we are."

"Gosh, it seems so long ago since we left home. I wonder if we shall ever get back there to see the folks again. Perhaps we could if we married a rich miner with chests of money. Oh, well," she said, sighing pensively, "I don't ask for Emil, and wealth, also. He is only working for a day's pay at the present time. He did say though, that some day he is going into the leasing game, and who knows… we might become rich!"

"Or poorer, still, judging by what the men were saying over their cups, last night," Engrid remarked. "I'll bet that most people hold the thoughts of going home with a bag full of money and gifts for the family. I'd travel first-class on the train and ship, too. Imagine the airs we could put on! That is something to think about!"

"And I," Louise added, "would like to strut up to that mean so-and-so that used to be so grouchy at the factory if we left our table too often. I would like to appear arrayed in a silk dress, silk coat, a pair of while slippers and a hat with tall feathers on it; you know, the whole she-bang. I would say 'hello' to him and watch his face while he tried to remember the shoddy-looking girl who used to roll cigars for him. Also, that cat of a girl who used to look at me over her long nose. I'd tell her a thing or two! She didn't like me because I wouldn't drink with her at the Christmas party a year ago. She got so sick that she couldn't work for a whole week. She always had the manager hanging around her, and he was married, too. We could work like dogs rolling cigars, and that one girl could sit and say sweet nothings to that lewd, pot-bellied old man, with him grinning and showing his yellow fangs as he told her dirty stories. She in turn would cackle like an idiot and look knowingly at the rest of us girls. She dressed better than the rest of us and I know it couldn't be done on the wages she earned. I had to save and scrimp for years to make enough to come here. Oh, well" she dropped her voice and added philosophically, "why should I talk about her? We have our life and she has hers to live. It will get harder as she grows older and is no longer as attractive. When that time comes, I hope to have a family and a man who needs me and loves me enough to stay with me."

Engrid sorted some of her things as Louise removed them from the trunk.

"Why don't you get a man?" Louise asked.

"If there is any getting to be done," Engrid snapped back, "the man will have to do it. I won't be like you; chasing him all the way around the world to make him marry me." Her eyes gleamed brightly and her lips straightened in mock severity.

Louise waggled a finger at her sister, "Now, Engrid, when the right one comes along, you'll follow him anywhere. When a girl gets in the habit of loving a man, her life is no longer her own. The only difference between you and me is that I was born knowing what you will have to find out."

"Are you certain that you have the right man?"

"That is rather hard to say; but I know Emil most nearly approaches my ideal, and I have had three years to find another. However, in that time, I have found that I love him more than ever."

"Does he love you?"

"More than he ever did," Louise stated, displaying a conviction that was at the basis of her irrepressible good humor.

"I'm going to heat some flatirons and press my skirts and blouses." Engrid held her wrinkled clothing aloft and turned them around to inspect them with a critical eye. "Do you want to press any?"

"I believe I will. There's practically nothing else to do until tomorrow," her sister replied.

"I'll be glad when I can buy some real nice clothes that are ready-made, and right in style. I'd like a blue silk cloak and a silk blouse like Rika's. I think the lace and the billowing sleeves of her blouse are too adorable for words."

"If you intend to be like other women, you'll have to get one of those things that they wear to make them appear so slender. Alena says they call them corsets," Engrid observed. "All of the women wear them; so I guess we will have to fall right in line and not appear different. However, I am going to use the clothes that I brought from home for around the house and buy others for dressing up."

In a similar vein they chattered while they borrowed Alena's ironing board and flatirons to press their clothes. They rubbed out some clothing in a tub, using home-rendered soap which was both active and yellow.

"This rubbing beats hitting the clothes with paddles as we used to do," Engrid observed, as after a preliminary demonstration by Alena, the girl became adept at rubbing. However, it required a measure of control to keep from covering the floor with a mountain of suds.

"I'll bet it will seem queer to the men who see strange women's underthings on the boarding house lines. The town's people will probably get the wrong impression of us if we stay here too long," Louis said with a giggle.

"I am glad that I am going to work, and you are getting married; or some of the men here may get the wrong impression of us, also." Engrid remarked.

Alena chuckled. "Perhaps it is a welcome sight to see something besides dishtowels and rugs hanging there. I send my clothes to a widow because I haven't the ambition, or the time to do them myself. It may be that the men will get ideas when they see your clothes waving in the wind."

"What ideas?" Engrid asked as they walked outside to hang their garments to dry.

"Pertaining to marriage." Alena answered. "You see, many of these men are not living in this, or the other boarding houses because they like to; they do so to keep from having to cook their own meals, and for the sake of companionship. Only a few of the older ones are confirmed bachelors, and that I doubt they would remain, if they could find a woman to have them. The younger ones would like a nice girl to come home to, and a couple of kids to climb up on their laps and pull their mustaches. I know this; because I listen to their conversations when they sit around in the evenings and have a few drinks to make them talkative. It isn't the lack of wanting; but the lack of women that keeps them from marrying."

"It serves them right," Engrid said in heated tones; "they run away from nice girls at home, expecting to find just what they are dreaming of over here; then they start dreaming of the girl they left behind. There are plenty of women at home who can never marry, and they grow old as 'Auntie so-and-so the old grouch;' as so many call them. I feel sorry for the poor old spinsters."

Say," Louise broke in cheerfully, "it seems that it is going to be good hunting for you in this part of the world; so it behooves you to move slowly and pick out some man with a large roll of money in each pocket."

She seated herself on a pile of rough, bark-covered poles and pulled at the outer covering. A strip several feet long came loose, exposing the light wood underneath. She held the bark to her nostrils and sniffed inquisitively. "My," she exclaimed, "this is fragrant! What kind of wood is it?"

"It is cedar; good only for firewood and fence posts. There used to be a lot of it hereabouts; but before the railroad came, the inhabitants of the town had to burn it for fuel and most of it is gone. What firewood we buy now has to be hauled by teams and it is a two-day job to haul a load from west of Tintic."

While tearing the piece of bark into slender strips, Louise glance up to see a file of men walking hurriedly downhill on the gravel road where prior to this moment, there was to be seen nothing except an occasional stray dog. "It seems as if there is a parade coming this way. Where are all of those dirty men coming from?" she asked curiously.

"From the mine," Alena answered; "heavens, I never realized that it was that late, and me without even having put the potatoes on; although I have them peeled and in cold water." She waddled to the house, scolding herself, while the girls remained on the pile of wood, enjoying the warmth of the sunshine. They gazed speculatively at the approaching men who became more numerous as they appeared moving down the road.

"Look at that one," Engrid pointed out. "he looks like he has the measles."

"He must work in a dirty place." Louise remarked as one figure detached itself from an animated group and moved toward the girls. Louise peered at the mask of dirt and concluded, "It looks like Emil," she said.

And so it was; but an Emil appearing unlike anything they could ever had imagined. His face, was coated with dust of a chocolate-brown and his arms and hands were the color of a negro's. His teeth gleamed a startling white in contrast to the shade of his face as he smiled and said, "Hello!"

"Oh," Louise exclaimed, "you poor man, you seem to have been doing all of the work with your face."

Emil grinned and moved forward to extend a grimy paw toward her, and Louise exclaimed, "Don't you dare touch me with your filthy hands!" He moved one hand forward as

Louise attempted to move back and away from him. The top log of the pyramid on which the sisters sat, rolled from under them, causing both girls to fall over backward with a suddenness that neither had anticipated. They squealed as their legs flew high in the air, displaying well-turned legs in a froth of lace-embroidered petticoats.

"Here, let me help you," Emil prompted with a chuckle as he walked around the pile and extended a hand to each of the surprised girls. They moved back again from him, and at the same time, pulled their skirts down over their ankles while striving to regain their feet.

"Don't you dare touch me with that filth," Louise admonished as she sprang erect, followed by her embarrassed sister. They brushed the dry bark and chips from each other's clothing and hair; meanwhile keeping a safe distance from the well-meaning man who was laughing boisterously.

"Why don't you clean up at the mine?" Engrid asked; then she started to giggle and Louise, infected by her mood, laughed also.

"Because we have no change room, at present."

"Where do you work to get that dirty?" Louise asked, quite recovered from her surprise as she again seated herself on a log that was separate from the others and possessed a substantial footing.

"Oh," Emil replied, with a long look about him, "I would say that we are about 600 meters below that schoolhouse." He gave his overalls a hitch; then raised a leg to rest on the log.

"What?" Engrid gasped, "how do you get down that far?"

"We climb down," Emil assured her with an amused smile.

"But it would take a half-day to do that and another to get back." Louise objected. "How could you get any work done?"

"I was only joking; we actually go down on a cage that is lowered by a steam-powered hoist."

To these girls who had never visualized a hole deeper than a shallow well, the words sounded unbelievable; and their gaping mouths showed their incredulity.

"I'll try to explain to you so… "

"Tell us how a hole can be dug that deep," Engrid pleaded.

"How do you know where to dig to find ore?" Louise asked.

"Wait a minute… one question at a time," Emil admonished. He tamped tobacco into a pipe, struck a match and sat beside the girls, puffing his contentment; yet taking care that he didn't brush against Louise with his dirty clothes. "We dig a hole from the surface in search of ore. As we dig, we shore off the sides with timber and lagging. The boards form the walls and the timber forms the sets in the shaft. The shaft is divided into three compartments if we intend to go to any great depth. Two of these are to run cages in, and the third contains a man-way with ladders which we can use to come to the surface, in case something happens to the hoist."

"Does anything ever happen?" Louise asked all ears.

"Oh, yes, the boiler blew up one time, and all of us had to climb out, or else stay down for the three weeks it took to repair it."

"How do you keep the cages from sticking in the shafts?"

"We string guides which are hardwood rails bolted on each side of the shaft, and greased for the shoes on the cage to slide over, holding the cage in alignment as it moved up and down."

"Shoes?" …this from Louise who wrinkled her nose with a perplexed frown.

Emil chuckled. "Not shoes like we wear; but u-shaped pieces of iron fitting over the guides. The timbers are held in place with blocks and wedges. If they become loose, due to the jolting of the cage, men work in the shafts from the time nightshift goes home until dayshift comes on, doing repair work. They tighten and align the timber. Loose ground may bring pressure against the timber, causing it to bow out, and this must be relieved by removing the broken ground. Then we place as much new timber in its place as we need until the wall of the shaft is again safe. It's dangerous work; but there is a fascination about mining that grips a man, and as a general rule, once a miner, always a miner!"

"Do you mean to tell me that men actually walk around on the timber with the possibility of falling that far if they lose their grip?" Engrid shuddered. "Heavens!" she gasped at his answering nod.

"Yes, he added, "sometimes they work off cages and at other times with nothing except the timber to hang onto. They even have to chop ice in the winter, when downdrafts of air freeze water in the shaft."

"How do you go through solid rock… you can't pick it?"

"We drill holes with an air-drill. In each hole, we place round sticks of blasting powder. In one of these we insert a primer, or blasting cap, with a fuse attached. We light the fuses and climb into a bucket that takes the place of the cage during the sinking operations. We pull on a wire that is hooked to a bell in the engine room on top, and the engineer hoists us to the surface. The next shift has to go down and clean out all of the muck that our shots break, and put in timber where it is needed. They in turn drill more holes and shoot the ground loose for us to shovel out."

"And how can the engineer tell where to stop the cage that is underground?" Louise asked.

"In order that the engineer may do that, he has indicators geared to the drum of the hoist; and he also has white lines painted on the cable, so if anything goes wrong with the gears of the indictor, he can still know where the cage is. That question reminds me of a little incident that happened, just a year ago," Emil digressed from his explanation to say. "I was on the fourteen-hundred level caging cars. It is wet on the station, and slippery. I stepped forward to throw up a guard rail that prevents cars from rolling into the shaft. My foot slipped; the cage was coming down with an empty car on it… it goes past the station to allow the cage rising at the surface to clear the top so the top man can throw in what he calls 'chairs'… they hold the cage level with the tracks running to the cage. Anyway, when I slipped, I fell under the bar and just managed to grasp the edge of the timber forming the station level. When I fell, I screamed, and for a moment was petrified with fright. Just as the cage was about to descent on my hands, and tear them loose, thus hurling me into the shaft, for some reason, the cage halted about two feet up! I managed to scramble to the level of the platform and there I lay for a minute, too weak and shaken to move. Finally, I summoned my nerve and pulled twice on the bell, and down the cage dropped as it should have done; then it rose above the station level, and I threw in the chairs and rolled the empty car off, and the full one on."

"Oh," the girls gasped together.

"That night, after I went on top, I walked to the engineers shack and I said, 'Ben'… the man's name is Ben Thurmon… 'for God's sake, how did you happen to stop the cage for a time above the fourteen-hundred station? If you hadn't, I'd have been a dead duck.' Then I told him what had transpired."

"'Emil, call it what you want; but a guardian angel must have made me stop the cage. I was just clearing the top of the shaft with the other cage, when something spoke inside of my head and told me to stop,' he said."

"He was certainly a happy man," Emil continued, "he said that he has been running a hoist for twenty-five years without a fatal accident!"

Emil looked from one sister to another and smiled as Louise gulped at the conclusion of his narrative. "Another day, and another dollar in the hole," he said blithely, "I am going to get cleaned up for dinner."

"Heavens!" gasped the girls as they looked at each other; then they laughed nervously at the simultaneous voicing of the same expressing.

Inside Emil deposited his empty bucket near the kitchen door; then he continued on to his room where he procured a change of clothes and walked into the wash house where he filled a barrel with warm water. By opening the spigot, he allowed a trickle of water to run on him and he scrubbed vigorously with laundry soap. As he attired himself in the clean clothes, he sang boisterously in a rich baritone,

> "Spin, spin, spin daughter of mine;
>
> Tomorrow comes that lover of thine;
>
> But though the daughter she spun
>
> While tears they did run,
>
> Never, to her, did that lover come."

"She came after him!" Emil boasted as he stepped from the kitchen door with a swagger befitting his natty appearance. "Me for a home with a bathtub if I ever find one," he remarked as he stroke toward the girls.

"When you settle down, it will be with someone else, if I hear any more cracks like that out of you," Louise said threateningly as Emil stood grinning before her.

Causing Emil to feel tongue-tied, Engrid blurted out, "If I could find a man like you, I believe I would get married."

"You won't ever marry then, Engrid; there is only one Emil in this world," Louise hastened to say as she stood up and encircled his waist with a slender arm. "Let us go in and give Mrs. Kosky a hand with setting the table."

Chapter 11

The sisters dined with the men who, although they had taken extra pains with their appearances, ate in silence after the manner of hard-working men the world over and consumed prodigious quantities of food. Faces that ordinarily were shaved once a week, at the barber shop, now showed the results of their own diligently applied straight-edge razors. After satisfying their appetites, the men walked outside patting rotund stomachs. Some played horseshoes; others sat indolently watching although now and then leaving their seats to settle some technical point regarding the distance of a shoe from a peg.

The sisters and Emil lingered over a second cup of kahvia. He enjoyed a cigarette, inhaling deeply and releasing the gray smoke in contented sighs from his cavernous chest.

"Did you girls get enough supper?" Alena asked as she puttered about the table scraping and stacking dishes.

"Oh, yes, more than enough," Engrid answered. "I liked the rice pudding."

"I can't see how you can make any profit feeding men who eat as they do, and that includes you, Emil," Louise argued.

"All hard-working men eat heartily, especially when they are young and doing the heavy work. We won't eat so much as we grow older; Alena can then get back all she puts on the table; if we live to grow old," Emil stated.

"What do you mean by that?" Louise asked as following her sister's example, she pushed back her chair and began to help the oldest woman.

"Exactly what I implied," Emil replied.

"And what was that?" Louise asked.

"The work underground is so hard; conditions so bad in regards to dust, machine oil, gas from the powder and lack of sanitation; that it seems improbable to me that a man should live very long."

"Emil is right," Mrs. Kosky observed, "I have seen the men come and go. When they get sick, they finally end up in the county hospital to die."

"Why don't you leave?" Louise asked.

"I'll get out of the mines someday, after I make a stake."

"How can you do that working for wages?" Engrid asked a she scraped the last dirty plate into a pan. Alena took the pan outside to one of the wooden swill barrels and dumped the contents; then she replaced the cover discouraging flies. Saturday, the owner of a herd of swine would collect the swill.

"I can't," Emil answered as she began washing dishes and Mrs. Kosky placed the leftovers on the shelves under curtains. "Someday I am going leasing; and if I strike it rich, I can move to the valley and buy a home."

Louise came to Emil when he beckoned with a crooked finger. They spoke in low voices for awhile, then at Mrs. Kosky's appearance, Emil informed her, "I am leaving you in the morning, Mrs. Kosky."

"So?" the woman said with lifted brow.

"When Louise and I took a walk last night, she promised me that if I found a house to move into, she would marry me. I found one today!"

"Where?" Mrs. Kosky asked.

"One of the miners said that he was moving to the state of Washington to work in the logging camps. He wants to sell me his house."

"How much?" she asked.

"Five hundred dollars for five rooms with a back porch, barn, coal shed and all the wood that he hasn't used. He's getting out of the mines for good, he says. He's made his in the lease game."

"And you're going to buy it?"

"Yup, furniture and all!"

"Well isn't that the luckiest thing that ever happened?" Mrs. Kosky exclaimed. She turned to Louise. "Why didn't you tell me?"

"Why I didn't know until tonight; Emil just told me."

"Oh, that is right; how stupid of me!"

"Are you sorry that you promised me?" Emil asked Louise.

"Oh, heavens no; you poor oaf, I'm so happy I hardly know what to say; I can't wait to settle down and start keeping house in a place of my own."

"That's better," Emil said as Louise squeezed his hand reassuringly. His face glowed with pleasure and he grasped both of her tiny hands to imprison them in one of his own.

Louise glanced at her sister to find her nervously twisting her handkerchief as she looked at the floor.

"Why are you so dejected?" Louise asked.

"I … I was thinking how nice a wedding would be on a midsummer day." Engrid answered softly with eyes averted. She sat silent for a moment, then excused herself and walked to her room.

"Engrid…" Louise called after her; but the girl continued to the door and closed it behind her.

Inside she stood with her back to the door her hands behind her as she struggled to regain her composure. "Oh," she signed profoundly, knowing disappointment that was intense. A feeling of depression overcame her; she regretted that she had given way to an impulse and came with her sister to such a forsaken hole as this mining camp, with its strangely living, uncouth inhabitants, halfway around the world from the sanctuary of her home. It was true that her sister had found happiness; but at the expense of her own, she reasoned. The future looked dark; forebodings pervaded her thoughts. She must go on alone, making her own life in this barren land where everything she ate, or wore, would have to be earned doing the hardest kind of work for others who spoke an alien tongue. With these thoughts crowding through her mind, she moved to the bed and gave vent to her feelings in a flood of tears.

Louise permitted her sufficient time to have a good cry; then she told Emil, "I'll go cheer her up. She sometimes has these moods; but she'll snap right out of it, gayer than ever, after a good cry and a night's sleep."

"Feel better, sis?" Louise said as she entered the room and she seated herself on the bed by the girl; stroking her golden hair. Drying her tears, Engrid sat erect; while Louise pulled her sister's face against her shoulder for a time; then she stood up to pace around the room. After a time, she quit pacing the floor to sit by her sister, again.

"You'll feel entirely different once you start going to dances, meeting some of the nice boys and getting acquainted. I suppose you know that this boarding house is not the only place of its kind here? There are others, and who knows, right in one of them tonight, there sits a man for whom you could care. Look at me," she said to Engrid, and placing a hand under the chin of her sister, she peered into her woebegone eyes. "I'll be back in a few days and come to see you," she continued. "Right now, I am so thrilled that I can't even sympathize with you. Get some sleep, or you won't be able to collect your thoughts for work in the morning."

Smiling faintly, Engrid dabbed at her eyes. "I'm just an old crosspatch, Louise. You are right; I will feel better after I get my mind occupied, but …"

"But what?"

"Oh, nothing; I was merely thinking about men. I haven't seen any here I could care to go with. That is definitely out; most of them are too old; there's only that John, whatever you call him, and he's got a girlfriend."

"Silly girl," Louise said as she sensed the passing of an emotional storm, "let's go help with the dishes; after that, if you still feel tired, you can go to bed. As for me, I have a lot to talk over with Emil."

"Are my eyes red?"

"Just a little; go into the washroom and bathe them with cold water."

Engrid did and then rather sheepishly she faced Mrs. Kosky, who patted her on the back and engaged her in a cheery conversation. When the dishes were clean, Engrid crawled under the covers and promptly fell asleep.

"Get up, lazy bones!" Louise sang out.

Engrid opened her eyes and stared indolently about her.

"Heavens above, child, get a move on you!"

Engrid yawned and rubbed at her eyes. "What is the hurry?" she asked.

"Hurry? You ask me that? Today is only the day that I am to go to the city of Salt Lake and get married; today is the day you go to work, or have you forgotten?"

"Easily! It isn't I who am getting married, and I don't particularly feel like cleaning somebody else's dirt while you are getting married, honeymoon and all, merely because it is the most convenient way out of working for someone else. Why shouldn't I forget?"

"Get up now; sister," Louise pleaded as she tugged at the covers and exposed her sister's form under its voluminous nightgown.

"You seem to be the originator of bad news; so remind me to have a medal struck for you," Engrid said wickedly as she caught her sister in the face with a deftly aimed pillow. In a moment, the room echoed to their laughter and squeals as they mauled each other in the manner of two kittens.

"What the hell is going on in there?" bellowed an irate male voice from an adjoining room. Although the words were in English, nevertheless, the meaning of the tone was unmistakable.

"Hush!" Louise hissed, "Let's be quiet before we get thrown out on our necks. The night shift men are still asleep."

Engrid ceased her scuffling and the two girls stood up. "Who cares?" she whispered with a nervous giggle. She remained silent, however, and promptly dressed; then they left the room and before long were blowing on their saucers of coffee.

"Emil will carry your valise and see that none of the dogs eat you alive; then he and I shall go to the station from there."

"Can we leave the trunk here; until Louise gets back?" Engrid asked of Alena.

"To be sure; as long as you like. It isn't in the way and no one will bother it."

Emil finished eating his breakfast and reaching into his pocket, he brought forth a roll of bills. "Here is my board bill to date, and for the girls' food and lodging," Emil said as he peeled the greenbacks and thrust them into the apron pocket of the woman.

"No, I refuse to take a cent for the girls. The bed and a meal or two I was glad to give you," she said to the trio. "Oh, how happy I am that you stayed here so that I could get acquainted with you." After looking at the money Emil had given her she said, "You have given me twice as much as you owe me."

Emil backed away from the woman, forestalling an attempt on her part to give him change. Thrusting her hands aside, he drew his lips into a firm line and said, "Go treat yourself to some candy and see one of those stage shows when it comes to the opera house. They have some mighty nice ones." With a chuckle he continued, "Some good looking women doing the singing and dancing, too."

As Mrs. Kosky continued to thrust some change his way, he stepped around a table; then he swept off his hat in a salute. "Mrs. Kosky," he stated with a dead-pan face, "it is with the utmost regret that I leave this haven of rest. Here I have spent the happiest years of my life. How well I remember the cold Christmas Eve when I staggered, gaunt and blue with cold, through your open door. You pitied me, fed me and poured gallons of steaming coffee into me; until my lost faith in mankind was restored. If it were not for you, I wouldn't be alive this day. With the anticipation of a honeymoon beckoning me away from the comfort and security of your domicile, I leave with misgivings and regret." Here he struck a pose with one hand tucked in a Napoleonic gesture inside his lapel, and the other carelessly holding his hat by the brim, he went on, "When I am suffering the tortures of the damned, as I try to eat my bride's biscuits, bread and insipid kahvia, I'll remember the past joyful days. Pray for me, I ask of you, and be not surprised if I return to the sanctuary of your home the first time that my wife strikes me with a pot."

Alena laughed until she cried; and then she laughed again. She dried her eyes on her apron saying, "Emil, I'll miss you around here for you do tell the damnedest lies in a pleasing manner. It was July; you paid your rent in advance; and you were fat as a hog when you walked in that door; now you are thin. You've hurt your lady by your remarks. I have never seen a Swede or Finn girl who couldn't cook anything from blood-bread to cured fish; so your bride will satisfy in more ways than one. Off with you, now," she said with a wave of her hand toward the door. "If you are going to carry Engrid's valise and still make the train, you had better hurry. Take care of this lovely little girl, or you will have to answer to me."

She wiped at her nose; then accepted a kiss from Emil and Louise on a plump cheek. She wished them good luck as the trio hurried down the track, and noted that the handsome, blonde giant carried the valise as if unaware of its existence.

"God bless you, my children, for all of your days," the woman whispered a she stared red-eyed after the departing figures until they disappeared from sight behind the house; then she hurried into the house to cook for the dayshift men who were up and coughing in an attempt to clear their lungs of dust.

Mr. Wilken answered the door with a polite, "Good morning," and admitted the girl. Engrid observed that he was an attractive man of average height. He was slender build; quite in contrast to that of the majority of miners with whom she was acquainted. He wore a tailored black suit, a stripped shirt of alternating black and white and a dark bow tie. His complexion was inclined to be dark, as was his hair which possessed a natural curl accentuating his suave features. A slender, well-shaped nose overlooked a waxed mustache of an iron gray color. Brown eyes glowed with a warm friendliness as their glance fell on the buxom figure of the girl when she entered. Saying something that the girl couldn't understand, he relieved her of her valise and carried it upstairs followed by the girl and Mrs. Wilken. After depositing the burden on the floor inside of her door, he withdrew, leaving Engrid and Mrs. Wilken to pass a superficial judgment on each other.

Engrid thought; "I would that I could talk to this lady, asking questions and being answered in turn; in that way, I could make out alright." She stared blankly, wishing that she were around the world in the house of her former employer. 'Now I know what a mute endures," she pondered.

Mrs. Wilken moving to the girl's side; helped her to remove her coat. She pressed it into the young lady's hand and pointing to a corner of the room and said, "Closet." Engrid took the coat and her scarf to the closet, repeating the word to herself under her breath. After that, she unsnapped the fasteners of her valise and opened the drawers of the bureau, preparing to put away her things; but the woman forestalled her with an imperative shake of her head and a tightening of already thin lips. She beckoned to the girl and started down the stairs. Engrid obediently trailed after her.

The first day, Mrs. Wilken initiated tasks in the sequence that she wished them completed; then Engrid continued where she left off. It was Tuesday; the sky was clear; therefore the bedding was removed from her employer's bed and at the woman's direction, taken out to air in the warm sun.

At twelve o'clock, the master of the house returned from the store where he worked as a partner of his wife's father. Engrid prepared lunch for the man, wife and a freckled urchin who had been christened Jerold. There was, Engrid found, another baby; however, as it was slightly less than a year old, Engrid did not have to feed it. Because the thorough training that she had undergone at home, stood her in good stead, it wasn't long before the novelty of adjusting herself to her work wore off. And the labor became routine of the hardest kind.

Mr. Wilken welcomed her presence in the house. Her willingness to please and her sunny disposition, coupled with humorous attempts to repeat words correctly after he had once said them to her, caused the man to look forward to meal times; while he told himself that only a healthy woman can create a congenial environment in a house, in fact, it makes it a home. His wife was suffering from some obscure ailment that caused her to act, at times, as though she were a bundle of nerves, and every one of the bundle, raw and exposed, in the bargain. Healthy women, on the other hand, must get rid of their energy, somehow, and Engrid certainly appeared to be using hers in a manner that was welcome indeed.

When breakfast; consisting of fruit, cereal, bacon or ham and eggs, was served to the gentleman's liking, he generally rewarded his cook with a kindly pat on the shoulder, and he added complimentary remarks, coupled with a friendly smile as he rubbed his waist to express contentment. Warming to his kindness, Engrid found herself liking to labor here a much as she had enjoyed working for her former employer.

Mrs. Wilkens personally cared for the baby girl. Engrid, at times, had her hands full with Jerold, who was five. He was a handsome little chap with red hair and a smattering of freckles; his disposition, on occasion, complimented his complexion. His time was generally spent in running away with the girl in hot pursuit, or in trying to shove the neighbor's cat down into the outhouse. He cluttered Engrid's clean room with a varied assortment of objects such as cat-faced spiders, stinkbugs, horned-toads, grasshoppers, centipedes and an occasional live mouse that he found in one of the numerous traps that his father kept set in the horse barn. Most of the time, the mice were dead, but occasionally, one remained alive. The boy would bring it into the house with a show of bravado and turn it loose. Engrid would promptly subject him to a blistering tirade in

Swedish, interposed with an occasional word in English; while the youth would stand with smiles reaching from ear to ear, his freckled nose twitching like a rabbit's as he imitated her vitriolic outburst in his own inimitable manner. When Engrid's patience would become exhausted at some such an offense, she would turn him over to his mother and the lad would enjoy the exiting spectacle of these two allies turned antagonist berating each other in different tongues.

The boy wasn't all bad, however; sometimes he would come to Engrid's room during her rest period. If the door was ajar, it signified that he might disturb her privacy if he so wished. Soon, after seeing the door open, his cherubic countenance might peep around the frame wearing a friendly grin and dark eyes aglow as he eagerly anticipated an exchange of confidences with this fair-haired foreigner. He would walk around the room, pointing to this object or that, calling its name in English. Engrid would respond with its equivalent in Swedish, and thus the two learned from each other. As their understanding of languages grew, a tie was formed between them. The boy soon learned what was taboo and what was not, so as a general rule, the home took on an atmosphere of serenity that was gratifying to the master and mistress alike.

After work, Engrid often visited Mrs. Kosky. They would retire to the woman's room, where they would sit chatting and knitting after the dishes were all done. If it chanced to be fine weather, they would sit on the front porch watching the sun go down. On one such an evening, while Louise and Emil were still on their honeymoon, a man walked through the gate and bounded up the steps to grasp Engrid in a tremendous hug, and before the men, who sat at the far end of the long porch with amazed looks on their faces could say anything, he kissed her soundly.

"Alex, Alex Nystrom!" she gasped. "What in the world are you doing here?"

"I came to town over two years ago; I have been living in a boarding house run by Mrs. Sumsion; right there it is," he said, pointing across town to another wooden frame building overlooking Leadville row.

"But how, when?"

"How did I know that you were here? In the store today, Rika mentioned the fact that you two sisters had come to town. She is quite the kiddo!"

"Yes, yes, of course she is." Engrid said, while striving to recover her composure and looking at the grinning boarders who were staring her way, knowing that they were discussing her and the youth who had so impulsively embraced her.

"Have a chair, and tell me about yourself." She invited as she sank into her seat. Alex looked about him and seeing none, he disappeared into the dining room and promptly returned with a chair which he set down a little removed from Engrid's. He rested his feet on the railing as though he had been in the habit of doing so all of his life.

"Are you acquainted with Mrs. Kosky?" Engrid asked the boy, who, for the first time, seemed aware of the third person's presence. Turning to the woman, Engrid remarked, "This is Alex Nystrom whom I used to go with in the old country. Two years ago he dropped me like a hot potato and ran off to this country. I received one letter from him afterwards."

"How do you do?" Alex remarked, acknowledging the introduction. He reached into his pocket and pulled out a pipe and a poke of tobacco; soon he was enjoying a smoke, doubly joyful because out of the clear, blue sky, he had been informed that his former sweetheart was living in the same community as he!

"I tried working in the logging camps; but that didn't appeal to me. I ran into Emil and nothing would do except that we should come west together to seek our fortunes in the mines, and am I glad."

"You found it?" Engrid asked.

"No, I found you," he remarked, as the smoke from his pipe rose in quickly repeated puffs as he surveyed the object of his past infatuation.

"Well, it is nice to know that you found something that pleases you," Engrid said with a smile looking at Alena; "as for me, I am working."

"Where?"

"For a Mrs. Wilken; her husband is partner in a store."

"I know the man, and I am glad for you. I work in that mine up from Church Street," Alex informed her.

"In that case, you'll have to climb up and see me sometime," Engrid said with a smile.

For approximately two hours, the couple talked, exchanged information, and reliving bygone days. During this interval, Engrid felt genuine happiness for the first time since leaving home. Suddenly life in the strange town blossomed with added meaning.

"Say," Alex proposed, when conversation began to lag, "how would you like to attend a dance at the Finn hall a week from next Saturday night?"

"You're selling tickets, I suppose?" the girl asked an amused smile tempering a trace of sarcasm.

Alex accepted the witticism in a manner that definitely told Alena he was at home in the exchange. "I am doing just that; and I was wondering if I could get you to buy a ticket. The price is fifty cents, and you may bring along an extra lady for a dime."

Engrid flashed Alex a quizzical smile. "How am I to know whether or not I can dance the way you do; if dancing is any different from our polkas, and folk dances. I refuse to make a fool of myself."

"Never fear," he assured her, "we dance the same here as we did at home; however, we have what folks call square dances and the Virginia reel. They are a great deal of fun, and resemble our folk dances. You'll catch on in a hurry. We have ladies choice every third dance. The dances are a lot of fun, and the beauty of it all is that we don't have to dance on the green, as we did at home, most of the time. We actually have or own dance hall that the lodge built just two years ago; so regardless of the weather, we can dance inside."

"The fifty cents that you speak of; the dime also, mean nothing to me. All I know of Amerikan money is that, in New York, before I boarded a train, they took what money I had and gave me some paper money and other coins. I shall not know until the woman pays me for a week's work just what I have coming."

"I was only joking about you buying the ticket; I do that. The fifty cents you speak of looks like this," He reached into his pocket and brought out a handful of silver and extracted a half- dollar, a dollar, and a ten-cent piece and held them up. "Two of those big fellows and the next biggest size is what you make in a week," Alena told her.

The lesson stopped abruptly when Alex found that his pocket money was limited to an amount less than five dollars. With that subject in discard, he turned to the original reason for his intrusion into the women's gab-fest. It grew dark, and a faint chill followed the exit of the sum from the sky. Purple shadows banded together and formed a veil through which the first stars of evening began to timidly assert themselves.

"Will you go to the dance with me?" Alex asked at length.

"But I have no clothes for dancing," Engrid objected. "All I have are the ones I brought from home. I would appear ludicrous were I to mingle with others in a garb which, though appropriate there, is entirely out of place here. No, I don't believe I had better go."

Alena watched this exchange between the youngsters, a sparring and fencing, each sought an opening in the other's armor of self-possession, the boy, who seemed eager and clean-cut, and the girl, countering each witticism; then hurling it back with perfect aplomb.

"Who will be going to the dance besides you?" the girl asked idly, although revealing a noticeable eagerness.

Alex told her; then turned to the mistress of the boarding house who rocked placidly back and forth. The boy's eyes finally caught the woman a look of pleading intermingled with hope that she would say something.

"It would be a shame to disappoint such a nice boy," the landlady thought as Engrid turned her glance to the older woman from which she received a nod of approval.

"I'll go," Engrid said turning to Alex, "even if I have to use the clothes that I brought from home."

"There is nothing wrong with your dress," Alex eagerly denied as he surveyed the girl's handiwork. "Every new-comer appears in the same costume; we make a welcoming night of it."

He looked wistfully at the girl. "I see no reason for not going, unless it is because you're asked to accompany me."

"It isn't that at all," the girl denied with a smile, "do you know where I am staying?"

"Just about; if you let me walk you home, I'll know."

"So," Engrid said, curving her lips until they appeared inviting and altogether desirable to the eager youth. She stuck her knitting into her bag, and stood up. "I think I will run along, Mrs.Kosky; it is much nicer to have an escort through darkened streets. Goodnight and I shall see you again."

"Goodnight, my dear, and do come again; I enjoyed your visit. Thank you for helping me with the dishes; if it weren't for your aid, I would just be finishing, instead of resting."

After taking their leave, the couple moved down a main street dimly lit in splotches of yellow where kerosene lantern shed their garnish glow. Alex walked slightly ahead; the girl clinging to his arm as he provided an opening wedge through the swirling crowd of miners who strolled in and out of the saloons. Through those doors came the tinny music of pianos, the rattle of poker chips and the whirr of roulette wheels. Tonight an atmosphere of peace lightly cloaked the town which seemed to be holding its breath until the Saturday, when it would expel it in dancing, singing, gambling, fighting and a general lowering of morals. Saturn's day rules supreme in a mining camp.

"Would you care for a bit to eat, or a drink?" Alex inquired as he drew to a halt in front of a plate-glass window of the Candy Kitchen where Engrid looked with a watering mouth on the tempting array of candies.

"No, oh yes, I guess I would like some candy," she replied as he opened the door.

"Hello, men!" Alex called to coworkers of another nationality who were seated at tables, and who stared with marked interest at the stranger with him. Alex swaggered to the display case and ordered a sack of assorted candies; while he leaned against the counter with one hand inside of a pocket and his left foot resting over the right.

Accepting the sack, Engrid waited until she arrived outside before munching on a chocolate. She gave an ecstatic sigh; then delicately licked her fingertips.

"Have you tasted chocolates before?" Alex asked in an eager-to-please voice as he accepted a sweet.

"Oh, Alex, if we could have had something like this in the old country, we probably would never have left to come here. I must remember to send some to mother and father when I get my first pay." She munched at the rich chocolate for a time; then commented; "They go down too fast; bite them once and they are gone."

As they turned from main street toward the Wilken house, Engrid looked up the hill where braced timbers reared above a waste dump. "What do you call that mine?" she asked.

"The Gemini."

"What does that mean?"

"The owner's wife called it that," Alex said evasively. "She is a well-read woman, and named it because of something to do with the stars, or something. They sank their first mine shaft down at the foot of the hill, and when they discovered they had ore in the ground, they found they had no place to disposes of the waste rock; so they went farther up the hill and sank a second shaft. The owner's wife named it because of the two shafts, 'the twins' is what the name means."

As they moved along, the girl looked up again, and to her imaginative mind, the timbers resembled a giant, leaning on two crutches against the hillside. To her ears came a rhythmical pulsation; a subdued undertone to the staccato exhaust issuing from the hoisting engine.

Her curiosity aroused, Engrid asked, "What is that?"

"What?"

"That noise." Engrid's face assumed an expression of eagerness and her white teeth gleamed between parted lips.

"Oh, you mean the sound resembling an engine? That is the exhaust of the steam hoist."

"No, there is another sound; a muffled throbbing and it can only be heard clearly at intervals when the hoist isn't running. It sounds as though someone was beating on a giant drum. There it is now; can you hear it?"

"You mean the air compressor," he laughingly informed her. "It pushes air through pipes to turn the drilling machines underground. What is so unusual about that noise?"

"Perhaps it is because I have never consciously noticed it before now. It causes me to feel peaceful and drowsy; soothing in much the same way as the breaking of the surf on a beach during a still night, or the muted roar of the fierce wind through the dark evergreens when heard through the heavy walls of home, or even the faint thunder of water falling over rocks by the mill. I really believe that I am going to like that sound; it will lull me to sleep if I open my window at night."

"You make things take on a new meaning," Alex observed softly as they meandered along under the over-hanging branches of trees. "I have never given things like that a thought; comparing one thing to another, and making beauty of them all; it is a gift, you have."

"But is there any other way that we can beautify many things in life that otherwise would be commonplace? If we take things for granted, we quickly tire of them and fail to properly evaluate their worth. Things change, such as the sun, moon, food, warmth, laughter and friends."

"That sound has a different meaning to me," Alex commented with a trace of weariness in his voice. "When I hear it chugging as it builds up a cylinder of air, I think of hard work and a bucking machine eating its way into the solid rock in search of ore. I see tired backs rising and falling to a never-ending succession of shovelfuls of ore that grow heavier while seconds drag along like they were hours. I remember ten hours of work each day, while heads ache from power gas, and foul air." He reached for a piece of candy, took a bite and then continued. "I think of darkness, heavy enough to almost prevent one from moving a hand, and the grim shadows of toiling men who drive their bodies harder than they were meant to be driven, and as a consequence, they become heavy drinkers to forget the toil waiting for them the following day. Finally, they end up by going to one of the brothels because there are not enough women to enable many men to have a wife. The next morning, half-dead from the toil of the day before, and a night of drinking and carousing, they return to work, carrying whisky or brandy to enable them to go on. Some of the men hardly ever draw a sober breath. Down there, also, there is dripping water that freezes a sweating man, and holes big enough to throw a huge building into. In these holes there are falling rocks to smash bodies; explosions that rend and destroy."

As they moved along slowly, Alex continued, "It is an awful sight to see one of your friends after he is blown to hell because a fuse has a missing center string. There are nights and nights when I go to sleep and listen before I do, to those who have been underground for too many years as they cough the night through, vainly trying to get rid of the dust and machine oil which gradually chokes them, and that, while they are still young men. Some wise fellow that has never done hard work may say that hard work is good for a person; but a poor working man soon finds that he can get too much hard work." Alex placed an arm around the girl's waist; then went on. "I am tempted to leave before it is too late. Go to some other kind of work; anything to get a job in the open air, even if I have to work for less money."

He glanced covertly at the girl. "This is a damn poor thing to be discussing on such a wonderful night with such a lovely girl." He spoke in a manner that caused her to turn on a smile.

"Go ahead and talk, Alex. Get it off your chest; I know what you mean. At home, I used to feel the same about the deep woods on the winter days and nights, when everything was frozen, and the 'lights' streamed across the sky. I used to go to my mother and talk things over with her and she always comforted me; then I felt better."

"But can you imagine darkness more fearsome than the darkest winter night at home?" he asked. "That is a mine; where only a flickering stick of a candle serves as a sun, moon or stars. The devil laughs with joy when the Tsar condemns men of Russia to a lifetime of servitude in the Liberian mines."

By now they had reached the gate, and Engrid went ahead of the youth up the walk. At the door, she inserted a key. "Goodnight, Alex; it was sweet of you to see me home."

"Never say it; I enjoyed this night more than I have anything in ages. I will see you on Saturday night, then?"

"You mean Saturday after next?"

"That's right," he informed her.

"Goodnight, Engrid," he said replacing his hat, he turned down her offer of more chocolates, accepting instead a quick kiss from the girl's soft lips; then he went whistling down the street with all sorts of thoughts whirling through his mind.

"A rather nice boy," Engrid mused as she watched his retreating figure. "He's depressing in some ways; isn't happy here, I suppose."

Chapter 12

Mr. and Mrs. Emil Flink returning after an absence of a week. They stopped briefly in on Engrid and invited her to visit with them that evening.

Engrid surveyed the couple with a mischievous smile. "You don't look any worse for the experience," she commented. "You are simply adorable," she complimented her sister who had purchased a suit whose color was the light blue of wood smoke when it enters a shaft of sunlight streaming through trees. Light braid neatly trimming the shoulders. "I see you have one of those shirtwaists that you longed for," she added as she fingered the frothy appearing ruffles of lace under Louise's chin. White gloves fit her wrists snuggly up to the sleeves of the jacket. A hat the same color as her suit and surmounted by feathers dyed to match the color of her hat, fit saucily on her head.

"My goodness!" Engrid gasped in amazement when her glance dropped to the white slippers that her sister proudly showed when she raised her skirt a trifle, "You are simply wonderful. What clothes will do for a woman."

"Do you like this?" Louise asked, pointing a finger at her head gear.

"Uh-huh, do let me try it on?" Engrid begged, and accepting the hat, she placed it over one eye.

"I guess it just isn't made for you." Louise said with a gay laugh. "Your head is large than mine, and your nose broader. You'll have to get one just a bit bigger."

Engrid gave her full attention to Emil who wore a dark suit, a bowler hat and pointed calf-skin shoes and a light shirt accentuated by a black loosely fastened tie.

"Do I look nice enough to kiss? I am your new brother, you know."

"Why Emil, you are perfectly handsome!" She threw her arms around her brother-in-law and kissed him soundly.

"That's one that Louise didn't get," he observed with a chuckle. "We are having a few of our close friends in for a cup of coffee and a drink tonight, will you come?"

"Certainly, brother; what time?"

"Anytime, come after supper."

Louise tittered; then burst into rich-throated laughter.

"Golly," Emil exclaimed, "I didn't mean that the way it sounds. I meant to say after the supper dishes are cleaned up; then you should come."

"Certainly you did. Alright, I shall be up tonight." She waved the pair away, and entered the house to prepare lunch for the family.

After the dinner dishes were washed and put away, Engrid changed from her work clothes and dressed in a dark wool skirt and blouse of white linen. She placed a white scarf around her waist and tied it at her side; then she ventured forth to do some shopping.

Uneasiness gripped her as she moved from one store to another, shaking her head as clerks accosted her with warm smiles. Feeling conspicuous, she vainly searched for some article that might make an appropriate gift for the newlyweds. She felt as if those whom she passed in her movement through the stores were looking at her alone, and she alternated between cold chills, and hot embarrassment when the clerks inquired as to her wishes. On each occasion, the timid girl could only shake her head in a vague gesture meaning anything, everything or nothing. For a long time, she vainly searched for some woman of her own race whom she might approach to translate her wishes into reality.

"If only I knew how to ask for something; how can I buy without being able to explain what I want?" In desperation she turned from an attentive male clerk and made for the door where Rika walked through and greeted her with an affable smile holding the door open for the girl to pass. Engrid laid a hand on her arm and explained her situation.

"Certainly I can help you; I would have been here before however, I was out to lunch. Wait just a moment until I discard my cloak." She walked into the back of the store but soon returned brushing at her hair with a slender hand on which the diamond scintillated.

"What do you have in mind?" she asked, displaying a smile that seemed a trifle forced.

"I thought that I might give them a durable gift; perhaps you have something in the store that I haven't seen?"

"I see." Rika reached under a counter saying, "How much would you like to pay?" She displayed some pillowcases. "These are embroidered by a local woman who specializes in that kind of work. They're not extremely expensive; only five dollars a pair."

Engrid felt uncomfortable under the girl's appraising glance as she ran a hand over the lace, admiring its incredible beauty. "Perhaps you have something," Engrid suggested, feeling her ears burn, "not quite so expensive?"

"Nothing fancy; useful though, I believe." She moved across the store and stooping over, rose up holding an alarm clock. "This is the only thing that I can think of, except silverware and dishes."

"That's just the thing!" Engrid exclaimed. "How much is it?"

"Two-fifty; too much?" Rika said with uplifted brow.

It was, until Rika questioned her; not now though. A week's wages! Ten-thousand scrubs with a brush on knees that ached; a thousand smug glances from an arrogant mistress, and insults of a freckled boy; a hundred buckets of water from a deep well; twenty-one or more meals over a hot coal stove; yard after yard of carpet rags; seven long days alternating between elation and despair; but loudly she decided, "I'll take it." She reached into her bag and fumbled around until she found two big silver dollars and a fifty-cent piece. The large ones were shiny in their newness, with 1897 stamped in clear letters below the face of the austere woman who looked impersonally to the side as though she cared not in the least whose hands carelessly tossed her with others of their kind on a gaming table, or clutched with fingers loath to release their grasp as did the girl who now stacked one on another, then capped them both with the half-dollar.

In her mind's eye, Engrid saw again the sturdy copper chest that her mother used to carry from the cellar each month upon receiving money from Anton. Marie would place it on the table after a preliminary glance through the windows assured her that there were no guests in the offing. With hands that trembled a she unhooked the clasp, she would lift the lid and add to her growing horde which grew in size over the years until at last she was forced to purchase another box.

"Allow me to feel the money," the children would plead, and at their mother's nod of assent, dip their hands into the receptacle.

"Yes, my children; feel the hard metal as it runs through your hands. Know that it represents the tired body of your father, who is earning more to enable us to live in a home near the city and to till more land. When we grow old, we shall not have to depend on charity or our children."

Sometimes Marie would mention further schooling for the children after the lower grades while she rubbed the palms of her hands together and watched with observant eyes as the children grasped the coins by the heaping handfuls, then allowed them to drop with musical tinkling sounds into the box.

"Learn well the meaning of money, how it is so hard to earn and easy to spend."

How her mother's eyes had gleamed with avarice as she added to the growing hoard; but how sad when forced to remove a portion of the coins when a log had broken Anton's leg. The house had been wrapped in a shroud of gloom for months. Finally money came again, and Marie began to act her cheerful self as she went about her tasks.

Engrid recalled that she, too, had saved and watched while a pile grew from year to year in her own secret box in their granary. Finally she had money sufficient to pay her fare to Amerika when Louise had encouraged her to accompany her. What a wonderful feeling it had been to arrive in this town with a little money over, and to find a job awaiting her, so that she, too, might begin saving. But what was there to save for, other than clothing? Unquestionably she could not purchase a home on her weekly stipendium. Perhaps a pair of horses black as midnight, and a black and red buggy such as this one passing by? Foolish thought; out of the question. "I can never save enough before I die of old age, were I to save for them out of my weekly wages."

Lost in Elysian ponderings, the girl arrived at her sister's house where Louise joyously admitted her with a huge hug, warm smile; then took her coat.

"And where is Emil?"

"The poor fellow is taking a nap; he helped me clean the house a bit. But, being unfamiliar with the work, it was too much for him." Louise allowed a note of sarcasm to creep into her words. "Come, let me show you around."

Louise showed her the cellar first of all. It led directly from the back of the kitchen, and its roof was dome-shaped and made of boards, covered on the top by rocks and dirt to the depth of a foot. The former owner had built well, without having to dig too deeply into the rocky ground and seemingly he had used the rubble from the hole in the ground to make the roof.

"Although I have to hoist the water out of the well, I don't mind it at all," Louise informed her. "Someday I shall have water piped into the house."

The bride pointed out geraniums, begonias, ferns and flags in lard buckets that had been painted attractively by the former owner, the colors harmonizing with the woodwork and paper in the different rooms.

"How does the place look to you, sister?" Louise asked anxiously. "I have worked hard all day to make things appear as attractive as possible. I have changed the furniture around a bit, scrubbed and cleaned, hung new curtains in the living room, and ordered and received about half of a grocery store's supplies, so we shall not go to bed hungry tonight."

Engrid's answer brought a gratifying smile and for the new living room rug with the figures of a huge dog and a boy sitting in the garden, her praise was vociferous.

"To think that we had to be satisfied with plain rag-rugs on our floors at home, and keep the most beautiful for decorative purposes on the wall."

"That reminds me," Engrid said, "Mrs. Wilken and I are cutting rags for rugs in our spare time. We are also using squares from suit-sample books to make her a beautiful patchwork quilt."

"Someone is coming," Louise exclaimed at the sound of footsteps on the front porch. Hurrying to the door, she threw it wide. "Welcome, John! Welcome, Rika! We have been waiting for you...Emil..."

"Yes, dear," came a muffled voice from a bedroom.

"John is here, you had better get up."

"Ah, let the poor fellow sleep," John said; "that's where I ought to be this very minute instead of paying social calls."

"Emil!" Louise called, going to the door of the bedroom.

"Yes, dear?"

"Get up, John's here!"

Running a huge hand through his tousled hair, and stifling a yawn with the other, Emil filled the door to the kitchen with his bulk.

"What's the matter, boy? Has the misses been too hard on you?"

"Oh, John." Rika remonstrated, "Don't say such things." Her voice reached Engrid's ears on a subdued note; but John unabashedly simpered at her; then winked at Engrid, causing her to blush.

Engrid laughed. "Just to spite Rika," she told herself.

"Go sit down while I comb my hair and slip on a clean shirt." Emil prompted through a splatter of water.

"You're splashing water on the new curtains that I tacked on the wash stand, dear," Louise fretted.

Emil mouthed something unintelligible; but Louise persisted. "Use a washrag instead of scooping it up with your hands, and blowing through it like a sea lion."

"Ah, hell, a man can't get clean using a washrag; they're for women," he stated positively as he dried his face and carried the water to the kitchen door where he sprayed the ground below the porch, and the water smell, rising from the dust, felt sweet in his nostrils. At his wife's plea, he mopped the floor around the bench and dried the top of the wash stand.

"It's fortunate for you I had a mother, or I wouldn't submit in such a docile manner to your bossing," Emil grumbled. "It seems natural for men to be bossed, and for women to want to boss them," he added with an engaging grin as he ran a comb through his thick hair.

The women naturally affirmed the wisdom of his remarks; but John protested, "Not by a darn sight; I don't want to be bossed, I think too much of my independence."

"Hmph!" Rika snorted, "You should talk."

"Where is Alex? Is he coming?" Engrid asked. "And by the way, Emil, why didn't you let me know that he was in town? He came to visit me at the boarding house the other night."

"I'm sorry, Engrid; I was so excited with your arrival, and my impending marriage that I didn't give it a thought. I decided to invite him tonight after I recalled that he was in town when Louise and I were talking things over in Salt Lake. He will be here anytime. I gave him the money to rustle up some refreshments before I went to sleep."

No sooner were the words out of his mouth, then Louise opened the door to admit the person under discussion; who was accompanied by a puffing Mrs. Kosky and the smiling "Toasty" Hansen who handed Louise a wrapped gift. Seemingly Alex was in fettle, his straw hat was cocked back on his head and under each arm he clutched a bottle.

"Hello people!" he called with an engaging smile as he came through the door and deposited his load of spirits on the table. "I sampled a little before I left town, and found that it is good brandy." He looked at Louise, "Here's a little present."

"Did you have any trouble finding it?" Emil asked as he picked up one of the bottles; he eyed the contents to estimate the extent of his friends "sampling".

"That I did. I tried at several places. All they had was whiskey; Smith had it, however."

Emil took the liquor into the kitchen where he filled a set of glasses shining in their newness. These he carried into the front room to be distributed among those gathered, and all of whom accepted a drink, with the exception of Rika.

"Won't you even have a tiny one to toast our marriage?" Emil coaxed in an affable voice.

"Nope."

"Why?"

"I just don't like liquor. Mother and dad do not use it; nor do they condone its use. They both belong to the Temperance Society."

"Alright for you," Emil exclaimed with a mischievous twinkle of his eyes. "I will drink yours then." So saying, he tipped the glass and smacked his lips. "Now, that is something!" he remarked running the back of his hand over his mouth. Setting the empty glass on the tray, he picked up his own and raised it aloft. "Here's to my wife's husband, the best damn timber man in the Little Chief mine," a puckish grin detracted from his flamboyant boast and he flashed Louise a quizzical glance.

"Let me make the toast," she pleaded.

"All right by me, my Svenska Flika!"

"Here's to our life together in this new land! May we never regret that we came here, and our decision to marry." She grasped her husband with a joyous hug, turned to her guests and said, "Here's to our friends. May they always be welcome here, and may they come often."

Glasses clicked and drinks were downed as a knock sounded at the front door. Emil lowered his glass and striding to the door, he threw it wide. "Come in, come in!" he boomed out, "You're just in time to have a drink. I see you brought your accordion, George."

"Without it and my wife, I am as lost as if I had forgotten my clothes," George answered as he shook the man's hand and congratulated him on his marriage.

Mrs. Swanson, her gray eyes darting here and there in a nervous glance that missed nothing, entered following her husband. She was a tiny woman with thin cheeks and her face at the juncture of her long nose was lined with tiny crows-feet. Hair that had been dark, showed traces of gray, and she wore it as other women customarily did; gathered at the top. Her breasts were so flat as to appear non-existent, even with the lift that her corsets gave to her form. At Louise's invitation, she removed a yellow straw hat and greeted the sisters in a nasal voice that caused them to feel uncomfortable. She talked incessantly, and if no one seemed to be listening she prattled on, asking questions and answering them herself if there was no response to her rapid-fire barrage; or, if one started to answer, in the middle of an explanation she would add similar words completing the conversation; always a half-word behind the other speaker, until the individual stopped in confusion; while she chattered on.

Engrid smiled at Louise, and in turn received a sagacious wink; both women realized that the woman was unaware of her fault.

George Swanson appeared to be about forty, or forty-five years of age. He was of average height, and his face, broad. His body was heavy, as were his arms. His fingers were short and his hands were smaller than is usual for one with such a strong-appearing torso. His dark brown suit fit him loosely, as though he suffered an illness or loss of weight since its purchase. His countenance was benign and his smile engaging, even when he opened his mouth to grin, displaying a paucity of teeth. As she watched him talk, Engrid mused that he resembled a baby; even to the scanty red hair struggling to maintain a foothold over each ear.

"Greetings, fair ladies!" he said after being told the names of the girls. "What do you think of this desert, so far from the lakes and green meadows of home?"

"And what caused you to come here after learning Swedish, as well as you native tongue?" Engrid countered with a coy smile.

"So you know I am a Finn, then? How do you know that I am not a Swede-Finn?"

"I can tell by your accent."

"Is that the only reason?" he inquired slyly.

"No, your build is different. It follows the pattern of all the pure Finns I know. You're heavier and look shorter than Swede-Finns; however, that is not to be deplored. At home during the dances, the Swedes had the devil's own time hanging on to their girls. I like you Finns," she added; "You're so vital, and full of life; your so friendly, sincere and above all honest."

"Not only that," Emil broke in to say; "they make the best muckers. They're built so close to the ground that they can work the pants off any other man with a shovel, and, when it comes to pushing cars, they can replace a mule."

George's features beamed in an unaffected smile, coming as the compliment did from one as sturdy as the speaker.

"I am in need of a good lawyer," he said casually. He sighed as though he were striving to quell forebodings. "Can you recommend one to me?" He paused, with lips ajar, and red gums glistening.

Emil appeared surprised, as did the others who flashed the man a look of commiseration.

"What need have you of a lawyer?" Emil asked. "Have you been in a knifing scrape?" His shaking head showed his concern.

"No, not that; I stopped using a knife on other people when I came to this country."

"For heaven's sake, man; tell us." Alex broke in, "We're dying of curiosity."

"I was thinking of suing the city," he said soberly, "That graveled sidewalk they built going from my place to in front of Job's store ..."

"Go on," said John after looking at the others and seeing the suspense growing in their expressions.

"They built it too close to my backside!" George blurted out.

"Ho, ho, ho," Emil roared with laughter as he slapped John a resounding thump on the back, "Did you ever hear anything the likes of George?"

"I got tired of sewing patches on my pants when my wife refused." George informed them after the laughter had subsided.

"That was a good one on us," Emil admitted. "Let us have a drink on it."

"What is the matter, Rika? Why didn't you laugh?" John asked of his companion who sat straight-laced on a new chair that had been recently unwrapped from its straw and paper cover.

"Because I fail to see anything particularly funny in the story," she said haughtily.

After her remark, the men fell into peals of mirth that threaten the safety of the walls.

"Nothing seems to be funny to you anymore," John observed with a wry twist of his mouth as he reached for a cigarette; then walked to the kitchen to procure a match from a holder on the wall. Returning, he inhaled tremendous drags of smoke into his cavernous chest, and with a deft motion, flipped the match into the spittoon by the kitchen door. He looked at Rika to find her mouth gathered in tight lines.

"You'd better run out the storm line," suggested Emil as he accepted a smoke with a provocative grin.

The lines faded from the girl's mouth. "No one could remain angry around you for long, Emil," she said.

"Well, I like that." Louise's expression seemed to suggest as she glanced at her sister.

Engrid engaged Mrs. Swanson in conversation which eventually embraced the others in its warmth. In a moment's time; there were cross currents of conversation flowing from one chattering woman to another. Louise became the focal point of admiring glances as the others examined her engagement ring. Her silk blouse, with blue crocheted floral designs of lace snuggly fitting the contours of her youthful breasts, evoked genuine admiration. A white tortoise-shell comb embedded with miniature rubies twinkled cheerfully at each eager movement of the brides head.

From the kitchen where the men had congregated, sounds of revelry rose as John's modulated voice ended on a note of laughter in which the other men joined.

"What are you men doing in there?" Louise called.

A click of glasses followed; then George's voice answered, "We are just making a toast to the state we live in." the men drifted en masse into the front room where George continued, "We've toasted Finland and its people; finally we have come to Utah which we like best of all. Do you want to hear the toast?"

"It appears that you have toasted too many countries already," Mrs. Swanson said with ill concealed disgust.

"Now, now, my dear; we just got a start." Turning to John he proposed, "Give us that toast again."

"First we must fill the glasses," Emil suggested and he tipped a bottle.

John raised his and looked at it gravely. "Here's to the sad state of Utah, when one man's death makes a dozen widows."

At this witticism, even Rika unbent herself, adding her voice to the gayety sweeping over the group, and drawing it close to the bonds of friendship. After mirth had shattered the numerous barriers that intrude themselves between strangers, John suggested that George play some music. "If you are able."

"Man, what are you talking about?" George blurted indignantly. "The only time I can play is after I have had a few drinks." He ran his fingers up and down the keys of the music box, causing notes to dance to the corners of the house. "What will you have?"

"Play a schottische," pleaded Rika.

George complied with gusto, and toes tapped the floor while Engrid's eyes followed his hurrying fingers. She glanced quickly around, wishing that someone would suggest they roll back the rug and dance. Such music as this man played should never be wasted!

"Such music must not be wasted," said Emil as if reading Engrid's thoughts. "Let's throw back the rug and dance!"

Cries of approval answered his timely proposal and in a twinkling the rug was rolled back to the wall. Emil poured the men another drink. The women declined a second one; however, not a dissenting voice was raised when George helped himself. "I'll just take this one as a primer," he remarked as he hoisted the glass and downed the drink with a sly wink aside at his wife. He handed the empty glass to Emil; after adjusting his chair in the doorway leading to a bedroom to make available the floor that could be used by the dancers, he began to play.

Alex extended his hand to Engrid as the other couples moved to the floor. In a few seconds, the heady music and exertion caused the girl's pulse to pound with a tempo surpassing the momentary glow of pleasure that the small sip of brandy had caused her to feel. Her breath came fast, her eyes sparkled, and her mouth, parted slightly, revealing her even teeth. She danced gaily, happily and unthinking; giving herself full play to her emotions, until the walls spun faster and faster as she and her partner whirled around and around. She gloried in the feel of Alex's arms about her. Oh, what fun to dance, to feel the jostling bodies of the other couples as they made for an open space on the floor, only to find that others with the same idea in mind, laughed gaily at the inevitable collision. The men's laughter; and the women's squeals mingled with the chanting voice of the accordion until all stopped in exhaustion; only to begin after the men had taken another drink and had changed partners. Mrs. Kosky too, joined in the gayety. For a woman of her age and bulk, she showed a recuperative power between dances that left the others gasping and giggling when the music stopped.

Engrid found herself nestled snuggly in John's arms, gliding in a slow waltz.

"You dance beautifully," the man whispered in a pink ear from which was suspended a ring of gold.

"Thank you, Mr. Semell," she responded, "you are doing nicely yourself." She shivered slightly at the feel of his mustache moving along her cheek when he leaned down to make himself heard above the sobbing accordion.

"I think your betrothed is a beautiful girl," she ventured, as her eyes followed Rika who danced with her hair pressed against the fair face of Emil.

"You, too, are beautiful," he replied warmly.

Engrid felt her ears glow hot until she wondered if the crimson that must, of a certainly be there, was discernable to her partner's eyes. She glanced into his handsome face, feeling a queer chill for an instant at the nape of her neck.

"It is kind of you to say that; but I will consider the fact that you have been drinking," she replied with an infectious laugh as she looked into his eyes. She lowered her glance and laid her head on his shoulder; her eyes unseeing as they waltzed about the room and her heart beat faster than the quiet rhythm of her gliding feet warranted.

"Engrid," he whispered, leaning low again, his feet moving slowly in a step that was grace itself.

"Yes?"

"Even before I had a drink, I thought you were beautiful," he whispered.

"You're letting the liquor talk, for sure," the girl replied as she noticed the intent look that Rika flashed their way when they came momentarily into the scope of the girl's vision.

"Thank you for the dance," she warmly said as John released her and she found a chair, feeling glad to turn to Alex as he sank beside her; mopping his brow.

"Your sister is a very nice dancer and so light on her feet." Alex remarked.

"Are you enjoying yourself?" she countered with a quick glance in Rika's direction to find that the girl was engaged in conversation with John and there seemed to be sort of an argument from the set of the girl's lips and the look of resignation on the man's face. "Probably she is lecturing him on the evils of drinking," Engrid thought to herself.

"Hear ye! Hear ye!" Emil's affable face lighted and his voice commanded attention. "Here in our midst there is a lovely lady with a lovely voice." He paused, his eyes resting on Mrs. Swanson. "All in favor of the fair lady favoring us with a song; make it known by silence; others applaud."

A splattering of hands caused all eyes to turn on Engrid who had inadvertently followed the habits of a lifetime, unaware that Emil had deliberately reversed a customary procedure for the resultant laughter.

"Why, you're the meanest man in the world." She gasped; then she laughed.

"Come on Nora," John called encouragingly to Mrs. Swanson. She rose and placed her hands with palms together and nodded to her husband.

"What shall I sing?" she asked as George squeezed out bubbling notes.

"Sing the Spinner's song," John requested.

"Do that," came a chorus of pleas and soon the plaintive words and music swelled into the room. Engrid felt herself gripped in loneliness that the music suggested as Nora drew a word picture of a girl in a barn-like room far across the sea, patiently, but with a growing feeling of hopelessness, waited for a lover who never returned to claim his bride. The years dragged on and finally when the woman lay on her deathbed, the door to her room opened to reveal a familiar figure that had been absent for fifty years. Although the image was a vision of her fevered imagination, the woman died happily in her lover's arms.

Mrs. Swanson concluded and seated herself in silence. So beautiful was the woman's singing in contrast to her speaking, that the girls looked with awe at a different woman.

"What a wonderful voice you have!" Engrid applauded. "I have never heard anything quite so enchanting and I have heard the song a thousand times."

"Thank you, Engrid; I am glad that you liked it."

George continued the movement of his hands. His eyes closed, and Engrid felt herself caught up by the sounds sweeping from his instrument as he summoned forth a surge of wild music in which huge pines bowed in a biting north wind. Snow swished in clawing, rasping streams through agonized trees. Towering waves beat with relentless fury against a dismal coast bordering the North Sea. Higher and higher they rose under the remorseless insistence of the violently howling wind. Spumes of spray sped through the air falling with tinkling sounds in a coating of ice along the shore. The wind song died, and George's fingers simulated the surf struggling futilely to free itself from the finality of cold that caused the sea to flow in sluggish swells, until, with a tired sigh of submission, it lost its urge to resist and fell into a profound slumber. Ocean and land knew icy death and spirits haunting the northland danced forth in weaving, swaying convolutions of the aurora borealis painting the stygian blackness with their garnish glow.

The music softened and flakes of snow fell soundlessly. In its smother, a wolf howled while at intervals, the response of other gaunt brutes that ran with gleaming eyes and slavering jaws to fall in savage fury on their quarry. Into the music-drawn picture came firelight dancing on walls of a huge room where sat an aging mother with her husband reminiscing on bygone days.

"God, you can play," Emil's voice rose above the hush filling the room at cessation of the music.

"Amen to that!" John added reverently.

"You liked that, did you not?" Alex asked leaning toward Engrid.

"That I do, Alex; it does something to me. I feel as though I had feasted following a protracted famine."

"Well, now," George remarked, "it's not good and it's not bad. Pour me another drink." With that he set his instrument aside.

Louise set the table with new cups and saucers on which were hand-painted bluebirds. When she retired to the kitchen to grind the coffee beans, Emil followed her. Soon he presented himself in a bib apron with two heart-shaped pockets of red blushing on their white background. On his head rested his wife's hat. He set a heaping platter of fresh donuts in the center of the table; a mischievous smile playing over his face.

"Do have some donuts," he invited in a falsetto voice," or would you rather have brandy?" Placing two fingers of each hand in the pockets he gave his audience a simpering smile.

Alex grinned appreciatively. "I've had enough of the hard stuff. I am going to try some of the donuts and coffee when Louise gets it made." He gazed longingly at the generously sugared donuts and sighed. "I hope that when the old baker dies, he will go to the same place as I," he remarked as he inserted half of a donut into his mouth, followed quickly by the other half. "Won't heaven be hell without his donuts, and wouldn't hell be heaven with them."

"I think you have something there, Alex; but wait, you haven't seen anything yet!" Emil cautioned as he walked back into the kitchen, catching his wife with a quick kiss before he again entered the front room with a tray of cinnamon rolls from whose icing-covered surface, raisins were fairly bursting. "Sink your molars into these rolls," he suggested as he picked one up. He grasped the outside and unrolled it until it assumed a clock-spring shape. "See the cinnamon between the layers? I believe he sells then at two-bits a dozen just to make people happy. Of a certainty, he couldn't make a profit at the price." He looked inquiringly at the others. "What do you think?"

The guests agreed as Emil extolled the baker's virtues. From the kitchen the aroma of coffee drifted in breath-taking fragrance. As the Asiatic uses incense to perfume the air; so the Scandinavian uses coffee, and over the homes of the old-county born hangs that all pervading perfume, mingled with the delectable odor of cardamom seed.

"John," Emil said as he licked at his fingers, "let's go leasing."

"It's too uncertain; the pay, I mean. I don't know what I would do without a steady wage coming in. I've done my assessment work each year to my claim to the north of here, and to do that, I have to miss my wages as a miner during the time that I perform the work. I just don't see how I could go leasing, right now."

"If you don't try it once, you'll never make more than the wages you are now getting."

"I agree," John admitted as he whittled at a match, "that what you say is true; but how would we know where to start? How will we get our machines for drilling, our powder, and the cost for timber, track, pipe and air? That's only a part of the expenses. I know; I've talked with many of the men who have tried their hand at leasing, and they have it tough-sledding. Do you realize that it may be months before we can ship to the smelter; if we are lucky enough to find ore? All we'll have, after paying for supplies, cost of hoisting, and the royalty, might not amount to much. Take for instance the powder bill that I run up each month for the company, why, if I had to pay for that myself, I'd have to be wealthy."

John sugared his coffee, stirred thick cream into it and passed the pitcher to Alex who sat in silence, listening to the conversation. The women dunked donuts and rolls while listening with half-bored interest to the topic that was the most common one in mining camps. Rika obviously showed distaste for the subject as she had told John time and again, "All you can think about, you men, when you get together, is mining and drinking. I suppose that when you are in the mine, all you talk and think about are women and drinking."

And her appraisal of the men did justice to their natures.

"You forgot to include eating," John would remind her.

"To put it bluntly," Emil continued, "for a man to make anything at this game of mining, he has to sacrifice security on a gamble to make more than a measly day's pay. He has to go in debt I'll allow; but brother," he said, and his voice fell to a whisper and his eyes assumed a dreamy expression, "if you ever strike it rich, you'll be sitting on top of the world. Instead of renting a buggy to take a sweetie for a Sunday ride, you could buy your own surrey and bobsled and spirited horse to pull them. Think of the summers when you could ride out into the hills to picnic, instead of walking. I get so much walking during the day in the mine; that I am certain I am losing the zest I used to have. I am so lazy off the job that I will soon have the wife bringing me coffee and cigarettes to bed, rather than go to the table." He looked sideways at Louise who wrinkled her nose in mock disapproval. "If I work it right," he went on, "I may even get breakfast served in bed."

John considered this idea commendable, and said so. "What to use for money to pay my board bill is my main worry," he said.

"Oh, man, nothing to it," Emil dismissing John's objection with a careless wave of a hand. "The storekeeper wants to get rich, also. He'll give any dependable person a hundred dollars worth of credit to encourage him to take a chance. If you need more than that, and you have ore on the road to the smelter, and can prove to him that you can clear about half of your bill, he will stake you to more. Look at the home he owns, and the family he is raising if you think that this leasing isn't profitable. Look around you and see the fine homes that people are building. You can't buy them for wages. There is Kearl, Saunders, Clegg, and Pendray; not to mention a few of those who have made good at the game. What do you say?"

John thoughtfully picked at his teeth, "I don't know," he said at length, "give me time to think it over."

The women shared a mild epidemic of yawning, and anyone looking at George where he nodded in the chair, could realize that the man would be better off in bed. His wife nudged him to prevent his jaw from striking the table as he fell slowly forward, and the men roared with laugher.

"Come on, life-of-the-party; let's go home so the newlyweds can get some sleep."

"I must go, or I shall never be able to do my work tomorrow," Engrid observed as rising to her feet. She stifled a yawn behind a hand. Alex sprang up and helped her into her coat. Goodnights were said all around and the couples took their leave knowing that before long, Louise and Emil would spend many joyous minutes looking at their gifts.

Chapter 13

Outside it was pleasantly cool, and the waning moon cast a hazy glow over the slumbering town. Alex extended an arm, as they walked along the railroad in silence for a time. A queer tenseness gripped the girl so at last she pushed the resurgent feeling aside with conversation.

"Isn't life the most amazing thing?" she asked. "Here we are halfway around the world from home, and yet fated to pick a tiny spot on the map and both come here."

Out of the myriads of starts overhead, a streak of light shot briefly into view, "Look," Engrid exclaimed.

Looking up at the girl's command, Alex was in time to catch the flash before it faded from sight. "Make a wish," he suggested, "and it will come true."

"Do you really believe that?" she asked.

"Don't you?"

"When I was a child, I did."

"And now?"

"I am in a quandary! When I was little, I used to believe in a God who sat on a throne, with angels who played harps and sang lonely songs. Now that I see all of the suffering that there is in life, and the way people and nations fight tooth and nail for an existence, I don't know what to think. Don't misunderstand me," she went on, "I do believe in God; but he is a God who allows things to happen in ways that are inexplicable. The whole of life seems crazy and unreal at times, and I find myself, as a consequence, not knowing what to believe."

"Explain yourself."

"Well, if some fiend commits a crime of violence, and does the same thing time after time; even though that individual is finally caught and made to pay for his or her crimes; still, the harm that has been done, cannot be undone."

"And the same with nations," Alex added. "What wrongs they do cannot be undone."

"Now if there were a God as we were taught to believe in when we were children, he wouldn't let these things happen."

Because that was food for thought, Alex pondered long on the girl's remark. Finally he suggested, "Seemingly intelligent people are too smug or too blind to live and let live; to know the meaning of love."

"Could be," answered the girl. Pausing momentarily; looking up and pointing a finger, she said, "Oh, Alex, did you ever see anything so beautiful?"

The youth looked at his companion as she stood poised, the moon adding a touch of unreal, almost ethereal charm to her features. "I have never seen anything lovelier," he remarked earnestly.

"But you're not looking," she objected, drawing her lips into a pout.

Alex obediently turned his head; followed by his glance in the direction that the girl pointed.

"What is there to look at on the hill?" he asked, and his eyes came back to the level of the girl's. "I'd sooner look at you," he exclaimed and reaching out to draw her to him, he kissed her.

"You are inconsiderate not to look at a cross that the snow forms in the hollows of the peak," she pouted. Vague emotions, stirring to life from a revived past, rose in her when his arm stole around her waist, and she allowed him to keep it there as they continued to walk.

"Do you recall how we first met each other, Engrid?" He moved to the fore in order to look at the girl's features. "Remember how I tried to turn on the ice and looked at you instead of the sail? The first think I knew, I didn't know anything." He chuckled engagingly and fell back again as Engrid continued to walk along.

"How well I remember. It was only luck that I avoided your careening ice boat. Why did you have to come so close to where Louise and I were skating before you turned?" Although she had asked this question before, yet asking again held the exquisite charm of remembering the past.

"I just wanted to see you close up. Everybody up the lake always had a nice word to say about the Isaacson girls; so, I had to find out for myself."

"And you found…?"

"That their appraisals of the two of you were understatements. I don't believe those boys in your neighborhood had much get-up-and-go to them."

"Well, I like that," she protested; "never were there finer men. I had more than one proposal of marriage that I turned down."

"You did?"

"Certainly. One of them was Conrad Newman, who inherited a farm after his father died. I turned him down."

"Why?"

"Oh, I cared enough to marry him, I suppose," the girl said thoughtfully; "but I didn't want to live there. Father had so much praise for this country, that he would never had returned to Finland if mother had only come over here. I would have been living in Michigan right now."

"Did Conrad marry?"

"Oh, yes, he married one of our friends; maybe you know Vinie Sundquist?"

"Yes, I danced with her on several occasions, and I took her on one or two picnics."

"They have two children," she informed him. "One of them is a boy."

"And the other?"

Engrid's gay peal of laughter at this satire; fell delightfully on the young man's ears; and the couple moved from the track to continue down the main road, then up the tree-shaded path leading to her place of abode; while spring magic danced along the bypaths.

"Isn't the night lovely?" the girl asked. "Nights like this could cause me to believe in wood sprites and angels and…"

"Love?"

"Yes, love, also," she said softly.

At the door, Engrid turned to face her companion; while he in turn looked intently at her.

"Engrid," Alex looked at the golden head bared to the moonlight.

"Yes," she answered softly.

"May I … can I …?" He faltered as Engrid became aware of expectancy growing in her being; and strangely, for the moment, she had no desire to rid herself of it. Alex removed his hat and moved closer.

"What is it Alex?" Her eyes glowed with a limped fire and the pulse pounded rapidly in her throat.

The youth dropped his hat on the step and placed an arm around her neck. He bent his lips to hers as Engrid relaxed for a time; neither helping nor hindering him in his hungry kiss. She felt his heart thumping wildly against her breast as he crushed her to him and a sympathetic trembling coursed through both of their bodies. Engrid felt a vague sense of alarm as his lips became more insistent, and his hands strayed around to the front of her waist, then toward her breasts. She pushed him from her with a frenzied burst of strength that left her panting.

"I love you, Engrid," he pleaded as he placed his arms around her again. "Say you love me, too," he urged, seeking to draw her closer; but the girl moved her head to the side as he sought to kiss her again.

"You've been drinking, Alex, or you wouldn't be this way. I thought you were drinking too much. It has given you ideas that you wouldn't have, otherwise, so don't!" She felt angry, as well as frightened. "You'll wake the Wilkens."

Alex dropped his arms to his sides as the girl inserted the key and turned it. She straightened up, saying, "I have to work tomorrow, so I must excuse myself."

"But sweetheart ..."

She cut him off, saying, "I'll see you dance night; good night dear."

Alex stood motionless; then he moved down the walk. Pausing at the gate, he ran his hand through his hair with an unconscious gesture; he felt dazed.

"My hat, I forgot my hat," he muttered as he moved back to the porch to retrieve it from a step. The door was already closed and the girl inside; probably in her room by now.

"Golly!" He ejaculated as he walked away, "she has done something to me, and what it is feels mighty nice!"

Happiness flooded through the youth. In his delirium of joy, he kicked an empty can. "She called me 'dear'," he said in a wondering voice. He followed the can where it glinted in the moonlight and he gave it a hefty kick again. The can landed in a ditch. He promptly disregarded it and hurried along, loosing his pent-up emotions in a cheery song.

Inside, Engrid stared out into the night with unseeing eyes; while joy and anxiety fought to a draw until she fell asleep.

The braying of the whistle at the Little Chief mine which sounding it was six o'clock; brought Engrid sharply to her senses. She dressed and after a dash of cold water shocked her awake, she laid the fire in the kitchen stove. While it burned, she hastened to the well and drew fresh water for the use of the members of the household. After filling a pail of clean water for drinking, she scoured the dipper and hung it on a nail above the bucket in the kitchen. While waiting for water to boil, she went outside to breath of the fresh spring air.

Gossiping in liquid tones, a pair of bluebirds flew from tree to tree. Pink splashed the sky where the sun pushed purposefully above the gray hills. Fragrant cedar wood smoke rolling from numerous chimneys ascended to a uniform height and drifted eastward where it dissolved in sage-scented air. Wagons rumbled over numerous roads, followed by barking dogs challenging horses that pulled loads of timber and supplies for the mines and prospects scattered throughout the hills. In a poplar tree at the front of the house, a robin sang its oft-repeated trill. Groups of men filed stolidly by and climbed trails winding around the waste dumps to the Gemini mine.

Here was life! Everyone up and doing something in an exchange of labor to make possible a thriving community, which had, but a few years before, been a lifeless wasteland inhabited only by wandering Indians and skulking coyotes.

Down the road and across the fence forming a corral, a man was busily hitching horses to a delivery wagon. Even from this distance, the team of blacks loomed huge and powerful appearing. "I'll bet each of those horses weighs as much as two of ours at home," the girl mused.

Clear on the air came sounds of hammering as houses were springing into completion almost overnight.

Engrid sighed with pleasure as her senses attuned themselves to the hustle and bustle of the waking town. After filling her lungs with cool morning air, she went into the house to find the coffee water boiling. She poured a handful of roasted coffee beans into the wooden grinder turned the handle and the box responded with a cheery, whirring sound. When the grinding was finished, she removed the drawer and dumped the coffee into the pot. She boiled the coffee for seven minutes; then she set it aside on the stove allowing the ground coffee to settle to the bottom of the pot.

At her knock, Mr. Wilken shortly appeared from his bedroom and after greeting the girl with his usual cheerfulness; he drank a pre-breakfast cup of coffee while avidly scanning the Salt Lake paper. So different he appeared to be from the men of her native land, holding a cigarette in a free hand with a debonair manner. There was fastidiousness about him, and his clear, appraising glance, impersonal, but friendly, warmed Engrid as he chanced to catch her eyes when she poured him a second cup of coffee after placing his ham and eggs before him.

"He is all that Mrs. Kosky says of him. I wish I might be able to talk with him. He seems so friendly and self-assured. I wonder if it is right for me to feel a secret admiration for this man who is unaware of anything but his breakfast and his paper." She sipped coffee and pondered that thought.

Mr. Wilken smilingly complemented her on her cooking; then moved into the bedroom to kiss his spouse and the children goodbye; with a nod for the girl, he walked briskly to his work.

That day, as always, there was an abundance of work to occupy the girl. The bare kitchen floor had to be scrubbed and dried until it gleamed white and clean. Engrid rested on her knees and one hand while vigorously scrubbing with a brush until every last grease spot was removed.

Mrs. Wilkin passed on a tour of inspection; she soon returned from the bedroom and summoned the girl with an imperious movement of one hand. Engrid followed her though the door; watched as her mistress, with a grim look of determination stamped on her features, tore the bedcovers off and piled them on the floor. She turned to the girl and took a stance, one hand on an angular hip and the other pointing to the window.

"Tuesday, line, Engrid, Line!" Her impatience, with the girl's seeming stupidity, engraved itself on her face and grated in her voice.

"Good heavens," Engrid said to herself, "it is Tuesday again, and she evidently wants me to hang the clothes up each Tuesday; but how was I to know that?" She felt humiliated and avoided a direct look at the woman as she gathered the bedding and carried it out to air; while she forced back tears of resentment threatening to break through in a flood.

"Do I hate that old witch?" she muttered grimly in Swedish as she went on with her work.

Gradually her resentment vanished, and Engrid amused herself as she swept through the house by visualizing herself in Mrs. Wilken's place, a she waited for him to return at night; they would then enjoy the interchange of gossip which must assuredly thrive among the English speaking peoples of this community.

As the day wore on, Engrid made her usual numerous trips to the well. While tugging at the rope, her arm brushed roughly by her right ear and one earring disengaged itself, falling with a faint plop into the darkness below. August clutched at her heart. It was one of the things of value that her father had given her as a keepsake; reposed forever beyond the reach of her straining eyes. A gloom, as profound as the darkness in the depths of the well, into which she vainly peered, fastened itself on her emotions when she picked up her bucket and moved purposelessly to the house. Her suffering became unbearable as she scrubbed and her tears mingled freely with the water on the floor.

Mrs. Wilken chanced to walk in on her while the girl alternately scrubbed and cried. "For the love of Mike," exclaimed the woman. "What is the matter? Why do you cry so?"

Engrid slowed the motions of the brush; however, the pressure of her emotions increased proportionately as the strokes decreased in rapidity. Standing erect, she displayed the remaining ring while pointing to the empty lobe. "Well," she said.

Understanding shone in Mrs. Wilken's eyes as she patted Engrid's shoulder. "Tonight Mr. Wilken will get it for you. Go on with your work and cease your crying."

At the mention of Mr. Wilken, the girl's equanimity was restored.

That evening Mrs. Wilken addressed her husband, gesticulated towards the well, and grasped her ear while explaining what had occurred. Engrid saw a smile of comprehension light his face as he went into the kitchen and procured a large mirror and motioned his wife to follow along. Engrid trailed them to the well where Mr. Wilken handed the mirror to his wife. He lifted the doors and taking the mirror, held it until the sun's rays reached the bottom. She spied the ring at the same moment as Mr. Wilken, and cried aloud for joy. He smiled understandingly; handed the mirror to his wife while Engrid pondered on the probable method to be employed in retrieving it from the well. Mr. Wilken went to the house and returned with a long piece of twine attached to a button-hook which he lowered. As the hook slid under the water, ripples moving to the side broke gently. The man moved the string this way and that in an effort to bring the hook to the gold band. Engrid strained this way and that as though she could will the hook to snag the coveted ring. She watched intently as the hook move closer and closer, finally touching the submerged object, then slid over it as Mr. Wilken grunted out an explosive, "Damn!" Again he moved the hook toward the ring and Engrid held her breath expectantly. After what seemed an eternity, the hook engaged the ring, and with a cautious tug on the cord, the man raised it from the bottom, carefully pulling until Engrid clutched it with trembling hands.

"Tank you, tank you!" she exclaimed fastening the beloved object in its place and flashed him a joyous smile. Again she felt life would go on.

The following Saturday, Alex promptly called for Engrid and escorted her to the Finn Hall. At the hitching racks, horses stood tied to buggies which had carried pleasure seekers from outlying mines. They impatiently stood in line for their tickets. Alex engaged in good-natured banter with less fortunate men who stood in line without companions; basking in their envious glances.

When they arrived inside the hall, Alex guided the girl to a cloak room where they hung their coats and hats on adjacent hooks.

"You had better take anything of value out of your coat," Alex warned; leaning close to the girl, he made his voice audible above the sounds of merriment coming from the ballroom. His words held a note of intimacy affecting the girl much as would a glass of brandy on an empty stomach. She felt vibrantly alive and expectant as she looked forward to the evening's festivities.

"You are eye-shattering in your skirt and blouse," Alex remarked with a warm cheerfulness as he gazed admiringly of her full-breasted blouse and the roses resting possessively in clusters over each mound.

"Thank you, Alex. I was a trifle afraid to come to the dance; being a stranger and all, however, I think I shall manage now." She smoothed some imaginary wrinkles from the front of her blouse, and plucked lint from her dark-blue shirt. A pat at a strand of golden hair before a tiny wall mirror hanging between two coats, and she followed Alex toward the hall. They attempted to squeeze through several men who stood smoking in an annex off to one side of the stage leading to the floor two steps below; but the men blocking the passage, greeted Alex with added warmth after seeing the girl.

"Engrid Isaacson, I would rather not introduce you to my cronies as they are bound to try to hog your time for the evening; nevertheless I will or the three of them will gang up on me and I dread the consequences." Alex said with a woebegone expression on his face. "This one here is Victor Johnson; this is Jack Olson and this is his brother, Frank. This grinning ape," he said wryly as another added himself to the group, displaying as he did, a mouthful of gold teeth, "is August Sunbloom." He patted the latter on the back and attempted to pass through the quartet but they restrained him.

"Wait a second, Miss Isaacson," the amiable August said, "I am asking for a dance. The others can take care of themselves."

"You may have the one following my dance with Alex, if you wish," the beaming girl replied as her eyes rested momentarily on the youth.

"Ahem," August grunted importantly as he straightened his tie and slicked at his hair, "a man has to be a fast worker around here to get a dance with a stranger that quickly."

Engrid eyed the others with an encouraging smile, and losing their shyness, they promptly claimed her for the three following dances, overruling Engrid's escort's objections.

"I will save the next one after theirs for you," she said quickly, "after all, were you in their shoes, you would want to dance also."

Alex a picture of dejection, led the girl through the grinning crowd of triumphant men, but secretly he reveled in the fact that he, and he alone, was escorting her that night.

A happiness that was indescribable caught the girl up when she moved down the steps, as a couple who danced by waved to Alex, then another, and another. Alex stood there beaming as he enjoyed to the fullest his moment of triumph; while the vivacious girl hung lightly on one arm and surveyed the crowd of dancers. One couple stopped beside them.

"Hello, Arvid; hello, Hulda; how are you doing tonight?"

"Fine, Alex," Arvid answered. "I have the round drilled and loaded; the platform is laid to catch the dust I kick up when I shoot. Introduce us." His glance looked Engrid over from head to toe with the frankness of an uninhibited married man.

"Engrid Isaacson," Alex announced, "meet Hulda and Arvid Swenson."

The girls chatted warmly for a brief time and Engrid learned that Hulda had come from Sweden. She enjoyed the girl's conversation, and the words that were different in many respect from her own.

"I like to hear you talk," Engrid remarked to the woman. "You sound so, what should I say, precise; that is the word." Hulda thanked her and Engrid felt they would become friends.

John and Rika were already dancing and the couples exchanged greetings as they passed each other on the floor to the strains of a lively polka. Emil and Louise came in after a time; whereupon Engrid and Alex moved to them as they stood on the steps waiting for the music to halt before descending to form the nucleus of a crowd of cheerful couples who shook their hands and pounded Emil on the back. From the stage where an American flag displayed its silken beauty, came the discordant screech of an accordion. All eyes centered on George, where he sat between two fiddlers by the piano. He laid his instrument aside and raised his hands aloft.

"Ladies and gentlemen, and fellow lodge members," he called, "I see among the familiar faces which I gaze on with much admiration two who are strangers to the majority of you gathered here to frolic and feast. Will Miss Engrid Isaacson and the former Louise Isaacson step forward so that we may all make your acquaintance?"

Engrid giggled self-consciously, while closely following Louise; she climbed the steps to the stage.

George beamed them a jovial smile, and again addressed the audience. "I have already had the pleasure of meeting these young ladies, and find them most charming. Louise has already run one of the town's most promising men to the ground. Emil Flink, will you please step to the stand?"

Friendly shouts urged Emil up to the steps to take a stance beside his wife. Bowing again and again, he accepted the plaudits of the crowd with upraised hands clasping each other in a gesture of a champion.

"Speech, speech," friendly voices called from all over the hall.

"Tell us how you came to get your wife, Emil. It's such a surprise to us all that there must be a juicy story connected with it," Arvid Swenson called loudly.

"Well, if you must know, I sent for her in answer to one of those advertisements that you see occasionally in the papers. I saw this particular one in the Helsingfors Bladet; so I answered it, and here she is."

"Oh, you contemptible brute," Louise cried with a look of shocked surprise and turning on her husband, she pummeled him with tiny hands balled into fists.

Uproarious laughter surged from the crowd, followed by silence as George again raised his hands.

"What did the paper say, Emil?" George asked in a falsetto voice that could be heard clearly as the crowd, holding its concerted breath lest it miss out on anything waited for the smirking groom's reply. George's eyes gleamed with a malicious light. He sucked air past his naked gums; then stepped forward and laid a hand on Emil's shoulder; and lowering his head in a discreet manner, he slyly winked at the audience. Emil leaned down to the level of George's ear with an impish twinkle of his eyes, and the two of them exchanged whispers until George drew back in mock surprise, saying in a shocked voice, "You don't say!"

"What did he say, George?" Arvid egged him on.

"I had better let Emil tell you because I don't want to have my neck wrung by his wife," George answered with a knowing look at Louise.

A roar of good humor rose from the gathering; then as Emil spoke, silence fell again.

"Well," his voice trailing off; he licked at his lips and glanced aside at Louise who, with a forbidding frown, stared over the heads of the audience to the back of the hall; while one foot tapped ominously on the floor, a warning signal of impending fury. "She said, I mean, it said, 'A lady desperately in danger of becoming an old maid, desires marriage with wealthy mining magnate in the country of Amerika; preferably in the state of Utah. I, however, even accept matrimony with a Morman and his families, if necessary!'"

With that, Emil made a break for the side of the stage, the infuriated Louise in hot pursuit. Safety lay in losing himself in the crowd as it opened and swallowed him. The men quickly drew together, blocking the irate woman who felt herself grasped by firm hands and placed forcibly on one of a pair of chairs bound together with a clothes line from the kitchen. Emil sat on the other. All at once, Louise felt a sinking, breath-taking sensation as she felt herself tossed high in the air, accompanied by cheers of mirth which swept over the crowd.

After what seemed to be an eternity of breathless rising and falling, during which time Louise hung on to the edge of the chair with all her might; then the music signaled the beginning of another dance. The woman was released, and the crowd dispersing, formed into couples that swung gaily around the floor.

"Oh, dear," Louise breathed as she followed Emil to the strains of a polka, "you don't suppose we will have to go through that again, do you?"

"Not unless you get married again, and that only happens once in the average couple's life," he said smiling.

As the dancing couples swung around, at regularly repeated intervals, the men stomped their feet three times in succession, and the floor thundered and vibrated with the third step which was heaviest of all. Couples whooped their exultation, the fiddlers played fast, in perfect time, and the piano thundered until, to the eyes of the uninitiated, the crowd seemed to be in a frenzy of excitement that could not be controlled. Faces perspired, mouths opened to pant for breath, and eyes took on a gleam of excitement as the men, furiously swinging their partners, on occasion, swept them completely off their feet. The women's faces glowed with pleasure.

"That sensation …," Louise gasped, "it's worse than any ride that I ever took; it's even more terrifying than when we used to grasp the arm of the windmill at home, rise up for about ten feet, and then plummet to the sands below."

"Something like the feeling I get each time I drop down the mine on the cage," he ventured.

"I would never work one day in the mine, then," she said in a determined voice.

"Oh, it's nothing," he assured her, "I just got used to it after a time. The man who rides the cage from level to level endures it without complaint."

At length the music stopped, and Emil took Louise to the east side of the hall where women sat on chairs off to each side of a huge pot-bellied heating stove.

"I'm going out for a breath of air," Emil informed her, as he motioned to Alex and John. They climbed the steps leading to the kitchen where Mrs. Kosky and Mrs. Snell, the latter a frail lady with thin care-worn features, were busy with preparations for the midnight meal.

"Hello, mother," Emil called; "Hello, Mrs. Snell," he greeted the second woman as he gave each of them a friendly squeeze on their waists. "Don't we have fun though?"

Beaming with pleasure, the women looked up and returned his greeting as the other men added their voices.

"My soul," Mrs. Kosky exclaimed, "how could you stand the tossing that they gave you?"

"I have done the same to others in the past, and to tell you the truth, I couldn't wait for my turn to come. It was hardest on Louise; she enjoyed it, however. She never knew what that banter was leading to. Boy," he said reminiscently, "have you ever seen anyone quite so angry? She almost burned!"

'Why didn't you drop a hint as to what it was leading to? The poor girl seemed to be half scared to death."

"And detract from the pleasure of the crowd? Oh, no!"

"I suppose you are right, although I thank heaven that I shall never have to go through that again."

"Don't be too sure about that," he replied with a sly wink at his male companions. "I have been aware of many miners searching for an easy living. They follow you around with their eyes gleaming in a manner that reminds me of a starved cat eyeing a huge steak."

"You get along with your joshing," Mrs. Kosky said in confusion. "I won't be a meal ticket for the best looking man in the world. I have had all I want of marriage. I'll let you younger ones try it for a few years; but mark my word it is a whole lot different than you think. Of course, I can't say that one try isn't worthwhile, when you are young and hot-blooded; but for me, a warm brick or two at my feet on cold winter nights; not some dirty old tramp miner whom I would have to force into taking a Saturday-night bath, or one whom I would have to drive to the barbershop at the point of a gun, or almost murder in an attempt to get him to sit in church on Sunday. Not for any man shall I go through that."

Emil laughed uproariously at the woman's homely philosophy. Turning to the smaller woman he said, "And what do you think?"

"I say she speaks the truth," the woman shyly answered. "I have a tough enough time supporting myself and the children without having to wash clothes to earn a man's living, in addition."

"I believe you are both right," Emil commented as he turned with a wave to his companions, and the trio went outside.

"Wouldn't it be hell to have to wash clothes for a living like Mrs. Snell does, or feed a bunch of wolves like Mrs. Kosky?"

John answered as he breathed deeply of the cool night air. "Life is certainly tough for a widow in a mining camp, especially if she has children who present her with the problem of how to stay home and care for the kids, and make a living at the same time. God," he said, "think of how many stinking pieces of men's mining clothes that Mrs. Snell has to wash for a dollar."

"Mark my words, fellows; the day will come and we can get congressmen in who will have brains and hearts enough to help women financially when they are left destitute after their man dies, or is killed in the mines."

"God hasten the day," Alex said as he followed Emil to the back of the dance hall where it was dark. He reached down and rolled a boulder away from the wall, and when he stood erect, a bottle gleamed faintly in the light of the stars.

"Have a swig," he said invitingly as he pulled out the stopper and passed it to Alex. "Drink hearty!"

Alex drank deeply; then he passed the bottle to John, remarking, "That is good stuff, Emil."

John sampled the bottle, taking a small swallow. Finding the taste to his liking, he drew deeply. "Brr," he shuddered, "I wish coffee tasted as good as that stuff and still caused one to feel as good."

Emil took his turn on the bottle. "Another shot?" he asked of his cronies. Their answer was in the negative, so Emil corked and thrust the bottle back from where it came; and then he replaced the rock.

"Cigarette?" John asked.

"Thanks."

Emil, feeling the mellow glow of the liquor moving through his system, lit the cigarette and inhaled deeply.

"I also have a bottle cached away," John remarked. "I hate to leave it in my coat pocket; because sure as hell, some thief will steal it."

"What do you fellows think of Engrid?" Alex asked casually.

"She is quite a kiddo," Emil answered. "Did you ever bundle with her?"

"Hell, no, man. She was never serious over me, as far as I know; so nothing like that ever took place. I sure would like to have the chance to marry her though. She is a good girl, and pretty as a picture. I believe I have gone over the deep end over her."

"Not a bad fix to be in, I would say," John remarked. "She has something about her that makes a man want to be in her company, if only to talk."

"Let's go in and dance. Damn, but those two swigs made me feel like a million dollars," Emil remarked, as he flipped the butt of his cigarette away and ran toward the back porch and the steps leading to the kitchen. He made the six steps in one stride, and burst into the kitchen with a shrill, "Ki-yi!" bursting from his throat. The other two likewise feeling their oats, were hard on his heels. They stomped on past the startled cooks; but reduced their speed to a walk circumspectly down the steps leading into the hall.

Engrid had by this time danced with those who had asked her, and she sat expectantly as John ambled toward the women with a nonchalant air. At first, she thought he might go to Rika who was watching his approach with a smile; however, almost to the line of women, he changed his course slightly and headed for Engrid. At that moment a figure interposed itself between them.

"Would you care to dance?" Glen Rostrum asked.

"I would love to," she replied with a quickening pulse; "would you care for the one following this?"

Glen thanked her and moved to Rika who accepted his proposal, and they danced away as John bowed and requested a dance.

"I would love to," she answered as she rose and moved around to the strain of a waltz.

"Why did you turn that other fellow down?" John asked.

"I didn't."

"But Engrid," he objected, "he asked you for a dance, did he not?"

"Yes."

"So you turned him down," he reiterated.

"I promised him the next one after this."

"Oh, I see; why didn't you give him this one?"

"Because it was my right to choose."

"Why did you reserve this one for me?"

"Because I wanted to."

"I think you are a flirt," John said with an appraising look into the girl's eyes.

"As you wish," Engrid said with a gay smile.

Trying vainly to fathom the depths of this attractive girl's mind, John looked at her, and she in turn gazed with eyes that twinkled unabashed.

"Well?" she prompted with a roguish smile. The music stopped and they circled as did the others, whistling and shouting for an encore. Again the music started and they waltzed. Engrid stole a surreptitious look in Rika's direction as she made a pretense of listening to her partner's conversation, and she was mildly surprised to find that Rika was doing exactly that herself.

"I believe you like me," John remarked with an infectious grin as he danced lithely, feeling as though his body was curiously detached from his feet.

"Foolish; I know you better than I do Glen. I only saw him once at the boarding house, and I have danced with you before. I like to dance with you because you are an excellent dancer."

"That is what all the girls say," John said smugly. "I believe it is because they like to feel my brawny arms around their lovely waists." His eyes held a mischievous twinkle as he spoke.

"You are thicker than two fish in a net with Rika, I have observed. When are you two going in for the chair bouncing, John?"

"You mean baby bouncing?"

Blushing furiously, the girl replied, "That comes a long time after you've been tossed on the chair, I presume?"

"If you are lucky," he replied cryptically.

The music blared to a halt, and Engrid was glad to drop the conversation which she felt was fast becoming too warm to handle. She seated herself, after thanking her partner for the dance, and John bowed before going across the hall to sit with the men.

"A rather intriguing man," Engrid mused. "I don't know how to take him, though."

Had she but known, John was of the same mind in regards to her where he sat by Alex, nodding occasionally at what appeared the proper time as Alex made some flattering remark about John's latest dancing partner.

"Here I am engaged to a girl; and for no particular reason other than the fact that it just happened," John thought, "what a mess; what a mess," he said audibly.

Alex caught the spoken repetition. "Who's a mess? Engrid?" he bristled.

"Hell no, man," John said smoothly, "she's an angel. I was just thinking aloud about something." He slapped Alex on the knee and strode to the kitchen from whence he emerged with Mrs. Snell who was glad for the opportunity of dancing with the young man.

Mrs. Snell having long since reached the age where she joined the other widows on the side line, gratefully accepted the opportunity to dance with any of the men who were not intoxicated in excess of a normal, recognized limit. If no dances were to be had, she joined with others in folk dances, square dances and the Virginia reel which some of the youngsters had introduced to their countrymen after visiting American dance halls. At other times, the widow sat on the side lines watching with varying degrees of pleasure almost amounting to self-hypnosis as other carefree dancers disported themselves.

For three hours, Engrid experienced the excitement of being sought after by every eligible young man in the hall, and many of the married ones who enjoyed her youthful good humor. She danced gaily across the floor to Alex when George Swanson announced that a dance was ladies choice. She moved on winged feet from one partner to another, before she had no more than taken a step or two with each of her partners during the tag dances which the men caused to be called often by George, providing they offered him an occasional drink on the sly. Engrid's laughter was gay, and her feet light as the hours sped into eternity.

"Coffee is served," George called out on the stroke of twelve, and couples hurried to be the first at the table.

An atmosphere of intimate friendliness, and subdued conversation enveloped the hall while the musicians dined. Engrid and Alex moved to a kitchen table where they found themselves across from John and Rika. A cheerful flurry of banter sped from one end of the long table to the other. Mrs. Kosky and Mrs. Snell moved from one person to another, filling cups with delicious coffee. Cups clicked on saucers and spoons tinkled; as copious quantities of sugar was half-dissolved in the fragrant brew.

"Are you enjoying yourself, Rika?" Engrid asked as she bit into a boiled ham sandwich.

"The same as usual. I believe I am a trifle tired tonight. We had a hard day at the store; things are always rushing on Saturdays. Ranchers and miners who live out of town come in on that day to take home their week's supply of groceries. They do have such large orders to fill. There are some outlying mines employing fifty or more men who board right on the grounds, and by the time I get all of those groceries packed, I have done a real day's work. Sometimes I have to run around the store a dozen times to complete a list. After doing that all day long and trying dresses on women who can't make up their minds, I hardly feel like dancing. I enjoy coming here though; I like to go with the crowd. You old-country people certainly know how to enjoy yourselves; that I will say!"

"And how do you like it here, by now?" John asked.

"For the first two days," Engrid informed him with a burst of musical laughter charged with happiness, "I thought I would borrow enough from someone to get back to where I came from. After I get acquainted, I am certain I am going to like being here. How I love the sunshine and warmth." She ceased speaking and her eyes roved up and down the table, to finally stop on a huge, white-frosted cake.

"What will you have, Engrid?" John's eyes followed her glance. "A piece of cake?" At her nod, he grasped her plate and served her with a huge wedge.

"Oh, how lovely it looks!" she exclaimed, "but I'm afraid that I can't eat it all though. Do take part of it with me, John."

"For certain; what will you have? Top or bottom?"

"Cut it down the middle and it will suit me fine."

"I'll have another sandwich and potato salad," Alex requested.

"Pass your plate and holler, 'When'." John covered half of the plate with a thick salad in which golden slices of egg-yolk beamed invitingly inside of white rings. He added a boiled ham sandwich to the plate; then he passed the food to the appreciative Alex who watched him with mouth watering.
"Next?"

"No other request is forthcoming," Alex replied for the group after a prolonged silence. "Now, you eat."

Engrid stole a look at Rika to find her gazing at her with a thoughtful expression on her face.

"What is the matter, Rika; aren't you hungry?"

"No, that is to say; I have had sufficient. I was just enjoying myself watching you eat. You seem to enjoy it so much."

Mulling over the girl's answer, Engrid vainly strove to find any hidden meaning latent in it; apparently it was spoken without guile. "I am eating food tonight that I never dreamed of having at home. Ham was an unheard of luxury over there. We got along as best we could on fish, clabbered milk, more fish, cereal and potatoes with more fish," the girl remarked, and the table rocked with laughter. Others too, had gone through the same thing before coming to Utah. When the laughter, in which Engrid joined, subsided, she continued. "Perhaps it is all of this excitement and the novelty of my surroundings coupled with the dancing that gives me such an enormous appetite. If I keep this up, I shall soon be faced with the question of whether I shall work harder, eat less, or buy a raft of new clothing."

John, laughing heartily, seemed to enjoy her summary of her dilemma.

"Oh, by the way, I was going to ask you if there are any Mormons here tonight."

"Why do you ask that?" Rika inquired with arched brows.

"Because there are so many things that I would like to know about this country?" she countered.

"There are a number of Mormons in the town; but they only have one wife each, as far as I know. Although, I know of none who are at the dance," Rika replied.

"Do you believe that their leader received a divine revelation in which he was told that members of his flock could practice polygamy?" she asked of Rika.

"I'm no Mormon," she said evasively.

"Why are there no plural marriages in this town?" she asked.

"Well, now," John said thoughtfully, "if a man is to marry more than one woman, he has to have ground on which she and the off-spring may work in order to earn a living. It is hard for a man to support one wife in a mining camp; without thinking of another."

Engrid looked at Rika and asked, "Do you believe that a man should have more than one wife?"

"Well," Rika floundered in confusion as the eyes of those at the table rested on her, "I suppose I don't."

"Why?"

"It doesn't make sense to me for a man to marry several different women. Women are by nature jealous of each other; I'd sure hate to be the man who tried to divide his affection between two of us, let alone a dozen."

"Men, being what they are, should find it intriguing," Engrid replied boldly. "I believe that I would be a polygamist, if I were a man."

"Engrid!" Rika gasped, "You surely can't mean that?"

"Certainly I mean it; otherwise I would never say it," she said brazenly. "Why should you consider their manner of living wrong? How do you know weather your way of living is any better until you try another? What proof do you have that our social customs are the best?"

"Because I have been taught what is right since I was a child," Rika said stubbornly.

"For the sake of argument, if you were a man, would you like more than one wife?" Engrid asked.

"Why … why… I hardly know," Rika floundered, entirely unprepared as she was for the thrust.

Conversation along the table had come to a halt as diners listened, and men dropped eyelids in covert winks, their eyes gleaming with interest and their faces wreathed in grins.

Engrid looked around and brushed over the faces of those on the opposite side of the table. Her heart seemed to do a flip-flop a she observed reproving glances in the women's faces.

"I think I would like to dance, Alex," she remarked as she observed the members of the orchestra leave the table to make room for others who lounged in the doorway leading to the hall.

"Alright," he said, reaching into his pocked and placing fifty-cents on a saucer for the sick benefit fund.

"Why did I have to start a discussion on a subject that I know nothing of?" she asked of herself as she departed from the kitchen with ears burning. Conversation hummed after her as she entered the hall, sounding like a swarm of bees.

Alex and Engrid wheeled around the floor. The man's face looked thoughtful as she asked, "Why the pall-bearer's mask?"

"I was just thinking," he replied vaguely.

"About what?"

"You."

"What about me Alex!" She read his thoughts and felt anger surging through her; however, with an effort, she controlled herself. Alex seemed to be finding it hard to put his thoughts into words.

"Say it. That I'm a bad woman. Is that it?"

"Aren't you?" he asked blandly.

"Alex!" Engrid's lips trembled a little at a losing fight to keep her anger suppressed, so that she wouldn't call more attention to herself.

"Oh, I didn't mean that, Engrid; I was only joking with you. You did shock some of those old hens, though," he said in a cajoling voice. "What you said sounds alright coming from a man; because women expect men to talk that way, but coming from a woman, and a young and beautiful stranger, at that, will set a lot of tongues to wagging."

"And when they are wagging about me, they will be giving their poor husbands a rest!" Engrid flared. "People are staring at us; let us sit down."

Alex escorted her to the side of the hall devoted to the women. She seated herself next to an elderly woman who also had been dining at the table while the girl was there. The woman ignored Engrid after sliding a glance down her long nose; then she turned her back after an audible, "Humpf," which held all the implications of an hour-long sermon. Had there been a convenient mouse hole for the girl to creep into, she felt that she could have done so, and with room to spare. Because her humiliation was more than she could endure, she stood up, and with head aloft, she walked proudly toward the dressing room with Alex following after.

"What is the big idea?" he asked as he caught up to her where she was pulling on her coat.

"I merely wish to go home, and please do not be rude; I have a headache."

"But ..." he started in protest.

"You may stay if you wish; I can make it home alright."

"I'll come," Alex said, faced with the alibi which Eve probably used for the first time in narrated history. He helped her into her coat, retrieved his own and also his hat. The couple went through the kitchen, thereby avoiding the crowd which had gone to the dance floor. They bade the lady cooks goodnight, and with a sigh of profound relief, the girl stepped into the cool air and friendly darkness.

Alex struck a match to a cigarette as they meandered along. Engrid breathed deeply of the fresh night air and looked over the slumbering town to the snowy cross where it glowed faintly. Staring, she felt a resurgence of rapture as a lone cloud crossed the ridge with a trailing shadow stealing breathlessly below. A breeze, impregnated with the odor of spring, wafted about her and disturbed a tendril of the girl's golden tresses in its passing.

"Oh, how exquisitely wonderful it is tonight," the girl exclaimed as the depression which had weighed heavily on her, winged away on the breeze. "I wish I could capture this moment and place it in a box, and open it when I am in need of solace."

When the couple reached the door of the Wilken home, Engrid inserted her key into the lock and turned around with her back and hands to the door.

"Engrid" Alex sounded disturbed as he moved closer and gazed with a troubled look into the girl's eyes.

"Yes?" she whispered, crossing her leg provocatively over the other.

"Did you mean what you said at the table about wanting more than one wife if you were a man?"

"Oh, you silly goose." She laughed softly,

As she did so, Alex felt he would never look on anything lovelier. At that moment, their past life together, their walks in the woods with other happy picnickers, the stars, the exciting odor of spring, and the beauty of the girl, all blended into a bitter-sweet concoction and he longed to embrace the girl, fearing, however, that he would be repulsed.

"Did you?" he persisted.

"Of course not," she assured him with a trace of irritation perceptible in her words; 'I find the subject interesting, that is all. I imagine there might be enough complications arise in marriage to make it interesting. Why do you ask?" She stood erect and placed her hand gently on the young man's shoulder while giving him a shy glance from blue eyes.

"I don't know, exactly," he pondered. "Maybe it is because I am trying to find an ideal. I hardly know," he said in confusion as he looked at his companion, and desire burned in him so fiercely that he felt as though he could grasp her and eat her a bit at a time until full. He could start with her smiling lips, of course.

"Why do you seek in me that which you speak? At home you didn't think enough of me to stay there. You didn't ask me if I would marry you, and then the two of us could have worked and saved, finally coming to this country as we both wished. All you wanted of me was my companionship, and that, only when you tired of girls who more nearly fulfilled your desires which were contrary to mine."

"But…"

"No 'buts' at all, Alex. When you couldn't get what you wanted from me, you turned to other girls who were stupid enough and unfortunate enough to comply with your wishes. What happened to them, after you left? I'll tell you. They continued as tramps, going with everyone who picked them up and gave them a drink."

"I love you, Engrid," he assured her humbly.

"I, too, used to be crazy about you at one time, Alex; but that was before I was old enough to know my own mind. Now, I am not sure what I think of you. I know I like you a lot, however."

"Give me a kiss, Engrid," he pleaded, "you used to do so at home after a dance."

"That was long, long ago, Alex. That was part of our past life when I thought that you were the most wonderful boy in the whole of Finland. I feel different abut matters now."

"You let me kiss you last night." he argued. "Why do you think that is right? Don't you care?"

Engrid remembered how her blood had pounded while he kissed her hungrily on her unresisting lips. "I do enjoy your kisses, Alex; but there is something I can't explain that keeps me from wanting to return them. I wouldn't be fair if I let you believe that I cared more than I actually do." She paused, choosing her words carefully. "I like you more than any boy I know. Let us drop it right there. I'm going in now; again my thanks for a perfectly grand time."

"When can I see you again?"

"Oh, I'll be over to the boarding house occasionally," she said evasively as the young man put on his hat and started down the boardwalk toward the gate.

"Alex," she called softly. She walked toward him and pauses where starlight shone between two lilac trees.

"Now what?" His voice was gruff.

"You're going to marry, someday?"

"I suppose so; if I can find someone who will have me."

"I want to marry someday, also," the girl said. "You want to be simply crazy and madly in love with the one you marry, do you not?"

"I suppose so," he replied with obvious reluctance, and quite unable to understand the trend of her conversation.

"I, too, wish to be mad abut the man I marry. I want to love him so much that I shall be unable to live without him. Perhaps I will end up by marrying somebody that I am that way over, and at the same time, he may not feel or act the same way about me. Be that as it may, I want to feel that way." She placed a hand on his shoulder, and raised the youth's face until she looked into his eyes and found them full of hurt. "If I haven't that feeling for the man I marry, life will not hold much meaning."

Making a reluctant admission, Alex said, "I suppose I know what you mean." He grasped her hand and kissed the back of it. "That is the way I feel about you, Engrid. I suppose it is too late to undo what I did before; but I'll certainly try. Right now I want you so much that I would marry you tomorrow if you would have me. I would even stay here and work in the mines to support you, much as I hate them."

To Engrid's mind jumped the memory of her father who had changed his mind, after finding conditions at home intolerable. She recalled the way her mother had bowed her head to necessity when it came to choosing between her husband's absence and her home. That did it.

"When the right man comes along," the girl said softly as she reached for a twig and began to peel the bark, "I will follow him to the far corners of the earth, if need be." She looked at the youth and he looked firmly crushed causing a surge of pity to rise in response to the sadness of his face. "Please try to understand, Alex, and in the meantime, let us be friends."

"Alright," he sighed. "I'm sorry and I know I wouldn't be satisfied with just a part of your affection."

"Goodnight and thanks, Alex."

"Goodbye," Alex mumbled despondently. He heard the door close and the latch slip into place. Then slowly, purposelessly he started down the road; where this time there was no can to kick there was only a rock to throw at a yellow cur that paused in surprise when it came face-to-face with Alex, one foot upraised as it rounded a high-board fence. The dog began clamoring for a chunk of the young man's leg; but Alex uncooperative and dejected, promptly favored the dog with a well-aimed stone that thudded solidly on the animal's ribs. The beast's angry challenge became a yelping of pain and surprise and it beat a hasty retreat under the fence, and around to the back of the house.

"That fixed the bastard," he muttered vindictively; then he lapsed into a dejected silence, wondering vaguely what hapless cat the animal might avenge himself on. "Oh, well," he said, shrugging his shoulders. "There are plenty more women in this world, not like her, though," he admitted sadly. He whistled purposefully as he reached the main thoroughfare and heard the music from the Finn hall coming faint from the distance. A drink or two in Smith's saloon would fix him up in top shape.

The drink led to the inevitable many more as Victor Johnson and August Sunbloom bewailed the dearth of young women; and the fickleness of women in general; while Alex bemoaned the like attitude of one in particular. Finally, in their inebriated condition, they wandered along the main street with their arms linked together, singing loudly. On one occasion, big, amiable August walked unsteadily ahead a he spied a lone woman of English extraction hurrying up the street from the direction of an American dance hall. He bowed gravely as he drew off his hat and swept it down and around in front of him. Then with the hat resting on his wrist in clenched fingers, he sang out, "I dream of Yeanie vith her light brown hair."

The startled girl halted momentarily; then the big man stepped aside, allowing her to proceed unmolested as Alex and Victor laughed uproariously. Although the girl giggled nervously, she passed and looked back over her shoulder prepared to run if need be, to get away from the drunkards.

"Hey, fellows," August exclaimed as he stopped his companions in their stride. "Let's do something I've always wanted to do. Let's go to Kitty's and sing a song!"

Walking with as much decorum as their condition would permit, the trio made their way to the Palace where they climbed a flight of stairs to the bandstand. As they blundered in front of the orchestra, the leader paused his fiddling and motioned for the other musicians to continue.

"What do you fellows want?" the conductor asked.

"To sing a song," Alex answered.

"Just one?"

Knowing the reputation of the trio, and wishing to avoid any unpleasantness from good-paying cash customers, he complied with their wishes.

"What would you like to sing?" he asked with a wink aside at the other musicians who by now had paused after completing their tune. They grinned dutifully.

"Da Polly, Vally Doodle song," Victor beamed.

"Alright, boys. Hey, folks," he called to the crowd on the floor below, "by request we have the three Finns to sing a song for you. This added attraction costs you nothing except your whole-hearted applause. Give them a hand."

Amid a whooping and whistling, liberally sprinkled with cat-calls, the trio moved to the railing which stood two feet above the platform, and with misgivings the leader directed the musicians who promptly swung into the catchy tune. Alex, putting his heart as well as his hands into the song, disengaged his arms from the necks of his companions to lean far out with arms extended in a gesture of pleading to the girls in spangled dresses who swept by below.

Catching the spirit of the unexpected entertainment furnished by the local talent, the dancers joined in the chorus and the hall rocked to thundering feet. Leaned far out, Alex, eyes seeing double of every girl who danced by, lost his balance and plunged head long over the balcony. The music stopped abruptly; cries of terror came from the dancers who hastened to Alex to observe the extent of the youth's injuries. Victor and August leaned over the balcony as the members of the orchestra crowded to the railing.

Alex sprawled face downward for a moment; then rising unsteadily to his feet, he looked around him uncomprehendingly, feeling portions of his anatomy and seeming not at all amazed in finding himself in one piece.

"Come on, fellows," he called motioning to his startled companions who, with slack jaws and bulging eyes, stared down on him.

As the trio disappeared through the door, the orchestra leader said, "It's too damn bad he didn't break his neck." Placing his fiddle under his chin, he struck up a lively quadrille, while the intruders wove a circuitous route down the street away from the Palace.

The next morning, Alex pondered at length on why it was so hard to arise. Finally, giving up his attempts in disgust, and taking a drink, he lay back down to sleep it off.

Chapter 14

With the weather growing progressively warmer each day, Engrid, Alex, John and Rika, as well as Emil and Louise made frequent hikes into the hills surrounding the town. On one such hike, the group scaled Packard Peak, whose snow-filled draws had formed what looked like a cross earlier in the spring.

Out of breath from their exertions, the group seated itself at the top to gaze with varied emotions for miles in every direction. The houses of Tintic huddled together like tiny models on a play table to the north; and to the south, a trifle closer, the town of Mammoth sprawled on both sides of a narrow gulch running in an easterly and westerly direction. At the lower end of the town, a cluster of red-painted buildings overlooking a huge tailings dump, proved to be the Mammoth mill, and figures of workers appeared as tiny ants where they moved about at their labors.

Turning to the north, again, Engrid observed the Teetro mine directly below. By looking closely at the sheave-wheels, she could see them turning and reflecting a dull light as the westerly sun rested momentarily before plunging behind the desert mountains.

Dry-farms, on which winter wheat grew, lay here and there in yellow patches, surrounded by cedars of a deep green. For a breathless moment, the fields borrowed a golden radiance from flaming clouds poised overhead. The hills assumed a violet tint, and a haze of the same hue gradually encompassed the west Tintic valley.

As an engine pulling a train of cars shuffled in sight through a gap in the hills far off to the north and west; the girl watched spellbound as four distinct streamers of violet tinted vapor signaled that the engine was whistling for a crossing near a grain elevator rearing its white bulk above the scattered ranch houses. Waiting long, the girl had finally decided that the distance was far too great for her to hear the sounds of the whistle; however, just a she was about to remark on the phenomenon, clear to her ears the notes came and rebounding from surrounding hills, a piping chorus of echoes created for her an illusion that the hollows were harboring Pandean creatures, who had waited for this hour of twilight to begin their playing.

Engrid watched as the train whistled at intervals while the group reclined in silence, relaxing and recuperating their energies. Smoke from men's pipes drifted in lazy spirals. A wind springing uphill rustled the scrub oak and pines, then swept onward. Forms became formless and the purple cloak became gray; then changed into a black void through which the engine's headlight seemed to almost stand still.

Rising abruptly and shaking the used tobacco from his pipe into one huge hand, John suggested, "Let's build a fire."

"Let's do," the women chorused, and yellow flames dispelled the darkness which was by now hovering over even this high peak. Coyotes quavered their lament of loneliness from the hills east of the fire, causing Engrid to shiver.

Growing warm after a time, she moved to sit on a rock out of the wind which seemed to take a perverse delight in blowing, now this way, now that. She fell to coughing, and the reassuring statement that, "Smoke follows beauty," coming from Louise helped not at all. Finally the wind shifted to plague others, giving the girl an opportunity to disengage herself in thought from small talk which lent an effervescent gayety to the little group as preparations were made for cooking coffee by Emil who poured water into the blackened coffee pot, and then fastened his eyes on it with such an intent look that Alex remarked he must be willing it to boil.

Engrid watched as myriads of stars winked to life, and as if in reflection in the dark pool of the village, yellow lamplight glowed faintly.

Emil added coffee when the water came to a boil, then placed a stick across the top of the pot to prevent the appetizing, aromatic liquid from bubbling over into the fire. Sighs of appreciation rewarded the blonde giant's labors as he sank back to the ground allowing the liquid to brew properly.

Engrid was content to say little, listening instead to the comforting murmur of conversation from the others. As always in spite of her wish that it might be otherwise her hearing attuned to each word and laugh falling with easy carelessness from John's lips where the man lay on the ground, his head resting in Rika's lap; while the girl ran her fingers though his blonde hair. Time and again, Engrid caught herself staring as one of the group tossed a branch of sage on the bed of glowing coals; and when darting flames leaped forth in hissing, sputtering fingers of light, John, whose features were thrown into bold relief by the flames, met her glance with a whimsical smile; and the girl self-consciously dropped her eyes.

Oh, how restful to breathe wood smoke from an open fire, and watch flames licking at a simmering coffee pot! How peaceful to listen to the murmur of conversation coming from young men and women reclining in various restful attitudes of repose.

Engrid actually dared, while sitting there beside Alex, to imagine how nice it would be, if she were Rika, and could run her hand through John's hair. To stoop low occasionally and murmur some precious observation in his ear; then watch his lips curl into a smile and receive one of his kisses which Rika seemed to enjoy returning.

The hauntingly sad tones of the village curfew bell on the city hall trembled through the hushed air from the village. In its solemn voice, Engrid senses loneliness similar to the restlessness breathing in the muted whispers of the night wind which played through the branches of surrounding pine trees.

At regular intervals, she detected the rumbling of cars of ore being dumped down the chutes of the Teetro mine, then the steady chugging of the hoist.

It was with reluctance that the men smothered the fire with dirt; then, after accustoming their eyes to the darkness, all trailed homeward down a ravine in whose coolness wild roses and blooming choke-cherries emitted their fragrance.

With a tired smile, Engrid bade Alex goodnight. He was content to enjoy her companionship under the conditions that the girl had tactfully laid down in an effort to save them both suffering. Theirs was now a platonic friendship, but not because the youth willed it so.

A week before the longest day of the year, Louise called on Engrid and greeted her with more enthusiasm than was customary.

"Guess what?" Louise exclaimed; "Saturday night we celebrate Mid-Summer Dagen."

"I am aware of the fact; but as we're not at home now, of what import is the day here?"

"Emil came home from the sick-help meeting last night and announced that all of the lodge members are taking a special train Saturday morning up the Spanish Fork Canyon to Castello resort."

"A…a special train?" Engrid gasped in amazement, ""oh, golly!"

"Oh, Engrid, won't that be fun? There will be car after car of people and we will stay all night."

"And the music?"

"The lodge will have its band; there will be barrels and barrels of beer, roast-beef sandwiches, coffee and oh, everything to make a good time for everyone."

"Suppose Mrs. Wilken doesn't let me off?" Engrid appeared crestfallen at the disturbing thought.

"She'll have to!" Louise exclaimed. "I'll have Emil write her a note; he's good at writing in English. He is secretary of the lodge, you know."

Engrid nodded and dropped her glance to the mop clasping her hands about the handle. "I'll have to have a complete new outfit; something light and gay," she pondered aloud.

"That's easy; go see Mrs. Kosky. She'll take you shopping."

"Alena will have to prepare supper this evening and so will I."

Louise thought for a time and found the solution. "Listen dear," she said, striking an open hand with the other balled into a fist, "come to the boarding house after you finish here, and I'll be helping Mrs. Kosky. In that way we can make it before the stores close at eight."

"That's settled." Engrid remarked hopefully as Louise, lying a bit of gaily colored silk on the porch, seated herself.

"They're wonderful." Louis said, "The lilacs, I mean."

"The yard would be prettier if there were grass growing around the house," Engrid observed.

"It would be at that; if they had enough water. There is talk of running a pipeline from a deep well adjacent to that mill in Homansville; then we can have all of the water we want. Just think what it would be like to just turn a tap and have water in the house. If I keep lugging buckets from our well, I'll put on muscles like a miner!" She flexed her arms causing her sleeves to bunch. Engrid giggled.

"But the soil, Louise; you can't grow grass on rocks."

"Emil can buy some from a teamster."

"I suppose so," Engrid said diffidently. "How do you like married life?"

"I wouldn't trade it for anything in the world," Louise replied glancing at Engrid who was slowly turning the mop. "Why don't you marry Alex and quit cleaning up dirt for others?"

"I intend to keep working," Engrid said as she absent-mindedly continued to turn the mop in her hands.

"I thought you had gone for Alex in a big way," Louise reminded her.

"I like him as a friend, that's all. I value my independence," she said. Not convincingly, Louise decided. "I will continue to do so until the right man comes along." She bit her lip and nervously twirled the handle of the map. "I don't care enough for Alex to marry him. If I ever do marry, I want to be as crazy about a man as you were over Emil; otherwise, I won't marry."

"If I remember right, you thought a lot of him at home," Louise pointed out.

"Until he left me; that was hard to take, believe me."

"Does he ever kiss you?" Louise pried.

"Of course, silly goose; all men kiss a girl if they like her sufficiently, given the opportunity."

"Does it thrill you when he kisses you?" Louise probed; all ears.

"Well," Engrid's eyes held a dreamy expression, "the night I came from your house, he kissed me and I felt something for him. The next time he took me to the dance at Finn Hall; it was all changed, somehow."

"I do believe you care for someone else." Louise chided.

Engrid glanced quickly at her sister's face in an effort to determine what meaning there might possibly be behind her words; but found an impassive mask.

"Do you?" Louise encouraged.

"I suppose I do, and I wouldn't have it any other way; but it's so hopeless," Engrid faltered, "I could just cry the way things have turned out for me. I wish I had never left home."

"Who is he?"

"If I told you, you'd not understand. You'd worry yourself sick because you didn't. I'd better not tell you; it will blow over someday, and I will see what a fool I have been."

"Who is it?" Louise insisted.

Engrid hesitated but knowing the persistence of her sister, she said, "It's John."

"John? Good heavens!" Louise gasped. "You can't do a thing like that, it isn't right." She shook her head. "Oh, sister, you must be out of your mind."

"I said that you wouldn't understand."

Engrid dropped her mop as the frustration and nostalgia she felt poured out in a flood of tears. Footsteps passed in front of the house, and she restrained herself with an effort.

Louise's face registered confusion. "Why, I hardly know what to say to you Engrid. I'm sure I didn't mean to hurt your feelings."

"You, have already said enough."

Louise suddenly saw the light. "Say, that explains your remarks that Saturday night at the dance hall; why you put up such an able defense of plural marriages."

"Maybe, I don't know. Who told you about that?"

"Everybody at the dance has been gossiping about it. One can't take a definite stand on a controversial subject like that without having to pay a price. You certainly set the women's tongues to wagging; however, the men sided with you."

"They would, the nasty animals," Engrid said in biting tones. "They would all be happy if they could paw over a different woman every single night."

"Oh, sister, what are you talking about? You don't mean what you are saying any more than you meant what people thought you did the other night at the dance. You know, deep inside, that you wouldn't want to share John with Rika."

"I suppose not," Engrid said glumly.

"Oh, you poor girl." Drawing her fair sister's head to her shoulder, Louise murmured consolingly, "Cry it out of your system even if the whole town passes by." She held Engrid close until the girl fell silent with a long-drawn sigh; Louise rose and smoothed out her skirt.

Lifting her face, Engrid shamefully looked at her. She wiped her nose then giggled nervously. Louise smiled understandingly.

"I feel better now, Louise. I have saved that up for so long that it just had to come out." She felt that weeping had solved her problem. "Perhaps it has," she told herself. "It's off my chest and no longer shall I have to feel like a thief." She shook her apron and grasped the handle of the mop in a determined grip. "I have work to do or Mrs. Wilken will pull my hair out, if she dares. I'll see you and Alena this evening."

"Goodbye," Louise said and she watched while her sister went around the back to draw a pail of water. "Poor girl," Louise mused, "I wonder how things are going to turn out for her; she deserves to be happy."

A western sun trailed a splendid scarlet cloak. Scattered patches of snow reflected a pink radiance under the masses of granite protruding like jagged teeth from the heights of the darkening mountains. Far off, the west Tintic Valley lay bathed momentarily in an azure sea which altered into dark formlessness as though some giant had doused the light with a quick swipe of its hand.

"Did you see how quickly the color of the valley below changed as the sun disappeared?" Engrid asked her companions. "It seemed as though someone dropped a curtain in front of a painting at which I was looking while I blinked by eyes just once."

"Yes, my dear." Mrs. Kosky puffed in reply as she walked. "I have noticed that since I first came to these mountains. I have never tired of watching the sunset and listening as the town takes on a peaceful tone. This used to be the hour I treasured most when Frank was alive. We'd sit and talk of things which all couples share after marriage." The girls trailed her bulk around sage and scattered cedars. "Yes", Mrs. Kosky continued, "there's magic in mountain sunsets, girls. A magic that makes one want to reach out and wash the naked body with that bowl of purple twilight until feelings of remorse, bitterness, and what we mortals share in common; 'sin' as we call it, has been washed away, leaving us clean and innocent. My husband," she said softly, "forever called this time of day, 'The Golden Hour!'"

As if having revealed an intimate detail of her past life, Mrs. Kosky, fell silent as she led the sisters down an alley enclosed by a high fence whose pickets framed coruscated strips of light sprinkled with stars.

"What twaddle I do speak," she said in disgust.

"It's not twaddle at all," Engrid objected. "I think what you have said is beautiful. It gives depth and meaning to the sky, the sunset, your life and mine. Nothing actually has meaning unless we can put our thoughts and feelings into words, music, and paintings; conveying a part of ourselves to others for their interpretation. Most of us actually see, or feel very much and unless someone interprets what we do see and feel, life loses some of its meaning."

"Do that, Mrs. Kosky," Louise encouraged.

"Hush, now, we are entering town," Mrs.Kosky admonished, "people will think we are crazy."

"It would be nice if everyone were as crazy." Engrid said with a disarming giggle as she drew abreast of the woman squeezing her arm and assisting her from the boardwalk.

They crossed the street between buggies whose lanterns cast distorted shadows before high-stepping horses. On the opposite side the girls trailed Alena down the middle of the walk where loitering miners moved aside before the woman like a sea parting before the prow of a majestic ship. Passing a barber shop, from whose crowded interior came singing accompanied by a banjo, the girls followed the woman who disappeared in the gloom of an alleyway for a brief interval, only to reappear in the lighted front of a saloon. Past this she strode pausing to open the door of a well-lit shop. "Lenore," she addressed a charming woman in her late thirties who stepped from the rear where she had been arranging her stock of slippers and shoes, "these girls want to look at some of your summer creations."

"Oh," said the saleslady, "you are the two sisters from Finland! I am from Sweden myself; I came here when I was eight years of age. Is there anything in particular that you would like to see?"

For the first time Engrid tried on a variety of genuine silk shirtwaists. Lenore called out prices and sizes. Engrid leisurely handled each shirtwaist where it hung on a wooden hanger reveling in a delicate feeling of suppressed excitement. She was to remember for as long as she lived, the unforgettable thrills attendant on moving around in a store, catering exclusively to women while the smell of new clothing vied with the odor of shoes and slippers as Lenore showed her pair after pair.

Here there was no standing, hour after hour, as her mother fitted a waist or skirt. Here mother was not saying, "Try this… see how this fits… a little more at the sleeves… hold still now, I said", a trifle impatiently. Then, "Move over… lean back just a little… now straighten out, and pull your stomach in, a person would think you were expecting!"

That was all in the past, and in this array of skirts, shirtwaists and dresses, Engrid had entered a woman's heaven. It was nice to finger the dresses on one side of the store and say casually, "Lenore, I don't believe I like any of these. Haven't you others?"

"Of course," Lenore assured her; "but they are genuine Japan silk and come at a higher price."

She showed Engrid several.

"Wait a second, Lenore." A note of excitement crept into Engrid's voice. "Hold that up to the light," she gasped as she looked at the shining material. "I want this if it fits!" She tried it on and it fit her perfectly.

The creation was of thin, gauzy material over silk. The princess slip of pale yellow silk was finished with a wide hem at the bottom. The over-dress of sheer French organdy; was cream-colored and attractively scattered over with flowers of violet color. The full skirt had a trimming of tiny ruffles at the bottom, a tight waist, and a front yoke of yellow chiffon. Ribbons of the same color ran over the shoulders from the belt ending at the back and front. Tiny bows of the same material rested on the shoulders, and the bottom of the yoke. The belt, too, was of yellow ribbon, with a large bow formed by clusters of loops at the back.

A hat to match was an airy affair of cream chiffon, yellow ribbons, bunches of French violets and aigrettes of white.

Lenore pressed upon her, and without a protest from the entranced girl, a silk parasol covered with white chiffon; white gloves and slippers completed her attire.

"They were made for you." Louise exclaimed. "Everything … the slippers, hat parasol and all… oh sister, you are divine."

Flushed with pleasure, Engrid asked, "Do you really like it?"

"Do I like it? Words can't express how you look. Wear that outfit to the Mid-Summer Day dance, and I swear you'll bring all of the men to their knees. You'll have to carry a spare hat pin to use in the clinches!"

"Would that be so mad?" Engrid asked with a facetious smile.

"It wouldn't be good." Louise said with a wink, "I'd better keep an eye on Emil."

"You'll be wanting a new outfit?" Lenore inquired of Louise.

"Oh, no… I don't have to deck myself out like a man-trap."

"Man-trap? I like that coming from you, Engrid muttered from the other side of the screen. "You are worse than that; a man-hunter, I would call you; you just… run them down."

"It appears as though you two truly are sisters," Lenore suggested with a lively laugh.

"I'm bankrupt," Engrid observed ruefully as she placed the purchase price in Lenore's hand, "but I don't know what else money is for. I'm certain I can't wait for the holiday now."

With Lenore's thanks loud in their ears, the trio picked their way through the Saturday night crowd.

The week dragged by on leaden feet for Engrid. However, she reconciled the slow-moving, drudgery filled days with evening visits to Alena and Louise.

In the meantime, Emil hurried importantly around the town, preparing for the gala day. Orders were placed with the butcher for the beef which was to be barbecued; then Emil instructed that the beef be taken aboard the special train the following Saturday. Leaving the shop, Emil placed an order for buns, donuts, and cinnamon rolls with the Vienna bakery.

"Poy," said the baker, "I'll hev to vork do shivts exdra pesides der von to mek da order. It's vort it, doe." Emil looked fondly at a tray of tarts that the baker was filling with a yellow concoction. "Hev von," the artisan urged in a guttural voice. "Dake a lot… cake do!"

At the saloon, "Hello, Emil," Jerry Malmstrom greeted him in an affable voice. "Have one on the house."

Emil nodding acceptance, grasped a dill-pickle and stabbed a hard-boiled egg with a long roasting fork and munched joyously after swallowing his drink.

"Set one up for the boys," he directed, and chairs scraped at a table where card players accepted the invitation.

"How much beer will it take," Emil asked, getting down to cases, "to keep the bunch going for one day and night of the picnic?"

"I don't think you will need more than a gallon for each. Most of the men have already ordered liquor to go with the beer. Do you want some?"

"Sure, save me a quart of brandy. If I don't drink it, someone else will."

Emil finished a second egg, paid for the drinks and left the saloon with a wave of his hand after the necessary details such as additional ice had been attended to. In the Tintic Mercantile store, he relayed an order to Rika who with eyes warm and friendly, put it down.

"How are the plans coming for the blow out?" she asked; after giving him a precocious smile. She pulled a pencil from behind a pink ear and leaned over the counter to translate Emil's instructions into a written order.

As always, Emil felt an undeniable attraction to her when in her presence, thinking "What a lucky man John is to have her for his sweetheart." Aloud he remarked, "Things are under control. This is the last order that I have to place. How are you fixed for dry onions?"

"We have plenty. How many do you require?"

"Enough to feed a mob," he replied. "You see we want dry onions, dill pickles, roast beef sandwiches and candy for the kids."

"Who is in charge of refreshments?" Rika asked.

"Charley Swenson is going to barbecue the meat, and five of the older men have been delegated the task of serving the beer. When I think of those dripping roast sandwiches, I can hardly wait for the day to come." Emil, like most of his countrymen, lived to eat.

"Who'll cook the coffee?"

"Mrs. Kosky and several widows. It will be a fine thing for them to be able to pick up a few extra dollars. Just think, Rika," Emil said with a smile, "all of the beer, brandy and coffee that I can consume at one time, and then not have to go to work the following day; there'll be dancing all night until the sun comes up. That's my idea of heaven."

The girl considered the simplicity of the big man's needs. "I wish that I were a man for just one night, and I'd really kick up my heels! I'd howl like a coyote and be going from one pretty girl to another, making love to them all."

"You would, huh?"

"Certainly."

"That might be a grand theory, but look what it has done for the Mormons," Emil said with a chuckle.

"Oh, to be a man for a night," Rika said with a pensive sigh. "By the way, who is going to take care of the boarding house?"

"You have overlooked the fact that the men will all be going; if they don't they can eat at the restaurant; that will teach them to appreciate Mrs. Kosky's culinary accomplishments."

"I believe you are right," Rika exclaimed with a mischievous smile. "What about accommodations for sleeping?"

"Sleeping?" the man gasped in dismay; "you don't suppose a bunch of Swede-Finns would take time out to sleep, do you?"

"I suppose not," the girl replied thoroughly enjoying the gab-fest. "What about the children, though?"

"Their mothers can make beds for them in the seats of the cars. Anything else you want to know?"

"N-o-o, I suppose not," the girl replied. She had never been restrained in her visible liking for Emil, and her look as it met his glance, gave eloquent testimony of her admiration for the big man. Emil's face colored visibly.

"Well, I suppose I had better be going; have those things sent up in time for the special, Saturday morning; it leaves at seven."

"I certainly will, Emil." The girl answered and her eyes followed the man with an infinitely remote look shadowing gray depths. She was startled from her absorption when a high, nasal voice intruded itself into her reverie as she leaned over the counter with her elbows; chin resting in the palms of her hands.

"Rika!" Mrs. Wilken snapped, "How long must I stand here before you get your eyes off that man and serve me?" The words were spoken loudly and of a certainty that the male clerk piling potato sack on potato sack as he made up an order for one of the outlying mines; heard her.

The girl blushing her confusion, faced the woman.

"What can I do for you, Mrs. Wilken?" Her voice dripped honey. Giving the thin customer a covert glance she turned a page and inserted the carbon between two successive leaves of the order book.

Mrs. Wilken regarded the girl with a cynical look containing veiled amusement. "Making calf-eyes at a married man," she thought. She sniffed with a jerk of her head, in unison with a snort of contempt.

"I was just discussing the coming picnic with Emil. It's quite an affair for the Swedes and Finns." She licked the point of her pencil, placed it on the top line after filling in the date and address then waited for the dour-visage woman's order.

"I suppose it is," Mrs. Wilken snapped out; "I'm forced to dispense with my hired girl's help for two whole days. I don't see how I can manage. She would pick an evening to be gone when I am to entertain my club. She'll miss the extra quarter I would pay her for her services."

"She'll also miss the cooking, preparing the table, dish washing and serving of the food," Rika said smugly to herself. Aloud Rika stated, "It isn't the girl's fault that the celebration comes at the time of the party. Engrid has looked forward to going, as have the rest of us. I, too, am taking the day off. I suppose you are aware of the fact that this particular celebration means as much to us as does an American's Fourth of July, or the Mormon's twenty-fourth of July?"

"Certainly, but it still inconveniences me, though" she stated; then gave the girl her order.

"Do you want to have this order sent up?" Rika asked.

"Certainly; that's what the delivery boy is for."

"Is that all?"

"Tell the boy to have the things there in plenty of time for supper."

"You old she devil!" Rika muttered, and after a surreptitious look around the store, she stuck out a pink tongue after the departing woman. "I wish someone would poison you," she hissed. With that, her thoughts reverted to the kindly man working in the other departments.

"How he can live with her; let alone sleep with her, is beyond my comprehension," she muttered.

Meanwhile, Emil, at the Finn hall, placed his hands over his ears in mock disapproval when he moved to the stage and stood grinning behind Roy Nielson, conductor of the lodge band. He waited until the thirty-odd members came to an ear-splitting finale before thumping the slender leader on the back. The man promptly turned and lowered his baton to face Emil with a myopic look through thick lenses.

"Hello, Roy; how is the band coming?"

"Hello, Emil, I would gladly enter them in a contest with any band in the state."

"Hello, boys," Emil called in response to a chorus of greetings from the men on the stage who looked trim indeed in their red and white suites. Their gold epaulettes gleamed when they moved about relaxed and chattering over a cigarette.

"Hey fellows," Emil called, I have made the arrangements for the eats and drinks at the picnic. Do you boys think you will be ready to take first prize? Yes? That's good. Park City, and Bingham are entering the contest, according to the word received from their secretaries; they're going to give you some tough competition!"

"We have one or two rough spots to iron out. After that, I don't believe there'll be a band able to hold a candle to us." Roy said reassuringly.

"I certainly hope not, old man," Emil smiled. "Well, I have to be hurrying along; I've been busy all day, and I'm afraid my old lady will throw me out if I don't go now. So long boys, so long Roy," he called and waving goodbye he strode through the doors.

The conductor tapped on his music stand, and the band blasted forth with a stirring march causing Emil to replace his hands over his ears. "Sounds alright from the outside; but it is too much to be cooped up in that hall," he said aloud with a twisted smile as he strode briskly along in time with the melody.

"Life is indeed wonderful!" he told himself gaily. Saturday was well on its way; one that couldn't come too soon for old and young alike. Emil whistled a bar of the march as he hurried home, harboring a glowing pride for the community of interests shared with his kind.

"Always on Saturday night we have fun!" he exulted, saying words that friends used as a greeting when meeting in the dance hall. "Always on Saturday night."

Chapter 15

A tenseness held Engrid on the evening prior to the excursion; some of which she dispelled by writing letters to her parents, and close friends. She wrote steadily until eleven o'clock; then afterwards she undressed and drawing a robe about her, she blew out the lamp. Pulling a chair to the window, she raised the blind and stared absently into the moon-flooded night.

Sounds of revelry from the main street reached her ears. The cheerful brass of an orchestra in a downtown dance hall accompanied by the muffled undertones of the bass drum rolled through the night; sometimes loudly, and at other times diminishing as if merrymakers were opening and closing doors of the hall.

Shouts of exuberance from an inebriated miner came clearly through the window, causing the girl to smile. Somewhere near, a rooster crowed in the false dawn. Others took up the challenge as Engrid gazed pensively at the moon, feeling a surge of rapture akin to worship rising in her; and almost unendurable in its poignancy.

Undoing her braids, she allowed her hair to hang in shimmering waves over which she ran a brush in a mechanically motion. "Tonight I should be with the one man whom I care for," she mused; "and regardless of right or wrong, I wish I were."

She imagined herself and John in a buggy resting on a side road overlooking the town. While he smoked, she would listen to his subdued voice enlightening her on his plans for their future, and at an appropriate moment, he would reach an arm around her and kiss her. Of course, she would show a proper reserve as his lips met hers for the first time. She would push her hands lightly against his chest and just when John had probably decided that her lips were not for him to bruise; yielding, she would give free rein to her pent-up hunger. After he had released her, she would look through half-closed eyes into his smiling face.

She pondered this as she laid her chin on her hands, resting her elbows on the window sill while sinking deeply into reverie. She was aware of how light frosted the house adjacent with a silvery iridescence, and cloaked the lilac bushes with bewitching clarity.

The lazy, clip-clop of a passing horse pulling a buggy, a trill of laughter bubbling from a girl's lips caused Engrid to say with a sigh, "Someone is happy tonight."

How life had changed for her in a few short months. A wave of loneliness engulfed her causing her to long for familiar faces and the comforting presence of deep-hued forests   shadowing myriads of sparkling lakes. To a great extent, she had altered her opinion of the somber tone of the land which she had left, after enduring a glaring sun that shone with surprising vigor.

Here there were no comforting clouds dispensing gentle rain daily, nor slowly billowing masses of cooling fog to moisten faces and collect jewel-like on grasses and trees. In fact, she pondered, there were not enough trees to make a measurable difference in the intensity of the oven-like breath wafting from the rolling sand dunes far to the west of town.

Oh, perverse, unpredictable Engrid whose thinking was contradictory; while she longed for her former environment , she thought how nice it would be to inform an attentive mother of emotions engendered by the sight of massive, snow-capped mountains shining in the distance, and of the blue, almost white haze where purple lingered a short time before. How delightful it would be were she able to tell mother that she had conquered fears which previously possessed her when looking at the towering heights. Now, she knew admiration and love.

However, the beauty of the night was far from perfect, the girl decided, as from farther up the tree shaded street, drunken voices raised in argument reminded her that all of life could not be lovely, nor would there be any good accomplished by telling her parents of moral and physical changes which acquisitiveness wrought in many men coming fresh and eager from green fields, woods and clear lakes of their homeland to toil deep below the valley's sun-lit surface, under terrifying surroundings, and with only feeble gleaming candles for their sun.

Necessity coupled with greed furnished an incentive to claw their way ever deeper, always farther, with drills, picks and shovels until they sank exhausted after a supper… if they could summon an appetite into overworked oft times sick bodies.

How could she tell mother of men, who, while lying on their beds after work, drank liquor to deaden throbbing pain caused by fumes of powder, and foul underground air? Emil had said that the act of running a hand over his forehead, after handling explosives, would cause such an excruciating headache that no relief except whiskey could be found. How could she tell her mother of the horrible odor clinging to miners clothes when they walked into the boardinghouse after a day spent in the mine? And if it were that strong in the open air, how much more severe would it be, if she, herself, had to work in such places? She shuddered, and told herself, "No wonder they drink…"

And yes, she thought, no wonder these wifeless men whipped tired nerves with prodigious quantities of liquor, and consorted with women in drunken orgies at Kitty's place and similar places, in an effort to forget the day of toil past and the one staring them in the face, if they but dared to look beyond the debauchery at the coming day… but enough of that.

Ah! If her mother and father could see what she would wear tomorrow! With these, and kindred thoughts tumbling through her mind, she finished combing her hair, and fitting a cap of lace and silk over gathered-up tresses, she fell into a restless sleep from which she frequently awakened with a start to look apprehensively at the clock; how many ties, she never knew, because her waking moments came and went in an endless procession. As always, on similar occasions when it came time to be off, she slept heavily and upon awakening found that the sun was shining full on her face through the open window.

"Heavens, I've slept in!" she told herself as she tested the alarm to find that it had run down at six o'clock. On winged feet, she breathlessly performed her toilet, slipped a few accessories into a bag, and hurrying out of the door, she walked rapidly in the elongated shadows of the houses bordering the walk.

A chorus of whistles; trills and chirps greeted her as the dulcet voice of a meadow lark added itself to the sobbing of gray mourning doves, and the incessant chatter of a band of saucy sparrows swarming over droppings on the dusty road.

A flock of gaily colored pigeons wheeled aloft from a dovecote; however, one pair remained on its roof, the male bird bobbing and bowing with a boastful, albeit obsequious air as it presumptively told its mate with a throaty garrulousness to, "Look-at-da-coon,"

Engrid smiling warmly at the strutting, audacious braggart; felt her spirits soaring and she found herself humming a song.

The day was already warm. Smoke from scattered chimneys shone blue, and changed to a dirty black as coal was added to flames and smoke penciling lines across the cerulean sky mingled freely with a mass from the mine stacks whose numerous guy-wires seemed an inadequate support for the belching cylinders.

Illusive stands from ballooning spiders, adhering to her face with an irritating stickiness, caused her to claw at the sparkling streamers with a feeling of loathing.

A boy delivering milk deftly tipped a five gallon can and poured a stream of frothy liquid into a two-quart measuring cup; then he climbed the steps to a house and emptied the contents into a dowdy-appearing woman's lard bucket while she yawned a, "Good Morning," in a hoarse voice that belied her words as she held a robe loosely over her breast with a free hand, while the bottom of the robe hung open to reveal a beefy leg. Engrid giggled.

The sonorous whistle of the Little Chief mine sounded seven o'clock. The mountains, chopping the sound into fragments, hurled them at her ears as she turned the corner by a red-painted warehouse.

The banshee-like screech of an engine panting on the track caused the girl to cover her ears. She increased her pace, although knowing at this point she had ample time because of the people who had yet to board the train. Her eyes darted here and there in search of Louise; and finally she found her standing a little removed from the crowd proceeding slowly to the steps of the last car.

"Yoo-hoo! Here I am, sister!" Louise called while waving a white-gloved hand.

"Whew!" Engrid gasped. "I didn't think that I was going to make it. The clock went off and I never heard it ring. It was the darnedest thing; I would sleep and wake a thousand times, only to doze off. Just when I should have been getting up, I must have dozed again. Can you beat that? I never even had time for a cup of coffee."

"You made the train, and that is all that counts!"

"Where is Emil?"

Louise pointed down the line of cars. "He is in the baggage car, presumably making sure that all of the things he ordered are placed aboard. I believe he is supervising the opening of a keg of beer, if you ask me," Louise looked at her sister's satchel. "Did you bring your plate and the usual?"

"Oh, dumb me," Engrid cried in an aggrieved voice; "I knew there would be something I would forget in the hurry. Oh, what shall I do?"

"Don't worry," Louise said reassuringly, "I put some extras into the basket. I like to do that the night before we go anyplace; because there is generally some poor unfortunate in our little crowd who forgets something." She smiled and pulling her sister to her, giving her a generous hug.

"That is you, over and over, Louise; always thinking of someone else. No wonder you are happy."

"Silly girl, that has nothing to do with it. I am happy because I am married to someone who causes me to be that way. Try it sometime," Louise said as they boarded the car and found a vacant seat across the aisle from Rika and Hulda.

"By the looks of things, most all of the men are supervising the loading of the baggage cars," Engrid remarked with a rueful smile, as glancing about her, she noted the preponderance of women's faces.

"Leave it to the men to find the saloon," Rika agreed, "even if it rolls on wheels."

A member of the band thrust a trombone into the door of the car, and gave a blast answered by a confusion of feminine squeals and giggles as protesting women covered their ears with their hands.

Somewhere along the line of cars, a rattle of snare drums pointed out the tempo of a quick march and boys, wriggling past their mothers, paraded up and down the aisle displaying shirts of checkered calico, heavily starched and meticulously ironed. From their shoes rose the odor of black shoe polish, a suggestion of exciting possibilities of a ride on a real train, with all of the sights and sounds accompanying it. From outside came the blast of fire-crackers as other boys burned what was the end result of nickels which had been saved from allowances for weeks and weeks.

A pair of whirling, snarling, snapping dogs came together in the road between the main line and the spur where they had been stating their objections to each other's presence in guttural growls. An interloper, summoned by the sounds of mayhem appeared on the scene, seemingly bent on taking the recalcitrant animals apart. The two dogs turned on the intruder, and in a few short moments had chases him up the road and around the warehouse in a flurry of dust; while boys crowded to the windows, shouting their encouragement and the girls gasped in fear.

Their objections to each other's presence apparently forgotten in a moment; the two original enemies reappeared leaving their calling cards on every pole and wagon wheel.

"That reminds me of Swedes and Finns who fight at every opportunity, only to turn on the Russians who try to go with their girls," Engrid remarked humorously to her sister. "Man has so much in common with his four-legged friends."

The engine loosed two peremptory toots and its brakes were released with a satisfying, hissing, spine-tingling sound. The children's eyes grew large as they tensed to the forward movement preceding an initial series of barks from the stack. Then the train rolled steadily onward, the engine whistling frequently for crossings. Parents pulled unwilling children to their seats lest they lean too far out of the open windows and fall out onto black cinders coating the right-of-way. On and on the engine went, its determined barking measuring each exciting foot of the distance traveled, and deluging the village with a cascade of pulsating roars.

At Summit the train paused to take on other passengers who swarmed happily aboard. Soon young men in rakish sailors vests opened stylishly, drifted up the aisles to converse with maidens while sitting on the arms of their seats. The girls responded to their conversation with peals of laughter, until the car was inundated in an atmosphere of conviviality.

Down past Pollywog Pond where there floated rafts made of railroad ties on which the city's youth whiled away many idle hours, the train rolled. Tunnels, where perspiring men were wheeling out debris from yesterday's round of blasts, fell behind the exhaust of the coasting locomotive. To the children who were all ears, noses, eyes and quivering nerves; this activity was holding them expectantly on edges of their seats, or leaning out of windows whence came the fragrance of coal-smoke blended with exhaust steam and the metallic essence of brake- shoes. Through tunnels they moved, and excited girls squealed when receiving what they had been waiting for from youthful companions; stolen kisses of several seconds duration.

As the passengers glued their eyes to the changing panorama, the train accomplished the descent from the mountain-locked village and proceeded cautiously around horse-shoe curves and over a series of skeleton-like bridges spanning the deep canyon. Finally the bridges were left behind, and the train rumbled down a sloping plateau.

Coming in a smooth, continuous chant, the vibration of the wheels deepened steadily until the children felt themselves rushing along at the terrifying rate of thirty or more miles an hour! Oh, the joy of it. How the telegraph poles flashed by and how awe inspiring was the clattering reflected from a string of ore cars behind a freight engine where it waited placidly for the special's passing at the Elberta sheep-shearing corral!

How the children squealed at the sight of bounding jackrabbits and crows flying at a gait equal to the train!

After the mountains had been left behind, those possessing musical talent now had a favorable opportunity to display it to advantage, as fiddlers, banjo players and accordionists roaming along the aisles, struck up lively tunes. Old and young alike joined in giving vent to their enthusiasm in a riotous outburst of singing that caused miles to vanish speedily as the train coasted down the long slant to the level of the valley floor in which reposed the waters of Utah lake.

Joking boisterously and engaging the girls in animated conversation, Emil, John, Alex and Arvid entered moving in an aura of good-fellowship, happy as the children around them because they, too, were enjoying two days of well-earned rest from their labors.

What joy was an excursion for the crowd whose only rides during the past year for the most part, were confined to jolting ore-wagons, buggies or the backs of horses rented from the local livery stable. Every turn of the wheels spelled adventure for the gay revelers.

As the train rolled through fields where the youth of the valley were bent in their labors, the boys on the train called derisively, "Hay-seeds, manure shovelers, beet-topper, web-feet"; and the farmer boys responded with shaking fists and grimaces from beneath ragged sombreros; while the girls in the cars shrieked their amusement.

Much to the women's disgust, and long before the train pulled into the siding of the resort, Emil, John and Alex had earned themselves the sobriquet of "walking delegates," whose steps were unmistakably erratic to a discerning eye.

Louise concealed her irritation at Emil's conduct when Engrid told her that a man should be allowed to enjoy himself once a year in the manner that he had chosen.

"But suppose he gets sick," Louise objected.

"He won't be the first, or the last man, to do so." Engrid said with a giggle.

Rika disagreed, saying that so many of the men were temperance men, and she could see no reason why all of them couldn't be the same way. However, she felt little comfort in her remark when the subjects of her discussion; an unbelievably large number of them at least, walked down the aisles in jostling, singing, weaving groups, slapping each other on the back with blows that would have felled a mule. These men apparently had forgotten vows made so fervently while enduring the throws of a "hang-over".

Engrid conclude that Rika was becoming such a paragon of virtue as to soon be intolerable to the average man who associated with her. Her attitude toward occasional drinking and the fact that she was a native of this country, gave her a certain air of superiority which she sought to impress on others, even on such an occasion as this. Engrid, naturally, felt her dislike for the girl growing; while she sensed that in some measure, Rika returned the sentiment.

At Springville, the train back-switched and followed the track leading to the resort. With mingled emotions, Engrid and Louise surveyed the situation where they had waited for the train on which they had ridden to Tintic. Since that day many changes had taken place. Engrid, had gone to work handicapped by the inability to converse with her employer and Louise had settled herself into the intimacies of married life; content with her decision.

As the train passed verdant meadows, Engrid gazed with a feeling of nostalgia at barns and sheds resembling those of her native land with the exception that they were built of thin boards and not of solid logs and many were merely windbreakers, open on one side.

The sight of grazing cows caused her to hold back tears as she pictured herself standing by her mother's side at milking time and her parent's deft fingers again directed alternate streams of creamy milk into the foaming pail with a gentle, hypnotic sound; while the cows placidly munching their mixture of potatoes and grain, turned occasionally to lick with moist tongues at their extremities when flies bit viciously. Many times in a spirit of fun, Engrid had stooped over, and her mother had directed a stream of succulent milk into her open mouth and the both had chortled gleefully when some had missed her reaching tongue and spattered over her face.

As Engrid had gasped and wiped her face clean. Her mother had assured her that it would give her a rosy complexion. Perhaps it had, Engrid pondered, and maybe the rich cream that they worked into their faces each night before retiring had helped also; because Louise's skin and her own were fair to behold.

When the train at last drew to a halt, behind two others, doors opened to disgorge a swarming, shouting exuberant mass of people. Colorful parasols blossomed above the gaily dressed throng, and children ran with shrieks of riotous joy to find a swing or teeter-totter. Friends met amicable friends from other towns, and the arriving party flowed smoothly into their predecessor's crowd in a spirit of goodwill. Men pounded each others backs and shook hands, the sincerity of their meetings being measured by the amount of bull-like bellowing infused into the conversation. Truly these people knew the meaning of friendship!

Boldly accosting acquaintances of the opposite sex with whom they had consorted during picnics of other summers, boys moved around in pairs; faces lit with happiness as conversation danced and sparkled like bubbles in a glass of champagne.

From the baggage cars, over-eager hands carried barrels of beer which had been cooling in huge wooden boxes of ice. The barrels were set up in a portion of the resort which had been gaily decorated with branches of aspen trees. Spigots were attached to the barrels, shelves were lined with steins, and the bartenders went to work in earnest.

Meanwhile, quarters of beef were carried by strong men to open fires and fastened to spits, and those who had contracted the job of roasting them promptly began their work. When the delicious odor of roasting beef began hanging tantalizingly over all, the day began with a promise of unprecedented success.

Engrid and Louise wandered about in the company of Hulda and Rika while their male companions sauntered off to meet acquaintances from other towns. Emil, reveling in his work, went importantly on his way to help secretaries of the other lodges set the scheduled program for the day in motion.

Bottles passed surreptitiously away from prying feminine eyes, as miners relived experiences underground with each other; and conversation reverted to by-gone days across the ocean. Every man was unified in expressions of liking for his adopted country.

"A good country, Amerika; why did we not come here sooner?" served as a form of greeting. The men toasted their mutual friends who remained in the old country, their lodges, their jobs, their health and the wonderful climate in which they found themselves. Here it was a joy beyond belief to be able to lay down the price of a ton of coal and not have to spend leisure time hauling and cutting wood sufficient to do them through a long winter.

Here, if one were fortunate enough to possess a cow, hay could be bought from the farmers; consequently there was no need to wade in the waters of swamps to harvest wild grass.

Here, one could live the life of a king, and not the drab existence of a serf, bound to unfriendly soil in the midst of deep woods.

Here, one could meet with kindred spirits on a basis of equality and personal initiative was the touchstone to prosperity; when each new day opened wide arms of opportunity to be embraced or pushed aside, according to an individual's vision.

Here, there was no bowing of heads as they were forced to accept the decrees of another nation. Here, in the great country to which they had journeyed, races, tongues, religion, work, pleasure, studies and business ventures flourished, offering every man or woman unheard of opportunities. There was timber to fell, new homes to build, roads to open isolated parts of this vast new state of Utah, coal to be dug, ore to be mined, business to invest in if one had funds and each could seek an independent means of making a living.

Here, Catholics could go to services, and across the street, the Lutheran church opened wide its doors. To men and women far removed from their homeland they found a bit of home in the sermons of the minister who talked their own tongue, as well as the language of their adopted country. Here they could likewise celebrate an ancient festival expressing gladness for the sun which was once again at its near zenith after a southern sojourn.

And thus the men proclaimed the virtues of their adopted country, while women, weary of their interminable praise, talked of simple things; dresses, shirtwaists, hats, children, hair styles and menfolk who were headed for the "dog house" with each passing moment.

Music from three bands, playing alternately, kept the spirits of the gathering at a cheerful pitch. In the babble of confused, carefree conversation rising and falling like the waves on a beach and spattering even the most sedate with drops of conviviality, an announcement was made, after a fanfare, crediting the band from Tintic with a silver loving cup for being the best. Beaming with pleasure, the director stepped to a stand which served as a hub for the crowd wheeling about the picnic grounds, and accepted the cup. John, Emil, Alex and Arvid cheered themselves hoarse with other of their comrades, and found in the announcement an excuse to share yet another drink.

Races were run on a straightaway along the edge of the park. Boys vied with each other to prove their fleetness of foot, and incidentally to boost the esteem in which other lodges would hold the winners. Small coins changed from judge's hands to outreaching, eager children. Girls handicapped by their long dresses, strove to summon boundless speed and partners who had practiced diligently for the three-legged race, teamed together with near legs fastened to each other by handkerchiefs. Rare was the case of a pair of boys who reached the finishing line without first sprawling on the ground in a jumble of flailing arms and legs; while the crowd whistled and cried out in enthusiastic encouragement. Eyes shone with excitement as bodies of the spectators tensed in sympathy with the straining contestants.

Shrieks of merriment accompanied the efforts of the women and men, carrying an excess of weight, who floundered, with breasts jouncing and buttocks quaking over the finishing line. In this particular race, Mrs. Kosky won by a waddle and was promptly subjected to the back-slapping of her boarders.

"You run like you cook, Mrs. Kosky; you're splendid!" John told the gasping woman who laughed and laughed as she accepted five dollars for transporting her vast bulk over the measured course faster than her rivals.

Then there was the prize for the oldest member of the crowd. A woman from Park City, answering to the name of Matilda Erickson, received a beautiful, all-wool blanket because she claimed an incredible total of ninety-seven winters. She had papers from her parish priest to prove that her claim was valid and her shriveled face and shrill piping voice gave truth to her assertion. The throng gave her a lusty ovation, and agreeably raised their life-expectancy for the time being. The aches and pains of those who were sixty-five-years young, were dismissed with a careless shrugging of bent shoulders and another swallow of beer.

An evidence of fertility, beyond the normal number of five to which the couples of the mining camps apparently were addicted, received a reward of five dollars for each child over that number in a family group. One couple with the proclivities of a hare and the enthusiasm of a territorial Mormon, laid claim to forty silver dollars, and as Emil looked at the sturdy woman in her forties, he came to the conclusion, much to the amusement of the crowd in which he stood, that, "The woman was good for a baker's dozen more, If the old man only holds out."

Following a fan-fare, a genial Swede-Finn with the inevitable blonde mustache and complexion made even more paled by work underground, motioned for silence.

"Ladies and gentlemen, friends and fellow lodge members; it is customary to meet together on this longest day of the year to celebrate in the manner that we were accustomed to in our fair homelands. It is fitting that we should celebrate the day as did our fathers; because it marks the day when the sun pauses in its northern-most passage from the south, and there are many of you here assembled who have basked in its glow around the clock. This day," he went on in a booming voice, "marks a time when the northland takes on green life under the urgency of the sun's rays, and once again those back home are lost in the spell of the midnight sun. Here we do not have that; nevertheless, we are favored by a more sympathetic sun, and for that we are thankful. I know of none who would willingly leave this benevolent climate to go back to that land resting under the frigid embrace for all except a few months of the year. We give thanks for the opportunity of living in this kindly land, with its manifold opportunities and obligations. Let us not, my friends," the speaker went on, pausing to clear his throat as his eyes swept the assemblage, "forget that wealth alone does not make nations and men strong. Strength must be a quality existing inside. Wealth makes for a more abundant life; that we have found since coming to this country, but not necessarily a strong nation or person. Let us be as firm in our allegiance to the nation which has accepted us as its own, as we were firm in the countries of our birth."

After a wave of applause had died away, he went on, "Now, after this address of welcome which I hope you have been able to endure without too much discontent, I wish to say that, as is fitting, we are to have a queen to rule for the day; and along this line of reasoning, in a secret vote cast at their respective lodges, the male members have decided on a fair daughter to represent their lodges and we vote for one of the three to be, for the celebration, 'Goddess of the Sun!' Three names will be announced and we wish the ladies who are unaware of their honor, to step forward so that the crowd may make your acquaintance and admire your beauty."

Picking up a scepter and crown, he raised them aloft. "This scepter and this crown, together with fifty dollars in credit on any clothing store that she may choose in her own town, will go to the winner. Only the men in the lodges may vote; because it is the opinion of the men that they alone are capable of judging the various qualities that make a young woman appear beautiful. We have here three boxes, and into these you may drop your pennies, or any amount which you might wish to contribute. The proceeds, outside of the prize money, will be divided among the three lodges for the sick-benefit fund."

The speaker paused, picked up a paper while clearing his throat; then he went on to say, "Let's buy votes with our pennies ... a penny a vote." Then, "Will the following girls please step to the stand? Hilva Oleson from Bingham, Annie Johnson from Park City and Engrid Isaacson from Tintic."

Wild cheers and murmurs of disbelief together with complimentary remarks followed the girls to the stand where they stood together, sunning themselves in the smiles of their friends and admirers; Annie in her dark loveliness and Hilva and Engrid in their blonde freshness. They took their bows, expressed their surprise and pleasure in a few nervous words; then they left the platform and returned to their own circle of friends.

To say that Engrid was stunned by the announcement that the men of her town had chosen her as a representative, would be a mild understatement. After returning from the stand, she basked in a feeling of rejuvenation and giddiness during the remainder of the day. Never, she told herself, would she be so incredibly happy again as she was at this particular time; surrounded as she was by the approving glances of the men, and the envious thrusts from the eyes of many women.

For fifteen minutes, coins of various denominations tinkled merrily into three sealed hat boxes, and before an hour was over, the number of votes was totaled.

Again the blonde gentleman said, "Ladies and Gentlemen, I have the pleasure to announce that pennies were few in the box as to be almost non-existent. Our sick-benefit funds are $987.36 richer than they were previous to this voting. That mind you, is after deducting the fifty dollars which the winner will receive at the store of her own choosing."

Such a whooping, whistling, waving of flags and bobbing of parasols, clattering and rattling of firecrackers, there was at his announcement.

"Ladies and gentlemen, please, please, let me announce the winner," the chairman pleaded as he waved his hands to hush some of the more enthusiastic of the drinking, hard-playing, carefree miners.

"For Hilva Olesen, 34,278 votes; for Annie Johnson, 32,679 votes; and for Engrid Isaacson, 36,779. Will the winner step forward and received her reward?"

"Oh mother, kind mother, don't shake me awake; don't make me go out into the forest dripping with sickening fog; don't force me to go to school, today; don't..."

"Engrid!" came Louise's voice through the giddiness which strove to overcome her, "didn't you hear what the man said? Go to the stand and accept your scepter, he's waiting for you."

"Then… then it isn't a dream," Engrid whispered as the fog dispersed from her vision and the singing in her ears vanished.

"Come on, John!" Emil bellowed and stooping he gathered the girl up, supporting one leg with a brawny shoulder, while John grasped the other, and the girl fairly swam over the roaring crowd, high on the crests of her supporters' shoulders.

Regaining her composure, the girl stood with a smile transfiguring her features and a rosy color returning to her cheeks; while the blonde giant set the crown on her head and passed her hat to John.

"As is only fitting and proper," John said with a wink aside to the audience, "Oh Queen, I kiss your majesty's hand." So saying, he stooped on one knee and lifted her hand to his lips.

"And I," she replied imperiously, quite catching the spirit of the occasion, "dub thee, Sir Little Chief, the Mucker."

Her witty response evoked a roar of mirth in the male portion of her audience for what is lowly as a green-horn who is fit only to shovel rock and substitute for a mule, while the lordly miner rules his with a continual reminder of his servitude.

At nine o'clock that evening when it was cool enough to make dancing a pleasure, a huge orchestra composed of accordions and fiddlers, gathered from the various musicians to the crowd, played continually and those who were able danced the night through, pausing only for juicy roast beef sandwiches, a drink of beer, or a few moments rest.

At six o'clock the following morning, a thoroughly spent queen left the gathering with her sister and promptly slumped into a seat. She and Louise were so exhausted that they hardly knew when the train began its journey back to Tintic, nor did they care.

The men, utterly weary and moving in a daze from lack of sleep and a day and night of indulgence, succumbed also; and with many protests, they roused themselves sufficiently to make their weary ways to places of abode while their women companions trailed listlessly.

Pausing at the door of her sister's house were she could sleep the day and night through, if need be, Engrid turned mischievously to regard Alex who was looking shaggy with a new beginning of a beard. His drooping mustache reflected an inner weariness, and now and again he hiccupped.

"Good day, fair lady," Alex said as he raised the girl's hand and kissing the back of it, "it's been a wonderful party." Bowing gravely, he adjusted his bowler hat and moved into the street where sparrows were flitting about in quest of another meal.

Chapter 16

Relations between Engrid and Mrs. Wilken grew increasingly strained as the summer wore on. Indignity piled on indignity; and even the intervention of Mrs.Kosky could not forestall an open break. Engrid found herself being denied her rest period which she had been promised; also, she found herself being ordered to cut rags for rugs and tending the infant as well as the irresponsible boy.

One day in September, Engrid was moodily rolling rags with a growing resentment smoldering inside her when Mrs. Wilken's mother-in-law, Mrs. Meyer, walked in to inquire of Mrs. Wilken's whereabouts. As the woman entered, the dog slipped inside and flashed Engrid a covert glance before disappearing into the bedroom.

"Out to town," the girl explained quite forgetting the animal in her dejection.

Mrs. Meyer moved closer to the girl and after a glance assured her that Jerold was playing outside; placed an arm around the girl's shoulder and asked, "Will you work for me in my hotel?"

"Vat?" Engrid looked up from the ball that she was winding. Her jaw fell slack and a startled look leaped into her eyes.

Mrs. Meyer licked at thin lips, her eyes gleaming with a perverse, though hopeful light.

Engrid felt the meaning of the woman's words sink into her brain. "Here is a woman offering me release from an intolerable situation. What shall I do?" she pondered. "Will the work and the surroundings be better or worse?" She played with the thought, testing it from every conceivable angle. After all, it was not the same as things had been in the old country.

In the old country, a person signing up as an indentured servant, performed work for a specified period of time, whether they liked it or not. Part of the pay would be lost if one quit before the agreed-upon time. But Engrid thought, "If this woman wants me enough to come into her relative's house and ask me to work I had better reevaluate my worth as a servant."

Pondering this, she rolled another strand on the ball of rags.

"How much do you pay?" studying the woman who uneasily walked to each door; looked down the road at the front and back alley, lest she be caught in her underhanded dealings with this menial.

"One dollar more per week than you are getting for this rotten work, and your rest period will be longer."

"When do you want me?"

"Tomorrow morning; eight o'clock at the Tintic Hotel; do you know were the hotel is?"

The girl nodded her head. "I will come," she said in a determined voice.

Mrs. Meyers gave Engrid a friendly pat on a shoulder as she slipped a silver dollar into her apron pocket and left by the front door. "Oh, how fortunate I am," she told herself. Shrugging aside a premonition that things might not turn out as she expected them to, she pictured with satisfaction changes that would take place in the face of her mistress; surprise, chagrin, anger and a desire for retaliation.

Engrid was lost in thought when the kitchen door slammed and the woman of her contemplation walked sedately into the room. Engrid made no attempt to resume her work. She sat with face smiling and head spinning under the realization that now was her moment of triumph and the woman's turn to taste bitterness and frustration.

The baby cried out from the bedroom, the boy slammed the kitchen door and attempted to wheedle a piece of molasses and bread from his mother and a thumping sounded from the open door of the bedroom when the dog jumped from the bed and headed with a sideways-slinking motion toward the closed kitchen door.

"Engrid!" the woman snapped with a glance at the clock after kicking the dog outside and soundly boxing Jerold's ears to silence his whining, "why did you allow the dog to climb on my bed? Why haven't you put potatoes on to boil? You haven't even got a fire laid; what in heaven's name is going on here, anyway? I thought I told you until you knew beyond question or doubt that the dog was not to be allowed in the house during my absence. Have you fed the baby?"

Through this tirade, the girl sat idly paring her nails with the scissors. She watched as the boy ran into the bedroom where he crawled under the bed, and was hitting his toes on the floor to show his irritation and pain. Added to these was the shrill wailing of the baby who believed, in his hunger pangs, that the adults of his world had deserted him.

Rising, Engrid tossed the scissors onto the chair which she vacated. Arrogance possessed her as she stalked up the stairs after flipping her skirts toward the woman in a universally understood gesture. She packed her things listening meanwhile, to the furor from below where Mrs. Wilken clattered stove-lids in a frantic attempt to accomplish what Engrid had failed to do in her absence.

Engrid, smiled smugly as she heard the youngsters giving vent to their desperation; then with a final look around the room which she had grown to hate because it belonged to a woman whom she thoroughly despised, she stalked down the steps; her valise crammed with her belongings, and her hat fastened jauntily to her hair with a long pin.

"Mrs. Wilken," she said in a fanfaronade previous to her exit, "it mek me heppy to qvit. I not like you. Tank you… I go to batter yob!"

"What in heaven's name is wrong?" the flabbergasted woman asked.

"I am sick of you and I leave you with your own dirt and nasty vords." Extending a palm, "Pay me!" she demanded.

"You can't do this to me; leave me like this before you have given me a previous notice of your intentions to quit," the woman exclaimed heatedly.

"Oh, yes I con. I pee mine own poss. I peck. I vant my monee," Engrid said in halting English.

"I won't pay you a thing!" the woman exploded.

"You vill pay; I am going." Engrid asserted tossing her head as she strode toward the front door. Passing the bedroom, she observed Jerold, his tears finally halted, lying halfway out from under the bed, and staring in her direction with open-mouthed amazement.

In the meantime, Mrs. Wilken had been thinking furiously. "This is a fine state of affairs, what with the sewing circle meeting tonight, and I unable to get another maid because my mother-in-law has been trying to do that very thing for several weeks."

She followed the girl to the door and watched with alarm as Engrid stalked down the steps on hurried feet.

"Engrid," she wheedled, "please stay until tomorrow." To herself, she thought, "If I can only get her to remain, I can convince her into staying by offering her fifty cents more per week, and giving her the rest period."

"Engrid, Engrid, don't leave me," Jerold cried frantically.

Engrid continued walking, although at a reduced gait.

"Stay and take care of me, and I will not make fun of your talk anymore. I won't drag dirt in on rainy days, and bring live horned-toads into the house to scare you anymore. I'm sorry that I put that one between your sheets and scared you until you screamed; you don't know how sorry, oh, Engrid," the boy sobbed through twin streams of tears finding a pathway over freckles at each side of his nose, down to his lugubriously contorted mouth with its two missing teeth whence issued choking, repentant sobs.

Engrid weakened, almost enough to retrace her way up the steps to where Mrs. Wilken stood with face devoid of emotion. However, the memory of her past few months coupled with a premonition that continued employment with Mrs. Wilken would eventually result in a replication of this day's events, overruled any kindly impulse which the boy's sobbing elicited.

Jerold ran down the steps; she kissed his wet cheek, rumpled his red hair and added a generous hug. "Dere, dere, Yerold, don't cry so. I vill see you sometimes."

Turning, she walked away from the house without once glancing again in the woman's direction. The boy's renewed sobbing grew faint in the distance where he slumped by the gate, watching her retreating figure through blurred eyes.

Engrid walked briskly along, swishing her skirt with carefree abandon; scarcely aware that her heavy valise was growing heavier as was the extent of her joy. Gradually the weight asserted itself in aching muscles of both arms and she changed hands frequently in an attempt to continue.

Finally she placed it down with a sigh and stared about her. Self-conscious she noted that a group of loitering miners were eying her and undoubtedly discussing her.

There John Semell found her as he emerged from the barbershop where he had been recently shaved. He flashed a friendly smile, then strode over in a debonair manner, and with a huge hand, never quite free of the rust color of ore, removed his hat.

"Well, my fine-feathered-friend," he remarked with a warm glance from her hat to her face, "why are you here in the middle of the hot street with such a big load?"

Feeling shyness replace determination, Engrid replied, "Hello, John."

"You're not by any chance tired of our fair city and taking leave of us so soon, are you?"

"Definitely not," she replied, "I'm going to Mrs. Kosky's place. I quite to go to another job. The lady and I had trouble; so I walked out."

"Permit me," he said with an amused smile as he picked up her valise; together the couple walked up the street. John smelled pleasantly of shaving soap, the excited girl observed.

The walk to the boarding house seemed far too short as she unburdened herself of her troubles into John's attentive ears.

"When are you and Rika going to get married?" she asked in a gay voice, however an inner emptiness belied her forced cheerfulness.

"I am not certain that we ever shall, by the looks of things," he answered giving her an amused glance causing her to blush painfully and look straight head. "She wants me to go to Park City and work in the store with her father."

"And what is the matter with that?"

"Oh, I just don't have the desire and patience necessary to serve people."

"What do you like to do then, John?"

"What I am doing now, mining."

They left the railroad tracks and ascended the steps of the boarding house. John stepped ahead and opened the door.

Mrs. Koksy looked up from the stove where she was stirring one of several kettles of bubbling stew. She smiled, added a measure of spice pellets; sampled the aromatic concoction and added salt.

"Sakes alive, child, what are you doing with your valise? You're not going back, I hope?"

"Nope; I'm merely changing jobs."

"So?" Mrs. Kosky eyed the girl and her grinning companion, speculatively.

"I have decided to work for Mrs. Meyer!"

"What? How in the world did that come about?"

The woman motioned to a chair, and Engrid explained the happenings over the inevitable cup of kahvia. Mrs. Kosky chuckled and wiped a flushed face on her apron.

"Well," she remarked knowingly, "Mrs. Meyer was not slow to take advantage of the fact that you wanted to quit working for her daughter-in-law; but what a nerve she has! What will Mrs. Wilken say when she finds that her mother-in-law has taken you on at an increase in pay? I would like to be there to see the fireworks," Alena chuckled as she shook her kindly head and accompanying the motion with a knowing look. Suddenly she was overcome with laughter as she pictured what might happen when the two got together and expressed indignation at each others lack of scruples.

"Do you think I did right?" Engrid asked in a concerned voice as she glanced from the woman to John and back again.

"Sure you did," John assured her with a grin.

"Of course you did, my child; of course you did," Alena said soothingly. "The way it has worked out sounds almost unbelievable, though. I had better rent a room in Mrs. Meyer's hotel to watch the battle of a lifetime. I understand that they barely tolerate each other as it is." She shook her head, still with that perverse gleam in her bright eyes. "I'll tell you, child; there's no love lost between them."

"I'm going to see Louise now," Engrid said after standing up, "and tell her about it. She has been trying to persuade me to quit for a long time; but I haven't done so before because of my inability to speak English as I should." She moved to the door where she hesitated for a time, "I wonder who put the woman up to asking me to work for her?" she pondered.

Alena enlightened her, "I ran into her yesterday while I was shopping, and happened to mention your dissatisfaction with the way that Mrs. Wilken was keeping you at work when you should be resting and tending to your own needs." Mrs. Kosky's eyes twinkled. "Of course, my intention was for her to have a talk with her daughter-in-law and see if she couldn't persuade her to be more lenient with you."

"Oh," said the girl. She flashed Alena a smile. "Could I leave my valise here until tomorrow morning?"

"Certainly, my dear and you are welcome to stay for supper; there is a bed waiting when you tire. When did you say you were going to work for Mrs. Meyer?"

"Tomorrow morning."

"So soon? Why don't you take a vacation?"

"I would sooner work, and besides, I promised the lady. I'll see you, and thank you for the kahvia and your kindness."

"No thanks necessary," the woman replied generously.

"May I accompany you to your sister's? I have to see Emil on business," John remarked falling in beside the girl.

"If you wish." Engrid's heartbeat quickened as she flashed him a coy smile.

Emil was sitting down to supper in his trousers, underwear and bare feet when John knocked on the door.

"Put on your shirt," Louise hissed, "John and Engrid are here."

"Hell," he answered with an affable grin, "Let them in; she has seen long handles before, and if she hasn't, it's about time." Nevertheless, he complied and facing the visitors with a sheepish grin, he buttoned a blue and white striped shirt, although stubbornly refusing to wear a tie.

"The old woman insisted that I put on a shirt; I can't say that I enjoy it... make yourselves to home and draw up a chair," he added gesturing to the table. "Louise will set a plate for you." He turned to John and said, "Come and have a drink."

In the meantime, Louise set two more places and they all seated themselves together; then

Engrid informed her sister of the events which had transpired. Louise congratulated her for her good fortune and common sense.

"I must have had a premonition that you were coming; I bought extra steak today. Emil writes down what we need, and I take the note and carry the groceries home if there are not too many. Generally we place a large order on Saturdays; so that we only have to buy meat during the weekdays," Louise chattered on in a cheerful vein as she passed potatoes, creamed peas, ketchup and bread to the visitors.

"Nothing's too good for miners," Emil exclaimed joyously as he stabbed a steak from where it swam in its juice on the large platter. "Let us eat while we still have our teeth; later we can drink milk and eat mush while we dream about steaks that we used to enjoy." He speared a thick slice of raw onion, bit half off, then grasped the t-bone in his fingers and tore hungrily at the delicious meat.

"I do believe you think more of your stomach than of me," Louise bantered as she watched her man do justice to brown meat and succulent gravy.

"More," he stated flatly.

"More?" Louise asked.

"Certainly, I have to first satisfy my hunger; then I feel like eating you, no steak no love."

"You certainly speak the truth, Emil. Before marriage you swore we would live on love. I do believe you stretched the point a bit. For awhile, our relations presented the aspect of a feast. Now, I have to take what crumbs you toss by the way as you go from work, to supper, to lodge activities, and thence to the saloon for cards and home to prepare for work again. I do believe that I like the change, though."

"Explain yourself." Emil wiped the film of brown gravy with a doubled slice of home-baked bread then holding aloft he contemplated its goodness before inserting it into his mouth.

"It's easier on me, you goose."

"In what way?" he asked through a full mouth with a wink aside at John.

"Oh, Emil, stop discussing our relations before company; you are embarrassing them."

"Who started this conversation?" Emil pushed back his chair with a contented series of groans; then reaching over, kissed his wife on the cheek saying, "That was a lovely supper. How you can cook!"

The men settled back to enjoy more coffee and a cigarette.

"Do you want to go leasing?" John put the question to Emil between sips of coffee and puffs on a cigarette.

"And why not? I've been waiting for you to get in the mood. I've had offers from other fellows; but have felt they wouldn't make agreeable partners for various reasons." Emil inserted his napkin through a ring and dropped it beside his plate.

"Let's go tomorrow and see what we can find."

"Alright by me, John," Emil answered jubilantly. "I'll be working graveyard tonight; but I'll meet you at the mine in the morning. We'll go down then and give the once-over."

"I'll be there." John pushed back his chair and graciously thanked Louise for the fine supper. "I have to rush along now; I don't want to seem rude; but I have a little matter of business to take care of downtown." He retrieved his hat, then pausing at the door, he remarked, "Rika is going to Park City to take over her father's store. He had a stroke."

"Damn!" Emil exploded, "when did that happen?"

"A couple of days ago; he can't speak a word, Rika said."

The sisters murmured their sympathy and Emil asked, "Why doesn't his wife run the store if Rika wants to stay here?"

"Her mother hasn't a business head, and besides, she has her hands full with her kids; six of them all younger than Rika. I'll see you, and thanks again for the nice meal."

The door slammed on his tall figure and Engrid gazed after with a look of hurt lurking momentarily in her eyes. Emil and Louise exchanged knowing glances; then Louise stood up and began clearing the table of dishes.

"Why don't you stay with me tonight, Engrid? Emil will be going on shift and I'll be alone. We can sit and enjoy a good talk."

Engrid accepted the suggestion eagerly, and the two of them fell to working while Emil went to town for a couple of hours at cards.

"Emil will probably get hungry tomorrow morning, I'll better put extra sandwiches in his bucket, as well as an additional apple. Get a bowlful from the cellar, will you Engrid?"

After the dishes were placed in the cupboard and the house tidied, Engrid sat while Louise worked on a beautiful piece of linen.

"What have you there, Louise? I haven't seen it before."

"A tablecloth for Rika and John. I thought it would be nice to make them something as I have plenty of time on my hands. Do you like it?"

Looking at the cloth with vague misgivings, Engrid ventured in a small voice, "But they haven't set a date; John told me that when we were coming here from town."

"That's right; but there is nothing like being prepared for an eventuality," Louise replied wisely. "As you say, there is nothing definite about it; although heaven knows they have had ample time in which to make up their minds; after sparking each other for two years."

"How did they meet?"

"John left here to work in the Park City mines. He met her at the Finn hall and they just naturally began going together. That's about all there is to it, except that as the Park City mines are too wet and cold, John had to leave because of rheumatism. Rika came down for a weekend after John came back, and as there was an opening in the Tintic store, she remained here."

"Did she come down just to see John?"

"No, her aunt lives here so Emil says Rika stays with her. She has a rooming house on Main Street by the lumber yard."

"And John, tell me about him."

"John was born in Park City. He father died when he was a youngster and his mother died three years ago. He is twenty-four, has a serious air about him, is handsome and, as far as I know, is well-liked by everybody. He never got a chance to go to college because his mother suffered for years and years with a heart ailment; so John went to work in the mines when he was sixteen."

"He was born here, then?"

"Oh, yes; although, like Rika, he has been interested enough in his parent's language to learn Swedish, first rate."

"Do you think she is pretty?"

"Who?"

"Rika, of course."

Raising her eyebrows, Louise glanced at her sister. "I think that she is about the loveliest, dark-haired girl I have had the pleasure of meeting. Of course, she has her faults; but I would attribute my recognition of them purely in the fact that as a woman, I am prone to look for something wrong in one so charming. Were I a man... oh, Engrid!" Louise exclaimed with a rapt expression on her face, "I would go for her in a big way. I'd rent a buggy each night and take her for a ride into the cedars, and what I would do I wouldn't want printed in papers."

Engrid appeared to be headed into a mood of despondency, Louise decided with an inward impatience at the girl's emotional difficulties.

"Engrid, you had better get John off your mind; their marriage was cut and dried before you showed up, and the quicker you get the notion out of your head that your appearance should automatically change the course of all your lives just because you want it so, the better off for all concerned."

These words, unexpected as they were, served to blow away the fog of Engrid's emotional confusion. She realized that wishful thinking was a poor substitute for the way things actually were. There was the new job with a raise in pay, and possibly the woman would be more considerate than the last one had been; whether because of kindness or a desire not to lose her. She accepted the rebuke with a laugh and her gloom dissipated itself. Eventually the sisters retired leaving Emil's lunch on the table where he would easily find it.

Chapter 17

John accosted his landlady at the breakfast table. "You won't have me bumming around even if it is my day off," he said making conversation.

"And where are you taking yourself to?"

"Emil and I are going down the Little Chief to look for a lease. I'm tired of working for timberman's wages; there is no future in it," he informed her between bites.

Alena accepted his statement without comment as she deftly placed platters of steaming pancakes before ravenous men who emptied them forthwith into puddles of syrup swimming on plates.

John wolfed down the generous meal, picked up his bucket and walked towards the mine, joining the group of men trudging slowly up the hill. These men moving with stooped shoulders and stolid footsteps would walk that way until they began their shift deep below the surface of the sun-lit ground. A half-hours work would set them to perspiring, and loosen stiff muscles. At the end of the shift, however, they would again revert to their weary, dejected gaits.

Chattering gaily as if they were children out for a holiday from school, a pair of boys who appeared to be no more than sixteen years of age, hurried past John. They were clothed in new caps, overalls and jumpers; each walked manfully in high-top boots whose hobnails left pockmarks in the dirt. In probability they were going into the mine for the first time, if looks of eagerness on brown faces were an indication of inexperience.

The mines wanted young men. It is the youngster who; bowing his back to the heaviest shovelful of ore, slave tirelessly throughout a shift under the supervision of older miners who has the youngster as a "man-Friday". The older men are incapable of doing the hardest and heaviest work.

"There they go in their ignorance and eagerness," John mused while remembering his first shift as if it were yesterday. "Thinking that no shaft is too deep to dig, or tunnel too long to run. When they find that the muck-stick is too much for them, they will become a miner for fifty cents a day more. What a hell of a future to look forward to; they'll work for a few years as a miner, then oblivion…"

However, there is a fascination about mining for the initiated; underground sounds and the penetrating and unique odor causing a miner to feel at home in the same manner that a fire horse is most spirited when surrounded by smoke from a burning building. There is idle conversation during the lunch hour concerning where fishing is best, which of Kitty's girls most companionable, and what brand of liquor most potent. And were all deer that miners have killed in conversations brought down the mines, not a soul could move through the shaft, filled as it would be with carcasses.

There is eager speculation concerning the discovery of bodies of ore in virgin ground; the deafening roar of the drilling machine, relentlessly boring into ground under the calm guidance of a snuff-chewing miner who is lulled into a state of hypnosis by the rotating drill sinking deeper and deeper into its hole. There are the frantic, hurried efforts of men doing contract work, who drill farther into solid rock then the proceeding shift which will in turn have to remove the biggest pile of muck before drilling again.

Above all, there is the unforgettable thrill when a leaser finds treasure that has been buried throughout eternity! Each day during the quest, another round of holes exposes changing ground; until finally a streak of quartz appears in dolomite on the face of the drift, causing a feeling of anticipation that is well-nigh unendurable. At that stage, the miner can hardly wait, after firing his round of shots, until the following day. Then comes the morning when returning to work, he finds that the tiny streak of the day before has broken into a full face of gold or silver ore. Here is the reality of dreams inherent in most of mankind, of finding buried treasure.

John saw Emil and waved at him while walking by the mine shaft, and together they went to the office of Charles Berquist, the Superintendent.

"What's on your minds, boys?"

"We are thinking of taking a lease," John replied.

The man nodded; then shoved a paper across the desk which would relieve the company of any responsibility for their safety underground.

"Sign here; take this map with you and give it to the shifter on the twelve-hundred level. He'll show you around. Grab a handful of candles as you go by the supply shed." The man dropped his eyes to a map he was studying.

"He seems pretty busy," Emil commented.

"He certainly is; but I wouldn't mind being as busy for the money he makes," John answered in reply.

"Where are you big Finns going?" asked the top station-tender who was running a heavy car on the cage. He slammed the cage bar down with a resounding clang, fastening the empty car in such a manner that it could not protrude into the shaft. He raised his hand in a flourish and the engineer in the hoisting room deftly caused the cage to be raised a foot or so. The top man jerked the chairs out, and the cage slid with a whispering sound of the shoes against guides, and a rattling of chains down the shaft. The heavy, grease-incrusted cable whipped by in a blur of shiny black; while the smokestack over the boiler room belched greasy smoke into the air. After a time, during which Emil and John made their wants know, the second cage, dripping glistening drops of water, appeared in the other compartment with startling swiftness. Under the able hands of the engineer, the cage rose high enough for the top man to throw the chairs under, then the engineer lowered the cage with a resounding jar. He released the cable a little so that the chairs held the heavy cage and the bottom of the car wheels level with the turn-sheet forming the floor.

The top man pulled the load of ore off, replacing it with the empty cart which a trammer had just returned from the ore bin overlooking the railroad tracks. The trammer exchanged his empty car for the load, deftly rolled it up the inclined ends of the steel rails, and away he went over a trestle until, at its end, the ore was dumped down a chute into a railroad car.

"There is a fine job for you," Emil remarked with a smirk.

"A fine job, hell," answered John voicing the distaste of an underground man for a top job. "It's hot as the hinges of hell in the summer and with the turn-sheet fairly cooking your feet. In the winter the snow freezes you to death, and with just a quarter-inch of snow on the rails after a storm, it takes three men to keep a car rolling."

"Look at all the fresh air you get," Emil pointed out.

"Yes, fresh air from the hot desert, and dust when you dump a car of dry ore and the wind blowing it back into your face. You can still give me the underground where the weather is the same the year around."

"That is all of the ore from the seven-hundred for now," the station-tender informed the argumentative men; "I'll send down a note and the cage-rider will go to the twelve. You fellows can go down on the next cage."

When it came up, the two men stepped on after the top man had closed the door on one side and hooked it with a chain; then he closed the second one, and grasping a cross-bar overhead to steady themselves during the descent into the shaft, the two men waited expectantly, their heads, shoulders and arms visible above the door of the cage.

The cage jerked aloft for a few feet, the chairs were withdrawn and blocked out of the way, and the panting of the powerful steam engine became inaudible as the men, taking one last look at the sunlit hills, swiftly descended into a gray hole which gradually became so black that eyes saw nothing but light splotches lingering on the retinas of their eyes. In the darkness, shuddering and rattling, the cage slid by places where the timber had lost its perpendicular alignment due to swelling ground. During this time, the slurping of the shoes on the wet guides accompanied the men in the darkness to their destination, twelve-hundred feet below the surface of the ground.

The mine smell, a combination of the odors of old fungus-covered timber, the fresh tang of new timber, the strong stench of sulfide ore and the fetid scent of burned powder rising on the up-draft, came to their nostrils in waves. Ears felt plugged and a ringing impinged itself on their consciousness. Water splashed on their faces, and involuntarily, they closed their eyes. A loud clanking told them that a loose slab of rock had detached itself from the wall somewhere above them, striking the protecting, inverted, v-shaped bonnets, and a shower of finer material bounced off the timbered sides spattering their caps and faces as it sifted into the cage. The second cage, rising, passed them with a clanking, jarring sound and was gone. The sensation of dropping through the confines of the shaft had long since lost its terror, although a queer emptiness of mingled pleasure and pain gripped the men's loins as the cage slowed abruptly, then stopping, left them jouncing up and down as a result of the spring inherent in the twisted steel cable.

"Damn that engineer!" John exploded indignantly, "I'll break his neck with my bare hands, or warp a length of starter-steel around it when we get on top. He ought to know better than to pick us up that fast."

"Ah," Emil said in a placating way, "he just had a grudge against the world this morning. Probably his wife didn't treat him right last night."

"Dammee… wot's doin' 'ere?" asked a little man who released them from the cage after spitting a generous gob of tobacco juice which shot between the rails at the bottom of the cage, barely missing the men's feet.

"Someday you're going to miss your mark when you spit like that," John said threateningly, "and you'll have a beautiful funeral. I wouldn't doubt but what they'd let the company men off for the day, and pay them wages in the bargain."

The cage-rider laughed shrilly, "I never 'its a man."

"You will someday, and then…" John made a suggestive motion with his huge paws turning in opposites directions as though wringing the neck of the fowl.

"Ye'll 'ave ter ketch'm first, 'n 'twould be 'n 'ard job; there's better neer three-hunnert miles o' tunnel ter 'ide in," the cage-rider said with an infectious smirk.

"Where is the shift boss?" John asked with a smile as he visualized himself racing through the dark mine, moving up slippery ladders, then sliding down ore chutes with intent to commit assault on the little man.

"'e'll be in the Delaware or Michigan 'bove sill-floor. A bit o' timberin' ter do."

John and Emil turned away from the man who was pushing one of several carloads of glittering ore onto the cage. They walked awkwardly between rails following the winding tunnel through devious twists and turns.

A rumbling that grew in volume and a dull glow, far ahead on a straight stretch of track, informed them that a trammer was bringing a carload of ore toward the shaft. Finding a wide part of the drift, the men stepped aside and allowed the car and the youth pushing it to pass. For an instant, they saw a begrimed, straining face down which perspiration rolled; then the young man was gone with a shout of "H'ya, fellows!" and the rumbling diminished in the distance.

The partners continued with lit candles flickering on dark walls. The tunnel twisted and turned as though the men who mined it out of solid rock had been drunk. In all probability they were; however, the twisting had followed breaks that were marked on the map where ore might possibly be found. Momentarily, the men came to the bottom of a wooded chute where behind broad gates, galena and silver ore glittered.

"This is the Michigan," Emil announced as he peered around at the heavy timbers forming the support for the chute. "Up we go!"

For seventy-five feet they climbed a series of ladders which were nailed to the heavy timbers. Ore was dumped from transfer cars rumbled at frequent intervals inside of the chute. Each time the men heard muck rushing down; they hugged the ladder and pulled their necks into their shirt-collars to prevent fine dust from trickling inside of their clothing.

"Nothing down but the fine stuff, and damn little of that!" John roared as a car rumbled to a stop overhead; a chain clanked as it was drawn from a handle and the laborer prepared to dump the load.

"C'mon on up; I'll hold it," said a muffled voice; thus allaying their trepidation.

At the top of the ladder they came face-to-face with a panting trammer who greeted them with a perfunctory wave of his hand.

"Hell, if I had known it was you and your square-head partner, I'd have dumped the whole damn load down the man-way."

"If you had, ass, you wouldn't live long enough to load the car again." John growled as he tapped the young man on the chest with a light blow which the grinning youth parried, then countered with a blow of his own to the big man's head. Then the trammer stepped back, hands in front of his face, on guard.

John failed to follow with another blow but asked instead, "Where's Pendray?"

Dropping his hands, the youth reached for tobacco and paper, "He's inside chewing the fat with the timbermen."

"Say 'Sir' when you address a miner," John growled.

"Sir!" the trammer sneered.

John thanked him and held the candle for the youth to light his cigarette; then the would-be leasers walked down the track their candles reflecting on the ebony sides of the tunnel until they came to a part of the passage where ore had been found. They traveled a few feet further; then John halted Emil.

"Take a look at that, will you?" he exclaimed as he pointed with his candle to where a statue of a woman approximately three feet high was sitting.

"White clay," Emil grunted, "I wonder where that young whelp has seen a naked female? Just look at that, every bit of the body is perfectly proportioned."

"The boy has talent," John said admiringly.

"Talent, hell," Emil grunted, "it's easy to see that his mind is on one of Kitty's girls."

"Roberta, by golly!" John kidded, "The Spanish dancer."

Jut then a car rumbled to a halt and the youth glanced from the men to the statue. "So that's how you spend your dinner hour?" John said, giving him a dig in the ribs.

"Certainly; why?" Max McCune answered. "A man can't spend a whole shift by himself and not have something to take his mind off work."

"Get out of this place and make your living at it!" John encouraged him; then they left the youth staring dreamy-eyed at the statue.

The pair of men moved under caps; heavy timber held in a horizontal position by sturdy posts. On top of the caps was lagging; forming a roof which was the floor for the square-set above. They climbed up ladders of the stope which had been divided into sets roughly six-feet by six-feet square and from which ore had been removed; then replaced by timber so that the men mining ore could follow its course up a man-made canyon. Timbers were butted against the solid ground by blocks and tightly driven wedges.

As they climbed from one square-set to another, muffled voices came from above and the swishing stream of each shovelful of ore falling past, showed that muckers were bowing their backs. Occasionally, the feeble gleam of light winked through cracks between laggings, far overhead. The picking sounded with heavier emphasis when a miner went to work in earnest and breaking a huge slab of ore which rumbled past, followed by a dribble of finer particles.

As a relative silence followed the descent of the slab, John called, "Is Pendray there?"

Pick sounds stopped and a voice answered, "I'm here; what do you want?"

"Come on, Emil," John said as he climbed up a ladder to emerge on the top of the last set where he stood panting under a mass of solid, shining silver and lead ore, shot through with streaks of blue.

"Well, boys, what in the hell are you doing here?" the clean-shaven, dark-featured man greeted them. Turning to Emil he remarked, "I thought you were working night-shift, timbering."

"I vas, but I'm going to find me a lease and git out from onder da shifter's heel," Emil said, mouthing each word as does a son of the north. He reached for a sack of "tobok" and carefully filled a pipe.

"More power to you, big Finn. If you can't cut 'er, the company will be glad to have you back again."

"Do you know of any likely-appearing places?" John asked.

"Did the Sup give you the maps?"

"He did."

"Let's go down on the sill–floor out of this noise and have a look," Bob said after a miner gave his machine an experimental burst of air and the huge driller roared its challenge to the rock tomb.

As the men began their descent, there hung a blue haze of acrid powder smoke and dust causing them to gasp, cough and wipe at tears.

"Gassy as hell in this stope," Emil remarked.

"Yes it is," Bob replied, "but we'll hole through with a raise at the far side of the stope in a day or two on the one-thousand; then we'll have a natural draft to take it out."

Down they went further and further.

"This is a mighty big stope," John remarked.

"One of the biggest in the mine," Pendray answered. "It will be bigger if the pay-rock keeps going up to join the stope on the seven-hundred, and I wouldn't be surprised if it did."

Emil produced the map and Pendray, unrolling it, spread it on the floor; then weighted corners with chunks of ore so that the print might be plainly visible.

"You men have timbered in most of these places; so both of you can find the spots that I point out to you; here, here, and here." He indicated the three places with the point of his sample-pick. "On any of these streaks that the company has by-passed to take the main body of ore out, you men have a chance to make some real money. You'll find tags on wood in drill holes at places indicated, and a sheet in a box showing the value of the streaks. All you have to do is follow one until you find a big ore-body."

"If there is any," John remarked.

"How simple it is to say," Emil grunted and poked the shifter in the ribs.

"Take it or leave it, boys. The engineer said the streaks were not worth bothering with; that there was no chance of ore making in their general direction. He claims that these are only feeders to the bodies of ore already taken out."

"And what does an engineer know," John scoffed; "he can only see as far into rock as we can. I remember..."

"Oh, hell," Bob broke in to say, "you Finns are all alike. Here, take the map and get the hell out of here before I throw you down a chute."

The shifter took leave of the men, to make his rounds through other stopes; muttering as he walked away.

"How any woman can mother a baby that will grow into apes as big as you are, is beyond me."

Emil grinned crookedly; then turned to his partner saying, "What do you think, John?"

"Let's look all three places over; then make a decision. I have a hunch," he pointed to one of the crosses that the shifter had marked on the blueprint, "that this one here is our best bet. Notice how the stopes, here and here, are made on the same fault. Let's go and look them over and if we have to, we can flip a coin. Ore is where you find it, and we don't find it by squatting here on our butts."

"Let's get it over with, then." Emil suggested and rising to his full height, he stretched powerful arms over his head.

By eleven o'clock the two men had definitely made their choice, and they sauntered down the track to where Pendray waited for the noon cage to take him to the surface for lunch; a privilege which only the bosses enjoyed. Other men ate lunch in close proximity to where they worked.

They notified the shifter of their intentions to take a particular block of ground and of their desire to start work the following morning.

"Go to the office and sign a lease." Bob directed them. "The supply clerk will fit you out with everything you need, except brains, and your mother forgot those."

"Oh, as if you had paid a dollar for your brains and got short-changed ninety-nine cents," John said with a chuckle.

"What are you going to do with all the money you make?" Pendray asked.

"Start a fund for broken down shift bosses who are too lazy to work," John replied.

Further disparaging remarks were cut short when the cage stopped and the men crowded on; six men standing in two rows facing the end of the shaft. Soon the partners; squinting their eyes at the unaccustomed glare of the sun, walked to the office where they signed a lease guaranteeing the company a flat royalty on any and all ores produced in addition to paying for expenses incurred in the process of mining and prospecting.

" It's lucky we're going into the leasing game before the farmers come to spend the winter underground," Emil observed as they walked away from the mine; "That's the life for a man; living on the farm and regaining your health in the summer, and coming up here in the fall, strong as a bull to make more money away from the cold."

"What do you mean, 'lucky'?"

"They'll jump onto these streaks and we'd have to work for the company."

"If we don't find ore, we'll be going around town asking for handouts inside of two months," Emil observed with a rueful smile.

"And whose fault will that be except yours?"

"What do you mean, 'mine'?"

"It was you who talked me into leasing."

"Go on back and work for the company, you big Finn."

"And watch you driving a nice black horse, and smoking fifty-cent cigars and drinking Scotch whiskey, oh, no!" John stated with a shake of his head.

Emil laughed heartily as they took separate paths; Emil to his home, and John to the boarding house where he bathed, changed clothes and went to town where he whiled away the remainder of the afternoon playing cards.

Ten minutes before Rika was due to leave work for the day, he crossed the street from the saloon and seated himself on a bench before O'Day's barbershop. When Rika made her appearance, he stood up, swept off his had and offered her his arm.

"Well," she exclaimed, "what are you doing here?"

"As it is to be your last evening here, I thought that perhaps you might like to dine at the restaurant."

"That is ever so thoughtful of you; however, I hardly think that I am dressed to dine out. Couldn't you wait until I change my clothes?"

"You look like a red rose and smell as sweet as a garden of them; and dressed the way you are, you're the most beautiful woman in town." John said gallantly.

That did it! The couple walked into the Chinese eating house and seated themselves at a table covered with a white and red checkered cloth. A wrinkled oriental came forward with an ingratiating smile and inquired of their wants. The couple decided on pork chops with apple pie for dessert; then the proprietor left to prepare their meal.

"What did you do today?" Rika asked as she gave the wheel of conversation a spin.

"I went to the mine and signed for a lease; Emil is my partner," John replied; then placing his tongue in his cheek, he warily regarded his lovely companion.

"No…"

"Yes," John replied in a matter-of-fact voice.

"That means…"

"That I won't be going to Park City with you."

"But mother and father planned on it," she protested with a hurt look from her beautiful eyes.

"I'm sorry, Rika; but I can't stand the thoughts of kowtowing to every old lady who wants a yard of ribbon or flannel for baby diapers. It would be like confining me in a dungeon. My interest is mining, not merchandising. I want to produce something and make some money at it."

Rika fingered her engagement ring and almost removed it on a sudden impulse; she changed her mind, however, as the cook came with their soup and she fell to supping.

"Why can't you come to Park City with me and work in the mines there?" the girl broke in on John's thoughts to ask. "You could be near me; we could be married. I want to marry you if you will come up there, and you don't have to work in the store. Work where you want to."

"I might be near you; but not in Park City," he replied.

"Why not, dear."

"I don't want to work there because the mines are all too wet; and in the second place, you object most emphatically to my drinking, moderate as it is. You and your mother would manage to make life a bit of hell if I came home, after working all day and insisted on having a glass of liquor to give me an appetite and take the chill from my bones. No, thank you for your invitation; but if there is going to be any planning as to where my wife and I are to live, I am going to have the say. It will be I who will have to support the family!"

"But," Rika said hopefully, "we wouldn't have to raise a family. I could go right on working and our combined earnings would amount to quite a sum."

"That's where you and I differ again, Rika. If it is just a woman, I could go to one of the sporting houses." John said, lowering his voice. "I want some kids to welcome me when I come home at night. If I didn't have them, all I would do is come home to a cold house; build the fire and have supper for you when you came home later on, or else eat in a restaurant. No, thank you; it just isn't my line of reasoning. It would be worse than living in a boarding house."

Rika continued to eat in silence; although she was tempted to take a vocal stand against what her companion was saying.

"Rika," John continued, "I have gone into this so many times that to speak of it is a waste of breath. I hardly know what to say anymore, or how to say it. If I go there and marry you; God only knows that I want to do just that, I'd be contented for just so long; then I would start hating those wet mines with their cold water. I'd blow up and come back here where conditions are more to my liking. Stay here and marry me, dear, please!"

Rika peered into the face of the man she wanted on her own terms. A film of tears showed in her eyes as she laid aside her fork when her meal suddenly became tasteless.

"I'd like to go, John; I've things to pack and I must get some sleep."

John helped her with her cloak; then he waited, hat in hand while she tied her belt, and together they walked up the street in silence, each deeply troubled with thoughts running in futile, wavering circles in their minds, only to come back to conclusions that were irreconcilable. Each felt weary with trying to find a means of breaking a deadlock that had grown to gigantic proportions since the girl's father had fallen ill.

"I wonder how things would have been if father hadn't become sick? Perhaps we could be married happily. As things are, who would run the store which I managed after leaving school? I alone know to whom to extend credit, who is worthy of more in an emergency such as illness or accident. Only I can follow the trends in styles and place orders for future deliveries so that, when inventories are taken each year, there will not be piles of useless articles gathering dust on obscure shelves."

To this reasoning, John sorrowfully agreed. Obviously, the young woman was "on the spot". The transient population of the camp presented a problem requiring the services of an experienced manager at a handsome salary which would have to be made up by an increase in prices. Price increases meant lost customers, and lost customers indicated eventual failure of the business.

"I am right back where I was when I started thinking about the whole mess," she said as she paused at the door of her aunt's house. Turning, she faced John who stood unyielding and dejected.

"Oh, sweetheart," she murmured, "I'm sorry things have to turn into such a mess. I'll go home and take charge of the store because I have to. I'll write you, and who knows, if we don't try to hurry life, we may come out on top of the muck-pile; as you have so often said."

John grasped the girl's hands in his own. "I don't know what to say, Rika; but I love you very much, how much I do not know; because there are as many kinds of love as there are people. Maybe if things pan out and I strike it rich, you'll forget about the store."

"I'm afraid not," she replied sadly, "I belong to my family. Mother and father as well as the kids, they all need me. Sometimes," she mused, running her graceful fingers over John's calloused palm, "I believe that God uses us as tools to work out his desires. Perhaps the things that he wants us to do are problems we failed to face in the last life, I don't know. We almost had happiness in our grasp; and I did intend to stay here and marry you, at the same time keeping my work at the store. We'll feel hurt for awhile, John," she said soberly; "but that, too, will vanish and things will turn out right for us in the end."

Her voice sounded weary in spite of the optimism which she tried to place into her words. Raising John's hand, she kissed it and a tear fell on his wrist.

"Are you trying to tell me that we are through?"

"Yes, dear," she replied with down-cast eyes.

"Marry me, Rika, tomorrow," he pleaded.

"No, John, I…"

"I'll come to Park City."

"We can't; we must not," the girl exclaimed tearfully, knowing full well the inevitability of a rupture in their relationship should they marry, and the resultant suffering.

In a daze and his face contorted with anguish, the big man raised his hands to his head and jolted his forehead. "Oh, God," he moaned, "why did I have to learn to care like this?"

"The ring… I'll keep it until we see how things turn out. Kiss me and go, dear, I feel as though I might cry, and I don't want to do it here."

"Here is one kiss no other man will ever take from you," John said in a husky voice as he folded the girl into his arms and kissed her brutally, while she hung limp and un-protesting.

"Goodbye, John…"

Turning down the street, John made straight for Smith's saloon where he drank several glasses of whiskey. Taking a full bottle with him, he went to his room and locked the door; then sank to his bed and sipped at the bottle while staring morosely at Rika's picture. At length he brushed at tears threatening to break into a flood; then he stretched out on his bed and fell into a stupor.

Rika laid wide-eyed watching moonlight creep across the floor. Finally she turned on her pillow and cried herself to sleep. Her restless slumber was filled with a dream which occurred again and again. Her lover was holding her in his arms and kissing her as he wrapped baby blankets and handed them to an endless line of Engrids who accepted the change that John handed back with each purchase and made for the door.

Such is the stern way of life where only in dreams can all mortal men realize wish-fulfillment. Wide-eyed and unseeing we stumble through our waking hours, toward some dimly visualized goal.

Chapter 18

The following morning, John stood on the front porch with a third cup of black coffee in his hand as the train thundered by. A window framed a white face waving a lace handkerchief. John raised his cup in a gesture of bravado that he did not feel and he muttered bitterly, "Skoal!" He drank the brew, threw the cup across the railroad track where it smashed against a barn; then turned his back and walked into the kitchen. He flipped a fifty-cent piece to a startled Alena saying, "Catch." Picking up a lunch pail with more black coffee sloshing around in its bottom compartment, he strode purposefully up the road to the supply room where they took stock of equipment.

"Everything is on the bill, fellows," said the clerk. "The bull-gang has put in a frog and switch to take you off the main line. I hope you strike it rich!" he said heartily.

"I'll buy yew a qvart of da pest viskey om ve do," Emil promised.

"By the way," the clerk called as they turned from the window, "there are three sets of drill-steel in the car with our machine. Send up your dull ones each shift and write your name on a piece of powder box attached to your dull drills and picks so we can get the right ones back to you."

The two men joined the throng of miners moving forward as the top man called out the level numbers in order that the men might board the proper cage. Finally it came their turn and they were to be dropped into the fetid vapor, rushing up the shaft. They waited until the supplies were delivered to the lower levels; then piled their equipment onto ore and flat cars. They pushed the cars back to the cut-tunnel adjacent to where they intended to work, and unloaded them. The graveyard bull-gang had already tapped into the four-inch air line; so they connected the hose to the machine after blocking a horizontal bar into place across the tunnel.

Together the men lifted the huge piston machine onto the clamp which was rigidly affixed to the crossbar by bolts. The bar had been set up approximately the length of a pick away from the face of the tunnel. John placed a candle into a crevice. Emil held the machine at an upward angle so that John could insert a starter; a drill approximately two-and-a-half feet long, into the end of the slugger. The steel hit bottom with a chocking sound and the men pointed the machine to drill upward on a thirty-degree angle for the back-holes. They tightened the clamp so that the machine would stay firmly in place. John screwed the machine forward until the drill touched the hard rock.

"Turn on the air, Emil, and I'll give it a try," he suggested after pouring oil into a cylinder.

Emil spun the valve, and air hissed into the hose. John shoved a lever forward until the drill began to turn with an ear-splitting clatter. The drill slipped out of line and stopped. John shut off the air.

"Collar the hole with a pick," he suggested.

Emil complied; then John barely allowed the drill to push against the ground. As it rotated, a hammer inside of the machine pounded at the base of the drill, causing it to strike the ground and a stream of dust flying from the hole, instantly enveloped the men. After the drill had gone forward as the set of the machine would allow, John withdrew the dull steel and replaced it with one a foot longer, although smaller in diameter at the end so that it would easily follow the hole. Finally after changes the men considered the depth of the hole sufficient.

They alternated at the task of drilling until by lunch time, they had the top half of the round in. After dinner, they lowered the machine to finish the bottom round. The lowest holes were pointed downward and outward a trifle.

"This rock is hard as Kitty's heart the day before payday," Emil observed as he loosened the machine. He disconnected the hose and attached an air pipe to it. After moving all equipment into the cross-cut tunnel, and at a signal from John, Emil turned on the air and John thrust the pipe into a hole. With a soughing, roaring sound, interspersed with sever thumping sounds as the end of the pipe struck the bottom of the holes and filled the tunnel with dust, John blow the debris out of the holes.

Into the detonating caps, the men inserted six-foot lengths of fuse and clamped the primer tightly over the one end of the inserted fuses. With a stick, they shoved holes through the powder and inserted the primers. They carefully slit the sticks with their knives, then shoved them cautiously to the far end of the holes, and tamped them fast with a long pole. In quick succession, Emil split other sticks, and John tamped them in until the holes were full to within six inches of the collars.

Eighteen white fuses protruded from the holes. John decided which of the three cut holes; those breast high and pointed downward, that he wished to shoot first. He whetted a knife on a stone and cut a foot off the fuse. Holding the segment next to the hole in his left hand, he coiled the fuse around so that it formed several concentric circles about five inches in diameter. He then twisted the end of the fuse through the rings and cut it down an inch exposing the white string running through the center and surrounded by black powder. This fuse, if not defective, would burn at the rate of a foot a minute. If the fuse was defective, the undertaker did a good business.

All of the fuses were cut in varying lengths so that they would explode in sequence; then the partners laid rails to the face of the tunnel. Over these they placed lagging to form a floor, and on the planks muck to keep explosions from raising them.

Most of the exploded rock would now fall on the boards and make mucking easier than if they had to shovel it from between the rails and off to their sides.

They waited until all miners had come up to their tunnel from farther back in the mine; then John asked, "Is everything alright?"

"Alright," Emil responded after looking around to see that everything was in the clear.

John took a piece of fuse and notched it along its length, then he set it afire and as the powder in the fuse burned, it showered fire out of each opening. When this occurred, the man calmly held the flame to the gaping ends of the fuses until soon he was engulfed in a cloud of blinding smoke.

"Fire!" he called, between spasms of coughing as he grabbed his jacket and lunch bucket then hurried out of the tunnel with smoke trailing him. After they had gone a safe distance around a bend, they paused; waiting for several minutes and during this time from the ground in every direction, came the muffled sounds of shots as rounds exploded.

A knocking sounded in the ground about them followed by a swooshing current of air that extinguished their candles and left them in Stygian darkness.

"One…" John and Emil said in unison, "…two, three, four, five," and so on, until all of the holes were accounted for. They drew relieved sighs, knowing that on the 'morrow they wouldn't run the risk of drilling into a missed hole with its resultant carnage. Matches flared, candles were lit and buckets in hand the partners walked toward the shaft, feeling thankful that the shift was over, but hoping, as all leasers did, that on the following day they would be back on the job, pounding each other's backs as they joyfully surveyed a rich body of glittering ore.

Squatting on their haunches, they waited for a cage to stop at their level. They watched loads of men from lower levels ride by, their snatches of conversation rising; then fading quickly leaving a tomb-like silence; broken only by monotonous drip, drip, dripping of water into a tiny pool beside the track. Occasionally a falling rock hissed by down the shaft. Finally a cage slowed and stopped at their station.

"Git t'ell out o' 'ere. I don't want to se yer bloomin' fice 'again," the cage-rider said with a grin as he reached up over the door and pulled John's hat down over his eyes. John's hands pinned at his sides bellowed an irate curse. "Suck in yer guts… 'ow in 'ell do 'e 'spect one to close the cige on ye? 'ow in 'ell did you mother belch sich a lout o' man?"

The cage moved swiftly up the shaft into the darkness; flashing past stations, the cage's occupants glimpsed tired men biding their time, their candles glowing like fireflies in the rocky chambers.

A pale gray radiance shone on timbers of the shaft, and with a few more wraps of the cable, they were on the surface; their eyes squinted in the strong light and breathing thankfully of air which felt comfortably warm.

At the boardinghouse, Alena divulged the startling information that Alex had departed on the eleven o'clock train for Salt Lake City, and from there he intended to go to Park City.

"So his landlady told me when I saw her in the store today," the woman explained. "She said that Alex had told her to send his laundry to him at general delivery, Park City."

"Well," John mused, "he could at least have told us goodbye. I wonder what his hurry was about"

"I wouldn't know," she said, "he slept late, ate breakfast with the rest of the nightshift; and after that, he wandered about nervous as a man after a week-long drunk."

"It seems odd that Rika and Alex should leave on the same day. Maybe the boy intends to work for Rika!" he said, "wouldn't that be something; he doesn't like the mines and his temperament is just suited to that type of work. I hope he makes a million! Maybe he might even marry into the business, now that there isn't much chance of her old man going back to work."

Alena regarded John with amazement. "What in heaven's name are you talking about, boy? Am I to understand that things are over between you and Rika?"

"I suppose so; she wanted me to work with her or in the mines there; I refused."

"Why, don't you love the girl?"

"More than any, but I don't like clerking or wet mines; besides, there isn't any leasing up there. She wanted everything her own way."

"I can see your point. I suppose you'll just have to let the matter work it's self out. I am sorry, though; I think that you and Rika would make a fine couple for a wedding." Mrs. Kosky heaved a pensive sigh.

"Aw," John chided her, "Cheer up; someday I'll meet the right one; then I shall have a wedding that will go down in the annals of this mining camp. I'll furnish enough drinks to float the Finn hall away, and the most beautiful girl in the world will share the chair tossing with me. I'll have the best music I can find and the biggest crowd of guests that ever packed the hall for any occasion. Could I get you to take care of refreshment?"

"My stars, boy, aren't you a little premature? You haven't even got the bride yet; you said Alex might have … just what are you talking about?"

"I'm just dreaming, just dreaming," John answered cryptically as he fingered leaves of the oleander; then hands in pockets, he started out of the window for a time. "What do you think of Engrid?"

He might as well have thrown a stick of dynamite under the woman with a short fuse ignited so startled was Alena's expression; as pausing in her dusting, she held a chair and the rag motionless. Turning, she peered into John's face.

"Satan will take you! What manner of a man are you, engaged to one and your mind on another, for shame!"

John's face was wrapped in a half-cynical, half-amused smile as he looked at Alena.

"When I became engaged, she took it more in the manner of a lark than anything else. It was just one of those proposals that she made the mistake of accepting on the spur of the moment. Neither of us knew very much about the other. She doesn't particularly care for me the way I am, and the longer we went together, the more obvious it has been that we just couldn't make a go of things. She has kept hammering at me, trying to cure me of a few of my habits which she has never condoned, such as getting drunk occasionally, playing cards for a pass time, and just plain hell-raising."

"I think a woman is to be commended for trying to make a man finer than he is." Alena said emphatically.

"You know, Mrs. Kosky," John went on, seeming not to hear her last remark, "now that I think things over, I can clearly visualize what would happen to me after I slipped a ring on her finger after marriage. She would probably insist on piercing my nose and staking me out in her dear mother's house; one of those that they rent to married men and use that wedding ring in the same manner that a farmer uses a ring to govern a bull. Probably the only time she would show me any love is when she would condescend to spend a night with me, because she happened to remember me between pounds, yards and dollar signs when she vaguely recalled that she had married someone, sometime. None of that for me," he said, raising his voice and dribbling small change through fingers into a trouser pocket. "I want a woman who will make me the center of attraction at home, and Satan can take me if I don't find one someday."

"Humph!" Alena sniffed as she vigorously applied the rag to a chair; then scraped a fleck of egg yolk from the seat, "you'd better become a member of the Mormon church."

"I want a woman," John continued with a devil-may-care expression shining wickedly from his eyes, "who will pull off my shoes and stockings when I come home so tired that I can hardly move; who will put the coffee pot on while I sit there thinking how lovely and kind she is; who will love me at night, and if it isn't too cold in the mornings when an extra hour of sleep is appreciated by a man, will make the fire, bring a cup of coffee to bed, kiss me good morning, light a cigarette for me so I can stir my stiffened body by degrees; while I think how marvelous it is to have a woman so attentive and kind. Boy-oh-boy," he sighed, staring off into space, not even seeing the wallpaper, his eyes rested on.

"Dream on," Alena scoffed, "Lincoln, I am told, freed the slaves."

Chapter 19

When Engrid arrived at the Tintic Hotel, Mrs. Meyers invited her to a cup of coffee before making her acquainted with her surroundings and routine. Engrid observed, as the woman pointed out, that the hotel was a two-story, wooden-framed building with twelve rooms on each floor. The owner occupied two rooms where she slept, cooked and supervised her business of making a home for occasional drummers, but for the most part, a hotel peopled by bachelor miners furnishing her with a regular income.

"My second husband left me this place when he died of a fall down the stairs. He came home one night, drunk as a hoot-owl. He probably tried to walk erect up the stairs; he lost his balance and fell backwards. When I heard the bumping noise, I found him halfway down the stairs, his head twisted sideways against the banisters. He died right there in my arms, poor dear." Mrs. Meyers wiped at red eyes.

"Oh," Engrid remarked, understanding only part of the monologue.

"Yes, that he did; but such is life," the loquacious woman added with a sigh. She dabbed at her eyes again; then pointed out to Engrid the men who came off nightshift to sleep, would hang a "Do Not Disturb" on their doors and the other rooms could be cleaned first. The sheets and pillowcases would be changed once a week, except in rooms reserved for guests not boarders.

While Engrid was busily sweeping an accumulation of dirt and papers from the boardwalk in front of the hotel, a familiar voice called her name. Turning, she stared wide-eyes at Mrs. Wilken who had come to her mother-in-law's to sob out her tale of woe; how the ungrateful girl had left her with hands practically tied to the point where she would be unable to entertain her club members.

"Engrid!" gasped the woman with both arms raised aloft, and her mouth forming a circle of surprise below the pointed beak of her nose; her jaw fell slack as consternation shone in her eyes.

The girl's eyes dropped for a moment; then the realization came to her that this woman had undoubtedly held a strong grip on her. She quickly shed embarrassment and a tiny sense of fear as she grasped the broom in knotted fists fastened near the end of the handle. She surveyed the woman with assumed nonchalance, somehow, managing a friendly smile.

"Well?" Mrs. Wilken snapped.

"Little vork, bedder hours, and more monee." Engrid said sweetly.

"Oh, you...you..." the woman stuttered and with fists clenched on the handle of her umbrella, she stepped menacingly toward the girl.

Engrid moved the broom to her shoulder, still grasping it tightly; then allowed her grip to relax as Mrs. Wilken glanced up at the open window where she caught a glimpse of her mother-in-law's head as it was pulled back through parted curtains billowing gently in a warm breeze.

Casting Engrid a look of veiled hate, Mrs. Wilken burst through the doorway of the hotel and up the stairs she hurried at a fast pace, her long skirts grasped in a hand. Engrid methodically completed her task; then, with bated breath and shining eyes, she followed up the stairs in the wake of the flustered woman.

Mrs. Wilken breezed into the kitchen where her relative stirred at a small pot of mush with an assumed air of sanctimonious innocence. Inwardly, a sense of guilt and apprehension clutched at Mrs. Meyers corset-encased stomach; however, at the approach of her kin, she turned and called airily, "Good morning, my dear, how are you? What brings you up so early in the morning? Have a chair." Turning she looked at the mush in the wake of her moving spoon.

"Good morning, did you say? What's good about it? How dare you make such a remark? How dare you pretend such child-like innocence after what you have done to me? You wretch!"

Feigning surprise, Mrs. Meyers, after pounding the spoon on the edge of the kettle, shoved it to the back of the small stove and looked directly at the face of her irate visitor. She moved to the side a few steps and leaned against the table.

"What in the world are you so upset for? Has my son gone on another bender?" she asked.

"You know as well as I that such isn't the matter. Why did you come sucking around my ingrate of a maid and lure her here to work for you, after I went to the trouble of breaking her in to the routine of my housework?"

"But I haven't forced the girl to come here; I merely told her that I would give her an increase in pay if she would come to work at a job that is easier and has shorter hours."

"Shorter hours, did you say? Less work; tending to a hotel this size? You have certainly got your crust!"

"Certainly; she will be through every day at two o'clock when she works for me because I will help. She has the rest of the day off except for filling lamps in the rooms each evening, and that won't take long. She's going to like working for me."

"You still have no business…"

"Mrs. Kosky put me wise to what you were doing to the girl, because you had her buffaloed into believing you were the only one who could use her. She told me how you have been forcing the girl to use her rest period to cut rags for rugs and mind the baby while you have gone gallivanting around town, using the excuse that cutting rags is not hard work. Don't think things like that can be kept quiet when there are so many women in need of working girls."

"You dirty son-of-a-bitch!" the accused cried advancing on Mrs. Meyers. Mrs. Meyers picked up a stove poker with which to defend herself. For the second time Mrs. Wilken found herself blocked by a weapon. She paused, clenching and unclenching her fists. Turning, she haughtily made for the door with her head high in the air, while throwing a pair of words over her shoulder which loosed the floodgates of Mrs. Meyer's fury. "You slut!" she spat.

Mrs. Meyer dropped the poker and her calculating glance roving about for something not quite so lethal in pressing the attack on her retreating daughter-in-law, chanced to see a pan of greasy dishwater saved from the night before. Grasping it in her hands, she turned into the hall where Engrid paused in her sweeping just in time to observe the water cascading on the shiny silk coat and straw hat whose feathers bobbed each agitated step that the woman took, "And, so help me," Engrid gasped and giggled later with her hand over her mouth, "squarely into the startled woman's face when she chanced to look over her shoulder."

Moaning like a wounded animal, Mrs. Wilken fled into the street where people looked at her with mingled amusement and surprise. The bedraggled woman, frantically removing her coat, entered an alley in order to avoid meeting a group of men striding along in the direction of the Gemini mine.

Mrs. Meyer swaggered down the slippery steps, a contemptuous air of bravado and arrogance in every movement. She tiptoed to the door, stepping gingerly lest she slip in the soapy water; and peered with a smug satisfaction after the fleeing enemy.

"She'll probably be so humiliated that she won't dare tell my son of this incident," she told herself. "I don't give a damn if she does; because she shouldn't have called me those filthy names; and her a society woman, too. It serves her right, coming into her own mother-in-law's house with hate in her eyes and murder in her heart. She'll think twice before she ever spits again on a woman whom she considers beneath her," she said with a glance at Engrid who peered expectantly down from the banister-enclosed landing. "All this because some people had to work for a living." Turning again to the door, she noted that Mrs. Wilken had vanished. "She's gone slinking up the alley like the cat she is!" she spat as she walked up the stairs.

"Clean up that mess, Engrid," the woman said to the girl who in all truth was glad to comply.

To think that she had found a champion and the in-law of her former employer at that! She met the eyes of Mrs. Meyers with a sheepish glance and a grin displaying a mouthful of white teeth. Mrs. Meyer gravely dropped one eyelid in a slow wink, followed by a smile which illumined her face as she went to prepare breakfast.

Engrid was called to breakfast after wiping the soapy water up and drying the banisters. She ate heartily of mush, eggs, bakery-made bread and ranch butter with a slightly rancid taste. The woman was actually cooking for her hired help.

Engrid wound up her work well within the predicted time so she left with a flushed face to see Mrs. Kosky.

After an exchange of greetings, Engrid inquired, "Would you be going to town this afternoon?"

"Certainly, Engrid; what would you be wanting? Some help with choosing clothes, perhaps? Oh, by the way, how do you like your new job?"

Engrid related the day's events, pantomiming the happenings and concluding her description with a sweeping movement of her arms in imitation of Mrs. Meyer's triumphal banishment of her visitor.

"Don't tell me any more," pleaded the corpulent woman who laughed until her figure threatened to burst from her corsets, while she wiped at tears streaming down her face. "Never have I heard anything so funny," she gasped. "Now, child, what is it that you have on your mind?"

"I want Mr. Wilken to know that his wife refused to pay me for this week's work. Will you do that for me?"

"Certainly, wait until I change dresses and wash my face," the woman answered jovially. She chuckled occasionally, recalling Engrid's tale.

At the store, Mr. Wilken appeared sympathetic as he opened his purse and passed Engrid a week's pay.

"She has been a big help in our home, and I hardly know what we will do without her. The boy will certainly miss her; he has learned to love the girl, and picked up the longest string of Swedish words that I have ever heard tumble out of one who isn't a Swede. He was a regular little hellion until he began taking an interest in Engrid. Right now, he is a trifle peeved because she has refused to divulge a collection of profanity in her native tongue." He looked at Engrid and smiled.

"It has been remarkable and laughable to watch the two of them together. She'd release a string of Swedish, interspersed with an occasional word of English, and I'll be darned if he wouldn't do her bidding, and I have no inkling as to what she is saying, it's amazing!"

Turning to Engrid, he said, "Come and see us, Engrid; we will miss you… just a moment." Raising a hand to stop the pair who prepared to depart and going to the grocery section of the store, he returned with a sack of chocolates which he presented to the amazed girl. Engrid turned with a glance of embarrassment to her companion as they left the store.

"You didn't tell him about this morning, did you?"

"Goodness no, child; he will find out in due time when his mother fails to visit and his wife has to cook up an alibi. Those women have never got along; jealousy, I suppose."

Engrid fingered an earring. "He has been kind," she stated simply as Mrs. Kosky halted at a window where fall clothing was on display.

"I certainly wish that women didn't have to wear those hideous contraptions," Engrid remarked pointing to corsets. "I'm tired of feeling like a pig in a barrel. We never used them at home."

"It is alright for one as young and shapely as you to say that; but I can't imagine living, walking and working without them. They keep me warm in the winter and support my fat in the summer. I am telling you, girlie, they are something!" The last word, she uttered as though it were a prayer.

"Mrs. Kosky, there is in me a desire to learn the Amerikan way of speaking correctly. I want to read papers and magazines and understand what you discuss with others. I like to read stories, I am weary of groping around in a fog and it makes me feel so futile."

"I'm afraid that I wouldn't make much of a teacher," the woman remarked with a throaty chuckle. "You might get John to help you though. Say, I believe that the best thing is to procure a book from the school. If you could get someone who knows how to talk both languages, it shouldn't take long to learn."

"I would like that more than anything," Engrid said; her eyes sparkled as she squeezed an arm of her friend. "I think you're the nicest woman that I know, Mrs. Kosky."

"Child, what nonsense do you prattle," snorted the woman; feeling warmed, nevertheless. She led the girl up an alley between a barbershop and butcher shop. From the back of the latter, the odor of smoldering wood, mingled with the scent of curing meats came in tempting, cloying waves. They crossed over Leadville row, and taking a pathway up a hill, soon came to a wooden-frame schoolhouse.

Striding boldly to the door, Alena gave it a determined pull and they entered a room echoing to the sound of children's voices reciting in unison.

With misgivings, and her heartbeat quickening, Engrid entered as a hundred pairs of eyes fastened themselves on her.

Turning his glance to meet the eyes of the advancing women, the instructor beckoned for silence. The students ceased their chanting, only to begin whispering.

"Silence!" The master bellowed, brushing a large ear with a quick movement of a red hand.

Engrid stifled a nervous giggle, as the room became quiet under the stern glance of the teacher who stood, haughty and impressive, his long nose protruding from a red, pock-marked face. His eyes of a washed-out blue were overshadowed by brows of white. He was a tall, muscular man and thoroughly competent to control children or irate parents; the kind of a tutor needed in this frontier town where various nationalities sitting next to each other nursed racial antagonisms, an inheritance from parents who had not been in America long enough to forget their pasts, and who reminded their children of it during the course of each evening's conversation. The parents succeeded in erecting walls almost as fast as the principal could break them down with the collection of hardwood pointers.

"Ah," he said, "Good day, ladies; what can I do for you?" He slicked at his hair, pulled at his mustache and straightened his tie, his gaze resting over-long on Alena's companion.

"Good day, Mr. Nole; I have here a girl from the old country. She is interested in learning to speak our language, and would like to purchase a book for that purpose. Could you be of help?"

The principal, reluctantly tearing his eyes from Alena's comely confidant, hissed, "Oh, yes, to be sure, of course, let me see, now…" He left the last word dangling then gazed abstractedly through several books, occasionally brushing at an ear with a big hand. "How would something like this be?" He asked at length.

"It is the first year primer?" Mrs. Kosky asked.

"From the first to the sixth," the teacher stated as he again raised his bull-like voice to bellow for silence, and whispering receded like spent waves withdrawing from a beach.

"That is the book that I would recommend, as the best. Of course she will be in need of instruction," he added regarding the attractive girl with a speculative glance. "I'd gladly help her," he added licking his heavy lips with a nervously moving tongue.

Engrid heard his suggestion with an inward shudder of revulsion as her companion relayed the man's invitation to her.

"Tell him that I want the book without instruction," she said in Swedish.

"The girl says to thank you for your desire to be of help; however, she has to work and couldn't arrange for instruction," Alena said diplomatically.

"Humph," the principal grunted, "that is too bad." He again licked his lips and he glance darted to the far corners of the room; students immediately found their books of all-consuming interest. "Tell the girl that I will gladly help her at any time."

Engrid managed a synthetic smile as she inquired about the cost of the book. At his reply, she laid a silver dollar on the desk and added fifty-cents and a quarter-dollar. Her spirits lightened as she regarded the volume. She thumbed its pages as she gave her thanks and made for the door, feeling only too glad to leave the room with its stifling atmosphere of discipline and visualizing pleasant hours she could devote to learning. Light would gleam brighter in the recesses of her mind, and one day, she would be a stranger in this huge country no longer. Oh, to speed the glorious day when periodicals and the daily paper would appear clear in her searching eyes. She would be able to get her citizenship papers!

"It sounds alright to me, when you say that I might get John's help; but suppose he is unwilling to put himself out?" Engrid asked as the pair trudged downhill toward main street, and a wind which had been blowing sporadically renewed its vigor and slammed the door of a shed.

"Leave that to me," Alena said patiently; "I am certain that he would sooner spend an hour with a girl, rather than waste his time lapping up beer and slapping dirty cards on a green table in some stinking, smoky saloon."

"I hope you are right; although I haven't the nerve to ask him."

"He will ask you one of these days, never fear," the woman said prophetically as a cloud of dust swept up main street, carried on the wings of the now blustering wind.

"Don't you feel that wind?" Engrid gasped.

"I'm glad for the protection of my corsets this very minute." Bowing her head as she spoke, Mrs. Kosky clutched at her hat after a glance up and down the street gave assurance that a team of horses might not run them down; moved toward a pair of planks serving as a makeshift bridge over the ditch draining the run-off water from the town and surrounding hills.

As another gust of wind swept up the street, Engrid paused momentarily with eyes closed; however, her companion lumbered forward, holding her hat with one hand and coat with the other. The girl staggered almost to her knees and grasped a hitching post to steady herself. Dust filled her eyes and spattered against her as she clung frantically to her new book. Her hat ripped loose from its restraining pin and disappeared up the road in a cloud of dust. She threw an arm to her face as the wind shrieked and rattled the sign at the front of the livery stable; above its roar, she heard her companion scream from across the dust obscured street.

"My God," she gasped, "what has happened now?"

Completely forgetting her hat, she hurried forward calling Alena's name; but only the wind answered with icy pellets striking viciously as they shook loose from inky clouds that had accumulated in a tumbling mass overhead. Drops of rain spattered dry dust leaving splotches large as silver dollars. A vicious flash of lightening struck a cottonwood tree beside the Vienna bakery; instantly there sounded a crack similar to a rifle shot, followed closely by an awe-inspiring rumble of thunder. Flash after flash of lightening tore the heavens into shreds. To the dazed girl, an ocean seemed to drop from the zenith. Through this ruthless manifestation of natures might, Engrid groped her way to the side of the ditch, and looking down saw below her the crumpled figure of her friend whose silk coat gathered hail stones in its folds. The woman's eyes were closed and the hat rested in a crumpled heap under her coiled braids. One arm was pinned under her as though she had reached down in a frantic effort to break the shock of her fall.

With mouth dry, Engrid slid into the ditch and tugged at Alena's head. She moved around to the windward side of the supine figure and sheltered the woman's face from the torrent.

"Mrs. Kosky," she pleaded. "Speak to me. What has happened? Can't you hear me?" Her voice was imploring and strung through with a piteous sound as she ran a hand over the woman's face and wiped away dirt. Tiny points of blood oozed fro Alena's forehead and a trickle of blood from one nostril dyed the hail on the ground. Her bosom rose and fell with regularity, Engrid noticed despite the horror gripping with a strange tightness over the small of her back. She realized immediately that she couldn't help the woman by herself. She glanced accusingly at the planks, one of which had slid from a crumpled bank when the woman had stepped upon it. Help for the woman was urgently needed. A doctor… where? Get out on the street… stop anybody that comes along…

Quickly she unbuttoned her coat and covered the woman's head, noting how the driving pellets of ice covered the robe. The wind, lightening and thunder persisted with a violence threatening to prostrate the terrified girl who, with a horrified glance, noticed a growing stream of water forming a puddle against the woman's body and moving out and around her legs!

"She can drown right here," she thought as she climbed the bank using the standing plank which had dropped an end. A hurried glance up and down the street assured her that no person was within the radius of her look; only a number of woebegone appearing horses with drooping heads who had turned tail to the storm where they coward at hitching racks before a livery stable.

Running with skirt clasped in hand to the door, Engrid tugged frantically, it opened unexpectedly, to reveal three men sitting on empty powder boxes playing cards. The trio looked up as the wild-eyed, soaked girl entered and grasped the nearest one by an arm, just as he was in the act of slamming down a red queen.

"Come, Mrs. Kosky fall, hurt!"

For a moment surprise registered on slack faces; but understanding came simultaneously to the men who pushed over their box and hurried to the door, close on the heels of the white-faced girl. The proprietor of the livery stable grasped a heavy overcoat, and giving it a quick shake, he hurried after the others who, disappearing around the corner of the building, had back-tracked the girl's footsteps in the heavy slush. He caught up to them as they slid down the ditch back. Stooping, he pulled the girl's coat off Mrs. Kosky and placed it over Engrid's shoulders. He covered Alena with the overcoat, and looking at the water which has risen halfway up on the woman's body, he quickly made a decision.

"We've got to get her out of here and into the office," he said firmly. "Two of us will get hold of the upper part of her body, and you get hold of her legs, just above the knees," he directed one of the men.

The girl watched helplessly as the three men raised Alena and carried her to the side of the ditch. After much pulling and lifting, they raised her up to the street level; then carried her across to the office and laid her on an old couch which the night-hostler used.

"You run and get the doctor, Vic; Carl, you beat it into the back of the stable and get a couple of horse blankets." While he spoke, the man stomped down on all three empty powder boxes and quickly built a roaring fire. This man, Engrid decided, was a man of action. And so he was; a lifetime of handling horses, mules and rough men, had trained him to quick decisions.

Having lost her fear when this man took charge, Engrid stood attentively by waiting in case she might be of some use after she had wiped the woman's face with her handkerchief. Soon the man who had been dispatched for the blankets returned, and the proprietor of the stable warmed and spread them over the prone woman.

After an interval of ten minutes during which the storm slackened, leaving only a faint, though almost continuous rumble of fading thunder, the door opened and in stepped a keen-eyed man with a full mustache and carefully trimmed beard.

"What goes on?" he asked noting the reclining woman and the bedraggled girl standing at the woman's side. In a well modulated voice he said, "Hello, Miss." As he removed his gloves and topcoat he said, "Mrs. Kosky, I see; too bad." He noted with approval the men's efforts to keep the woman comfortable; then stooping, he raised an eyelid. He released it, grasped a wrist and felt of her pulse. Laying her arm down, he examined the bruise on her forehead; after that, he ran exploratory hands under her neck, then up and down both legs and the arm on which she had lain. He removed her shoe and slit her stocking to expose an angry appearing, discolored swelling around her ankle. "Hmm, it seems as though she must have dropped on a rock sticking out of the sand; her ankle is broken."

From his buckboard, the doctor procured splints and a stretcher; with the help of two men who held the leg, he applied splints and yards of restraining bandage. He turned to the gashed forehead cleaning it, applying antiseptic and bandaging it, He then placed a blanket on the stretcher, and the men lifted the woman into the buckboard. The storm had blown over, leaving several inches of hail on the road. Engrid climbed in the front seat at the doctor's invitation and the men climbed in back.

At the boardinghouse the girl opened the door to the woman's bedroom where the men carefully lowered Alena; then retrieved the stretcher. Several of the boarders came to inquire about the accident and Engrid explained in detail.

"Isn't it hell? Who's going to take care of the boardinghouse? She'll lose her men," Engrid overheard one of the men say.

"Anything else that we can do?" Dan Lucas asked; as hat in hand he stood at the door of the bedroom.

"No, I think that I can handle the rest with this girl's help. Thanks a lot, boys; maybe I can help you all in the same way, someday," he said with a humorous smile.

"Heaven-help-us-no," Dan protested as he retrieved his odorous horse blankets and hastily departed with his companions.

Engrid completed the cleanup of Alena with the doctor's aid, removed the woman's clothing and got her under the covers. The doctor gave Engrid instructions for the care of his patient; but not knowing what Engrid could or could not understand, he instructed one of the older men who relayed the information to the girl.

A long time after the doctor had taken his leave, Alena stirred and groaned. She opened her eyes and fastened them blankly on the ceiling; finally, she moved an exploratory hand to her bandaged head and said wonderingly, "I'm still alive." Then, "What happened?"

Engrid explained and directed her to take some pills and water.

"What time is it?"

"I'll see." Going to the kitchen, Engrid procured the woman's alarm clock and placed it on the bureau facing the patient.

"Four o'clock? Good Heavens!" she gasped, "The potatoes aren't on and the buckets for the nightshift are yet to be put up. What shall I do?"

Engrid looked thoughtfully through the window at the white hail and the sullen sky. The room was silent except for the ticking of the clock, a murmur of conversation from the dining room where men were playing cards, and an occasional moan from the pitiful figure on the bed. Turning to Alena, Engrid told her that she would cook the supper, put up the buckets and take charge of the boardinghouse until the woman was able to do so.

"But," Alena protested, "what about your job at the hotel?"

"Don't give it a thought. That woman can get along by herself until she finds another to help her; and you are in no condition to help yourself. Perhaps you have someone else whom you would like me to call to help you?"

"You know that there is no one other than yourself; but I don't see why you should quit such a nice job to work for me; I am not even sure of how much I shall be able to pay you."

Engrid overruled her objections, and going into the kitchen procured a pitcher of water and placed it on a chair by the bed. She filled a glass and said, "Take your pills and get some sleep. I'm perfectly capable of doing the work until you can handle it and that won't be for a long, long time."

"Oh, lord, girlie, I guess I shall have to give in to you; but it doesn't seem right, somehow; what will I ever do?" Mrs. Kosky's voice was laden with anguish and tears rolled down her cheeks. "Get me a hanky from the top drawer; I'm no better than a baby."

"If you ask me," Engrid said with a rueful smile, as she went to the bureau, "you are through doing for awhile."

Alena nodded her head and gulped some pills. Engrid inquired of her further needs and after opening a window to air her room; then she went to the kitchen and placed potatoes on to boil. In the box of groceries, she found a huge package of round steak which she cut, pounded and placed in several frying pans. While the meat was cooking, she set the table and measured coffee into the gargantuan pot, added water and set it on the stove.

The mouth-watering aromas of coffee, steak and onions flooded the house as the miners walked in. When they inquired about their regular cook, Engrid explained and the men soberly drifted to their rooms and prepared for the evening meal.

Engrid speared the steak and turned it over as John entered. One slice which had cooked faster than the others, she placed on a plate, and using a fork and sharp knife, she cut a piece and passed it to John who leaned indolently by the door.

"Well," he ruminated, "I suppose a taste won't prove fatal." He chewed at it and said, "M-m-m, that's good!"

"It ought to be; I've cooked for some mighty fussy people, both here and at home. I think I am a pretty fair cook."

"Pretty, and a cook, you should say. Well, I suppose I had better wash or I shall miss out on the rest of the steak." With that he drifted off leaving Engrid warmed by his kind expression.

While John was performing his toilet, he found himself thinking of Rika and her poised, although oft' times irritating, self-assurance.

"Now Engrid," he reflected as he dried himself carefully after shaving, "is eager to learn, cheerful and with a childish interest in life that is as refreshing as a mug of beer on a hot day; still, she's a woman."

He went to the dining room, seated himself and promptly felt a strong awareness of the girl who, while moving purposefully about her tasks, adroitly turned the quips and friendly banter of appreciative men, into a pleasant chatter. More than once speculative pair of eyes rested on her briefly and dropped again to loaded plates when her frank glance met theirs.

After deciding there was sufficient food on the table, Engrid went to the kitchen where she picked up five dinner pails. For the top section of each she made a sandwich and added an apple. In the bottom section Engrid poured coffee. About a half-hour before the men would eat their lunch underground, they would hang their buckets over a lighted candle and heat the coffee.

After finishing with the lunches, Engrid went to Alena's room and found her fast asleep. Because the room seemed a trifle chilly, she placed a quilt on the bed taking care not to put weight on the injured leg. Pity welled in her as she gravely regarded the woman; however, controlling her emotions she went to the kitchen where she prepared water for dishes. After the men had finished eating, she cleared the tables.

After a time John, puffing on a pipe, entered the kitchen. He stood in the doorway contemplating the busy girl with an air of calm detachment causing curious little shivers to play up and down the nape of her neck. After she scalded a pan of dishes, and picked up the towel, the silent man wandered over to her side and removed the towel from her grasp; then without breaking his silence, he grasped five plates and wiped them dry.

"Has the cat got your tongue?" he drawled, placing cup in cup and plate on plate as he stacked them on the shelves of the cupboard.

"You don't have to wipe the dishes," she replied evasively. She felt ill at ease in this young giant's presence and hardly knew how to put herself in a restful frame of mind.

"I'm aware of the fact," he commented. "Occasionally when Mrs. Kosky seems to be under the weather, one of us gives her a hand. I thought that you might appreciate a little help; what with all of the excitement and the unaccustomed work that you let yourself in for."

"But you still don't have to do it," She persisted.

"Oh, I'm not putting myself out in any way; we drew lots and I just happened to be the loser." Engrid glanced at him and perceived a twinkle of veiled amusement in his eyes.

"I do appreciate your help as I have to go down and let Mrs. Meyer know that I shall not be able to work there. If I get through here quickly, I can be back before it gets dark." Meeting his eyes in a direct look for the first time since he had started helping her, she asked, "Would you do me a favor?"

"I might, and then again, I might not; it all depends."

"Would you write a note for me, explaining Mrs. Kosky's predicament to Mrs. Meyer? Tell her I am sorry that things have happened as they have; that I shall not be able to continue working for her because I am going to keep the boardinghouse running until Alena gets well."

"I'll bet you're just using this as an excuse to be around us men," he suggested slyly.

"Listen, you big Finn," she retorted, "I am doing this to hold you men here so Mrs. Kosky can get by until she is well again. If her boarders leave her, she won't have a cent of income, and she will be dependent on the goodness of her own nationality for her livelihood. I can't stand idly by and see that happen."

"Admirable reasoning and right to the point," he admitted. He grinned at the angry glance the girl shot his way as she slammed a pan onto the top of the stove. "I was only joshing, you know. I'll do more than write a note; I'll walk down with you and carry your valise, if you want me to."

"Would you do that?" she bubbled happily; "You're a dear. Wait until I get my coat and hat and I'll be right with you." she said thankfully. Taking a final sweep at the table with a drying cloth, she entered Mrs. Kosky's room and glanced at a film of perspiration showing on the woman's brow.

"Poor dear, so much trouble she has had; yet, how kind she is in spite of it all," Engrid pondered as she primped before the bureau mirror.

She left the room and walked to Mr. Hansen, one of the boarders, who was studying the evening paper. "Mr. Hansen, will you be going out for awhile?"

"No, I can't say that I will; why?" he replied, meeting her look over the top of his reading glasses.

"I just wanted to have someone tell Alena, if she wakes up before I come back, that I have gone to the Tintic hotel to get my valise; and to tell the woman there that I shall be working here."

"That is good news, Miss Isaacson; I was just wondering what we were going to do; none of us like to eat in the restaurant."

"Thank you, kind sir; I'll continue to cook if you men can eat it."

"Now, Miss," he said reassuringly, "don't you worry about that at all. We just like plenty of food. Go along, and don't worry about Alena. If she is in need of help, I am sure that I can oblige." As the man turned to his paper, Engrid took her leave.

Outside the hail was cut by ugly wagon tracks and the hoof prints of horses, and the road had the appearance of a quagmire; therefore, the couple gravitated to the railroad track as others had previously done since the storm, judging by the well-beaten path between the rails. They walked in on Mrs. Meyer to find her sipping a cup of black tea. John explained what had happened, and why Engrid had decided to help Mrs. Kosky.

"I am sorry to lose you, girlie; but I do understand," she exclaimed in a sympathetic voice as she laid a hand on Engrid's shoulder. "Here is fifty-cents for the day's work. I do hope that Mrs. Kosky gets along fine, and tell her that I will be up to see her soon."

Leaving Mrs. Meyer staring blankly at the door, the girl and John procured the valise and took their leave.

"I'll be damned and double-damned," the woman muttered to herself as she heard the lower door slam behind the couple. "Just when I had the help I needed, after running my nose into trouble to get her, fate steals her away. I'll learn to poke my nose in where it doesn't belong. I'm on the outs with my in-law, and I've lost my hired help. Damnation!"

Moving up the street, the girl chattered gaily. John spoke but only to fill gaps in the rambling fence of Engrid's garrulity. Upon their arrival at the boardinghouse, the girl stoked the big heater in the dining room; while John carried in extra coal and wood.

"There!" said the girl in a satisfied voice as she sat down to take up her knitting.

John glanced at the twinkling needles, "What are you making?"

"Just a wool sweater for myself; winter is coming, you know."

Without further comment, John settled himself to read the paper which had already been perused by other men who had left for town.

Finally he laid the pages aside saying, "It's late for a working man; I believe that I had better go to bed or I'll be useless tomorrow. By the way," he said with a grin, "don't forget to pound on my door at seven o'clock and have my breakfast ready when you do. Bring me a cup of coffee and a smoke when you waken me, huh?"

"Who do you think you are, the Tsar?"

"No, just a poor working man trying to get along, goodnight."

"Goodnight, John, and thanks for the help."

"No thanks."

Engrid put aside her knitting and prepared a sandwich for each of the men who would be coming home sometime after two o'clock; then, after making coffee for them to warm, she banked the stove and went to the washroom where she filled the barrel, and allowing a trickle to fall on her, she took a refreshing bath. After dressing for bed, Engrid opened the door between her room and Alena's and locked the doors leading to the hall. She wriggled under the covers with an appreciative sigh, and her clean feet explored the limits of the sheets, then she found a comfortable spot on the hard mattress in which to rest her hips. She felt weariness but likewise satisfaction, as she realized that for once, she had a definite purpose, and not just a job. Without her help the slumbering woman would be destitute.

Sometime after she had fallen asleep, she heard footsteps of boarders coming off shift; then mingled with the clicking of cups and saucers as they enjoyed the snack that Engrid had set out for them in compliance with Alena's wishes. Subdued voices of men came in comforting waves from the kitchen.

Chapter 20

Awakened by the shrilling alarm, Engrid dressed and went to the kitchen where she laid a fire. She kindled one in the huge heating stove in the dining room so that the rising miners might be comfortable when they crawled from their warm beds. Going at the proper time to the doors of those who were to work, she knocked until they responded sleepily. Then she stood by the kitchen stove after putting up lunches and cooking breakfast and watched the amusing spectacle of growling, yawning men who trooped into the room in their stocking feet long-handled underwear and trousers, while carrying boots to warm at the stove.

"Just like children," she told herself, "I think Mrs. Kosky has spoiled them into expecting a warm stove with the first chilly night."

She set heaping platters of yellow pancakes, three large bowls of prunes, three pitchers of milk, and platters of bacon and eggs on the table; while the men sounded a curt greeting as they languidly pulled on boots; then went to the washroom. There was an air of easy-going indifference about these men who spoke in monosyllables as they ate. How they differed from Mr. Wilken and other business men with whom she had become acquainted! These men were, for the most part, silent to the point of taciturnity while dining. Just as silently they withdrew from the table and sat for a cigarette before picking up their buckets and climbing the road leading to the mine. The only time these men appeared sociable as a general rule, was when they had been drinking; then they reveled in joyous self-expression, every man talking at once, and none seeming to listen. Close and constant association as a group had led them to the realization that there was little about each other that all did not know. However, they seemed to break loose from their shells when tramp-miners joined the group for a few days' lodging, and they became voluble indeed as they listened to news that the newcomers had gleaned during their travels from one mining camp to another. When these individuals' innermost thoughts, philosophies and experiences had been related a sufficient number of times, so that all could digest them and present observations of their own in turn, the men would accept them as one of the group. About that time, the miners would pack their rolls and continue with their restless nomadic wanderings, in all probability to make their appearance again after a year or two.

John, much to the girl's surprise, seemed no different from others merely nodding a greeting as he chomped on a mouthful of food, and as a consequence, Engrid was actually startled when, after picking up his bucket, he paused at the kitchen door and told her that her breakfast had been excellent.

"I shall see if I can find you an ore specimen; would you like that?"

When the girl replied in the affirmative, John trudged away through the slush, his brown-stained boots leaving dirty marks in the white pellets covering the ground. Hardly had the last man departed when Mrs. Kosky's voice could be heard, calling the girl's name.

"How are you this morning?" Engrid asked cheerily as she breezed into the woman's room.

"Bad, very bad," the landlady complained as her helper deposited a dish of warm water on a chair by the bed; then proceeded to wash the woman. During this time, the girl carried on a cheerful one-sided conversation, because she felt buoyant and refreshed after a night's sleep. The invalid punctuated her sentences with an assortment of sighs and groans. After washing Alena, Engrid brushed her hair and allowed it to hang in two braids tied with ribbons.

"There," she said, "I believe that you are going to feel better. Now, I shall give you a cup of kahvia; while you are drinking it, I'll prepare some breakfast. You are hungry?"

"Certainly, it is my leg that is broken, not my stomach, thanks-be-to-the-lord. Merciful heavens, what about the men?" Her voice trailed the girl who left the room to prepare the woman's breakfast.

"All taken care of and safely off to work; their stomachs are full and they seemed to be satisfied." Engrid called over her shoulder. "In fact," she added with a note of joy, "John complimented me on my cooking and said that he would bring me a pretty specimen of ore if he runs into one."

The girl, her head in the clouds, boiled eggs and browned toast on a wire-toaster held over hot coals in the firebox. After dishes were cleaned, and the kitchen floor scrubbed, she entered the rooms of men who were at work.

While glancing curiously over the contents of John's room she was surprised to find several well-thumbed and much underscored books including a dictionary, two books on mathematics, and treatise on mining and another on metallurgy. Two novels attracted her attention, and as she thumbed through them, she told herself," Someday I may read them!"

To all appearances, the man put part of his leisure into something other than card playing and drinking.

Engrid felt a catch in her throat as her glance fell on two pictures reposing on the dresser. One was a group picture with the boy John standing between his mother and father, the girl surmised; however, it was the second photograph which gave the girl pain. In it stood an attractive Rika in skirt and white shirtwaist, and on a finger held to the front of her waist was the diamond ring that John had given her. Engrid felt a sense of emptiness, as studying the picture she observed the affectionate scrawl in ink at the lower right-hand corner, "With all of my love to John, Rika."

With an effort, Engrid tidied the room and made the bed neatly; then she went to other rooms giving them the same care. After that she mopped the dining room and swept the halls upstairs and downstairs. Before she was aware of the passing of time, she had to prepare breakfast, which was actually a lunch, for the late risers. Afterward she went to each room and put them in order; then she poured oil in all of the lamps, trimmed the wicks and began a much needed job of window washing.

The doctor came during this time and gave his patient an examination; then he left with a word of encouragement and more pills. Later, Louise dropped in and ran into her sister who was polishing the front windows.

"Good heavens, sister, what goes on here?"

"Work."

"What about the other job? Why did you quit? Where is Alena?"

Engrid had to explain while Louise clucked her tongue and shook her head sympathetically; then Louise went to listen to the injured woman's version. For a time Mrs. Kosky basked in the attention which her visitor willingly gave her. Finally, Louise announced that she was heading for town.

After inquiring about the contents of the larder, Mrs. Kosky wrote a list of groceries and gave it to Engrid who went to town and placed the order. Upon her return from the store, she took a jar of yeast culture and mixed a huge batch of bread. That evening, she had the satisfaction of watching the boarders enjoy the products of her culinary skill. After supper, John went in turn to visit the confined woman.

"How is the lease coming?" Alena asked as she shifted her body and groaned.

"Things are fine, Mrs. Kosky," he declared as he stared contemplatively at the woman. "In another ten days we ought to put out a sixty-ton shipment; it will net us much more than wages, after expenses are paid."

"I am glad to hear of your luck. My husband hit pay-rock once and purchased this place. All of his leasing after that; brought nothing."

"But," John pointed out, "that was before there were any well-defined ore channels and a man didn't even have a feeder to prospect on."

"That is too true," Alena agreed; then her mind reverted to herself. "I am tired of being in bed already." She eyed the man for a time, and making up her mind, she said, "John, would it be asking too much if you were to spend an hour occasionally helping Engrid learn English?"

John's brows lifted in surprise, only to revert to normal as he placidly puffed his pipe; while giving the question his attention. He smoked in silence, the woman waiting for an answer. After all, he decided, there was nothing of importance that he really had to do of an evening, and perhaps it would be good for the girl to study a bit. In fact, it would help him as well to discuss languages with the girl, because as he was aware, the teacher also is taught. What would the rest of the boarders think? Well, he didn't particularly care, and come to think of it, the others would jump at the chance to be of service to this friendly girl. John visualized himself in the roll of teacher and was surprised when a glow of interest fanned into desire.

"I believe that I could devote time to teaching her; although I must say, I am not the best."

"It's good that you are willing," the woman said warmly.

"I'll be seeing you," John said as he stood up, "I'm going to town and play a few hands of poker; in the meantime, I'll think things over."

After he departed, Engrid tidied Alena's room; and while she moved about her tasks, she heard Alena say with a profound sigh, "I would certainly like to have some blood-bread."

"Where could we get some beef blood in a town like this?" Engrid asked.

"There are three slaughter houses on the other side of Summit; we can buy whatever we need from one of them."

"I can make some this weekend."

"I'll write a note for the butcher and you can give it to him tomorrow when you place an order. He can deliver some in a five-gallon milk can," Mrs. Kosky informed the girl.

Before noon of the following Saturday, the can was delivered to the kitchen. Pouring it into a pan through bleached cotton material to remove the clots, Engrid added blood in place of water to mix with the rye flour which she sifted into the mixing pans. She added salt and home-cultured yeast. She went to work with a will, kneading the dough and adding more flour and blood until she felt satisfied that there would be sufficient for all.

When the dough threatened to overflow the pans, she shaped it into loaves. After it was ready for the oven, she punched a fork into the loaves, baked them for an hour; then she rubbed the bread with rye flour and placed it on the pantry shelves.

"I'll bet the men will be pleased at breakfast tomorrow," she told Alena gleefully that evening. "I won't say a word until I serve them."

"That they will," the woman replied, "and so will I. there is nothing like blood-bread to give people strength. I have had enough work baking plain bread, and if it weren't for the bakery, many times I would be without bread on Sunday mornings. Lately I have not been able to perform all of the work that I should. I'm getting old, fifty-five next July."

"You're just old enough to give some bachelor ideas," Engrid chided her.

The following morning, she cut several of the loaves into chunks approximately an inch square; then placing them in kettles, she added hot water and salt. In a short time, the chunks became soft; then she spooned them into bowls and with a lid over each, she set them on the table with ham and eggs.

For several moments, Engrid watched with a mischievous smile as the men, still rubbing sleep from their eyes, sat down and indifferently lifted the plates off the bowls thinking, perhaps, that the bowls held the inevitable prunes.

"Blood-bread; Collar-stiffener; Brain food!" came amazed cries from the boarders, and reaching for the chocolate-colored concoction, they filled their plates to the depth of an inch. Over this they lovingly laid eggs, then broke the yolks and watched the golden color merge with the brown. On top of this, they poured a flood of ketchup and spearing a slice of ham, each man began to feast.

"Oh, you wonderful girl," Mr. Hansen breathed between mouthfuls, and Engrid could not restrain a bubble of laughter when the other men chortled their glee, sounding like a bunch of youngsters at a picnic.

And needless to say, every Sunday morning after that while Engrid worked at the boardinghouse, breakfast was a blood-bread special. In preparation for the event, all went to bed after deliberately eating less than usual; so that they might indulge in the luxury, which is to a Scandinavian, as caviar is to Russian nobility.

One morning, shortly after blood-bread breakfast became a weekly ritual, Engrid noted with a start that Rika's picture was missing from John's bureau. Decorum prevented her from asking what had become if it; however, John casually mentioned that Alex and Rika had sent him an invitation to their wedding.

Finally, the day which the girl longed for came when John asked, "Would you like to have a little help with your language studies? Mrs. Kosky mentioned that you were interested."

Engrid's heartbeat quickened. How could she tell John that she envied Rika's ability to both speak and write two languages?

"Oh, John; would you?" she asked tremulously.

"And why not?"

"But I am afraid that you will find the teaching an unwelcome burden," she objected.

"I believe you can safely allow me to judge that," he said jauntily.

"Oh, John, you have no idea what this means to me; I want to learn so I can associate with other people on a common ground. I want to be able to read newspapers, and uphold my end in conversation with women who are born and raised here. I want to be able to purchase things at the store intelligently; discuss prices and materials. I don't want to stay in a rut. Who knows," she mused aloud, "someday I may even be a clerk in a store; get away from cleaning people's dirt. I can meet lots of people in that way, and life will hold meaning greater than I have ever dreamed." Giving him a wistful smile, she said, "But most important of all, I want to be a citizen."

John looked at the starry-eyed girl until she blushed and dropped her head. "I guess that will hold me," he said with a whimsical smile; "your aims aren't too high. When do you want to start?"

"Anytime."

"On the other hand," John considered with a look of mock severity, "I don't believe I should help you."

"And why not?"

"After you learn to talk without too much of an accent, you'll start going with Amerikan boys, and the first thing he'll teach you to say is, 'Yes!'"

Engrid giggled. "Would that be so bad? I have certainly seen some handsome ones."

"Here goes; have you that book Mrs. Kosky was telling me about?"

Engrid went to her room and procured the book which was no longer new after suffering the downpour on the day of Alena's accident. John showed infinite patience with the girl, sometimes devoting more than an hour of each day with her. She was eager, willing to please, and consequently, much midnight oil was burned. At times, Engrid was so weary that she fell asleep listening to the man's modulated voice, as he read to her in English and compelled her to repeat it back to him, as well as she was able.

October came, maple trees in the hollows of the hills assumed their ravishing hues. John asked Engrid if she would care to go pine nut hunting. "We can take a coffee pot, frying pan, steaks, potatoes, onions and cook our supper in the hills."

"Who will be going?"

"Emil, Louise, Hulda, Arvid and us; if you will go."

"But, what about Sunday dinner for the men?"

"I have already talked to them. They agreed to cook the chickens, if we'll share the nuts we gather with them."

"You're quite a promoter," Engrid observed.

"A man has to be to get what he wants."

"And suppose I do not go," she suggested with a factitious frown.

"School will be dismissed," he countered.

"I'm beaten; what time do we start?"

"After breakfast we will stop at Emil and Louise's then pick up the other two as we cross town. We're going to climb that cliff over there," he promised, pointing to the yellow bulk of Cole Canyon Cliff protruding above the second line of hills, north of town.

"I don't know about that; I have never climbed anything so high," she objected timidly.

"Oh, you'll like climbing when you once start," he assured her. "By the way, we mustn't forget to take a pound of lard to loosen the pine-gum from our hands; and see if you can rustle some old rags to wipe away the grease and pitch so we can have clean hands for dinner."

They bent their heads to studies until Engrid grew sleepy and John's words failed to make sense.

A bond was developing between the young couple in spite of John's reticence which heretofore had characterized the man's attitude toward anything bordering on the intimate. In spite of the fact that he had been impersonal to Engrid since Rika's marriage to Alex, John found himself weakening. Of late, John had found thoughts of

Engrid's beauty pervading his waking hours as well as his sleep. Emil, on occasion, chided him about it at the mine.

"If you don't get petticoats off your mind and get that muck out, we'll never make this next shipment on time," he would observe cynically as John, leaning on the handle of his shovel and chin resting on cupped hand, would stare with unseeing eyes at his partner.

"Ah, go to hell, you big Finn," John would say in a factious voice; nevertheless he would bow his back and ore would fly over his shoulder faster than before, as powerful muscles threatened to burst through his grimy shirt. Emil would grin, take a hunk out of a plug of dark tobacco, replace a worn drill that had caused him to halt, and give the machine the air until the drill churned in the hole.

Sunday morning, the couple met with Louise and Emil. The men gathered up empty potato sacks and placed in them cooking utensils and food. They stopped for the third couple and continued on their way to climb over the first line of hills. Here the strong scent of flowering sage rested heavily in the air. The sun shone warm, causing the woman to remove their sweaters. As they walked in single file along a trail which horses had trod through the brush, cotton-tail rabbits flashed across open spaces, and chipmunks darted by. Occasionally jack-rabbits would lope away, to freeze abruptly as one of the men whistled shrilly; but as the party drew near, the nimble creatures would again run into the sea of blossoming sage.

John kicked into a huge ant hill; and Engrid stopped to watch as its inhabitants, rushing here and there in pandemonium, finally settled down to begin carrying eggs underground through hole openings on the exposed portion of the hill. Other ants, heaving dirt aside as they broke into the open, added to the existing furor.

"And why destroy what they have worked so hard to build?" Engrid asked as they moved on at an increased pace in an attempt to overtake the others in their party obscured from view by tall brush and cedars.

"Oh, I don't know," he answered with a boyish grim. "About the only fun an ant gets out of life is when someone creates a diversion; breaking the routine in which they find themselves. I believe they are much like people who get in a habit of doing the same thing, day after day, and the first thing they know, they are in a rut whether a good one, or bad, depends on the individual's intelligence."

Gradually succumbing to the peaceful serenity of their surroundings, the couple again slowed their pace, and at John's quips, Engrid's gay laughter rang on the air. Horned toads clambered awkwardly from their path. Moving lizards paused with uplifted heads, the buttery yellow of their throats pulsating visibly. A hawk circling high overhead; screamed repeatedly in warning to its nesting mate as it propelled itself on motionless wings. Engrid paused to watch it until her eyes watered.

"I wish that I could take wing, looking down on others who crawl below," she said raptly as John, watching her, thought that here was a girl who could make a fitting goddess for Ukho, into whose vault the girl's desire was ascending after the wheeling bird.

"Come on, dreamer," he broke in on her rapture; "there is a lot of hard climbing to be done, and staring at birds won't give you wings, you'll find. Let's go, or the fun will be over before we can catch the others."

"Hal-o-o-o, John," Emil's voice came from far up the hillside.

"Coming," John answered in a normal voice as he grinned at his companion and allowed her to pass him on the trail. "Get going before they get crazy ideas about our tardiness."

"Such as?"

John failed to take the bait; so falling silent, Engrid saved her breath for the steep climb ahead. Up the mountain they went, with Emil and Arvid helloing in boisterous voices until surrounding hills rolled back their sounds in a mocking chorus.

"Do you want to climb the cliff; or should we go around?" John asked as they paused in the talus at its base.

Engrid stared up at the forbidding mass, meanwhile striving desperately to overcome the fear she felt at the mere thoughts of what John suggested; but he assured her that there was a passageway up, offering firm hand and foothold, which other girls had frequently climbed.

"I'll try it if you want me to," she said, but not without trepidation.

"Good girl," he said warmly. "I'll go first to give you a hand if you need it."

She watched where John placed his hands and feet, and before long she found herself enjoying the novel exercise. Crevices, where rock had oxidized and worn away, were numerous enough to offer firm support. Engrid experienced a feeling of exhilaration a she felt the pull of muscles responding in healthy cooperation with her thoughts. They continued steadily until they came out on a narrow bench approximately halfway up the cliff. Here, pausing for a time, they leaned with backs against the cliff to rest; and Engrid gazed at the slope below, marveling that she had climbed so high without fear. She breathed deeply, and her heartbeat was strong; while she reveled in the breathless excitement which the climbing had induced.

She elevated her eyes to look far across the valley, observed the panorama stretching from the slope; lying roughly three-hundred feet below, to the blue line of the Wasatch Mountains thirty miles to the east. A rain storm, which had washed the valley three nights before, had blanketed the far turquoise mountains in a mantle of snow partway down the slopes. Above the sheen the sky was immeasurably bluer by contrast. Clusters of trees from which snow had melted, formed black patches on the frozen background. Composed of three distinct peaks of uniform height, one mountain stood in virgin beauty, its divisions resembling the crests of spume-capped waves. Below its undulating slopes gleamed a tiny lake; so small was it that had the sun not been reflected in its waters, at a definite angle; it would have been invisible.

Eyes weary, Engrid dropped her glance to find ease in a casual survey of closer sage-covered hills where cedar and pinion pine vied with each other in varied shapes and greens. Wherever she looked, flaming maples nestled in cloistered hollows, and the ridges projecting above the trees appeared yellow and vibrant with blooming sage. Beyond the first line of hills, looking back over the pathway which she had taken Tintic's dwellings seemed toy-like, much like the miniature houses that her brother had played with as a child in the long winter evenings.

Engrid sighed as her glance going to John's face, found him regarding her with an amused smile.

"Do you like it?"

"Oh, John," she breathed, eyes glowing with a light similar to that of the tiny lake at which she had stared, "never did I realize that from one point a person could look on so much beauty."

There before her eyes was a reminder of all seasons. Spring and summer grass was green below; across the way hills were glowing with a riot of yellow, red and gold which autumn had painted with a profligate hand; and on the far mountains, winter had dropped its glistening shroud.

"I too, like its beauty," he remarked; "but being a man, perhaps I'm concerned more with practical things. That white mountain over there, which by the way, is called Nebo, furnishes water for growing things during the long hot summers when the only water we get is that coming from heavy cloud-bursts. I think you have overlooked something unusual, however."

Engrid stared questioningly.

"No, not here; it is there," he said with out-flung arm. "See that mountain over yonder? turn sideways; you won't fall, and besides you can't see it unless you turn; that is better," he encouraged as she turned her back on him, and his hand pointed over her shoulder to the north of the country which she had previously surveyed, to a mountain far across serene Utah Lake.

Engrid stared long at the mountain which John pointed out; but for a time, all she could think of was the fact that one of John's hands rested lightly on a shoulder to keep her from leaning out too far from the cliff. Her heart pounded wildly for some unexplainable reason, and she felt a desire to crowd closer to him and feel the nearness of his body. She shook off the thought determinedly and paid attention where his finger was pointing; although, at first all she could see was a snow-covered mountain several miles in length.

"I see it! It appears as if the whole mountain is supporting a recumbent figure shrouded from head to foot with snow. Is that what you mean?" she asked breathlessly.

His hand tightened on her shoulder, and he breathed the odor of her hair coming to him in exciting waves. "That is it; it's most beautiful when the snow covers the body in fall and spring. That mountain rises about a mile and a half above the valley floor. The other side has snow on it the year around. The snow on this side generally lies in the hollows until sometime in August."

"Imagine that!" she gasped, comparing his statement with the memory of tiny hills of her homeland which were no more than a few hundred feet high, at the most, and not carved in solid rock as were these.

"There must be a name for such a beautiful mountain?"

"The Indians call it Timpanogas, the sleeping woman."

"Hey, John," Emil called, and the couple looked up to observe their companions lying prone, evidently, just showing their heads.

"Coming," John answered; then turning he moved a few steps along the ledge to a route which enabled them to circumvent the sheer cliff. Panting heavily, they reached the top where the others met them with cries of mock disapproval.

"That's a fine place to corner a girl," Arvid chided; "you should at least have waited until you had her on level ground."

"John and I have been admiring the scenery," Engrid protested heatedly. Her explanation, however, was greeted by a chorus of ribald laughter.

"I used to think that John was a lady-killer; however, after watching his conduct when he had you on that ledge, and all he did was put a hand on your shoulder, I am forced to change my opinion of the man. Now," Emil said with a sly glance at Engrid, "if I had you where he did; halfway up the cliff, and no place for you to go except toward me, or else jump to get away from me, I would have kissed you!"

"Man, oh man," John said reflectively, glancing at the girl who dropped her eyes and her face colored.

"You would have kissed me, had I allowed you to," Engrid said with a smirk at Emil.

"Coffee?" Hulda asked.

"No thanks, I'm hot enough from the climb; I'd like a nice big drink of water, though."

"Follow the leader," John said, as standing up, he led them to a tunnel under a grove of willows, the bottom of which held water as far back as they could see. "This is one of the first prospects in the district," he informed the girls. "Joe Cole, one of the first men to enter town following the discovery of ore, came here to run a tunnel and all he found was fresh water. Of course there isn't enough to run out in a large stream; however, there's always a cool drink for whoever comes this way on a hot day. I've been drinking here since I was a kid when we used to come out to hunt rabbits and roll rocks down the mountainside. Have you women ever rolled rocks?"

"No," they exclaimed in a chorus; "let's do!"

And like a group of children who have discovered a fascinating pastime, the group labored industriously, rolling huge boulders to the east of the cliff where they would give them a start; then stand erect, faces flushed from their exertions, and eyes sparkling as they watched the boulders bound down the mountainside; clattering, bouncing, smashing through branches of trees, and sometimes disintegrating as they spun through the air.

"Oh, but this is fun!" Engrid exclaimed as she watched one pancake-shaped rock fly through the air and shatter as it struck the bottom. She wiped a dirt-covered hand over her perspiring brow, leaving a long dark streak of dirt which enhanced her beauty as far as John was concerned when he stole a glance in the flushed girl's direction.

"Godfrey!" Emil gasped, "Talk about the proverbial sailor taking his sweetie for a boat ride while on his vacation, here we are, hard-working, hard-rock miners toiling our guts out rolling rocks for the fun of it, and in the mine we get paid for it."

"But it's such sport!" Hulda exclaimed.

John, meanwhile, cast his eyes around until he found himself looking longingly at a huge boulder resting on the hillside a little removed from the cliff.

"Emil," he said in a positive voice, "that particular boulder there…"

"That big one?"

"That's the baby; I have wanted to send that down over the cliff; I've tried it with kids, and we never made it budge. Let's see if we can move it and if we can, holy-hell, what a smash that will be!"

Infected with his enthusiasm, "Let's!" Emil exclaimed.

Together, the brawny giants placed their backs to the huge rock. "Now!" said Emil. The men's bodies quivered with the strain that they threw into their attempt.

"It rose a little!" Louise said breathlessly. The men tried again, but succeeded only in raising one edge a trifle.

"If you men will admit that you are licked," Arvid said carelessly, "I will give you a hand."

The three of them succeeded in causing the rock to move, and slowly they forced it to the edge of the cliff. The women, in a fever of excitement, lay on their stomachs at the cliff edge and watched expectantly as the rock, with tantalizing slowness, rolled a little then seemed to jerk itself off, to hurtle down with startling swiftness. It struck at the foot of the cliff and amid a shaking, clattering upheaval of shattered talus dust and broken boulder, found its rest.

"Oh!" gasped the women at this climax to their rock rolling. "I wish we had been born here!" Louise ejaculated.

"Stuff like this is what makes big men," John boasted as he flexed his arm muscles. "I was raised on rock rolling."

"What do you say we find some pine nuts?" Arvid suggested after a look at the sun.

His proposal was met with enthusiasm. John and Engrid climbed one slope and others took their chosen routes to groups of trees which attracted them.

Staring up into the trees, Engrid's sharp eyes presently discerned green, glistening cones, and she notified John of the fact.

He chose a tree that was burdened with cones, and up he climbed; while the watching girl occasionally directed him in his efforts to fill the gunnysack. Those he could not reach because of slender branches which couldn't be trusted to bear his weight, he knocked off with a long branch of dry pine which the girl passed to him. These cones Engrid gathered in her apron until she had collected a substantial pile.

"Do you think we have enough to fill a sack?" John inquired.

Engrid surveyed the results of heir efforts with a judicious eye and shook her head from side to side.

"We'll try another tree," he concluded. Halfway down the tree he stopped and procured a chunk of hard pine pitch. "Want some?"

Engrid nodded and he threw a chunk to her. The girl chewed and expectorated in imitation of her companion, and found the act contained a particular pleasure in keeping with the surroundings and her effervescent spirits.

"I'm taking some with me," John said as he dug several pieces off and placed them in a shirt pocket. "This is great stuff to chew when I'm working in the dust."

Under the next tree, Engrid settled herself on a carpet of needles and gazed about with contemplative eyes. She observed a squirrel scampering across a clearing and disappearing in a jumble of weathered rocks, its whistle piercing the sylvan woodland drowsing under the autumn sun. Perfumed with the odors of pine, warm air wafted to her nostrils; and the buzzing undertone of deerflies added a note of incomparable peacefulness. Sounding richly charged with happiness, women's laughter interspersed with the muffled conversation of men came from further along the hill.

Lazily stretching out on the warm pine needles, Engrid stared through half-closed eyes. Peace filled her soul as she felt herself attuned to a feeling of harmony lying over the tree-shaded slope dipping to the top of the huge cliff. A faint breeze moved the grass as it drifted over a neighboring hill, and whispered through the trees with a soughing, hypnotic sound. The tired girl slept.

In the meantime, John finished picking all that he could reach; so taking his stick, he began to belabor the outside branches. A startled cry came from the girl who had awakened at the first blow in time to open her eyes and close them again instinctively as cones flew through the air under John's determined swipes.

"What is it, Engrid? What is the matter?"

"Oh," she cried, "one hit me in the eye."

John hurried to her side and without thinking grasped her fair head in his pitch-covered hands and forcing her to raise her face. "Let me see where I hit you!" he exclaimed in an agitated voice.

Engrid, trying to open the bruised member, removed her hand from her eye. She found the pain too great, and was forced to press the back of her hand to her eye again.

When John stood up, she uttered another cry, and the amazed man found that his hands had pulled several strands of hair from her head. John ruefully striving to pluck hair from his hands failed. He stooped and grasped dirt and rubbed his hands vigorously; then he made his way to where the others had built a fire and procured a water bag. When he returned to the girl, he soaked a handkerchief and directed the girl to apply it to her eye.

After a time, she removed the rag.

"You have a black eye!" he said in amazement. "Gosh, how could I be so careless?"

"I was the one who was careless; I shouldn't have lain under the tree. What a rude awakening that was! I dozed off for a moment with the most restful feeling imaginable; then this had to happen."

"Can you see with that eye?" he inquired anxiously.

Engrid opened it with difficulty and found that she could.

"That's fine." John exclaimed in a relieved voice; then chuckled nervously, as he looked at the woebegone girl.

"That is the blackest blue eye I have ever seen on a girl," he remarked.

"And what is so funny about getting my eye blackened?"

"It's not that; it's just what the others will have to say about it, that's funny. It is a beauty!"

"And what will they have to say?"

"They will accuse me of poking you in the eye because you wouldn't let me kiss you," he chortled. "Let me see it again."

Sheepishly, Engrid displayed her orb; John took one look and promptly began to roar with laughter. At first Engrid felt humiliated; then catching the humor inherent in the incident, and John's remarks, she too laughed.

"This is no place to be sitting while I starve to death." Engrid said at length. Standing up she proceeded to gather pine nuts until the bag was filled. John tied the sack with a shoelace, and they made their way to the fire where he threw sticks on the coals, removed the pitch and dirt with lard and rags and placed steaks in two pans. The odor of the meat combined with the scent of cedar wood smoke, and the aroma of warmed-over coffee made Engrid's mouth drool in anticipation while she watched the gallant man prepare dinner. Into another pan he sliced onions and potatoes; he gave the contents a generous sprinkling of salt and pepper; then placed a lid on the pan allowing it to steam. Occasionally, he raised the lid and turned the food over. Engrid's heart warmed to John's kindness.

When the other members came from the trees, Louise looked at her sister ad gasped, "Good heavens! What has happened to your eye?"

"I hit her," John said in a matter-of-fact voice.

"You hit her? What for?" Hulda asked in alarm. This was unheard of; men just didn't do things like that.

Emil seemed perplexed; Arvid looked askance at the man and then the girl.

"Why, I never heard of such an outrageous act!" Louise gasped, "What did…"

"Oh, can't you take a joke, you dumbbell? John was knocking pine nuts from a tree with a long stick, and fool that I am; I fell asleep off to one side. A cone hit me just as I opened my eyes."

"That is the blackest blue eye I have ever seen," Emil echoing John's summary remarked, and healthy laughter attended further preparations for dinner.

"Sakes alive!" Mrs. Kosky gasped, "Who gave you that?"

"It's a present from John." Engrid then related the day's happenings to the amused woman.

"Is there any chicken left?" John, perpetually hungry, asked.

"I think so; although the boys have been piecing all afternoon."

Leaving Alena, the couple went to the kitchen and fell to eating all over again. When they went in to see Mrs. Kosky again, she informed them that Mr. Hansen had fixed her the nicest dinner, and it had been such a beautiful day, and that she had several visitors, including Mrs. Meyers. She had read the Sunday paper and Mrs. Snell had dropped in and left papers from Finland stating that trouble between Finland and Russia was becoming graver all the time, with the Russians threatening to take the whole country over.

"Let's roast some pine nuts," the girl said at length.

"How should we cook them? Baked or boiled?" John asked.

"Whichever you prefer."

"Baked ones have the brownest, nuttiest flavor," he informed her knowingly.

"How about the pan to bake them in?" she asked.

"Mrs. Kosky will raise fancy hell if we use a baking pan; I'll go out back of the coal shed; I think that there is a pan there that we can discard after we finish, if some kids haven't taken it."

Out back, he rummaged around and found a piece of tin which he decided was good enough. He covered it with cones, and placed it in the oven.

"This is no fun," he exclaimed; "let's build a fire and roast them in the backyard!"

They lit a cheery fire, and buried the cones in the coals, and as the men came from town, they gravitated to the circle and began to munch on the nuts.

Engrid tried to crack the nuts between her fingernails, after removing them from the cone.

"Watch me," John directed as he placed a nut between his teeth, and biting gently, he cracked the shell; then turning it a half turn, he bit again. One-half of the shell came off in his fingers, and with a deft twist of his tongue he rolled the nut end-over-end and pulled the second half of the shell off. After a few tries, Engrid found herself doing it as he showed her.

"There's only one thing wrong with eating pine nuts, Mr. Hansen exclaimed, "they don't grow as big as peaches."

"If they did, people wouldn't enjoy pine nut hunting," John replied.

Engrid went to work and removed a cupful of nuts from several cones and these she took into the thankful woman who sat in bed, watching the group around the dancing flames. One on the men began to sing, and others joined in, and for an hour or more, the neighborhood rang to cheery voices. Finally, with the last nut gone, Engrid and John found themselves alone by the dying coals after the others had retired. She went silent, filled with a sense of peace. John in a talkative mood, spoke of his lease, and told the girl amusing incidents which had befallen him and Emil. He chuckled reminiscently and when Engrid asked him what he was laughing at, he told her.

"When I was in Park City, Emil and August Sunbloom went on a bender, one Saturday night. We were staying in the same boarding house. I had been up town, hoisting a few drinks, and it began to rain cats and dogs. It rained so hard, and the water in the creek rose so high that it swept several of the outhouses away and down the creek. Instead of digging outhouses as we do here, they just stand them on timbers over the creek and the water serves as a sewer. Emil and August felt the urge to go places, so in the pitch darkness, and both drunk as all get out, they started for home. To get there, a bridge crosses the old mill pond. It's easy enough to walk in daylight, when one is sober, but it is a treacherous bit of footing at night, even if one isn't inebriated. I think it was an hour later that I decided that I had better go home. The rain had stopped by this time, and about halfway across the bridge, I observed a figure lying on its belly on the wet bridge. I asked who it was and what was the matter, and Emil's voice answered me. I struck a match, and the damnedest sight I have ever seen met my eyes. Emil was holding an umbrella over August Sunbloom's head, and August was standing in the mill pond, up to his neck in dirty water. 'What in the name of hell are you doing?' I asked.

'August fell in, and I'm keeping his head dry,' Emil answered soberly. Of course I fished him out, but it was a tough job and a tougher job still to get them to the place where we were staying. Now, if you want to get Emil's goat, all you have to do is ask, 'Do you think it will rain, Emil?'"

Engrid laughed until tears ran down her face; then she, with a great effort, restrained herself and asked, "Any others like that?"

"Yes, except that this concerns me, this time, and August. We were in the leasing game together, and shortly after the railroad came to town, a circus with all the trappings paid a week-long visit. August who hated the fact that he had to work on the streak of ore which was only about four feet high, got the idea in his head, after seeing a midget, that he would make an ideal man to push the wheel barrow full of ore down our tunnel. We had been drinking, and together we approached the midget on the last evening that the circus was in town. August asked if he wanted to work in the mine, and the midget stated flatly that he wasn't intending to do any work harder than shoveling beans at the supper table. After the show was over, and having previously reconnoitered the grounds, August and I sneaked into the tent where the little fellow was sleeping. Our intentions, of course, were to abduct him after we had got him sufficiently drunk. August shook him, and the little fellow woke up."

"'What in the hell are you fellows doing here?' he said."

"'Shh!' said August, placing his hand over the little fellow's mouth. 'We merely wanted you to know that there were no hard feelings, and we have a drink for you.'"

"The little fellow decided that he had better get up to do his drinking, and he suggested that we go to the creek below the circus ground so that his wife wouldn't see him. How the man liked his whiskey! Well, after a time, August picked him up and carried him to his buggy, and away we went to Kitty's place. What an evening!" John exclaimed with a pensive sigh. "We got the fellow up on the polished oak bar where he danced, sang, made love to one of the girls and presented a sideshow that kept the crowd roaring with laughter. Just as we got ready to go, a crowd of those tough circus roustabouts came in with blood in their eyes, after having first gone through every saloon in town."

"'Sparrow', he said, walking up to the pint-sized man, 'who kidnapped you?'"

"Sparrow pointed to me and August."

"'Take them, men!' the circus owner called to his gang who were in an ugly mood after searching the whole town and drinking at each saloon."

"What a glorious, free-for-all, knock-down-and-drag-out affair that was! Those circus toughs, about fifty altogether, tangled with about an equal number of miners. One picked up the Chinese cook who poked his head out of the kitchen door and threw him through a window; after that, I was to busy with my fists to remember much; and when the city marshal and a dozen-odd deputies got there, late as usual, to restore order, the floor was littered with the wreckage of broken bottles, shattered chairs and overturned gaming tables. From where I raised my head in an attempt to get up, after I had knocked the circus owner out with a hefty right to the jaw, I could see Kitty's girls staring down at us from the balcony of the second floor. Some were frightened, some excited, and some glorying in the action and bloodshed that had taken place. Kitty just stood in the middle of the crowd of girls with a cynical smile on her lips, after she had sent a runner to get the law. I struggled to my feet, and lo' and behold, the midget was the only man from the circus crowd still on his feet, and he was on the top of the bar. As I stood erect, he raised a bottle of whisky to his mouth, said, 'Skoal!' and fell off the bar, dead drunk."

"And who paid for the damages?" Engrid managed to ask after she had dried her eyes following a period of prolonged laughter that left her feeling weak.

"Kitty was nice about it; she made it up on the gaming tables in about one hour's time the following payday."

"And did you get the little man to work for you?"

"Nope; the marshal gathered up the circus men and took them back to the circus grounds with orders not to come back downtown again."

"You mean for the circus not to come back to town again?"

"No, just that particular crew of rough necks."

Engrid fell silent and watched where the handle of the big dipper framed the top of a mountain in the north of the town, as though the black mass of rock were supporting a comb, incrusted with diamonds. She signed at length and stood erect.

"I'd better go in now; and I have had a wonderful time."

John stood erect, and moved to her side. He gazed long on her fair face and her star-lit eyes. "I'm glad," he said, and as the girl turned to the house and her bed, he drew a bucket of water from the well and doused the fire. After that, he stood for a long time, watching vapor rise from the dying coals. Satisfied that the fire was out, he too, went inside.

Chapter 21

As time went by, other men came to stay at the boardinghouse, and Mrs. Kosky gladly took down a sign saying "Rooms for Rent With or Without Board." She retained Engrid, paying her four dollars per week, and Engrid was glad to remain.

Simple, heartwarming things did John and Engrid share and with that sharing, a bond grew between then.

"Look inside!" John said one day when he passed Engrid an empty dynamite cap box containing something that proved to be a loosely piled jumble of gleaming threads.

"What is it?" she asked, probing the mass of wires with a forefinger.

"It is wire silver; occasionally we come across it in the richest part of the ore bodies; although generally shooting destroys it."

Engrid's warm smile and thanks amply rewarded him for his thoughtfulness.

Although the young woman progressed with her English, she found learning tedious, tired as she was from the daily repetition of hard work. John encouraged her, however; until finally she could pick up the Salt Lake Express and read in halting words sounding harsh to her ears. She would read sentences aloud at John's insistence, pausing and rereading, savoring the words with her tongue, over and over; until their meaning in Swedish and English tied together in her mind.

John took her to the assay office where she peeped through a hole in the furnace at ore samples melting in fire-clay cups. These were dumped into indentations on a metal tabletop, and so hot was the ore that it flowed like syrup. The liquid solidified as she watched; then the man struck the glassy surface with a hammer, exposing metal in the bottoms of the receptacles. She watched, wide-eyed as the assayer pounded the pliable fragments into cubes of various sizes up to a half-inch in thickness. These were placed on cylinders of bone char that were saucer-like, indented at the top. After being inserted in the white heat of the furnace, the lead was absorbed into the char leaving buttons of gleaming silver resting on the surface. When they were allowed to cool, the man picked them up, with a pair of tweezers, and placed them on delicate scales housed in glass lest a current of air throw them off balance. From the weight of the buttons of silver, each representing a sample from different working mines, the total amount of silver in a ton of ore could be estimated, thus eliminating the possibility of mining valueless rock.

"Here," said the assayer opening a cigar box, "take a look at these. I do them in a spare moment."

Peeping inside, Engrid marveled at an assortment of rings, earrings, broaches, belt buckles, miniature animals, quaint men and women made of silver. They were so soft and pliable that they bent easily under pressure. With a tiny punch, the metallurgist had inserted intricate designs into their surfaces.

"I save the stuff from the samples, melt it, and beat it out," the metallurgist stated in a matter-of-fact voice.

"How would you like one for a souvenir?" John asked of the dumbfounded girl.

"Oh, I couldn't even dream of it," Engrid gasped as she fondled the various pieces, turning them over and over; while she marveled that here was metal which gave value to her work, and measured services rendered by people the world over. Here was metal her mother had hoarded so that she might have a home in her old age. Here was a metal that gave power to nations and individuals who possessed it, and made obscure and unknown those who had it not.

"How much for the bracelet, Bob?" John asked.

"Fifteen dollars, and that don't pay for the actual time I put on it." The man answered promptly.

"Here you are," John remarked peeling off a five and a ten; then he said to Engrid, as he placed a stuffed wallet away. "Choose the one you like."

Engrid complied hesitantly, and John placed the soft metal around her wrist, then molded it to fit.

"You shouldn't purchase a thing as expensive as that for me; it costs as much as my month's wages," the girl objected.

"But not for me," he replied pressing the band firmly around the girl's wrist, "there, that was made just for you. All I ask you to do is give a thought to the poor suckers who each sent a sample up so that you might wear the silver on your wrist. Most people who buy jewelry think nothing of the men who dug it out for them. If they did, they would look at their ornaments with a feeling of profound awe, and feel reverence when they realize that some man with a houseful of kids to feed, dug the metal because he loved them, even though he hated to slave in darkness to keep them from starving."

"But I do realize that," she replied with a wistful smile, "and I do cherish it." She glanced lovingly at the two hearts which were interlocked and wondered if John appreciated the symbol.

"It's right pleased your misses is," Bob said after deftly directing a brown stream of tobacco juice through an open window and into a pile of shattered clay cups.

John smiled, thanked the man and led the girl out of the comfortably warm assay office into the brisk autumn air.

Christmas proved to be an occasion of particular significance at the boardinghouse. Preparations started on the first of November with the purchase of gifts for loved ones in Europe.

Engrid sent her mother a silk coat; her father five pounds of tobacco which John recommended, and her brother was to be gladdened with a silver initialed ring purchased from the assayer. The latter she bought large enough so that it might be cut down, if necessary.

On the first day of December, Mrs. Kosky placed an order for dried stock-fish.

"This is the time of the year I appreciate old-country customs," the butcher chattered as he led the woman and Engrid to the rear of the store. He showed them cord after cord of dried fish piled, much in the manner of stacked firewood at home, high to the ceiling.

Mrs. Kosky placed her order, and when the fish were delivered that afternoon, she laid them in three tubs in which she had dissolved a quantity of lye, causing the water to feel as soft as rain in her hands.

"Maybe we can't have fresh fish," she observed, gesturing to the yellow slabs; "but by the time we change the lye water to lime water and bleach the yellow color out in the process, we're going to have some mighty tasty dinners! Of course, we'll have to soak them in several changes of fresh water; but we can wait. I am so hungry for fish other than smoked herring that I feel like chewing on a piece the way it is."

For several days the fish swelled and smelled, necessitating an additional pair of tubs; then, following the prearranged plan, the woman threw out the lime water and put the fish to soak in fresh water. During the waiting period, the boarders made daily visits to the tubs, poking the fish with an air of deliberation; then wandering into the dining room, they discussed the advisability of cooking a portion of the fish before it was sufficiently treated.

"It'll give you the worst gut-ache you ever had," Mr. Hansen gravely warned John when he suggested that they experiment some night after the landlady had retired. John's yearnings for a mess of the under-soaked fish bowed to the older man's reasoning.

Falling steadily all day and night, snow appeared ten days before Christmas. Engrid rose in the cold dawn, shivering as she laid fire in the cook-stove. Regretfully she suppressed a desire to snuggle under blankets warm from the heat of her young body; instead she opened the door on the pot-bellied heating stove and vigorously shook the ashes, then dumped a half-bucket of coal on embers which quickly burst into flame, and a steady droning of the fire dispelled bitter cold from the room.

Engrid removed ashes from both stoves; then set the pans down by the kitchen door. As she tugged, the door flew inward, followed by a mass of powdery snow that had banked against the door during the night. Grasping a broom, she swept vigorously until the porch was clean; then she went on to clear a path to where the buried ash-pile thrust its cone-shaped whiteness above the level of the yard.

Stars shone in frosted brilliance from a clear sky. On the hills warm air from mine shafts coming in contact with the frigid atmosphere, created billowing volumes of vapor.

All that had been angular, irregular and unclean had been obscured by the falling flakes. Symmetrical curves of white on the eastern side of snow-covered objects, deepened to a pale shade of blue, as night dissolved slowly over the mountains whose once dark, pine-covered crests, seemed to flow and merge into the isomeric stillness of the valley.

From the hollow above the Blue-Bell mine, an owl hooted mournfully; subtly echoing the spiritual feeling of peace enfolding the girl, the compressor of the Little Chief mine puffed rhythmically as though the very earth were breathing sighs of contentment as it snuggled under the white blanket.

"If I had a talent for painting, what a picture I would do," Engrid said aloud as she stood with broom in hand, drinking in the beauty of the overall transformation of the village and hills long since denuded of autumn coloring. She gazed spellbound at chalk-roofed houses and huge drifts which wind had swirled into sloping banks against the side of the boardinghouse, obscuring many windows of the first floor. On the west of sheds were bare patches of ground shaped like half-moons overlooked by serenely poised drifts.

Turning from her reverie, Engrid glanced toward the dumps of the Little Chief mine, and on its road saw a blotch of darkness which, moving nearer, resolved it's self into six straining, heavily breathing horses from whose flaring nostrils, vapor gushed spasmodically. The horses were pulling a v-shaped wooden plow weighted down with boulders enabling it to cut a deep, wavering swath in the drifts as the animals spurred on by guttural shouts of a heavily wrapped teamster; moved around the intersection, then in the direction of the depot they disappeared from view. Engrid, tearing herself from her reverie, went into the house, grasping the pans of ashes and with a twinge of regret, scattered ashes over the priceless beauty of the yard.

"Engrid," said John, after partaking of several cups of coffee, "how would you like to go for a sleigh ride this evening.

"On a small sleigh?"

"I'll rent a horse and sled at the livery, and we can take some supplies out to a fellow who is working for me."

"Is it far?"

"About an hour's ride, I should judge."

"That's alright with me," Engrid said.

"We'll have to get there before dark; you had better see if Alena will let you off."

Mrs. Kosky received Engrid's request with elation. "A ride in the brisk air is just what you need, poor girl; you've been working without a day off for a long time and it's about time you were having some fun. Do go and have a good time."

Engrid found herself snuggled under a huge lap robe of bear skin; the horse going at a brisk trot, the cheerful clamor of bells announced their movement past cliffs marking the exit from town. Between the city dump and the cemetery they hastened, and Engrid shivered as she stared at several mounds outside of the fence surrounding the main burial ground when John informed her that they were the graves of girls who had catered to men's desires.

After pulling off the main road; they headed in a northerly direction. They followed a narrow road that was otherwise undisturbed except for occasional rabbit tracks and dog-like prints, which John informed her that they were coyote's. At one place the snow was splotched by red where the hunted had been overtaken by the hunter, and the victim's flailing legs had threshed about.

The sled moved swiftly along, with a fine spray rising in the couple's faces, and sprinkling the robe with tiny pellets. Drooping under their crystalline burdens, cedar trees formed a canopy under which Engrid surmised it would be sporting to plow from one to another in a game of hide-and-seek, were she a youngster with several children accompanying her.

Sage was bowed under the snow's weight, and in places burned-over patches of brush protruded through the mantle. Wild oats, reared sere stalks in rigid clusters above the surface where restless tumbleweeds had ended their wind-driven wanderings.

A pair of crows, their croaks sounding rusty, wing beats appearing sluggish; waded by overhead.

The faint shushing sound of wind brushing the girl's face grew louder as the horse increased its pace; and flying clods of compressed snow from the horse's hooves thumped on the guard.

Engrid's gloom slid away as effortlessly as the runners sliding over the snow; she felt elation when they descended at an increased pace to the bottoms of washes; and rose with startling swiftness over the crests.

Finally, while clouds of vapor rose from its steaming body, the horse slowed its pace of its own accord to regain its wind.

Breaking the long silence, "Does it cost much?" Engrid asked abruptly.

"What?" John asked blankly.

"Prospecting. Tell me about your claim," she answered brushing an accumulation of snow from the robe.

"Oh," he replied, "my mind was a thousand miles away." He slapped the horse with the reins and the animal obediently increased its lagging gait. "The work is hard and slow and the cost, enormous."

"Oh?"

"Barrett, he's working for me, puts the holes into the ground with hand-drills, hitting the head of the drill with a hammer, or single-jack, as we call it. After each blow, the drill is turned about a quarter-turn; then he hits again. After countless hits, the hole goes into the rock a few inches. As for cost," he reflected, "an engineer at the Little Chief mine once told me that there has been more work done, valued in dollars, then the total of all silver and gold ore which has been mined the world over. I can easily believe that when I look at dumps scattered over the entire country. Men have spent their lives without getting a fraction of what their work is worth. Until a couple of years ago, all of the drilling was done by hand."

He pointed at the mountainsides from which they had descended. "Those dumps scattered along the hills are only a few of the monuments which prospectors have left to mark their passing. Those dumps, where ore was never found, will lie forever where they have been shoveled by half-starved men who preferred the solitude of the mountains and deserts, and the song of the lonely wind, yapping coyotes, to the cheerful atmosphere of a home and a woman's lullaby."

"But what manner of men are these who prefer to live as you say?" Engrid asked with a shiver. Pulling the robe closer, she snuggled against John's big body and felt the gratifying warmth when legs came together under the robe.

"They are set in their ways," he replied. "Some have a deep lying anti-social streak deeply ingrained in their natures. There are some who have been wealthy and live in dreams of finding another fortune. Quite a number of these men have ended up here in the mountains and desert wastes to get away from past lives. Some are murderers and criminals; although you wouldn't know it to look at them. There are some whom God made almost self-sufficient; however, most require the companionship of a dog, burro or horse and their dreams."

"What a horrible life to contemplate," Engrid remarked. Peering over the valley, she sensed the brooding desolation and timelessness of these wastes which had swallowed wanderers who had spent a lifetime scratching a pitiful obituary on the mountainsides. Yet, she knew, if it hadn't been for these same dreamers, the earth's wealth would never have been tapped, pouring a silver and gold stream into its commerce. Emil would never have come to this place, Louise would never have followed him, and she, herself, would not be riding along this road by the side of the man she loved.

But what of this man? Dared she hope that their desires were alike? True, they had often been together since Mrs. Kosky had met with her mishap but that was as far as matters had progressed.

Perhaps he had made no attempt at intimacy because she had not thrown herself at him. Maybe she had not used her feminine allure. Silly thought; she couldn't be any different than her natural self. She would have to continue with a pretense once she started. Of course, by action she could brazenly express a desire that she felt with increasing urgency; but in all probability, such a course of action would drive the man away in disgust.

Maybe his experience with Rika had embittered John. Perhaps he had given himself to her; and then, after wearying of his attentions, she had dropped him.

Engrid dismissed the thought with a shrug. Girls are either all good or all bad she decided; but are they? Rika had seemed all good. It showed in her face and actions, except for that smug air of superiority which was so hard for one to overlook. There was the marriage to Alex soon after the break with John. Could it have been that Rika, using John, had hoped to establish a bond strong enough to force the man to comply with her wishes? That could be possible, Engrid pondered, glancing over at John steering the course of the sleigh with firm hands.

Because Rika was a proud woman it wasn't at all impossible that she had misjudged her hold on this man, and finding too late that she would have to bow to his wishes, rather than he to hers. She had chosen marriage to Alex who was attractive in his way, although different in most respects from John who balked at being led by a female.

Perhaps Rika had used him as she had used John, thereby solving some rather pressing problems. Engrid smiled at the thought. After all, anyone who had been around this man sitting beside her, couldn't help knowing that if some woman decided to follow him, he would take her without much thought into a life of his own choosing.

"I could follow him anywhere," she told herself as fear encountered desire and the ching, ching, chinging of bells on the horse beat time with her buoyant thoughts.

The horse turning toward the hills, settled into a slow walk as the contour of the country became increasingly steeper, and the snow deeper when they entered a narrow canyon. Here the animal pulled mightily to surmount the high drifts; and just when Engrid concluded that the horse could go no farther, the sleigh rounded a cliff and halted before a one-room cabin from whose tin stack, smoke rose into the air. A hound with flopping ears boomed a challenge which the hills swallowed.

"Hello, Spike," John addressed the animal warmly as it lunged through the snow and in a frenzy of excitement it jumped at the man and tried to lick his face. John was forced to restrain him so the dog turned to the girl.

"Get down, Spike!" a heavy voice boomed from the opened cabin door.

John waved a greeting as he tied the horse to a pine tree, slipped a nose bag containing a generous serving of oats over the horse's head and the animal began to eagerly chomp the grain. John rubbed the horse down; then tied a horse blanket over the steaming animal.

John picked up a box of groceries, sack of flour and a sack of doughnuts. Engrid carried a roll of newspapers. Engrid followed John as he plunged into the snow, while the dog cavorted playfully running from the visitors to its master in its enthusiasm.

"How are you, Charles? Meet Engrid Isaacson."

"Howdy, Miss, I'm pleased to make your acquaintance; come in, come in," Charles replied.

Because the cabin's occupant had held the door open since the dog had announced their arrival, Engrid at first found that the air in the cabin seemed a welcome relief; but as Charles talked, she became increasingly and uncomfortably aware of odors; the putrescence of rancid grease which had soaked into the wooden floor during preparation of meals mingling with powder gas clinging to the miner's work clothes, and the sickening stench of unwashed sweat.

Engrid held a perfumed handkerchief to her nostrils at intervals, seeking to overlook the collective smell. Peering around the room, she noticed the small stove whose lids glowed red over the coal fire. A powder box, emptied of its original contents, and filled with cedar wood kindling, reposed in the corner beside three others heaped with coal.

On a wooden scabby green cot lay three straw-filled burlap sacks, two filthy blankets and a patchwork quilt. From the walls were suspended weathered clippings showing mustached men with clenched fists and wearing long, skin-fitting tights. They were posed in various stances denoting their professions, and each displayed rhinestone studded belts.

In various, voluptuous appearing stages of undress, several pictures of women also hung listlessly from the walls. One smoke stained window emitted an unreal twilight into the room. One bottom pane had been broken, and a sack of straw filled the gaping hole. On a rough table sprawled a jumble of dirty utensils. In a pan reposed a portion of brown beans covered with a dried surface.

John paused in his conversation with Mr. Barrett and returned some fragments of rock to the man who tossed them into a box on a shelf near the window.

"Charles wants to know if you'll have a cup of coffee and a plate of beans," he said with a sly wink. Engrid declined with a shake of her head; almost gagging through a forced smile.

"Would you care to struggle through the drifts while I look the diggings over; or would you sooner wait here where it is warm?"

Restraining a shudder, Engrid jumped at the first suggestion, with a vigor which caused John to smile knowingly. The miner pulled on his coat, cap and gloves then directed the dog to go outside and watch the cabin.

"I'll bet my clothing will stink forever," Engrid told herself as she fell in behind the prospector and John's insistence. She floundered along catching toes in sage all but concealed by the fluffy burden of white. Walking was tedious, and she strained every muscle to place booted feet into footprints of the man ahead who moved up the mountainside retracing a barely discernible indentation marking his passage from the mine after the storm.

"How are you doing?" John asked after a time.

"Fine," she managed to gasp; "It's better than sitting in that overheated cabin with a family of stinks. Heavens, doesn't that man ever clean the place up, or take a bath?"

"I suppose not," John chuckled, "he has no woman to take care of him, and many bachelor miners are the dirtiest animals on two legs. They work so hard, they don't have the energy to put out after work to clean up. They get supper cooked and the floor swept occasionally, and haven't time to bother with niceties."

"Whew, I'm losing my wind." Engrid gasped.

"Go slower if you must; you can't expect to keep up with that man. I'm walking behind in order that you may set your own pace."

Engrid conceded the wisdom of his words, plowing forward. Finally, she came to a wind-swept ridge. Pausing, she looked over the Tintic valley, which had donned a robe of purple haze.

"Oh, how inspiring! See that spiral of white smoke, way off through the trees. Isn't it wonderful how distance changes things? Down among the trees, at times, I felt moody and depressed. Up here, I feel joyous. Why is it that people's moods change so quickly?"

"Some people's moods don't," he declared; "perhaps it is something you ate," he added with a whimsical smile as he pulled her to him. She came to him unresisting, and John stared searchingly into her face. Engrid peered into his eyes and knew only that she was near to him and happy. John kissed her tenderly at first and then brutally. The girl's arms crept about him then closing her eyes, she returned the kiss; a long, unforgettable embrace it was, and pregnant with yearning. Association with this man who seemed concerned primarily with work and men's affairs, had gradually created in her a fierce hunger which now cried for consummation of their relationship here in the cold on the wind-swept hill. John held her close for a time, smothering her with hungry lips that strayed over her closed eyes, her face, and down to her warm neck where the pulse beat madly under the creamy whiteness of her skin.

"Whew!" she sighed, pushing him away. Turning her head, she avoided him as he sought her lips again; while her heart pounded madly. "We've climbed this hill for a purpose, you know," she gaily reminded him.

"By the way you kissed me; that must be the purpose of our climb. Let's do it some more."

"Oh, no," she laughed, "I can't take it." Withdrawing from his arms, she moved away in footprints rapidly being obliterated by snow, as the wind, dashing up the hill, caused the surface of the white burden to creep with a whispering musical tinkling, so fair as to barely be perceptible.

"Did… did you mean that kiss?" he gasped floundering after the girl who moved on at a faster pace, buoyed by the cold and their first embrace.

"Certainly I mean it; I don't go about sharing kisses with men just for the fun of it. Did you mean it?" she asked ducking under the waving branches of a cedar as it showered her with snow.

"What did you say? Stop a minute so I can hear you," he implored.

Pausing, Engrid repeated her question.

"Of course I meant it, you adorable girl. I'm mad about you, and I want you to marry me."

"When?"

"Today, tomorrow, as soon as we can," he suggested eagerly with a look of yearning filling his eyes. His arms again encircled her in a fierce grip, and he bent to kiss her time and again, until again she was forced to push him away. Pulling the wool scarf closer about her throat, she sought to shut out the bitter wind striking with knife-like thrusts.

"Let's get that sample you were talking about, and we can discuss the matter later," she proposed with pretended calmness that she was far from feeling. Turning, she moved again, and John fell in behind her feeling strangely elated. Along the ridge they went, and into the deep snow beyond where wind was dropping its burden. She moved laboriously forward, shrugged and came to a stop. John viewed her predicament as he plowed to her side, then shoved past in order to break a trail.

"Are you enjoying yourself?" he questioned with a boyish grin, the snow on his mustache quivering as he spoke.

"I wouldn't miss this for the world. I haven't had so much fun since the time you hit me with a pine cone. This time you made up for that injury! You kissed my eye."

"The kiss didn't hurt?"

"On the contrary, it was nice; why didn't you kiss me when you blackened my eye? I am certain that it might have relieved some of the hurt," she smiled demurely as she pulled herself up a steep section of the hill with the aid of scrub oak standing sturdily in the whipping wind.

"Did… did you want me to do that?" he gasped as the girl turned to look where he stood in slack-jawed amazement, staring into her twinkling eyes; and to the man, her laughter was bubbling water falling into a pool.

"Of course I did," she laughed.

"Gosh-oh-golly," he breathed; "how can I be so dumb and still be living." He climbed hastily to where she clung to her precarious foothold, and reached to grasp her again. A foot slipped, then a second, as he grasped her arm; and with a squeal the girl went tumbling down bowling him over into the deep snow at the foot of the slope. Engrid squealed with delight and pawed at snow covering her face; then opened her eyes to find John flat on his back, trying to remove the snow from his face. With her glove, and lying prone beside him, she brushed the snow off. He opened his eyes with a chuckle. "That does it," he exclaimed, "that will cost you a kiss." He grasped her and pulled her to him and kissed her soundly.

"Of all the places you could choose to be romantic, this is undoubtedly the craziest," Engrid giggled as she rose to her feet and clawed and scrambled her way up the hill again, her feet slipping on concealed tendrils of wild roses sleeping safely away from the biting wind. When she arrived at the summit, Engrid paused and looked back over the erratically meandering trail they made during their ascent. John eyed her and said, "I wanted to kiss you so much that day when we were halfway up the cliff, and I would have, but those other apes were lying on their stomachs, peering at us and wishing that I would, so that they might have something to kid us about. I decided that I wouldn't give them the satisfaction. Right then when you looked over the valley, I wished that I were a painter and could catch the happiness covering your face when you told me that the view was the most beautiful that you had ever seen. Oh, Engrid," he said softly, taking her in him arms, "you are the most bewitching creature I have ever laid eyes on. Say that you love me, please!"

Evading his command, "Was that the only reason why you didn't kiss me?" she asked with Rika in mind.

"Well," he hesitated.

"Well, what?"

"I was afraid to," he answered boyishly; "afraid that you might repulse me, and I would sooner go on thinking that I might have done so."

"Silly boy." She stood up on tiptoe and kissed him gently.

"Give me a big kiss, like you really meant it," he pleaded.

"On one condition,"

"I promise," he vowed.

"That we continue with whatever business you came here for. We might be in love; however, it is a poor substitute for warmth and food. I am freezing, starving, and growing weary."

After a moment snatched from eternity, John released her and climbed ahead, pulling the girl up places where she slipped on concealed branches. They crossed over a last ridge to find themselves at the mouth of a tunnel with its pile of waste running out from the hillside and spilling down into a hollow.

At the mouth of the tunnel, the prospector held three candles which he lighted.

"We follow behind him," John directed, "and watch the candle grease doesn't drop on your coat, or you'll have a devil's own time removing the spot."

The trio walked along for about a hundred and fifty feet in air which was apparently warmer than the outside; although smelling of underground and the musty odor of powder gas. Walking with cautious steps, Engrid followed in the pattern made by the wheel of the barrow in which the man hauled out the waste rock.

"Watch your step that you don't turn an ankle," John cautioned as one foot rolled on a rock in a pile of rubble near the face of the drift.

Engrid coughed, gasped and wiped at tears; while a feeling of dread subtly permeated her being as she imagined she was smothering when she closed her eyes against the stinging powder gas. She pictured huge boulders falling from the back of the tunnel forever shutting her away from contact with the outside air and the glorious sunlight.

"I'm afraid, John," she gasped.

"Nonsense," he rebuked her; "you'll never make a miner."

His words restored her equanimity; although she crowded closer to him and gasped his arm tightly. "I might not be one," she corrected him humorously, "but I'll bet I can make one."

John laughed heartily, then turned from the girl who succeeded in conquering her trepidation enough to become interested in her surroundings, as she glanced back to where they had made a turn in the tunnel; and she discerned the outside light illuminating the bend.

"Why did you turn the tunnel from the straight line that it was following?"

"Look above your head here, I'll show you," he replied as borrowing a sample pick from the miner, he exposed rock coated with dust. "See this streak of brownish-looking rock paralleling the center line of the tunnel? That is the quartzite that the man is following. It carries values of twelve dollar a ton in silver, copper and gold. That is what we are following in hopes that it may develop into something."

"Oh," Engrid replied, understanding what he was saying. She took a chunk of the rock which John had scratched loose and compared it to the gray lime incasing it on both sides. "This, then, is ore?"

"Right."

John moved to the end of the tunnel and scratched at the face. A series of exploratory jabs with the pick showed him that the vein of quartzite continued ahead as it had since the tunnel had been turned following the cross-break. He picked at the streak of ore and placed the fragments into a sample sack which the prospector held until the bag was full; then he tied a piece of shoelace about the top and jounced it up and down in a hand.

"There," he stated in a satisfied voice, "I'll take this in and have it assayed. The first thing we know, we'll have a mine here." Turning to the prospector, he remarked, "You will be coming in for the holidays?"

"Oh, yes; I'll see you around, and we'll have a drink of Christmas cheer. I wonder," he added hopefully, "if Mrs. Kosky could set an extra plate for me? I would sooner eat a Christmas dinner there than at a restaurant."

"She'll be glad to," John said heartily.

After relinquishing their candles to the man who placed them on an overhead timber, the couple started the return trip to find that the wind had stopped.

"It'll be cold tonight," John said knowingly; "I'm glad that we have a good lap robe as well as the bear skin to snuggle under on the homeward trip."

Darkness had all but wrapped the barren country in its toils when they reached the cabin after sliding down the last hill. At this particular elevation, the girl romped along, plowing through the smother with carefree abandon, and her laughter pealed cheerfully as John made awkward attempts to overtake her on a dare. They paused at the cabin for the leisurely approach of the miner whose face was wreathed in a huge grin.

"My, what fun you youngsters do have! I wish I were half my age, and I'd join you."

John removed the blanket and nose bag from the horse; as the horse nickered delightedly at his approach.

"I have some cheer for you," John said, as pulling off a glove, he thrust a hand into his coat pocket. "I thought that you might be in need of a drink."

"Bless your soul," the bachelor said with eyes alight in anticipation as he accepted the bottle. He thanked John profusely and concluded; "A spot of liquor is a fine thing to have after work when one is cold and tired. It was kind of you to bring it. Have a drink."

"No, thanks, I'm not drinking tonight," John said with a glance at Engrid.

The miner tilted the bottle and helped himself to a hearty swig, then he replaced the cork and opened the door of the cabin.

"Won't you come in?" he asked as the dog bounded from the door and fairly swarmed over him whining its joy at the man's return.

"We'd better be getting along," John said diplomatically. "The girl has to get back to work." Engrid climbed in and John adjusted the blanket about her feet, then climbed in beside her.

"I'll have these samples run," John said as he clucked to the horse eager to be on the move again. "So long, Charles, and take care of yourself."

Charles waved a hand and disappeared inside. Engrid perceived a faint yellow light shining bravely through the gloom just before they moved from the canyon and onto the valley floor. She shivered at the thought of living as did the man back yonder; then she faced forward, watching trees whose forms seemed close and comforting after the experience of climbing the wind-swept hills.

John held the horse in, until reaching comparatively level ground, he loosened the reins a trifle, and the animal broke into a fast trot. He turned to the girl his face framing a disarming smile, "Couldn't you get a bit closer?"

"I'm practically in your lap now," she objected; nevertheless she snuggled against him and he ran an arm around her neck. "Gosh, I'm hungry, John; I can't recall ever having been this hungry before."

"You had a chance to eat some sourdough biscuits and beans," he reminded her.

"I wouldn't drink a cup of coffee in that hovel," she snorted, recalling the disheveled room and its rank smells. She breathed deeply of crisp air and looked where the sky gave promise of an early moon. "Why do men have to be so dirty?"

"I suppose all of us would be the same way if there were only men in the world," he replied kindly.

"And I suppose all women, if there were no men," Engrid added, knowing she spoke the truth. A feeling of pity for the man who drank to break the monotony of his existence came over her. The thoughts of his loneliness depressed her, and then caused her to feel glad that she was not living as he.

"I suppose he wouldn't be happy living around others," she ventured.

"That's right, my dear; right now he wouldn't trade places with either of us. He has a tragic past."

"Oh?"

"Yes, you see, he sent for his sweetheart, and the ship that his sweetheart was coming on was lot at sea. He never got over it, and he craves to be alone. He comes in about every four weeks to get thoroughly drunk, poor fellow." John fell silent for a time, then turning to the girl, he suggested, "How would you like to stop at the restaurant and have supper? If we go to the boardinghouse, we'll have to be satisfied with leftovers. I want a piping hot meal. I could certainly go down on a steak and finish with half of an apple pie and a gallon of hot coffee!"

"That sounds wonderful to me," Engrid replied as John goaded the horse to a faster pace with the whip.

"Get up, you; two people are starving and you just jog along."

Engrid heard gayety in her companion's voice, and responded with a sigh of bliss. "Gosh, I'm happy, John."

"Now what?"

"Oh, I was thinking of the pleasure of riding with you for the first time. Somehow, I feel that I would like to have this ride go on forever, just the two of us, riding as if in a dream." She idly watched dark trees falling behind each side of the road. "Do I sound demented, or something?"

"Or something," he responded.

"Why can't things be beautiful, inspiring and wonderful, always?" She pondered aloud. "Why must there be sorrow, pain, hate, ugliness and greed to cause people and nations such trouble?"

John ventured no opinion on the subject; he merely pulled her closer with his free arm.

The deepening darkness was dispersed by an almost full moon brazenly pushing over a high mountain. Up a canyon the lights of Mammoth blinked cheerfully for a time, then were obscured by a hill which seemed to intrude between the pair and the town, as the horse trotted steadily onward. Past the graveyard whose headstones gleamed dully in the light, the horse trotted, its hoofs thundering over a wooden bridge spanning a gulch. The moon was momentarily obscured by a calmly moving cloud whose edges gleamed like silver lace.

"Are you happy?" John asked gaily as the horse, reaching the well-packed stretch of road connecting Mammoth to Tintic, increased its pace.

"Too happy," she responded, and at her reply, John kissed her full on the lips. "Surely," the girl told herself, "I must be dreaming." She snuggled even closer to her companion, and at his suggestion, she stretched out over his lap, feet curled on the seat and blanket tucked under her chin. Between kisses, she watched the glittering moon-path scintillating like jewels on the snow. Cloud shadows trailing across the valley and up the hills moved slowly until they were gone; and all too soon the couple found themselves riding under a bridge crossing the road at the lower end of town. Engrid sat erect to restore a semblance of respectability.

Overhead, as the sled went under a trestle, a car of ore rolled on thundering wheels; and when it reached the end of the run, the door opening, spilled a deluge of glittering ore into the railroad car squatting on steel haunches below the chute.

Children by the score, taking advantage of the first heavy snowfall, converged on the main road from every trail and path their shrill cries causing others who were walking uphill, to move. As many as could promptly hook on the back of the horse-drawn sled availed themselves of an enjoyable ride uphill. The horse pulled harder with each addition, until Engrid found herself wondering if the animal would be able to surmount the steep road. It succeeded, and the youngsters dispersed to ride downhill again.

The horse walked for a time, after reaching relatively level ground, then broke into a trot again, slowed to a walk, trotted again and breathing heavily, it slowed to a steady walk, as lights from the houses fell behind. Engrid felt as if she were making her debut when they drove up main street as John called cheerful greetings to friends they passed before stopping at the livery stable.

From the livery stable, the two went to the restaurant for their late supper; and as on another occasion that John had cause to remember, the yellow-faced man with pigtails came forward with a bow.

"Soupee?" He asked with an ingratiating glance from one to the other of his visitors.

"Soupee," John stated, holding up two fingers. Turning to the girl as the waiter took his leave, Have you ever been in here before?" he asked. Engrid shook her head from side to side.

"Would you like a spot of brandy?"

"Do they serve it here?"

"Only with meals; if you want to get drunk, you'll have to go to the saloon."

"I'll take one drink right here," Engrid answered.

When the waiter brought the soup, John made their wants known and the man hastened forth with a bottle of brandy and two glasses.

"It is rather daring for me to be drinking in public, isn't it?" Engrid asked doubtfully.

"It is perfectly proper," he assured her; then, "Skoal!" they said in unison as glasses clinked together. John tossed his off and watched his companion's face; he laughed heartily when she chased her drink with a glass of water.

"Whew!" she gasped, "I would hate to make that a habit."

"I wouldn't want you to," he assured her earnestly; "because it is a bad one." He stared at her, his eyes filled with a tender light. "Engrid," he said, "I am certainly a fortunate man. The lease is paying better than wages, and there is as chance of my claim panning out into something big. Would you marry me if it did?"

"I will, even if you are penniless," she said brightly.

"When?" he questioned eagerly, and running his hand under the table he closed it over his sweetheart's small one. "Tomorrow?"

"Oh, no, John; tomorrow is too soon. I'll marry you next spring, sometime."

"And why not tomorrow?" he asked glumly.

"Because," she replied, withdrawing her hand as another couple entered the establishment in search of a late supper, "I have waited this many years for that which I want to have come only once in my lifetime. I don't feel like matters should be rushed. I want to be able to talk intelligibly so that I may associate with your friends, and simple as it may seem, be able to purchase necessities without being embarrassed. Learning to talk as you do, is hard John; you have no idea how difficult. I think I have a word, and congratulate myself on mastering it, then before I know, it slips my mind; and I am compelled to learn it all over again."

"But that shouldn't prove to be an obstacle in the way of our marriage. You can learn as fast if you are married, as you can single; in fact, you will have more time to study."

"Oh," she said, casting him a provocative smile causing her to appear even more desirable, and unattainable to the man, "I beg to differ with you. I can keep my ears open around the boardinghouse and pick up a lot when the men talk with each other."

"Perhaps the conversation that you hear there is, should I say, a trifle coarse?"

Engrid's gay laughter filled the room. "They don't use profanity, other than the usual words around me, silly. They are all well-mannered men; especially the ones from the valley."

"So?" said John with an up-lifted brow.

"Yes," she replied; "Harold Bechtol wants to take me to the Christmas dance. He said he would like to take me to the church services first, and either the Finn or the Amerikan dance hall afterwards." She sat for a time, surveying John with a mischievous twinkle in her eyes. "He doesn't drink, either."

"Remind me to throw him out of the boardinghouse when I get there." John grumbled dourly.

"What? And lose a customer for Alena? Not on your life, I won't." She regarded him playfully. "You know, you might find that difficult; because he is built like a bull."

"Well, I like that! Just for that I will throw him out!" John fairly glowered as he looked at the girl.

"Not and have me for a friend. Look here, you big Finn, you can't go throwing people around just because you hate the thoughts of competition."

"Are you going with him?"

"I will unless…"

"Unless what?"

"Unless you ask me and promise faithfully to go to church without a drink. Of course you may drink a little at the dance but don't get drunk, or I shall refuse to go home with you."

"You remind me of someone else," he grumbled as he fairly rammed a cut of steak into his mouth and chewed hastily.

"Quit acting like a spoiled child; or you'll be going to the dance with someone else. I want you to take me, dear; but you've got to remember that you can't go with a girl and expect her to accept you in the same condition that you present yourself when you're out with a bunch of boys to raise the roof in a saloon or Kitty's place."

Giving the matter his attention while eating, John came to the conclusion that it wasn't getting drunk on Christmas which sounded intriguing, but going with Engrid did; so he promised her faithfully that he wouldn't become intoxicated.

At the boardinghouse kitchen, John placed the sample with his lunch pail. "Remind me not to forget to drop it off at the assayer's in the morning," he admonished Engrid as he chucked her under the chin; then he gave her a fleeting kiss after glancing into the dining room to assure himself that no one was loitering there. "I believe I had better go to bed; I won't help you make the sandwiches for the men tonight, goodnight, my snowbird." He looked deeply into her eyes. "Are you happy?" he whispered.

"Happier than I have ever been," she replied; and rising on tiptoe, she gave him a kiss, then washed her hands and prepared sandwiches as the man took his leave. "Good night, sweetheart," she breathed in a voice audible only to herself as with radiant eyes, she watched him climb the stairs.

For the girl a wonderful event transcending all others of her past life, had taken place. Today a ride through the purple west Tintic valley had miraculously altered her outlook; now life held an overwhelming significance.

Chapter 22

On the Sunday morning before Christmas, the sky filled with gently falling snow after wind had raged furiously for three days and nights.

John barged into the kitchen where Engrid was rolling out twists of coffee cake. "Emil and I have rented a bob-sleigh and team to get a tree for Mrs. Kosky, one for him and Louise and another for the Finn Hall. Do you want to come along?" he asked and removing a rag from a can of waste fat, he vigorously greased his boots.

"But it is storming," the girl protested.

"Snowing is the word," he corrected.

Engrid looked through the window and observed large, beautiful flakes falling so softly that they appeared to be pondering as to whether or not they should touch the ground.

"Now is the time to try your sweater. We'll take a coffee pot and sandwiches, and build a fire. There is a road almost to where we want to go We'll take a tarpaulin and some blankets and fill the sled with clean straw." Giving the girl a look of pleading, he asked, "Now, do you want to go?"

Engrid, noticing that her reluctance was causing him concern, tossed John a provocative smile. "So much the better," she thought as she deftly twisted dough into figure-eight knots and placed them into a well greased pan. "I'll go after breakfast dishes are washed, providing you come back in time for me to help Alena with supper."

"It's a go!" he exclaimed grasping her in his arms, he forced her to waltz about the room.

"You crazy man!" She laughingly tore herself away and placed the rolls on top of the stove to rise; while John sauntered into the dining room and shared a Sunday paper with early risers.

After breakfast, the couple rode from the livery stable in a bob sleigh, accompanied by the cheerful jingle of harness bells. In front of Emil's house, John whistled until the pair made their appearance. Emil carrying a double-bitted axe with a handle thrust through the handle of the much-used coffee pot; Louise clutching a sack containing the makings for a tasty snack.

The quartet was carefree and chattering as John whipped the team into a fast trot. Before they had traversed a third of the distance up the road leading around the mountain to the east of town, a string of ten or more sleds on which sat or lay in "belly-booster" fashion, fifteen deliriously happy children had attached behind with their ropes. The road skirted a deep wash until it topped the rise overlooking the east valley. Here John pulled the horses to a halt and allowed the youngsters to untie their sleds. The adults watched as followed by dogs, the urchins sped down the steep grade, a fog of snow rising from dragging feet.

"I'd certainly like to ride down a hill like that," Engrid told John whose glance lingered long on the youngsters speeding away.

"We'll try it one of these first weekends," he promised. "We'll rent one of those sleds that ten or twelve can sit on; we'll get several couples, and will we have fun!" To the horse he clucked, "Get up!"

The road wound around several mountains, and the horses, walking steadily, picked their leisurely way; while the occupants of the sleigh continued on with their conversation. At intervals, the runners grated over iron rails crossing the road to waste dumps from mine tunnels. They saw piles of timber which had been hauled in during the summer weather; whose tops were heavy with snow. Over all hung a peaceful Sunday silence. An occasional watchman waved down to them as they moved under ore bins, then retired to the warmth of the stove in his shack.

John pulled the team to a halt and pointed up a ravine. "There we shall find the trees we are looking for," he remarked. "But first, I'll cut wood enough for a fire." So saying, he grabbed the axe and soon the hills echoed to its metallic ring as chips flew from a dry windfall. In a short time, he had a roaring fire going.

The snowfall stopped as the men, struggling through waist deep drifts, climbed the hillside.

Engrid filled the coffee pot with water from a bag; then she laid a blanket on a fallen log near the fire and sat beside her sister. The women watched the men move up the slope until swallowed by trees; then turning about, they gazed from their vantage point upon the scene lying below which was flooded by dazzling sunlight causing them to squint. A road leading from the hills stretched in a straight line for fifteen miles or more; then curved around an irrigation dam and straightening out; passed through a cluster of dwellings which the girls recognized as Goshen. From there, the road crossed the valley, apparently losing itself in the foothills bordering the Wasatch Mountains. At intervals along the road black dots changed their positions so slowly, that Louise surmised they must be peddlers from the valley with apples, eggs and vegetables for tomorrow's trade.

"We should never have seen anything so breathtaking as this, had we remained in Finland," Louise observed as she pointed to Timpanogas reclining in a virgin shroud, and to the right where Mount Nebo loomed in dazzling, cloud-free majesty against a turquoise sky. Absorbed in silent contemplation of the grandeur of the wintry scene, the sisters sat for a long time, wrapped in a feeling of immeasurable peace.

"At home there would be sullen skies and low banks of fog," Engrid commented with a sigh.

"Would you like to be there?"

"Oh, I would that! I'd like to spend a week with mother and father. I'd like to tell them of all the fun that I have had since coming here, and of my job at the boardinghouse. I'd like to tell them of my work for Mrs. Wilken and how I quite working for her and went to her mother-in-law's; then I'd tell her how the woman lost me because Alena was injured. I'd like to start talking," she said wistfully, "and never stop for a week straight. I'd do it, too!"

Around them, snow slid from over-burdened branches and made plopping sounds in the deep drifts as warmth from the fire spread throughout the trees. Louise slid one foot back and forth over snow which she had scuffed into a pile, until it gleamed hard and smooth.

"When do you think you will have a baby?" Engrid asked curiously as Louise stopped her scuffling and resting her elbows on her knees and her chin in her upturned palms, stared moodily into the distance.

"That is hard to say; I thought for a time that I was going to have one, but nope, so far, it isn't in the cards, and both Emil and I do so want one."

"I have heard of people being married for several years before the woman got that way. It was two years after Vinie Sundquist was married before her first came, so you have no reason for losing hope."

"When are you going to get married?"

"When I name the day. John has already asked me."

"Congratulations!"

"I have decided to wait until next June. I don't want to rush into it," Engrid informed her listener.

"So the fisherman has caught the fish and intends to play with it a while before landing it," Louise observed dryly. "Just watch that the fish doesn't bite you before swimming away."

Engrid's gay laughter at her sister's remark rang bell-like in the hollow. "I suppose, to put it bluntly, you are right; but allow me to tell you something," she added by way of reprisal; "I didn't ask him, or chase him down. He asked me."

"Don't get too big for your bonnet, all the same. It all amounts to the same thing in the end; but really, Engrid, I am glad for you and think that you shall make an ideal couple."

"What are you buying Emil for Christmas?" Engrid asked.

"A new overcoat; the one he owns appears to have been used in the mine. What are you buying for John?"

"I have almost decided to buy him a silver ring, Engrid said hesitantly.

"And hope…"

"That he might return the favor in the form of an engagement ring," Engrid broke into her sister's conversation to say.

Looking up the hill, they perceived Emil striding along carrying a tree. "There," he remarked as he unburdened himself and stomped his feet to rid them of snow, "I'm going for the second one for the Finn Hall. John has had to seek further for the one that will be satisfactory in the boardinghouse."

So saying, he sniffed at the coffee pot and hurried back up the hill from whose summit, John appeared with a huge tree in tow. Emil accepted the axe from him, and with a few, well-aimed strokes, felled a tree and followed John who arrived at the fire breathing heavily and complaining of a ravenous appetite.

After enjoying coffee and sandwiches, the group stacked the trees in the back of the sled with the end-gate lowered; then they started their return trip. Engrid stuck up a Christmas song in Swedish, and the others joined her, causing the hillsides to echo as their youthful voices blended with the jingle of the bells on the spirited horses. The men for the most part, sang in rich baritone voices; however, John occasionally rose to a clear tenor.

In the shadows of tall cliffs, a cold breeze wafted a flurry of snow over them, and the women withdrew under the blankets with excited squeals. When the sleigh began the descent leading to town, John held the horses in the deep drifts off to the side of the road, so that the youngsters who were playing with their sleds, might whiz by without danger to themselves or the team.

Upon arriving at the boardinghouse, John fashioned a stand for the tree while Mrs. Kosky and Engrid popped corn and strung it in strands with cranberries and paper chains of various colors. A man that worked in the shop at one of the mines, took paper and making a paste of flour and water, sprinkled paper stars with granulated crystals of glittering lead and suspended then from branches after drying them in the oven. Small candles in holders were affixed to the tree. The decorating required two evenings, and it was a well-pleased girl who stepped back to watch stars turn in scintillating flashes of light as the wind found ingress through doors opening and closing when men filed in and out.

"Well, John," Alena beamed, "the only thing missing is a big open fireplace at each end of the room and a Yule log. I suppose we shall have to strike them off the Christmas 'musts'; nevertheless that is the loveliest tree that I have ever had in the old boardinghouse."

"Go on with you," John exclaimed, "you say that every year." He sounded pleased because the woman expressed her appreciation at his resourcefulness. "Maybe we haven't the fireplace and the log; but I have saved a drink for the occasion." Going to his room, he returned with a bottle of whiskey. He poured a small glass for the decorators of the tree; then he wished them all, "Merry Christmas! May it be the merriest ever!"

Alena brought forth a cake with three layers which she had taken great pains to decorate. "Here is your reward for the tree," she remarked, and placing it on the table, she cut it and served coffee.

The days trod hard on each others heels, and before Engrid knew it, it was Christmas Eve and Luti-Fisk dinner! Mrs. Kosky had invited many of her friends, and the boardinghouse resounded with exchanges of good wishes for the holiday. Glasses tinkled to the toasts of, "Glad-Yule." George Swanson outdid himself as a leader of singing which took place while the crowd waited for supper to be served. At the moment when the men were properly fortified with spirits, the women came from the kitchen with white linen table clothes. Numerous tables lined end to end up and down the room, groaned with platters of white fish, potatoes boiled with jackets on, rye bread, coffee rolls impregnated with the delectable odor and flavor of cardamom seeds, knakabord, milk gravy with slices of onion swimming in each bowl and beside each plate, a pudding whose main ingredients were prunes and rice piled high under delicious whipping cream.

At the conclusion of the feast, John and Charles lit candles and extinguished the oil lamps and the tender, nostalgic strains of "Silent Night, Holy Night" swelled through the room. In the soft radiance from the light of the candles, John came to Engrid's side, and drawing her, unobserved by the others who had their eyes glued on George's accordion, to the back of the group, he blended his clear voice with hers. As they sang, he placed a solitaire on her finger then bestowed a kiss on the ring.

Engrid felt life sing triumphantly through the whole of her being, and her spirits soared when the music echoed the singing in her heart. John placed an arm about her while singing. Candle set fire briefly to green needles which hissing and sputtering, filled the room with the fresh, clean tang. When the candle stumps were extinguished and lamps lighted, the gathering was made aware of Engrid's present, and congratulations were vociferous. Brandy was served again and toasts given to the couple; then the crowd moved as one to the Finn Hall where they danced until the following morning when the weariest, although happiest girl in Tintic received the day off as a Christmas present from her mistress. She slept the day through, and that night attended church with John.

Twelve o'clock, New Year's Eves in Finland had meant only that a new year had crept in during the coldest part of winter when people, feeling no urge for celebrating, hugged fireplaces and only did necessary chores. Here, it was different! Engrid ran outside with the throng at the stroke of twelve when the orchestra paused and the night was rent with sound from a dozen mine whistles. These was distinguishable; the deep bass of the Blue Rock mingling with the baritone of the Gemini, and the clear lead of the Little Chief, combined with the high note of the Tintic Hill. Overwhelming these at regular intervals, crashing explosions of dynamite rolled thunderously over the town and all except bed-fast invalids, hurried into the crisp air to call, "Happy New Year!" to their neighbors, while they watched the exciting flashes of the dynamite on the crest of the snow-covered hill west of town. Along with these overwhelming sounds, tubs were thumped, horns blared from the doors of dance halls, and the rattling of small arms and dynamite caps filled the gaps between the explosions.

Engrid stood vibrant with excitement on the back porch until the sounds reached a climax after fifteen, exciting minutes, leaving only the far-off wailing of the whistles from the Mammoth beyond the hill and the howling of indignant dogs. Finally, when it became to cold to remain outside, the girl went in with John delighted that she had shared in the enthusiasm.

"What a country to live in!" she told her finance as she flung herself with abandon into a schottische.

After agreeing to marriage on the first of June, Engrid lived in a state of breathless excitement; almost unbearable in its intensity during the remaining few hours prior to the ceremony.

Entertaining him with a lecture on conduct expected of a bridegroom, so that John might face tomorrow with more than his usual equanimity, Emil ceremoniously accompanied John on a tour of saloons.

The next afternoon, how handsome John looked in his swallow-tail coat, black bow tie on its spotless, white background and trousers of dark gray with pin-stripe lines causing him to appear even taller than his six feet. His hair was neatly plastered down and parted, and his face scented with lavender after a recent shave at the barber shop where he had been subjected to good-natured bantering of his cronies.

Shortly before the time set for the wedding march destined to go from Louise's home to the Finn Hall, John and Emil surveyed each other out of appraising eyes; and John shrugged off Emil's ribald remarks with an airiness which was, perhaps, a trifle strained, because he fidgeted nervously.

"What a fine pair of men you both are," Louise commented with a giggle; "you both act as though you were going to a funeral instead of a wedding."

Engrid laughed nervously as she pirouetted before the mirror and critically examined her white silk dress, mutton sleeves and bodice that was shirred and trimmed with white and jet beads.

"Take it easy, man; take it easy!" Emil said to his uneasy companion. "Here, have one more drink. After all, you are only going to be married, not to give a speech at the lodge. Here, let me straighten your tie."

Although John forced himself to endure Emil's kindly ministration, as soon as the latter was finished, he was again tugging nervously at his collar, while perspiration broke out in large globules on his forehead.

"I'd swear that you were working, and not just standing around," Emil said reprovingly. "Why didn't you take a cold bath after that warm one?"

"I did, you big bum. You stood there and watched me empty the tub after I finished the cold one. I am inclined to believe that you are more than feeling good."

"Maybe so," Emil agreed blankly, "because something tells me I'm going to be a weak kitten before this day and night are over. I believe I shall end up nursing a hangover."

John released his tension in a boisterous laugh; reached into his pocket and procured the ring. "Here, old man," he directed, "hang onto this with your life, and don't forget that I kiss the bride first." He looked at Louise and gave her a wink.

"You can depend on my memory, if not my judgment," Emil, looking at the radiant Engrid, assured him. "This will be a pleasure, and I'm going to give her a smack right on the lips even if no one else gets the chance."

"You big stiff," Louise reprimanded him affectionately, "straighten yourself and button your coat; here comes the music."

Engrid gave one last look at herself in a mirror; then she picked up her bouquet of flowers and went to meet John. As she grasped John by the arm, George Swanson, accompanied by two fiddlers, broke into a joyous wedding march, reminiscent of other preludes to marriages back home. The Snell girls scattered flower petals as they moved down the center of the dance floor between the guests. The couple sank to their knees on cushions before the Swedish minister, the music came to a halt and in the silence broken at intervals by Emil's hiccups, the minister intoned the lengthy Lutheran ceremony. John placed the ring on his fair companion's finger. Engrid threw her bouquet from the stage and the crowds surrounding the couple surged about them to offer congratulations and the men to kiss the bride. The crowd followed after the musicians who played all the way to the boardinghouse where Alena had taken John's money and instructions to prepare a feast which should truly set a precedent for other wedding suppers to follow.

"By golly," Emil exclaimed between hiccups, "they threw enough rice at you when you left the hall to feed all of the people in Finland." As he spoke he looked longingly at tables laden with rice pudding, boiled chicken, rolls, creamed potatoes, creamed peas and a variety of liquors and wines.

After the bride and proud groom had seated themselves, George Swanson stood up to say, "I feel that I must say a word or two to you, inasmuch as I have been delegated the honor of welcoming this young couple into the society of married people. It required all of us men to make this girl queen at last Mid-Summer Days' picnic and celebration. And then see what happens; along comes one fortunate man who gets her as queen of his home, merely by asking if she would like to be. Our best wishes for the happiest couple in this gathering of happy couples. May they always remain that way!"

After applause and a flurry of chattering died away, at Mrs. Kosky's request, the minister bowed his head and said a blessing; while Engrid told herself; "Perhaps happiness is a person of moods and whims; but this day shall I remember with its breathless tone of excitement, forever."

Then just as she picked up a glass of liquor in response to the first toast of the dinner, a bedlam at the front of the building transcending the chattering of the guests, caused a diversion, and people looked about with knowing smiles.

"Heavens, what is that?" Engrid exclaimed.

"That is the young ones who have come to charivari us," John informed her with a grin. "Let's go and throw them some money so that we may hear ourselves think."

"No, wait; wait until the noise has told the whole town that we are married," Engrid pleaded. "It is only once in my lifetime."

John laughingly agreed to her proposal, and after ten lively minutes had pounded into eternity, the couple arose and walked hand-in-hand along the hall. Engrid held her breath for a moment as she stood on the front porch to survey a hundred-odd youngsters whose shouting, tub and pan beating and rattling of cow bells increased at the couple's appearance. And these youngsters told the community in no uncertain terms that another pair had joined in the greatest adventure that life can hold. Firecrackers exploding at the foot of the porch caused Engrid to back away with a gasp of fright; but John stood firm, and reaching into his pocket, he said, "I have prepared for this."

He passed his wife a pouch and told her to throw the coins out to the throng. She did so, taking care to scatter the money in the area lighted by the lamps which Alena had thoughtfully placed especially for this event. The children dropped their noise-makers to dive for the shower of dimes which the girl in white threw with a series of sweeping gestures in the immediate vicinity of the porch. A scramble of pushing, pulling and shouting took place, until the scattered coins had been retrieved from the hard-packed dirt; then Engrid paused for a moment, her poke half emptied.

"We want money, we want money," the children chanted, and Engrid finally dispersed the remaining coins; and such excitement, fun and furor the girl had never seen concentrated in one spot as the eager children, in a frenzy of excitement, dove to the ground to retrieve coins from the hard-packed earth again. Those who landed on the bottom were quickly smothered by the bodies of others who threw themselves onto the pile out of sheer desire to enjoy themselves, and John was forced to descent from the steps and pull the top ones off lest those on the bottom of the pile be injured.

"That is all," Engrid called, waving the empty pouch, and the pyramid of boys strung out in a ragged line, trickling toward the Candy Kitchen and the delicacies which would come from the twenty dollars in dimes which Engrid had broadcast. The couple stood for a time, watching the boys disperse, and more than one youngster was wiping away tears because some other boy had stomped on an outreached hand as he had grabbed for a coin. Philosophically, the injured youngsters decided that the reward was worth the pain, for tears quickly ceased falling as their thoughts preceded their running feet, and their babbling voices faded in the starlit night.

Happiness was there in the eager, upturned faces of the departing children who boasted of their collections of coins and compared them to each other's. Happiness was in there where diners ate of the bounteous dinner, and laughter rolled through the door of the front porch. Happiness was here, too, as Engrid clutched her husband's big calloused hand and turned form the porch to hurry inside and eat chicken before the rich gravy cooled.

Chapter 23

Oh, what a night, this night of nights, and ending with the last of the exhausted crowd leaving the hall at sunrise. In the gray dawn, Emil walked unsteadily about the hall, peering under chairs, making certain that there were no smoldering cigarettes which might cause a devastating fire. He pulled down blinds over the numerous windows to discourage gangs of snooping boys who wandered about town looking for something to do, preferring mischief as a pastime.

"My, I'm tired," he sighed with a shake of his head. "I admit that I have never had so much fun; at least not since I was married, however. We can just leave your wedding gifts on the tables. I covered them with some dishcloths and we can carry them to your home after we get some sleep. You are intending on going to Salt Lake for your honeymoon, I suppose?"

"That we are," Engrid assured him as she sat slumped on the top landing of the high porch, looking wearily over the town at smoke rising from houses of men preparing to go underground.

"Here you sit like a pair of deflated sails after a storm," Emil observed as he eyed the bride and groom from blood-shot eyes. "As for me, I have nothing more to look forward to but work. I'm going to bed and sleep all day and night. I'm tired."

To the west and north of town, the tip of the mountains acquired a momentary glow of pink as the first rays of sun lit the valley with tremulous fingers. Robins raised their spirited voices from scattered cottonwood trees lining the main street a block below. A pair of prowling dogs appearing suddenly around the corner of the hall, paused at the sight of the couple, and at a gesture from the bride, departed unhurriedly in quest of scraps at a neighboring garbage tub. From a barn across the tracks came the stomping of cloven hooves as cows got to their feet when a door slammed open. Faint on the air was heard the sounds of milk frothing into an empty pail. Engrid snuggled against John and watched in idle preoccupation as a boy who delivered milk for Carpenter's dairy, came by; his horse driving to a habitual halt at the house adjacent to the hall.

"I'll have to start taking milk a soon as we get settled," she mused. Turning she looked at her husband who slumped in sound sleep, his hair hanging down over his forehead. Assuming a copper tint in the light of the dawn, his mustache hung limply, and a faint stubble of beard protruded visibly on his strong jaw to naught yesterday's careful preparations for the wedding. One arm rested heavily on Engrid's shoulders, the other on the porch.

Engrid's eyes grew tender as she surveyed her man. "John, dear, wake up; we've got to get to Louise's or we'll be the laughing stock of the town."

"What? Oh, I see, yes, let's get to bed."

Struggling to his feet and affixing his hat firmly on his head, he escorted his wife to Emil's house where they washed, then pulled down the blinds of their temporary bedroom and closed the door to the kitchen after first raising the ventilator to the outside. John was already asleep when Engrid slipped shyly into a silk embroidered gown which her mother had sent as a wedding gift.

She crawled into bed and gripped by breathless excitement lest John awaken and see her. She had barely settled herself when a knock sounded at the door. Again, it was repeated, louder than before. John stirred; then opening his eyes, he glowered in the direction of the disturbance.

"Who in hell can that be?" He growled as he slipped into his trousers and ran a hand through his disheveled hair. Engrid hurriedly clothed herself in a dressing gown before John threw the door open to find the top step of the front porch occupied by George Swanson, his accordion resting beside him. George was bending over and preoccupied with some task which piqued John's curiosity.

"What in hell do you mean by wandering around in a drunken stupor and waking people who have been out all night?"

George, swaying to his feet, stared at John and chomped his gums until his chin touched his nose. John saw that the man was engaged in, of all things, winding a shiny new alarm clock which ticked merrily.

George assayed an owlish grin and puffed his cheeks full of air. He swayed backward and forward, and as he almost fell from the porch, John was constrained to steady him. George swept off his hat, bowed gravely and moved through the door and John, watching with bewilderment, scratched the hair on his chest. George bowed to Engrid then moving unevenly across the floor, he placed the clock on the bureau. Turning with an admonishing shake of a forefinger, he said, "Don't forget to wind the clock!"

At this succinct reminder of a groom's nuptial duties, "Well, I'll be damned!" John ejaculated as he ogled the visitor.

Engrid broke into a ripple of laughter. John, after following George to the door, smote him soundly on the back and guffawed without restraint. He observed the man as he adjusted his accordion on a shoulder and playing a sprightly polka, danced down the street away from the house. John laughed until tears filled his eyes. He closed the door and looked at his wife who shyly watched him. He noticed how her skin became tinted a delicate shade of pink above the lace of the gown; and with a suddenness that startled her, he crossed the room in three strides and kissed her violently. He felt soft flesh under his hand, and picking her up despite her pretence of reluctance and admonition, "Don't wake Emil and Louise," he removed her robe and snuggled into bed with her.

"Oh, you lovely, adorable creature," he whispered, as he kissed her repeatedly.

"I'm so happy," she breathed, and losing her shyness, she returned his caresses. Her heart beat rapidly. Time ceased to be as she closed her eyes. Pain, followed by ebullient rapture, caught her up on wave after wave of intensely pressing breathlessness, and wordless was her joy until at length she sank into exhaustion with a child-like smile hovering abut her lips and a tear welling from a corner of each blue eye.

"I'll not forget to wind the clock," John's voice murmured from a dreamy distance as she snuggling on his shoulder. Engrid shivered her delight sighing as a child after a protracted period of sobbing.

Engrid opened her eyes and looked about the room until her glance came to rest on the clock. Smiling, she noticed that the clock's hands rested on two. From the kitchen came rattling of stove lids, and from outside, sounds of horseshoes striking pegs, and the excited chattering of boys as they followed their thrown shoes from peg to peg.

Rising, the bride slipped into a frothy, blue silk dressing gown, and without disturbing her husband who lay on his side breathing heavily, she opened the door and walked through the front room into the kitchen.

"Well, Mrs. Semell, how did you sleep?" Louise inquired as she opened the door and replaced the emptied pan.

"Like a log, sister; did you know that John went to sleep on the steps of the hall, while I watched the sunrise?"

Louise placed the kettle over an open hole. "I'm sorry that I couldn't be the last one on the dance floor; but I was so tired that I had to come home." She moved as she spoke while setting the table for four.

Engrid told her of George's visit; then both of them spoke of the past day and night. Engrid reviewed preparations for the wedding including the modeling of her gown by Elinor, and the breathtaking experience of being tossed on the bridal chair. Snatches of joy bubbled through her conversation, and tender memories evoking queer echoes of desire, caused her to shiver.

"Are you cold, dear?" Louise asked in a concerned voice. Perhaps you had better put on more clothes. We had a nice rain along about ten o'clock . I had to get up and partly close my window because it was coming in on the floor."

"I never heard a sound." Engrid said, "I slept too well."

"Aren't you chilling?" Louise insisted.

"No, dear, I just want to sit here and dream a little, while the coffee water boils."

Her face held such a rapt expression that Louise let her indulge in the luxury of her mood. She experienced happiness because her sister was happy. She pulled the blond head to her and ran her hand over its shimmering waves.

"I'm certainly glad that my sister got such a fine man; I like him very much."

Engrid looked up and smiling her thanks, she grasped Louise's hand and squeezed it gently.

John's voice broke in on them from the bedroom. "Come in here, dear; where are you?"

"I'm waiting for coffee to boil."

"I want a drink," he called.

"Here is a bottle," Louise said, reaching into the cabinet. Engrid went into the bedroom carrying the glass and bottle. She set glass and bottle on a chair beside the bed; then she uncorked the bottle and filled the glass. John thanked her and pulling himself erect, he downed the drink with a wry grimace.

"Hand me my cigarettes out of my inside coat pocket, please; there are some matches in my pants if the sweat hasn't spoiled them."

It had; so Engrid procured others as Louise ground coffee. Engrid eying John with an amused tolerance felt deep affection as she struck a match and held it.

"I have achieved a life-long ambition," John assured her. He inhaled deeply, then blowing smoke up towards the ceiling; he leaned back against his doubled pillow.

"I enjoy doing little things for you," his wife stated simply.

"What is on your mind, Engrid?" John asked idly flipping ashes onto the varnished floor.

Engrid gave him a look fraught with disapproval and procured a discolored saucer from the bureau. "Use that," she suggested with mock severity, "or Louise will never invite you to sleep here again."

"We won't have to," he objected; nevertheless he flicked the ash onto the saucer and indolently poured a neat, three-finger measurement into the glass. Drinking it, he asked for water.

"I was thinking that we shall have to get those gifts from the Finn Hall before nightfall, or they may be stolen."

"We won't dare take them to the house until we return from our honeymoon, or somebody may do it even then," he reflected. "Throw me my pants and I'll dress."

Engrid laid his trousers on the bed and retired to the kitchen, closing the door behind her. Emil called for coffee and grasping the whiskey, John went in on bare feet to offer his brother-in-law a drink of his own stock.

"How are you feeling?" John asked as he filled two glasses.

"Ugh," Emil shuddered, "my mouth tastes like the inside of a mule barn smells, and my head feels like miners are hammering inside my brain. Aside from that," he reflected, drawing a hand over his brow with a gentle touch, "I'll survive. What a wedding that was." He shook his head in an abortive effort to rid himself of that particular feeling.

"That's the friskiest I've ever seen you, Emil. You did get a little more than you could stand along toward the last."

"You should say I was the biggest fool you've ever seen; and you'd be telling the truth," Emil soliloquized. He ran a hand over his face. "I need plenty of black coffee and a good shave." He looked at his companion, who stood grinning down on him soberly shaking his head. "Help yourself to the razor if you can make those women stay out of your way," Emil said with a gesture toward the kitchen.

"Coffee is served," Louise called as she entered her and Emil's bedroom with a tray and placed it on a chair near the bed. "What will you two dissolute men have for breakfast?"

"Ham and eggs," John replied promptly.

"Nothing for me," Emil protested with a dismal groan. "I have no appetite. Perhaps another drink will straighten me out, or maybe the coffee will. Something has to, or I refuse to continue living."

Louise glanced at him severely. "You didn't have to make a hog of yourself."

"I didn't, hogs don't drink."

"But…"

"Alright, don't make me listen to a lecture on temperance. I'm suffering enough as it is. Never again, though; the next time someone gets married, I'm staying underground for the night."

After the woman left the room, Emil dressed except for his shirt; then wandered into the kitchen in his bare feet to wash and comb his unruly blond hair. "You're going to Salt Lake, I suppose," he asked.

"That's right," John replied.

The odor of the sizzling ham Louise was cooking wafted through the house making Engrid realize how incredibly hungry she was. John took his turn with the wash dish; then he donned a clean shirt and a semblance of respectability clothed his features as he peered into the mirror to part his hair. Louise glanced at Emil who evidently felt better after his eye-opener.

"Will you eat now, dear?" She asked again turning the ham, whose moisture sizzled with added emphasis in the smoking grease.

"I do believe I'm hungry now," he answered. Taking his place at the table, he invited the others to join him. The newlyweds complied willingly, starting with a cup of coffee. Louise fried an even dozen eggs which disappeared during the course of the meal.

"Men have to eat," John observed as he crammed a huge piece of succulent ham into his mouth, followed by half an egg which dangled momentarily on his knife then vanished.

"And drink," Louise added with a meaningful glance at Emil.

"A man can't just work all of the time; he has to have some fun," Emil said defiantly while defending the inclination of miners who indulge in something more potent than coffee on occasions such as Saturday night dances, holidays, workdays, mornings and evenings.

After the women had cleared the table of dishes, the quartet went to the Finn Hall where Emil raised the blinds. The inside of the hall brooded in the air of loneliness characteristic of dance halls when the music and laughter of the dancers are stilled. Crumpled flowers lay here and there under chairs where carefree feet had rudely pushed them. Shining in slanting bars, gray sunlight revealed particles of dust suspended in the dry air. The group moved to the tables which held the gifts.

"It appears as if you have enough stuff here to start a store," Emil said picking up a coffee grinder and a rolling pin. Holding the latter aloft, he remarked, "Here is your first line of defense against unruly husbands." He gave the handle of the grinder a twirl while regarding three coffee pots appreciatively. "Keep them full and you shall never lack for friends." He eyed several frying pans, cooking kettles and a large clock whose bronze weight was suspended from a stained, wooden shaft. "I like those clocks," he commented. "Home doesn't seem to be home without one." Turning to John, "Who gave you that?" he asked.

John wrinkled his brows in a frown of perplexity. "That came from Alex and Rika," Louise informed her audience. "I received it yesterday and a note declining the invitation with the excuse that they were unable to get away from work."

"Oh," said John, with tongue in cheek he glanced at his wife who fingered a tablecloth embroidered with quaint, gold colored windmills, similar to the mill at home where she used to go with her mother to have their winter's supply of grain ground into cereals. Figures of girls in pointed bonnets and checkered dresses paraded one after the other, around the border of the cloth.

"You gave this to us?" Engrid asked softly. She turned to her sister with tears brimming in her lovely eyes. She struggled desperately to control her emotions upon remembering countless hours that Louise had worked on the cloth in preparation for John's and Rika's wedding. Now the cloth belonged to John and her.

"How generous you have been to us. You must come to the house the first time we use the cloth for a dinner." Moving down the table, the girl's glance fastened on a set of silverware. "I don't know how to thank you, Louise and Emil. Why couldn't you have been married in the same manner and received these splendid gifts?" She held up a set of exquisite tumblers whose facets glittered with red, blue, orange and green colors in a shaft of sunlight.

Moving to a set of fragile china on which bluebirds winged their way around cups and saucers, she fingered a card. "Look at that, would you? Mrs. Kosky has used a week's profit to purchase that for us, John. Oh, but she shouldn't have done it." Engrid sensed a feeling of shame; to think that the kindly woman liked them enough to spend that much on them. "Just read what the card says, 'To Engrid and John; May you find life beautiful, and always walk together through an enchanted valley, where love heals all hurts, and each day's ending erases trouble as sunlight dissolves the mists.' Isn't that too beautiful? She remembered that I told her how I shared in the same feelings as she does when I look down over the valley at sundown. How utterly unselfish all of our friends are." Engrid dabbed at her eyes and felt a sob caught in her throat.

"Hey, what goes on here?" John asked. He put down the set of whisky glasses he had been admiring. Crossing to the bride, he asked, "Why are you crying?"

"Because I don't deserve all of this kindness. I haven't done anything to deserve it."

"Look, dear, you took care of her when she was an invalid, and worked without pay until the number of boarders increased; making it possible for her to repay you."

"But these others…"

"Listen, dear," Louise broke in to say, "you aren't in the old country where only intimate members of families give wedding gifts; on the contrary, you are in a country where everyone earns more; therefore have more to give. Just consider," she reminded her sister, "how much did you earn during the first year that you worked out as a servant?"

Engrid pondered briefly. "Twenty-five dollars."

"There's your answer," Louise assured her. "In due time, you will be called on to go to weddings and showers for newlyweds; then you will be on the giving end."

"Behold the rewards of virtue!" Emil mocked. His face held a cherubic expression as he rose aloft a vase of bridal wreath to better display the clustered, tiny white blossoms completely covering the green leaves. "If you hadn't been so eager to marry me, you too, could have had a formal wedding."

"Why you disgusting, conceited brute!" Louise exclaimed, and grasping one of several brooms, she ran after Emil who sprang up the steps to the stage. Emil turned to face his wife, and as she swung wildly at him, he grasped the broom in a big hand and firmly removed it form her grasp; then holding both of her hands behind her back with one of his big ones, he kissed her soundly while she sputtered impatiently. John and Engrid watched this from the floor of the hall where they stood, each with an arm about the other's waist, as they laughed happily.

"I believe we ought to stop this foolishness," Louise protested at length, "and get these things over to the house. Engrid and John can take them to their home after their honeymoon." She turned her head to evade her husband's bruising lips.

"Alright, come on, John, let's get some of these boxes and stack the things in them."

"What about the vases?" Engrid asked.

"The women who clean the hall will lock them in the cupboard. They belong to the lodge." Emil informed her.

It was necessary to make several trips before all the gifts were removed. Afterward, Engrid and her husband paused at the door and gazed about. Red roses, pink roses, bridal wreath, lilacs, ferns and corn lilies continued to remind them of yesterday although dried petals had even now begun to fall, causing a breath of sadness to take possession of the bride. The silent hall lay in an aura of loneliness, accentuated by the white bars of sunlight streaming through the windows. The America flag, however, hung resplendent in the gloom of the stage.

"Oh, John," Engrid sighed, "I hate to leave this hall. It has been such a wonderful day and night."

"Take a last peek at the hall decorated for our wedding," John answered and walked to a vase where he procured two pink rose buds. He affixed one to his lapel and gave the second to Engrid who inhaled its delicate odor. Happiness and sadness were strangely mixed as she stepped through the door. John closed the door and shook it to assure himself that it was fastened.

"I'll press this rose in my bible." She breathed.

"Come on, kiddo, the fun's just about to begin. We've got some honeymooning to do! Did you ever see cars riding on rails and drawn by mules? No? Well, Salt Lake has them and we can rent a buggy to see the sights. There'll be dancing, dinners and nights together in nice hotels." He squeezed her to him with one big hand.

"Oh, sweetheart!" she breathed.

Yup, we'll really put the mormons to shame when it comes to making love!"

Chapter 24

When the first baby, a boy, was ushered into the world by the doctor, with the aid of Louise, John stoically helped with the delivery. After the child had been bathed in sweet oil, John carried him to show Engrid; who ventured a tired smile upon being informed that he was perfect physically. When Engrid relapsed into a deep sleep, John poured whiskey into two large glasses.

"Have another, doc," he suggested as he helped himself to a second. A feeling of calm replaced the tension that had gripped him for almost twenty-four hours since his wife had begun to feel the pains of labor.

"No thanks, I'm due to attend two more deliveries, before the day is over," the doctor replied, and picking up his bag, he promised John that he would return the following morning.

Thoughtfully, John's eyes followed the buggy as it pulled away from the house, the location of which Engrid had chosen so that she might have a sweeping view of the west valley as well as varied activities of her neighbors. Two elm trees were spaced on each side of the pathway leading up to the house from the road. Lilac trees lined each side of the walk, and two huge beds of flags stood bravely in soil which John had hauled from maple guarded hollows in the hills. Turning from his preoccupation, John asked, "Is there anything that I can do to be of help?"

"Get me buckets and buckets of water to soak the sheets," Louise replied standing over the red-faced and soundly sleeping infant.

"Gosh," John breathed in an awed voice as he stared down at the child. "He looks like me, except that he hasn't the faintest trace of a mustache."

Giggling, Louise waved him away to do her bidding. Between trips to the well and back, John hovered between his wife and child. Love, of intensity and depth such as he had never deemed himself capable of feeling, overwhelmed him.

"God, little woman," he whispered through tears when he looked on his wife's wan face, "what a time you had, poor girl." Leaving them, he wandered aimlessly about the house until Louise tired of his restless pacing.

"You might stop off at the house and leave a note on the table telling Emil where I am; and then you had better get these groceries for Engrid will be waking, and she'll want you."

"Alright," John replied, accepting the list; then walking on tiptoe to the cradle, he gazed down into the face of his first-born. John felt insignificant, confused, humble and proud all in the same moment. He child was sleeping soundly, a scant shimmer of blond hair barely distinguishable on his head.

Going to Louise and Emil's, he experienced elation when he scrawled with a stub of a pencil, "Listen, you big ape, come over for supper and meet the new boss."

From there, he went with hurried steps to the boardinghouse. He took the steps four in a stride, and rushing into the kitchen, he grabbed the startled mistress and raised her from the floor with a hug that set her to gasping.

"What is heaven's name has got into you, John? Oh, I'll bet it is a boy!"

"Right on first guess!" He expanded his chest. "He's a husky, too, ten and three-quarter pounds, the doc says. He was an instrument case. Engrid certainly had a tough time of it. She's sleeping now. Come over after while and see her."

"Tell her I'll be over in about four days. Visitors ought to have sense enough to stay away and let her rest; but mark my words," she said knowingly, "they'll come flocking like a bunch of crows around a sheep herd at lambing time."

After procuring groceries, John stopped at Smith's saloon where he set up a round of drinks and purchased a box of cigars. He surveyed his reflection in a mirror and smugly concluded that he was quite the man.

"How is the wife and kid doing?" the bartender asked taking a swipe with a towel at the ornately carved, hardwood bar. And though this man had asked these same words hundreds of times of others; still they held a particular significance for the beaming father who seemed jovial as if he were the only man to be questioned in this manner.

"Oh, fine; the kid will make the best damn miner in the camp; he's got shoulders as wide across as a barn door, and a squawk like the Little Chief whistle."

The grinning bartender hoisted one on John whose enthusiasm couldn't be dampened by the good-natured ribbing which he suffered when Frank Fuller, an unobtrusive bookkeeper at a mine, instituted a long-winded discourse of how he had sired twins, three different times.

Setting his glass on the bar with a careless flourish, John picked up the box of groceries and walked with self-assurance through the batwing doors. Outside, he gravely decided that his first born should have a gift; and on a shelf of the Tintic Mercantile, he found what he considered to be appropriate. When he returned home, the baby was crying; and opening her eyes weakly, Engrid gave him a faint smile as she stretched out a pallid hand.

"I have been to town," John volunteered as he sank beside the mother and enfolding one of her small hands in his huge paw. "I saw Mrs. Kosky; I also bought the boy and you presents."

He handed her a sack of chocolates, then tore the wrapper from a wooden box, and allowed the paper to fall on the floor. He raised its lid and proudly displayed a chest of miniature carpenter tools.

"You big bum, the boy can't use them until he is older," she whispered, tears brimming from her eyes; "then he'll take that little hammer and mar the furniture, not to mention the windows that you'll have to replace."

Because John appeared crestfallen, Engrid pulled him close and whispered; "We'll buy new furniture and windows; now, are you happy?" Feeling better, John assured her that such would be the case.

When Emil arrived for supper, he endured John's account of the momentous event with an air of good-natured tolerance. After supper, he strolled to town leaving behind him the fragrance of cigar smoke; while John leaned backward in a chair on the front porch, his feet resting on the railing as he, too, smoked a cigar and carelessly, even a little disdainfully, regarded passersby with an air of overwhelming, self-importance. Each time the baby whimpered, he made haste to see what was wrong. Louise, however, made light of his trepidation as the infant, on one occasion, breathed with difficulty; and the woman was compelled to insert her finger into the baby's mouth to remove mucus. John stood tensely by his brow beaded with perspiration, expecting the child to succumb.

He went to work the following day; but only after Louise had assured him that if anything untoward should happen, she would send for him immediately.

And then came that day of days when John purchased a buggy and a handsome, coal-black gelding with four white-stocking feet and a blaze on its forehead. Driving up in front of his house, he whistled until his wife came to the door. He watched as her features expressed pleasure comparable to his own inner feelings; and nothing would do but that they must take a ride to the city of Mammoth, to the south around Packard peak, and back. No Longer did they have to depend on an occasional ride in a rented hack.

Each Sunday they drove to church, and after services, providing the sky favored them with a promise of fair weather, they drove to Knightsville Park where they enjoyed their dinner. Life seemed wonderful!

Since the arrival of the baby, Johnny they called him, Louise spent such a large share of her time at Engrid's house, that John made the observation he hardly knew whether the babe belonged to Engrid or Louise; because the latter was forever knitting sweaters, booties, and crocheting bonnets which the boy rapidly outgrew. Engrid carefully washed the articles with loving hands, and placed them in a separate drawer of the bureau for use on others who undoubtedly would appear in due time.

On the first day of October, John found himself unable to rise from bed following a feverish night and for the first time since her marriage, Engrid experienced fear. She dispatched Emil for the doctor, and Emil followed to watch as the physician examined his partner. Emil's eyes met Engrid's and flinched at pain lurking there.

"Pneumonia," the doctor announced flatly, confirming Engrid's fears. The doctor ordered her to prepare a mustard plaster. He prescribed whisky in hot water; then he took his leave after telling the woman what to expect during the course of the sickness. Emil accompanied the doctor to town for a bottle of whiskey.

Engrid and Louise cared for John with a tenderness which only they could show; and after the crises was over, the doctor told them reassuringly, "He'll be all right now, but I am afraid that he can't go back to work in the wet place where he has been. He should have plenty of sunshine and fresh air, as well as a nourishing diet."

John weakly nodded his head and closed his eyes. Engrid felt the tension under which she had labored spend itself. "Would you fix me a hot toddy, Emil?"

Emil brought her a drink and she sipped it, feeling warmth steal restfully through her body and relaxing nerves that had refused to do so previously.

"Now, I can go to work," Emil remarked; "we can't make any money this way."

"But you can't work alone," Louise objected.

"I wouldn't think of it; I'll hire a tramp miner for a time. There are plenty of them about town, looking for a few shifts and a little stake so that they can go on to some other town. I'll get along until John gets on his feet again."

"But the doctor advised him not to go back to work in the same place."

"I know it, Louise. We'll see how he feels after he has a chance to get on his feet; get some sunshine and fresh air. There is a lot of dead work to be done; moving waste rock, timbering and a new chute to build. We'll get caught up on the work that we have neglected doing while pouring the ore out."

Engrid finished her toddy. She looked at John whose pallor was accentuated by his siege of sickness. She shivered at the thought of what might have been had he not survived the illness. A great weariness took possession of her; he eyes closed and slumping limply to the floor, she shattered the glass against the bed.

"Emil, catch her!" Louise called in a startled voice; but the man moved too late.

"Gosh, the poor girl has fainted. Here, let me carry her into the other room and lay her on the couch. It didn't take much to put her out like a light," he chuckled as he looked at the almost full bottle. "She'd never make a miner." He placed her on the couch. "Undress the poor thing and let her get a good rest. I'm going home; get some sleep, and see if I can find a man to work with me."

"Don't stay out too late, or you'll never hear the clock ring." Louise cautioned.

"I won't, dear; do you need anything before I go?"

Louise assured him that she didn't; and after Emil's departure, she banked the fire, opened a window an inch and turned the lamp low. She felt the need for a good night's sleep herself, and it wouldn't require liquor as an inducement, she thought. Sinking on the couch beside her sister, she promptly fell into a profound slumber.

Although John resolved that he was going to work before long, the day never seemed to arrive. Too much underground work had run him down to the point where the doctor feared tuberculosis. A feeling of listlessness, a weariness that was hard to shake off, gripped him. Engrid encouraged him to wait until the holidays at the year's end were over before starting to work again, and, as money was no immediate consideration, they both agreed that he could well afford more rest.

"What are we going to do about a tree this year?" the man asked one morning of Engrid who was kneading a batch of dough for coffee cake.

"Would you care to drive out in the buggy and get one, just the three of us?"

"Let's!" he exclaimed. "Taking the baby will be fun because the weather is so nice." He looked through the door at the village swimming in bright sunshine. "I'll hitch the horse."

Engrid dressed the baby warmly, and taking an extra pair of wool blankets, she went out on the front porch. John was not long in coming and soon they were rolling behind the impatient, high-stepping horse who proclaimed a definite need of exercise by attempting to take the bit in his teeth. John restrained him until they reached the main road leaving town.

"How nice the day is," John commented; "but I am afraid that it might be the lull before the storm." He pointed with his whip to clouds stretching from north to south, and separated by patches of sky which gave one the impression of white combers rolling up on a blue beach.

The horse slowed his pace to a dogged walk as it reached the steep grade down which children had ridden on their sleighs. At the summit, the man halted the horse to look down into the valley clothed in the haze of Indian summer. Directly below, and to be reached by a winding road, Knightsville Park where they had enjoyed so many Sunday outings, glowed with a seductive red which dame nature uses lavishly. Ridges ran from the park, and thrusting boldly upward, blended with the bulk of a ponderous mountain, also shimmering in subtle yellows, warm oranges and vibrant shadings of carmine.

"How overwhelmingly beautiful it is," Engrid gasped as the horse continued on; its breathing had become regular. "We missed pine nuts this year."

John shook his head, "There wasn't any crop, so the boys about town say. There wasn't sufficient rain during the past summer."

"I'm glad that lack of water needn't bother us; I'd just as soon have a mild winter."

"The farmers will suffer," he said ominously.

"Let us pray that there is plenty of snow, then," Engrid breathed. She could easily feel concern of late, because John's health, up until now, had been poor.

"Engrid, have you been reading in the paper about the irrigation project that they're starting on the west side of Utah Lake?"

"I can't recall, why?" She thought for a moment; then burst out, "Say, didn't it say something about pumping water from the lake and running it above the land to be irrigated?"

"And from there through diversion ditches to the farms," John added. "I was thinking about buying a farm."

The horse was content to pick his own gait around the hillside, now in sunshine, and now in shadows of scarlet maple leaves clinging tenaciously to branches, forming a mottled pattern of quivering lights and shadows when a breeze moved gently through them.

"Do you think you would care to live on a farm again, Engrid? It will be back to the routine that you got away from when you left your father's farm. But, you would be working for yourself."

"You would like to get out of the mines," she stated.

"Yes."

"If we don't do something, we'll eat our little savings up; then you'll have to go back to the mines, or else to the west coast and the lumber camps. Everyone tells me that it is rainy and foggy the whole winter long, ugh, I wouldn't like that a bit. I love sunshine," she emphasized.

"You'll get all you want on a farm," John said with a chuckle. "At the place they propose to irrigate, rabbits carry water bags the year round."

Smiling, Engrid gave him a searching look. "Would you like to farm?"

"Yes, mother, I would. If we hadn't had some money put away when I fell ill, we would have found ourselves living on charity, if we could even get that. The store would have let us run a month's grocery bill, and then cut us off. The life of the average miner is just a matter of being out of debt for awhile, and then plunging into it again, if sickness or accident overtakes him. I know many men about town who would be going hungry if their wives and kids were not earning a few dollars."

Engrid, pondering over her husband's words, shivered when the buggy entered shadows cast by high cliff and rumbled over a wooden bridge spanning a deep ravine. She wrapped the blanket snugly around the baby who was placidly watching the changing scenery. As the buggy rounded a point, the horse drew to an abrupt halt upon finding itself face-to-face with the leaders of four pairs of mules pulling a cumbersome wagon heavily laden with glittering ore. John pulled back on the reins, the horse reared high on his hind legs. The mules halted while John spoke soothingly to the trembling horse which backed the buggy until it rested on a shoulder somewhat wider than the rest of the road. The teamster, at a wave from John, popped his whip; and the wagon rumbled past, its huge hubs almost jamming into the buggy wheels, while Engrid sat frozen in fear.

"Howdy, John," called the skinner as he deftly handled the maze of lines clutched in calloused hands. The wagon, towering far above the buggy, tiled and seemed to sway toward the woman, who uttered a startled cry; then it was past and solidly hugging the center of the road.

Grinning at his wife's alarm, John drawled, "It seems as if the Iron Blossom is shipping today. We picked a rather bad day for the trip."

The next time John discerned a wagon coming around an out-thrust hillside where they would shortly traverse; he pulled the horse into a wider space; and Engrid sat apprehensively as the wagon thundered past. This John did six times in all as heavily laden wagons passed them, huge wheels grinding on the rocky road, and boxes shaking violently. The mules strained in their tugs; ears twitching alertly forward as the animals pounded toward the buggy, and flattening as they shied aside to pass in clouds of enveloping dust mingling with the unique stench from the mules' powerful bodies.

"Fresh air is good for the boy," John remarked humorously as the last wagon rolled on and a glance showed their objective with no more wagons in view.

"It's good for all of us," Engrid laughed; "but how those mules do stink, and I mean really stink."

"About the same as usual," John observed; "they've been grained heavily for the work, I suppose." As they drew to a halt and stared up a hollow, John asked, "Would you care to walk up and choose your own tree?"

"But I can't very well carry the baby," she said hesitantly.

"That's no problem; let us leave him here in the buggy. I'll tie the horse to a tree and it won't hurt if we leave the buggy for half an hour, or so."

Assured that the drawstring on the sleeping bag was firmly tied, Engrid laid the baby on the seat after tucking the blankets in front of him so that he might not roll from the seat. She told the child in honeyed tones that she wouldn't be over-long; then she followed after John who climbed the hill on a game trail that was clearly marked with the imprints of deer. In places along a tiny stream, the spoor was plentiful where deer had habitually come to drink. As the couple rounded a shoulder of the hill, preceded by the shrill cries of a flock of arrant blue jays, Engrid uttered a low cry of amazement, "Look there, John!"

"It's a deer," he said in a hushed voice; "don't speak or move lest we frighten it. See how he stands, dipping his head to browse and raising it to look around. If the wind were from us to him, we would never have seen him. Look closely; there may be others in the vicinity."

"Psst!" Engrid hissed as a twig cracked in the ravine below, "there is another below us. I can see its head move as it eats." Excitement gripped her. For the first time she had seen deer whose grace made the reindeer appear as lumbering oxen by comparison.

Looking at his wife's flushed face; the man saw the same breathless excitement which had characterized it when they had stood together on the ledge of the cliff during their pine nut hunt.

"You are more beautiful than the deer," he said softly, and she turned her radiant glance toward her man who kissed her, lightly at first, worshipfully, then hungrily. He released her and she turned to look at the big buck as it ambled over a ridge out of sight in search of further browse. "Shall we frighten them and watch them run?" she whispered mischievously.

"Do that," John answered.

"You do it; I can't call loudly enough."

John hurried to the next rise of ground over which the trail meandered. He whistled and shouted vigorously; then out of the draw below several more bounded up the hillside as though propelled on steel springs.

"They are as birds flying; so effortlessly do they jump." Engrid exclaimed. "How can anything be so beautiful? And to think that some people kill them for sport."

"And to eat; every time I see them run, I think of a frying pan, coffee bubbling in a can at sundown, and a buck hanging from the branch of a tree after a successful hunt."

"Always, it is your belly that you think of."

"And after that, my wife," he informed her as he folded her into his arms and turned to watch the fleeing animals racing each other up the side of the mountain. Two of the number did not bound; they ran like gaited horses pulling a chaise, heads thrown back and carrying their antlers proudly as they entered a grove of scarlet maples. The branches swayed momentarily as they swallowed the fleeing animals. The hillside drowsed, lifeless and waiting patiently for further movement on it stage. It seemed to the woman that the life she had witnessed was but a passing figment of her imagination, so still was the sun-bathed slope opposite.

"Gosh," Engrid sighed; then remembering what she had come for, she cast her glance about the grove of balsam until she found one suitable. The scent of the trees hung heavily in the air. Warm waves of spicy sage smell wafted to her nostrils. Deer flies droned comfortingly. Maple leaves whispered in the draw below as a freshening breeze bent cheat grass and whispered through stalks of dried sunflowers. Engrid felt John's arms steal about her from behind. Her heart beat madly with desire that had been suppressed by fear and worry since John's illness. She sank to the dead leaves under a towering balsam with her man's lips frantically conveying his need for her.

"Do you think you should?"

"Love me, Engrid."

And over all, the breeze pressed insistent hands. Cheat grass whispered as it bowed in undulating waves, and rose again, and fell again; and curiously, Engrid was aware that her husband's body moved in sympathy.

Rising, their desires fulfilled, they headed back towards the buggy with the tree in hand.

Coming in sight of their buggy, the pair listened for infant cries; but heard none. The horse nickered a welcome when Engrid placed the axe in the rear of the buggy and peeped with sparkling eyes into the seat where the baby looked at her briefly; then dropped its mouth back to the blanket, and continued to extract what satisfaction it could from the wooly nap.

John tied the tree and helped Engrid into the seat after freeing the horse. He gave the baby a quick kiss and drove from the grove of maples whose leaves rustled giving notification of the impending storm. A sullen appearing cloud obliterated light and peering into the zenith, John perceived that it was no small one; stretching from horizon to horizon as far as the eye could see and the sun flowed faintly with a copper-colored hue through the dark mass of vapor.

"It's going to snow; we'd better step on it."

"It's snowing now," Engrid observed as the buggy rounded a point and she could see for several miles to where a ragged curtain of white trailed in bowed waves from the clouds to the ground. A few, idly drifting flakes danced hesitantly before gusts of wind prior to finding a resting place. Their numbers increased until soon the carriage was rolling along over ground blanketed in an inch of snow. In it, the wheels picking up dirt and snow, left wavering dark lines as the buggy progressed.

"When we get out from behind these hills and start downgrade, we'll feel the full fore of the storm," John predicted. "Bundle yourself and the baby up in the blanket, and I will get this robe up on our laps."

Engrid draped the blanket over her head; however, much to John's chagrin, there was no wind when they reached the ridge and began the descent. Instead, they found themselves riding along in large, slowly falling flakes that white-washed the back of the mincing horse and transformed the drab grays of the sage covered hills with sheer loveliness.

"This is fun!" the woman exclaimed gaily in answer to a query from John as to the child's welfare. "I wouldn't mind riding in this storm forever. Just look at your mustache; you look like a snowman."

Chuckling, John brushed at his mustache; whereupon his wife laughed out of sheer joy, then settled herself to enjoy the novelty of moving in a quietly falling sea of down which impressed on her a feeling of comfort and intimacy.

"We could have put the top up," John belatedly pointed out.

"And missed this fun?" Engrid exulted. "Not on your life!"

At home, she carried her mood into the snug living room where bare wood floors were covered with woven rag rugs. In a rocking chair, his stocking clad feet resting on a stool, John puffed at a pipe which persisted in giving off smoke which was anything but mellow or so Engrid mused while mentally criticizing the advertising of the green tin in which the tobacco came. But it was nice to have a man of ones own who lounged around in his stocking feet and smoked a pipe.

Darkness fell quickly, aided by the hills which served as a passageway over the mountain range, for a violent wind which started to rage through the town. The wind whooped and roared its intentions to lay all dwellings flat, and from inside the house Engrid watched apprehensively as a section of the factoring tore loose from restraining tacks, causing the paper on the walls to bulge out and in with each successive gust. The wind found a space under the front door and threatened to dissipate the warmth of the room. Snow hissed at the house, and fine particles of hail rattled at the windows, causing Engrid to recall another storm which had brought her companion misfortune, and her, good fortune, in her association with John. If the wind hadn't blown so viciously that particular day and moment, Mrs. Kosky wouldn't have broken her leg, and Engrid wouldn't have been thrown into close contact with John. "Let it blow," she thought as she found an old pair of trousers and stuffing them into the crack at the bottom of the door. The wind rushed past the stove pipe, occasionally forcing its way down against the draft and pushing out in puffs of odorous smoke.

"Darn it," Engrid said irritably, quickly forgetting her warm appraisal of the wind as a harbinger of good fortune. "If they made houses like this in Finland, the Finns couldn't live through October, let alone a winter."

"Houses in mining camps," John said in placating words, "are not built for permanence. It doesn't pay. Just suppose the ore in the producing mines here should be exhausted in another year or so; there wouldn't be any use for fine brick homes. The populace would have to move elsewhere to find work, leaving a handful of leasers trying to scratch out a living on what little ore there would be left."

"And does that happen to many mining camps?" Engrid sounded surprised. Coming as she did from a land where everything was built for permanence.

"All of them, in the course of time. There will be ghost camps all over these western states when the ore runs out, or water fills the lower levels. After that happens, all one can do is pack up and go to some other place to look for a job. When a man makes a little stake at leasing, instead of wasting it in search of more ore as most of them do, he should buy a piece of ground someplace and settle down to making a living as a farmer." He looked at his wife with thoughtful expression for a moment; then went on, "The Chief is stopping leasing operations on the first of the year."

"Does that mean..."

"It means that our income as a co-leaser with Emil is coming to a halt."

"Oh," Engrid sighed dolefully, "I never dreamed that such might happen. I had just expected that the money would continue to come in until the ore ran out."

"The leases we signed can be renewed, or not, as the company sees fit at the beginning of each year. From then on, all of the leasers will have to work for the company if they want to continue mining."

"Is that what you intend to do?"

"I have been thinking about it."

"You shouldn't go back into the mines," Engrid said thoughtfully, "you're not as strong as you used to be."

"Did I appear to be a weakling today?" he asked, and laughed uproariously at her blush.

"But isn't there something else you can do?"

"Several of the men I know are taking their savings and buying into that farming project," he informed her.

"Let's do it! Imagine having a piece of ground of our own, a garden to pick fresh vegetables from and all of the fresh eggs that we want."

"We've got to do something. Some day this will be a ghost town with nothing but a few rubbish-filled holes to mark the place where homes and businesses prospered. There will be dumps of refuse and broken bottles, jackrabbits will prowl through sage filled streets. The mine shafts will cave in, leaving miles of underground tunnels, with nothing but darkness and water dripping into invisible pools and falling rocks sloughing off the sides and backs of stoops where men are laboring at present. Down below town there will be a few hundred, deserted and neglected graves. Not a cheerful prospect to look forward to, is it?"

Engrid's shudder was sufficient answer. "Do you think you could farm by irrigating?"

"Certainly, those who came here as pioneers learned how; I have their experience to draw on."

"Do you know what to grow and how to grow it?" she asked. "This climate is so different from that at home."

"Oh, yes, let me show you. I have talked with many of the men who come up from below each winter to work in the mines. They all pretty well agree on one point; if a person has ambition, he can make a good living on a forty acre plot of ground." As he spoke, he moved his chair to the dining room table and drew a sketch. "They claim that an ideal farm should be laid out about like this."

"Right here," he said, drawing a rough rectangle and pointing to the top portion, "I would raise ten acres of oats and wheat. Barley yields more bushels to the acre, however. I would also plant five acres of corn for hog feed. We can raise five acres of potatoes. Of course, we would reserve enough for a garden spot for other vegetables, if you so desired, instead of planting all of five acres of each of those crops. Along the lake side, where the run-off water would settle, we'd have twenty acres of pasture land which would take care of ten head of cows and four horses. We'd sow this in clover, a portion in orchard grass and blue grass. Timothy grows well in bottom land."

"My heavens," Engrid exclaimed, "you sound as if you have been farming all of your life."

"No," he chuckled, "I've asked questions of every man that I have worked with, and from their ideas I have a composite in my mind of what is best. That is all there is to it, except for a lot of hard work."

They sat discussing the project far into the night, heedless of the blizzard threatening to shake the house to pieces. Engrid could hardly restrain her enthusiasm over the plan. She retired to dream that she was located on land of her own, standing in the white sunlight watching the wind caressing fields of golden grain.

"Best of all," John said to her in her dreams, "you won't have to dry the crops as you did in your country; here the sun does it."

Chapter 25

Marriage and a child cast a new slant this Christmas. For Engrid, there was no longer the expectancy occasioned by thoughts of meeting a congenial male as there had been when she was waiting for the right one to come along. Marriage had its compensations; yes indeed! Now it was not necessary to appear gay or vivacious, nor did she have to run competition to women such as Rika. No, that was all in the past. All yearnings accompanying pathetic loneliness were gone. Immeasurable peace possessed her after suffering from feelings of futility, homesickness and lack of purpose. Where she had previously wondered whether or not she might be attractive to men, and whether this one or that one might reciprocate her feelings, that need no longer concern her. She belonged to her man and child. Oh, blessed feeling of contentment.

Louise and Emil dropped in to exchange presents on Christmas Eve. Because of the tiny infant, John and his wife tactfully declined an invitation to attend the dance. After the two loquacious visitors made their departure, John persuaded Engrid to draw her chair close to his; and over brandy, he encouraged his wife to reminisce about Finland.

"Wouldn't it be nice to be home tonight and tomorrow, or say, for about a week?" As she spoke, a note of wistfulness crept into her voice. "Imagine gathering around a big open fireplace with the lamp turned down as we watched the flames dancing about the Yule log. How nice to sit snug and warm in a solid log house. Wouldn't it be fun to arise tomorrow and find that St. Nick had come and gone, removing hay from our stockings and replacing it with hardtack candy, or an apple on a stick, smothered in that hard syrup. Imagine how my parents' faces would beam if we drove up to the door in a hired sleigh and walked in on them with boxes and boxes of presents. Oh, what madness and celebration and talk, there would be! No one would be able to sleep a wink for a whole week."

John listened to his wife, and hoped that such might be the case sometime in the coming years. He nodded his head thoughtfully at her words as he sipped at his brandy. True, he thought, they were not going to the dance hall to whoop it up, but he felt content and hoped that his wife did also.

"Come for a moment," she pleaded; "let us stand on the front porch. Wait, I'll throw a coat over my shoulders."

They stood for a time and listened to the music and occasional shouts from the main street indicating that happy-go-lucky neighbors were converging on dance halls.

"I feel far removed from the spirit of revelry, John. I feel peace suggestive of moonlight on snow. I almost expect to see St. Nick come flying over the hill. I feel that the real spirit of Christmas is contentment. Look there," she said with extended arm pointing to where warm air from mine shafts far up on the mountainside rose like smoke from the shepherds fire.

"But everyone doesn't feel as you tonight," John protested. "I believe that old age is creeping up on us. Listen to the children sleigh riding. Hear the sleigh bells. It might be the old whiskered gent himself making the rounds, although I'll have to admit that it must be a bunch on a good old hayride."

Overhead a ball of fire flashed across the sky with startling suddenness, leaving a glowing, phosphorescent train in its wake.

"Someone has died; so they say at home when a star falls," Engrid said with a shiver. She snuggled closer to her husband.

"What rubbish they taught you. If a star fell every time someone died, the sky would have been a black void long ago. Besides, what you call a shooting star is a particle of rock," he informed her smugly, "I read about it in my geology book."

"Let's go inside; I'm cold."

Hardly had they settled themselves when from outside came the jingling of bells. As the bells stopped, a chorus of voices singing a carol came through the walls. They looked at each other, smiled, then stepped through the door again to behold a sleigh load of people whom they recognized as the lodge chorus. After waiting until the song was finished, the couple shouted in unison, "Merry Christmas! Come in and warm yourself with a cup of coffee!"

"And what else?" George Swanson called.

"What do you think?" Engrid called gleefully.

"Here we come," George said as he heaved himself and his accordion to the ground.

Engrid and John greeted the heavily wrapped visitors as the sleigh debouched its load. The horses heaving sighs at being able to halt, rested on three legs, as with stomping feet and a cheerful exchange of repartee, the guests overflowed the front room. Such gesticulating, back-slapping, wishing of Christmas cheer there was, and such crowing over the babe who lay wide-eyed in the bedlam.

"This is the last stop," George declared. "From here we're going to the dance."

"If there were any more stops, George would have to stay in the sleigh." His wife ventured, as John, aware of the man's capacity for hard liquor, filled his glass a second time.

When the men had downed their drinks, the women herded their mates through the door, although the men seemed reluctant to leave while there was still more liquor in sight. As the sleigh bells faded into the distance, John tamped his pipe and puffed contentedly. "Maybe next year I'll want to go to the Christmas dance," he ventured. "Maybe I shall also enjoy being intoxicated."

"I'm glad you're sober tonight."

"Let's light the candles," John suggested; "I'll light the top ones that you can't reach."

After they had covered the tree with twinkling tongues of flame, John doused the light and picked up the infant to show him his first Christmas tree. Engrid watching the child's eyes gleam with reflected light, and she realized she had found the spirit of Christmas.

John went to work in the mines on the first of the year in order to get by until time for him to move to where he intended to buy land and erect a home. On the first of April, when it had warmed sufficiently to make living in a tent comfortable, the trio moved their few personal belongings to the site of their future home on the west side of the lake. He went to Lehi, after pitching a tent, and ordered sufficient lumber to build a one room house, a barn for a team of work horses and six cows.

He labored industriously, and when one room was completed, the family forsook their tent as did other neighbors, and then he plowed the ground.

Electricity was available, the same electricity that turned the motors on the huge pumps at the lake's edge. Engrid's happiness was almost more than she could bear when by turning on a switch; John flooded the room with a light which outshone their oil lamp.

The following morning, Engrid looked out on sage-covered ground stretching for ten miles to the bulk of the Oquirrah Mountains. Turning to the east, she discerned the lake shimmering in the sun. Along the shore, tall grass reminded her of that covering the swamps of her native land. But this was different; in the warm air, a damp smell from the lake held a brackish odor, far different than had been the fresh, clean smell of the lakes at home. Gulls flew about aimlessly, uttering their raucous plaints. Off in any direction other than that of the lake, came the sounds of hammering as other settlers finished one room in which to live.

"What do you think of it?" John asked as he came from the house and seated himself on the top step of the porch.

"I hardly know what to say," she admitted. "It's so barren, so empty. At home the trees in the summer seemed to shut one in from the solitude. Here there is nothing to look at for miles and miles except the sage. Even in Tintic it was different," she mused; "at least we had the tall mountains shutting us in."

"But you're the one who was always telling me how you hated that feeling of being enclosed by the forest back home. If I remember right, you also told me how wonderful it is to be able to look for miles and miles over the valley while you admired the scenery and enjoyed our frequent hikes."

"But this is different; everything is different; the enchantment goes when one gets too close to something beautiful seen from afar, and scenery becomes toil."

John shook his head with a show of irritation. "We'll plant trees all around the house and raise a garden; then you won't be so aware of the distance; but even at that, I'll venture to state that as soon as trees and shrubs obstruct your view, you will come out of the house, walk beyond the farthest trees and stare off into the distance." He looked about him and said buoyantly, "We have one room built; in due time we'll add others as we plan on doing. Right now I have to get busy and plow and harrow the ground if we expect to get anything planted."

"I suppose it is that I have grown to love that dirty little mining camp and its friendly people," Engrid said as she looked about her at smoke coming from other one-room residences. "I'll learn to love this place in time."

When she went into the house and began tidying the kitchen, John hitched up his team and plowed a furrow. He paused occasionally to allow the team of horses a chance to break into the work gradually. Each time he stopped, he visualized broad acres of alfalfa, groves of apples, peaches, and stretches of ripened grain between him and the lake where all of the waste water would drain into the low lands.

That summer brought to the woman more toil than she had experienced since leaving her childhood home; however, she quickly adapted herself to the quiet and orderly existence of the countryside that contrasted to the feverish activity of the camp which she had left. Whatever time she could spare was spent in her vegetable and berry garden where she planted every type that her neighbors advised her to. She carried on an unrelenting war against weeds and insect life and became familiar with dirty gray squash bugs which threatened to overrun her vines. Getting down on her hands and knees, she hunted out every pair and took a malicious delight in smashing them into the ground with a stick until after a week of hunting; she had destroyed every vestige of pests. The work in the garden was tiring and the heat oppressive; but she felt relief momentarily at an occasional shower of rain which caused the tang of the sage to renew its fragrance, likewise her morale.

Always night came with welcome relief from the blazing rays of the sun; but warm weather brought hordes of mosquitoes, and she found it impossible to enjoy an evening out of doors without a smudge to disconcert the intruders.

"I don't know which is the worst, to be smoked like a side of bacon, or to be eaten a bite at a time," she told John ruefully.

Evenings, one of their neighbors would drop in, or they might visit with them in turn. They would chat for awhile on a front porch, watching the moonlight play on the waters of the lake. A lull in their conversation brought to their ears the shouts of children who gathered to swim in the moonlight by the pump-house. Sometimes the youngsters made camp fires and pretended that they were pioneers camping along the wayside. Starlight in the summer brought relaxation, women's chatter and the subdued conversation of men enjoying a homely exchange of wit and wisdom.

With the end of June in sight, John and Engrid received a letter from Louise and Emil in which they insisted that the couple attend the coming Fourth of July celebration in their home town. Enclosed was a handbill outlining the day's program?

John's pricked his ears at the mention of a drilling contest open to the general public as Engrid read Louise's letter.

"We won't take no for an answer," she had said in conclusion before signing her name.

John, grinning boyishly, looked at his wife. "Do we or don't we?"

"We do."

"Who'll take care of the livestock?"

Engrid's eagerness diminished as she stared moodily toward the mountains from whence had come the invitation. "Will all of our neighbors go?"

"I don't know," he pondered. "Say, Peterson can't go anyplace; his wife just had a baby and he'll have to stay home. Let's go see if he will take care of the cows and chickens for the three days or so that we will be gone. He can take the milk and eggs for pay. I am certain that he will do it, if someone else hasn't already asked him to."

While Engrid visited with Mrs. Peterson, John inquired of one of the Peterson brood as to the whereabouts of his father. The child pointed up country to where his father was irrigating. John went to the road along side of the fields and accosted the man. He came straight to the point after an exchange of small talk.

"Sure," the man replied, "I'll do it, providing you bring me a snort. I haven't had a drink since I moved down in March."

That evening an air of suppressed excitement charged the Semell home as Engrid wrapped two pounds of fresh butter in wet cloths, and placed several dozen eggs in a wooden box. In a crate, John placed a dozen chickens. He pastured the horses, and sunrise the following morning found them well on their way in the direction of Tintic. Engrid leaned close to John giving him an enthusiastic hug as they drove onto the highway. "Oh, it will be wonderful to see Louise and Emil, and Mrs. Kosky and the others again. I've been longing for a day away from the place. At times, I have felt as though I might be going mad."

The buggy rolled into a wash that was a hiding place for early morning shadows and quickly ascending the other side, then again coming once more into the faint light of dawn.

"I would like to sink my mustache into the foam of a schooner of Smith's beer. Better still," he added with a chuckle, "I would like to stand the barrel on end just as it comes off the ice and catch the contents in my mouth. I am so sick of alkali well water that if it weren't for coffee, I would dry up and blow away."

"Won't Emil and Louise be tickled to see us come? I am ashamed to think that I haven't written so much as a word for a whole month. If that attitude keeps on, we'll be a pair of hermits. I was so tickled to leave the town, in some ways; but I am happier to be going back, even for a visit. There is something about the friendliness of people who live in mining towns that gets in ones blood. I miss the excitement that the town feels with the beginning of each new day; and the air of expectancy as the community awaits the results of development work. I miss…"

"Perhaps it is the work that is getting you down, Engrid; you have certainly lost weight. Too much work in the sun; and too much loneliness are doing something to you that aren't good."

"On the other hand, you have gained weight; you look as you used to when I first met you." Engrid said generously as she looked at him from eyes which seemed larger in a thin face. "You're brown as an Indian."

The horse jogged along at a steady, mile-eating pace. The sky lightened; the sea of sage donned a cloak of silver. Once a coyote walked into the road where it paused until it was in danger of being run over; then it leisurely ambled off with a sideways swing of its body.

"Smart animals," John commented as he passed his wife the reins while he filled his pipe; "If I had a gun, we wouldn't get within a half-mile of it."

Daylight streamed into the valley, dispelling the light dew. The travelers welcomed the warmth for a time; however, in a half-hour it had grown unbearably hot. The baby lay in the crook of Engrid's arm, saying, "Ma, ma" while pointing to an occasional cedar tree. Flies came from nowhere to swarm about the horse and buggy. For a time, tiny gnats caused acute discomfort as they settled in eyes and ears.

At intervals they halted to give the baby some milk which Engrid carried in a sealed jar wrapped around with a wet cloth. On one such stop, the parents munched an egg sandwiches and washed them down with insipid water from a bag.

"About seven more miles," John remarked as they entered one of a series of draws leading toward their destination. Those past miles on the prairie had seemed endless. Now, as they moved on up the road, two engines, pulling a train of coal cars, box cars laden with food and machinery; as well as several flatcars of lumber for the mines, furnished moving relief from the monotony of the barren, sun-baked hills, when they chugged above on the mountainside. Gradually they left the travelers behind; and it was another hour and a half before the jaded horse broke into a trot as it recognized familiar country and the top of the long, uphill pull.

Engrid expressed a desire to engage several of her friends in conversation. John shook his head when she waved at them. "You've got three days in which to talk, he protested. Right now I want to wash the dust off my tonsils," he growled.

"Alright, dear; I merely wanted to ask Mrs. Bloomquist how she was getting on. Her husband died two weeks ago, according to Louise."

"Supposing he did? He is where he doesn't need a drink of cold beer. He drank enough while he was alive to last him for eternity; fell off the saloon steps and broke his neck, didn't he?" John growled testily.

"Oh, John, please don't be grouchy. I was only trying to be friendly. It wasn't the saloon steps, at all; it was the church steps he fell from."

"He had no business treading unfamiliar paths," John objected.

Engrid burst into a merry peal of laughter, and John's good humor was restored as they pulled into Emil and Louise's place. Before the buggy could halt, Louise ran across the yard and reached for the baby to smother his plump neck with kisses. Both women talked at once, and as John started to unhitch the horse, Emil, rubbing sleep from his eyes, looked through the open bedroom window.

"Greetings, hayseed; have you been traveling all night?"

"What time is it?" John asked, and when Emil told him, he said, "Not bad; four hours for a twenty-five mile drag in this heat; not bad at all.

"Would you like a drink?"

"Does a bachelor want Kitty?" John remarked wryly. "Wait until I get this sack of bones rubbed down, watered and fed."

He stripped the horse of its harness and neck yoke; then released it and it trotted eagerly into Emil's corral and nuzzled Emil's horse. While John filled a trough from a well, the horse lowered itself to the ground and began to roll in the dust, grunting its contentment. It stood up, shaking itself and made for the trough where it drank thirstily, its velvety nuzzle barely touching the water. John threw it a flake of hay, and poured some grain into an empty dynamite box, then went to the cool interior of the tree-shaded house.

"I'm not thirsty," John denied as he reached for a mug of beer. The beer was flat as it had stood since the previous evening; but it was cold, however.

"That is a fine cellar," he remarked as he rolled the cold liquid around and savored its flavor.

"Cellar, nothing; I have one of those new iceboxes, come see it." He led John to the back porch and pointed to the varnished box with a pan catching the steady drip of water underneath. "It holds a hundred pound chuck of ice and keeps meat and such from spoiling." He opened the door and displayed the various shelves containing edibles. "The cold drops down from the top and nothing can spoil before we use it."

"And what happens to the water when the ice melts?"

After Emil showed him, John asked, "Why don't you hook a pipe to the hole in the bottom and let it drip over the edge? It will save you watching that the pan doesn't run over."

"I never thought of that," Emil pondered; "I shall do it."

John felt himself important. "By the way, we've got a few things we can put in the icebox, providing you can do the dirty work." He showed him the chickens; then placed eggs, a jar of top cream and two pounds of butter in the icebox. He helped Emil dispatch the fowl; they cleaned and washed them and added them to the icebox, and Emil chortled gleefully as he allowed his glance to caress the chicken.

"And now for a real surprise," Emil added mysteriously as he ushered his friend into the front room. He walked over to a table and showed John an instrument with a horn attached to an arm resting on a disk. He turned a crank; moved a lever and out of the horn, when the disk began to spin, came a selection by a band.

John stood with mouth agape. "Heavens!" Engrid gasped.

"Do you hear what I hear?" John asked his wife, in all seriousness. "Well I'll be damned; what won't they think of next?" He examined the machine. "I've got to buy one of those things to amuse the wife." He exclaimed. "No more lonely evenings for us at home. Will people enjoy visiting with us now?"

After breakfast was over, Emil played and replayed his meager collection of recordings while they consumed the pail of beer; then he went after another; and thus they spent their day.

That evening, Engrid allowed John to accompany Emil to town where he renewed acquaintances over a countless number of mugs of beer, and Engrid smiled her contentment when John, removing his shoes as quietly as possible, slid into the bed, uttered a hiccup or two and almost immediately began to snore.

Chapter 26

Take eight-thousand people of diverse nationalities, almost all of them immigrants and, as a consequence, harboring pride in their uniqueness. Remove many inhibitions; inculcate in them love for freedom; instill in them a feverish desire for wealth pouring from the earth in a mountain-enclosed town, two miles long and a mile wide. Let a huge fault line, known as the Beck Fault, and extending east and west, mark the dividing line between the north and south portions of town. Watch winter's snow transform ugliness into picturesque beauty; and during the summer observe as unexpected cloud-bursts, draining through the business section, washes through establishments, and litter them knee high in debris despite flour sacks full of dirt piled in doorways to ward off the muddy water.

Give the bread winners a job so that they may allow their children a few coins to spend on a celebration. Note how the newly installed poles of the power company have been wrapped in red, white and blue bunting. See with a feeling of pride and a catch in your throat that Old Glory flutters proudly from each flag pole, or is displayed in pairs at residences.

Rouse the expectant populace at sunrise with the smashing rumble of dynamite blasts set off by volunteer firemen who, race to fires pulling hose carts. Listen to window panes rattling in sympathy with concussions reverberating like rolling thunder in confused waves from mountain to mountain. Watch a herd of goats run wildly downhill to get away from the disturbance. Note as eager children, springing from their beds, stand shivering in their underwear which are last winter's, now cut off at the knees and full of holes where pins have been fastened countless times. Listen to their excited cries as they admire mushrooming clouds of dust rising above the camelback mountain west of town. Watch juvenile faces as dynamite, spread proportionately across the top of the mountain, explodes with well-timed regularity. Hear dogs set up a chorus of frenzied howls at the smashing sounds falling with deafening impact on sensitive ears, just as a red sun touches the mountains with its first feeble rays.

Inhale cool sage-scented air coming over the town and sniff lustily at the odor of burned powder mixed with clouds of dust. Oh, glorious Fourth of July!

Watch the children who stand entranced until the last explosion and echoes die away. Follow them to their mother's bed as they wheedle, "Please, ma, get up and make the fire and dress us."

"It will be hours before the parade starts," she objects. "Go back to bed."

Impossible!

"But mother," the children inform her in wheedling voices, "we want to shoot firecrackers with the rest of the kids before they buy the stock out."

As if they could buy the stock out. The manager of the IXL store has his storage room full of firecrackers, pin-wheels, snakes, pink and purple caps, sparklers, torpedoes, stink-bombs, sky rockets, roman candles and itching powder to sprinkle down the necks of unsuspecting girls.

If you have been a reasonably well-behaved girl in preparation for the event, and have a father, you find yourself in possession of a pair of red stockings and gleaming red shoes which shine with newness. You also have a new, crinkly, frilly dress with its belt tied in a fluffy bow at the back, and a new straw hat. On the other hand, if you are fatherless, your mother polishes your black shoes with an odorous liquid which gives them a blue-black luster; but you forget they are old when your mother gives you a nickel, or even a dime to spend for candy or ice cream, or perhaps a box of pink popcorn.

If you are father of a family, you wake to your kid's insistent urging and help with their dressing; however, your aid is not forthcoming until you have helped yourself to a Coffee Royal; a cup of coffee, heavily spiked with whatever whisky you can afford. Then you send the biggest boy with your dinner bucket, its crown rubbed with butter as a foam preventative and assurance of full measure, to have it filled with beer for fifteen cents.

Mother fries pancakes to a crisp, golden brown; and if you are a boy and fail to consume a dozen saucer-size cakes floating in golden syrup, your mother remarks that you have lost your appetite, and that evening gives you a big dose of salts after first bribing you with a nickel. Meanwhile, you rush off, eager to get away from sisters so that you might join your friends and shoot firecrackers behind the backs of girls whom you secretly admire. Wait a minute! Wait a minute! Your friend has to milk the cow before he can go with you; so you block the barn doorway in a high pitch of excitement, watching and nervously chewing at your fingernails, while your companion works the creamy milk from the cow's udder. You stand on one foot, then on the other, listening to the exploding firecrackers made of old Chinese newspapers filled with black powder, and feeling inordinately afraid that you are going to miss something.

At your pleas that he hurry, your friend turns one baleful eye on you, the other has been disfigured as the result of an experiment with dynamite caps and says testily, "Aw, keep your shirt on; the parade doesn't start until ten."

You look at your friend accusingly, wondering again why he had to lose most of his fingers in the same explosion. It slows the milking, doesn't it?

Johnny, startled by the explosions, woke his mother with his cries. Engrid slipped into her dress; while John lay languidly in bed, secure in the knowledge that there were no chores to be done other than tending to the needs of his horse, and that could wait. He stretched, yawned, watched unconcerned with what almost amounted to boredom as Engrid ministered to the child's needs.

A rapping at the door announced Louise's entrance into the room. "Are you decent?" She set down a tray on which reposed a bottle of bourbon, a glass and a pitcher of ice water. Wonderful sister-in-law!

"Oh, you angel," John chortled pulling himself up in bed. Adjusting a pillow behind his back, he asked, "Where are your wings?"

"I thought you would like an eye-opener before breakfast, and I'm only treating you the way that you would us were we to visit you. Pour your drink and I shall have coffee ready before long."

John poured himself two drinks; then he leaned back against the pillow after glancing at Engrid who was busy with the baby, until Louise taking the child gave it a great deal of affection. "There, little man," she cooed, "I have to grind coffee; but I will be back soon."

John pondered over the fact that he had arisen at dawn each day since moving to the farm, and had worked until after dark each night. "Don't you wish you were a man to be waited on hand and foot by a sister-in-law?" he asked with a smirk.

"I have an idea I shall get it back on you in the next world." Engrid replied, feeling content that she was not due to work in hot fields as she pinned the diaper on the child's chunky body.

John lay in bed, feeling the mellow glow coming from good liquor wisely used and musing over his good fortune. It promised to be fun with crowds, a round of beer with friends, and small gossip which binds people together in small towns where almost every man at sometime or another, has worked together.

After a time during which the aroma of coffee drifted through the door in cloying, mouth-watering waves, Louise reappeared bearing a tray on which reposed a pot of coffee, two cups and saucers, a bowl of lump sugar and spoons to stir the cream. She set the tray down saying, "There, I hope you like it."

"Is Emil awake?"

"Awake and has already taken care of the horses. Right now he is washing and polishing the buggies."

John twitched his nose and remarked that they were going to have burned ham for breakfast.

"Oh, good heavens," Louise exclaimed, hurrying from the room.

"I'm hungry," John exclaimed, "where's my pants?"

"In the valise with the rest of your dress clothes. You'll have to wear your riding pants until I can press the best ones out."

"No rush, I'm going to wear my old ones until the drilling contest is over," John stated while getting himself up to parade about in the room in his trousers breathing deeply of cool air wafting in through an open window. "Oh, this beats the steaming air on the farm." He seated himself on the bed and blew on the coffee for a time; then he drank with gusto.

"You're not serious about entering the drilling contest? You haven't swung a hammer since you left the mine; in fact, it was a long time before you left."

"That doesn't mean a thing, my dear; just because a violin player doesn't touch his violin doesn't mean that he can't still play. I feel the same way about drilling. Just let me swing one of those hammers for a dozen strokes, and I'll be right in the pink." He flexed his arms and gazed with no small measure of conceit into the bureau mirror as he thumped his huge chest with clenched fists. Catching Engrid's eyes in the glass, he winked.

"You men are vain."

"When we have something to be vain about."

"And what have you to be proud of?"

"My muscles."

"I'd admire you more if you had sharp brains and small muscles."

At Engrid's remark, John released air from his cavernous chest. Engrid's words had been the pin-prick deflating his bubble of self-esteem. "Now, I like that," he stated in a sulky voice, his features assuming a gloomy cast. Engrid went to him and placing her arms about his waist, she kissed him. "You are like a small boy; you mustn't take things to heart when I'm joking."

Childlike, John's face brightened. "Leaving all joking aside; I believe I have an edge on the men working underground. I have put on a lot of weight since leaving the mine, and it is all muscle. The last time I stepped on the grain scales at the feed store in Lehi, I weighted two-twenty-five. I believe that Emil and I have a better than average chance of winning the prize money, and if we do…" his face lifted and his eyes held a faraway look. "Boy, oh boy!"

In the kitchen they found Emil sipping a cup of coffee, and Louise dropping yellow batter onto a griddle. On a plate reposed a huge pile of golden pancakes. On another, piled high, were several slabs of ham a half-inch thick and swimming in golden grease. John's mouth drooled when he stared at the food.

"How are you doing, Emil? Think you can swing a hammer with the best of them?"

"With the best? I am the best! Do you think you can turn steel?"

"My baby can turn steel for what drilling you can do."

"Aw, hell with you, sit down and eat. Louise, fry a dozen eggs for each of us."

John slapped him reassuringly on the back, and at Louise's invitation, he washed, and then sat down; and what the two men did to the plates of food, was amazing!

After breakfast, John took the baby outside while the women put the house in order. When their wives joined them, John and Emil pulled their shirts on and the father carried the babe during the stroll to town. For the better part of an hour, the rumbling of drums had accompanied the efforts of the director of the parade to make order of the milling mass of people, horsemen and floats. Up and down the main street with monotonous regularity, a wooden sprinkling-tank drawn by two mules; had sprayed the road until there wasn't a chance that dust would annoy the participants of the parade, or the onlookers who, in a dense mass, lined both sides of the street.

Engrid, as well as her companions, found a point of vantage on the steps of the City Hall. Her eyes, eagerly searching the passing throng, fell on the one person for whom she was searching. Her frantic, "You-who," caught Mrs. Kosky's ear and the woman moved toward the girl to grasp her in a massive embrace. She greeted the others warmly; then she relieved John of the baby and her praise for the infant was effusive.

"I'm sorry that I didn't catch you home last night," Engrid said, "Where were you?"

"I was out for a ride with Mr. Hansen in his new buggy; we're going to get married on the fifteenth of July."

Mr. Hansen's red face verified her statement.

"Congratulations!" The quartet chorused, and Mr. Hansen submitted to a number of blows on the back which left him visibly shaken. The timely appearance of a handsome woman riding side-saddle on a palomino mare heading the parade, in all probability saved the man from being injured.

Next, from outlying ranches and forming a gaudy, colorful, animated part of the parade, cowboys on cavorting horses came in sight. Their shrill cries, and frequent shots from revolvers, caused admiring youngsters to resolve, that they, would become cowboys. Two men dressed as clowns advertised the rodeo that would take place during the afternoon in which the wildest horses that they could gather, would be ridden for the amusement of spectators who were willing to part with fifty-cents for a ticket of admission.

Then, in the order decided by drawing of lots, came the various floats representing societies, lodges, business houses and mines. Between each float, clowns and bearded prospectors leading jackasses ambled along. A huge fat man, whom Emil said was the proprietor of a newly opened eating house, bore a sign, for and aft, proclaiming that he ate his own cooking. Next, the members of the miner's baseball team, followed by an out-of-town group from the valley; who were to engage the local idols in a double-header game. Interspersed along the line of marchers were various bands, and John's and Emil's cheers were loud and long when their lodge band passed by, adding to the din.

There were floats for boys and girls. The Mormon Church had a float with a beehive mounted on a stand, around which were seated children, and this drew both cheers and laughter when the spectators read a banner stating that this was "Tintic's best crop!"

Next, drawn by high-stepping white horses, the surrey of the popular mayor, then the local chemist in a buggy drawn by a prancing team of blacks. On each side of his buggy reposed two signs reading, "I make the pills to cure your ills." Next, the doctor's buckboard with a sign stating, "I prescribe the same cure for the wealthy or the poor." And finally, the undertaker, driving the shining black hearse through whose gold, framed windows, red dressed imps with horns and long tails grimaced, causing the children to squeal in fright. His sign, "You did what the doc said? I bury his dead" brought roars of mirth from the bystanders. People who had not yet seem the sign craned their necks so that they might witness that which provoked the outburst of progressive merriment.

Next, evoking excited cries from the youngsters; a dancing bear displayed by a swarthy-featured son of Italy.

Ponies, guided by the pressure of Indian riders' knees, came down the street and on a splendidly proportioned white horse rode Chief Tintic; for whom the town had been named. And trudging behind came squaws and children, a happy crowd because they had been given free rein to eat all they were capable of eating at any restaurant. The committee heading the festivities had agreed to foot the bill, if the tribe would make the frontier town colorful by their presence.

The parade moved down the road, accompanied by the rattle of fireworks and the crackling of twisted papers full of powder which ignited when ground underfoot.

Engrid went with the women to enjoy a dish of ice cream at the Candy Kitchen; but the men still feeling comfortably full after breakfast, declined the invitation to accompany them, sitting instead on the steps of the City Hall watching people who walked by, greeting those whom they knew and gazing speculatively at strangers.

"The idea of this contest," announced the man to his attentive audience; "is to see who the best mucker in the district is. Will five men who know they can swing a shovel, please step forward?"

A dozen promptly answered the summons, some with a determined look on their features, and others in an attitude of assumed nonchalance as they disregarded words of encouragement and jibes of derision.

"We need three more men," the announcer called, running his eyes over the throng. "How about you, Semell, or would you sooner shovel manure?"

"I'll enter the drilling contest; mucking is for green-horns like you."

At this exchange of repartee the crowd laughed uproariously.

"You tell him, John," and, "That's telling him, you big Finn," came from several spectators.

"Did you hear what he called me?" The announcer bawled through his improvised megaphone; "He said I was a green-horn!" He looked aghast at John. "I've a notion to break him over my knee." He paused for a moment to let the import of his threat impress his listeners, "I would if I weren't so busy," he boasted.

The crowd, comparing the diminutive barber with the colossus whom he disparaged, roared its approval.

"Well," the announcer said, "this is no time to be brawling." He winked slyly at the crowd. "Let's get on with the contest, so that John can make good his boast."

After being encouraged by friends, three additional men joined the ranks of the would-be champion shovelers, who drew lots indicating the order in which they would compete. The first five favored to display their prowess, went to a box of new shovels, feeling for one that felt just so.

"Now men, here are the rules; you have before you five boxes about six feet long by four feet wide. Each has the same amount of muck, a mine-car full. You first contestants will take your places at one of the boxes; and when I give the word, you will start to muck. At the side of each full box is an empty one. You will muck from one to the other. When you finish, and there must not be more than a shovelful left in the box you are emptying, you will hold your shovel aloft for the judges, the local jeweler and the foreman of the Little Chief mine, to see. The first prize is fifty dollars in silver dollars. Second prize will be twenty-five dollars, and consolation, five dollars." He scanned the faces of the men who had taken their places by the five full boxes, waiting for the signal to begin.

"Are you ready?" The announcer held his hands aloft. "Get set, go!"

In a growing crescendo of whistles, shouts of, "Throw your ears back," "Give it hell!" "Pour it on!" and "Get the lead out of your pants," five men clawed furiously and awkwardly to reach bottom. When they succeeded dirt flew and to the onlookers work appeared unbelievably easy, as shovelful after shovelful was thrown from one box to another in quick succession. Some men used knees as a fulcrum to drive shovels to the hilt. Others leaned over in a bow from the small of their backs driving the shovels with a swing of their arms. The spectators waited expectantly for the finish, glad that they were not contestants, and yet, wishing they were, as the hubbub surrounding the men rose to a din in which it was impossible to catch individual words when an increasing clamor measured the rate of progress.

Here was action; flying arms, showering spurts of dirt and sweat-soaked shirts; screaming, whistles, cheering audience; and over all, a cloud of enveloping dust.

The announcer's revolver cracked and the crowd fell quiet.

"Three minutes and ten seconds," the announcer bawled. The winner stood flushed of face and triumphant, breathing like a spent runner.

Cheers rose for Aurellio Vasquez, a brown faced, pock-marked Mexican who possessed rippling muscles under a colorful, red, silk shirt and whose squat stature had given him a distinct advantage over taller men who were slower.

The next five contestants took their places. The judges spread dirt and rocks evenly, making it necessary for the shovelers to scrape, as had others, in order to reach smooth shoveling. Jim Hansen, brother of Mrs. Kosky's suitor, dropped his shovel after raising it aloft when not more than a shovelful was left in the box; and the judges agreed on a time of three minutes and thirteen seconds. Immediately, the Mexican still flaunting his superiority; was surrounded by a band of his fellow countrymen congratulating him in liquid Spanish.

In the last heat, Frank O'Brien, winner of last year's contest, entered.

"Get down on your knees and shovel if you must, O'Brien," called a spectator, "but beat that Mex. I have a hundred dollars on you."

"Another hundred on O'Brien," called a butcher. His offer was promptly accepted by a Spaniard, who managed one of the town's brothels and for a time, the crowd was concerned with heated betting.

At the signal, the audience went berserk when O'Brien did his best, throwing huge shovelfuls. Faster and faster he worked as he warmed to the task, and finally raising his shovel, he dropped it and stood erect, wiping his brow with a begrimed hand.

"Three minutes and eight seconds!"

Pandemonium reigned as several of O'Brien's friends grasped the spent mucker and two-time winner after he had collected his winnings, and flocked to the nearest saloon.

"Ladies and gentlemen, the next event is one we have been waiting for. You will see the best teams of double-jack drillers in the country! The grand prize will be fifty dollars in silver to each of the pair comprising the winning team. We have here twenty slabs weighing five-hundred pounds. Each pair of contestants will be provided with a double-sided hammer, double-jacks, we call them, and three pieces of drilling steel. There is a short drill, starter, we call it, and two others of greater length, known as a second and third. The men will see to what depth they can drill into a slab in a half-hour's time. These men, each taking a turn at holding and drilling, are allowed to change with each other at will. There is only the first prize offered so that there will be no inclination on the part of any of the men to take it easy at all, thinking that they might possibly take a second or third prize. In other words, ladies and gentlemen, for one-half of an hour, you are about to witness men doing the hardest work in the world, if you doubt what I say, step right up and try it for five minutes, as fast as you can." The announcer looked over the crowd and heard not a dissenting voice; nor was there a voice raised in ridicule. These men knew for themselves.

"Will you hard-rock miners please step forward and take your places?"

At the invitation, sixteen drilling teams stepped from the throng, John and Emil among them. They looked along the line to see men of different races picking up hammers and swinging them in arcs, then hitting the ground with dull-sounding thuds to loosen their muscles. John and Emil exchanged grins as they surveyed the crowd and their competitors. Their knowing glances fell on their wives who stood, with alert faces, waiting for the dropping of the starter's arms. The women returned their reassuring smiles; although not feeling confident as to the outcome of the grueling event.

"Aren't there four more sets who would like to enter?" the announcer looked the crowd over, and found the spectators indifferent. "It's a shame to let those four rocks go without being used," he coaxed. Receiving blank stares from disinterested men; he stated, "Stand back and give the drillers room; get the kids back, if a hammer slips or breaks, we don't want anybody hurt."

The crowd became a milling herd as those at the fore attempted to move back from the line of miners, and those at the back resenting the movement attempted to push forward. The sheriff appeared on his gelding; then the mass did fall back, leaving room to spare as the horse advanced with dancing feet.

"I'll take the first heat," Emil stated, removing his shirt and exposing a hairy chest and bulging muscles. John nodded and grasping the drill, placed it at the center of the cross made with chalk on the face of the rock. This mark had been placed there by a judge in order that the depth from the face of the rock to the bottom of holes might be measured with a fair degree of accuracy. John realized that the men who stood along the line were well-versed in the work to which they were about to devote themselves; however, he exchanged banter with them off to each side.

"Drills on marks!"

Calloused hands grasped drills. A hush fell over the crowd, broken only by squalling babies and the ever-present banging of firecrackers.

"Hammers ready!"

Sixteen men tensed, spat on their hands, and eight gripped hammers, prepared to swing.

"Swing your hammers!"

"Thud, clang, thud, clang," the hammers spoke to the shining steel all along the line. They swung up, around and down, flashing in glistening arcs above the miners' heads and striking drills which would be turned a quarter-turn between blows. The hammers struck again, making a second ring, then another, another and another.

Smothered cries arose from a portion of the audience as an over-eager hammer man failed to hit his steel squarely, and the hammer knocked the drill aside, gashing the wrist of the helper who gritted his teeth and cried, "Mud!" as he placed his drill hurriedly into the hole, crying, "Hit it!" as he squeezed tears from his eyes and continued with his turning while the hammer man re-doubled his efforts to overtake the other contestants. The on-lookers murmured their sympathy. "Thud, clang, thud," the pounding went on in irregular strokes. Sweat poured down flushed faces, and hammer men shook their heads to divert perspiration away from eyes, and failing, made hasty swipes with hands as wet as their brows. A long drawn moan ran along the jammed crowd where a man, blinded by sweat, missed his blow and flattened the wrist of his helper against the slab of rock with a sickening crunch. The injured man dropped his drill, his partner released his hammer as the helper attempted to grasp the steel again and failing he stumbled through the crowd to the doctor's office up the street, aided by his sorrowing partner, concerned wife as well as a throng of morbidly inclined witnesses.

"Poor bastard," thought John steadily turning the drill, "a broken wrist and a broken heart. It could have been me, suppose it was me! Who would take care of the farm?" A cold sweat broke out all over him at the thought. However, it was no time to quit; no time to show the yellow streak hidden from view in every mortal man, so he continued with his turning. "Hit it, Emil; hit it, Emil; hit it, Emil." He chanted with every blow struck. Emil's face was taut with strain, and the muscles in his neck and jaws pulled rigidly with each down stroke.

"Take her, John, I'm winded," he gasped.

John jerked the drill from the hole which was now an inch deep. He glanced at the end of the drill, noting that it was losing its edge. "No time for a change yet," he decided. He took a spoon and scraped powdered rock from the bottom of the hole; then he grasped the hammer. How strong he felt! Grinning down at Emil who now held the drill, he ventured a blow; then blow followed savage blow as he settled into a rhythmical swing, striking again and again, inhaling on the up and overhead part of the strokes, and expelling the air out of his barrel chest on the downward strokes with gusty, "Ugh, ugh, ugh…"

"Feel how raw your throat is with each indrawn breath. Your heart is jumping out of your breast, John. The sweat is pouring into your eyes. You can feel it running in tickling streams down your chest and belly and farther to your loins. Your socks are squishing in your shoes, John. Who is ahead of you? Emil called, 'Stop!' He's cleaning the hole of the fines. 'Hit it,' he calls. The rock is as hard as Kitty's heart the morning after payday. Damn those flies, they're eating me alive… steel dull… doesn't cut… bounces. Who's ahead? Wish I had a drink of that Hommansville water… better than beer. God… missed the steel… mustn't hit Emil… break his wrist. My wind… I can't get enough air… too much smoking… gosh, my breathing's easier; I've got my second wind. I'll hit harder now… 'Whoa,' Emil said. Five jerks with a spoon and the hole is clean. He's putting in the second drill. I mustn't hit it so hard at the start, or it will bind and we'll lose out. I can actually see the drill sink with each blow now. I'll hit it harder, and harder, and harder…"

"What a fine partner and brother-in-law," John told himself as he found himself turning the drill after he had signaled for a change of positions. He watched as the drill-head gradually mushroomed outward under the impact of the pounding hammer. Hot chunks flew off with every stroke. "I wish the leases hadn't been canceled on the first of the year. We'd be sitting on easy street by now, with a dozen men mining ore for us instead of the company." Aloud he called, "Mud!" The drill had stuck. Something was wrong! The other men continued to turn with clock-like regularity; but he couldn't budge the steel. For a few seconds that seemed days, he nervously watched as Emil struck the drill on each side, and between blows, tried to pull the steel out. John's agitation transmitted itself into action, and grasping the drill, he shook it vigorously. His nerves tightened at the thought of the other drills relentlessly biting into the rocks. Emil tapped the steel gently as onlookers fastened glances on the pair who were beset by misfortune, then crowded in to offer advice and encouragement. The drill broke loose under the urging of the hammer, and Emil pulled it out of the hole, exposing a broken corner on the cutting edge. John prayerfully fished out the chunk with the spoon after several agonizing attempts; while the hammers to the left and right sounded remorselessly in his ears. Sweat broke out from sheer nervousness. Throat dry and pulse pounding, he picked up the third pieces of drill steel and inserted it in the hole with an invective for the smith who had turned out a faultily tempered drill.

"Hit it!"

Emil responded with lusty blows, placing all of his weight into his swinging, and John is firm in his belief that at the split-second of contact between the ponderous hammer and the drill head; Emil's feet actually raised from the ground, so heavily did he follow through with each stroke.

"Five minutes to go; five minutes to go!" The announcer's shout rolled like the voice of doom over the contestants' heads. A murmur, swelling in John's ears like roaring surf, steadily increasing in intensity with the passing seconds. The crowd, over eager to witness the finish, moved in dangerously close, causing the hammer swingers to be distracted. The officer, almost bowling over many of the throng as they edged nearer to the contestants, drove his horse firmly along the fringe of the crowd. The people moved back momentarily, then like water behind a moving spoon, they fell forward again with the passing of the horse.

"Let the damn fools get their heads broken," the man with the star muttered as he sat sedately watching the finish of the contest.

All along the line men changed positions; but John was still weary, and Emil only now swinging into his stride, his reassuring smile told John.

"God, what a hammer man he is," John breathed; then he called, "mud," as he jerked the drill out. A quick glance told him that the edge was holding; so he scraped the powdered rock and quickly rammed the steel back in. He winced as Emil struck off center; and a piece of rolled steel bit agonizingly into his wrist.

"Two minutes to go; two minutes to go!"

Emil exchanged looks with John who released the drill at the electrifying cry. John swung faster than he had ever swung before as the crowd became hushed.

"Crack!" the announcers pistol broke the silence into fragments and the crowd surged in with enthusiastic, back-shaking thumps on weary men.

Hammers slithered from hands weary to the point of paralysis. Many of the men slumped to the rocks beside their drills, too spent for the time being to show interest as the three judges came along, gripping slender rulers in their hands. As the three measured each hole when scraped clean to the bottom, the announcer wrote the names of the men down, and the depth to which the drills had ground into the solid rock.

Emil rose from his knees, leaving his drill in a clean hole. Throwing his arm about John's shoulders he remarked, "Win or lose, John, that's the most fun I have had drilling since my honeymoon!"

John, gasping for breath, ventured a weak smile as the hammer slid to the ground, leaving his fingers curved to the shape of the handle. He straightened them by pulling, and flexed them several times, then helped himself to a drink of warm whisky as he and the other contestants had countless flasks thrust upon them by their admirers, most of whom drank. As the drink reached his stomach, he immediately began to feel better.

"That's the best drilling I have seen in twenty-five years of mining!" said Mr. Hansen approvingly as he pounded the partners resoundingly.

"You'll neither one of you be able to do a lick of work for a week," Louise commented, her lovely eyes dancing over John to rest on her husband's face. The two men merely grunted.

"That's a man for you," Engrid chipped in, "you put out all of that work and call it fun, and cry like a lost soul if I ask you to wipe a dish."

"I can't even get you to spade my flower garden," Louise exclaimed severely.

"Aw, quit your kicking and hire John for the job; I'm no farmer."

"Let's go see who won," Engrid suggested a she grasped John by the hand.

The announcer carefully checked his notes; concurred with the judges and climbed to a platform gaily decorated with bunting and flags. Holding up his hands, he called for silence. After a brief speech in which he paid glowing tribute to the participants in the past event, he said, "I know that I speak for you all when I say how sorry we are that Ingwall Headman suffered such a regrettable accident; a compound fracture of his wrist. But now for the good news..." The announcer looked at the expectant crowd while savoring the honor attendant on being the focal point of all eyes. "The management has decided to donate the profits of the dance tonight to the unfortunate man. In the meantime, if any of you would care to chip in something to a pot for the man, I will start it off with a silver dollar."

Amid cries of approval, a hat was passed, and silver dollars, as well as an occasional twenty-dollar gold piece, clinked into the hat until it grew heavy as it moved through the crowd. The gloom that the assemblage had felt as the consequence of the accident was promptly dispelled.

"And now, to announce the winning team. I might say that the contest was close, and the winning pair was a little less than one-half inch deeper than those who came second and third. When the devil invented work, he made horses, jackasses and Finns to do it." Pausing, he waited for a storm of mirth to subside; then he continued, "Will the manure shoveler from the valley, John Semell and his partner, Emil Flink, step to the stand? Sheriff, pay the men each fifty silver dollars out of your prize money bag."

With the plaudits of friends loud in their ears, the partners strode forward to accept the new coins. They each counted out ten-dollars and placed them into the collection which had been gathered for the injured man. Emil jerked off the announcer's hat and exposed a bald head. He pretended to use the dome for a mirror; while John held the impotent, strenuously objecting man in a firm grip. Emil wiped at his face and ran his mustache between his fingers. How the crowd liked that bit of by-play.

"Charge him a dollar a peep," called a miner in the crowd. "Come to the dressing room of the Finn Hall and we'll hang you on a nail for a looking glass," derided another. "I can use you in the dressing room of the women's clothing department," called Mr. Wilken from the seat of his surrey.

John released the spluttering announcer and jumped from the stand, followed by Emil as the announcer missed with a hastily aimed kick at the latter's posterior.

Regaining a sense of composure and picking up his megaphone, the announcer called, "We will now go to the vacant lot by the Vienna Bakery, and I'll guarantee that there'll be enough free beer and barbecued sandwiches for all."

Like a breaking dam, the crowd flowed into the street, making their way to the designated spot where since early morning, skilled cooks from a cattle ranch had been roasting numerous quarters of plump beef.

"Me for the bath tub and a change of clothes," John protested, and Emil agreed.

The sisters looked at their grinning husbands who jingled their winnings in their pockets. Their eyes expressed pride and avarice as the men thrust out their chests and crowed over their accomplishments. And well they might!

"Give!" Engrid commanded, her lips drawn tightly together in a determined line.

"Now, mom, you…"

"You needn't entertain the idea for one moment that you are going to take all of that money and blow it in drinking liquor and beer; while you leave me and the baby to wander the streets like lost sheep. I know you too well. You can buy what you want and bring it up to the house, otherwise, drinking is out."

"Why don't we invite some of our friends to the house for a blowout? Bring the drinks and we women will fix up the chickens and have a grand dinner," Louise stated.

"Now, you're talking," Emil said enthusiastically, "name them."

Louise quickly named several couples, and John and Emil promptly went in search of them with a promise that they wouldn't end up in a saloon.

Chapter 27

Each winter, for four consecutive years, John added another room to their home. Each winter he performed his annual assessment work on his west Tintic claim. Once or twice weekly, he peddled his produce in Tintic, and when the weather was mild, Engrid occasionally accompanied him and visited for the day.

The second child, Gertrude was born when Johnny was two year old. A second daughter named Agnes was born two years later. During these years, rainfall was sparse until in February, only the peaks of the mighty Wasatch Mountains were capped lightly with snow. The settlers congratulated themselves that they were drawing water from the lake rather than from dwindling streams as were farmers across the lake. Because they had ample water, their crops were abundant and brought top prices in the mining camp which had come to depend almost entirely on peddlers for basic food supplies.

However, the unexpected happened.

"The crickets are on the march this spring; they've reached as far as the foothills back there," the mailman informed John with a jerk of his head as he handed him a letter addressed to Engrid.

John observed before putting the letter in his pocket that it bore the postmark of Jacobstad. He stared blankly at the cadaverous man whose jaws moved rapidly in a nervous, fitful motion as he nursed a chew of tobacco. The point of his chin almost touched his slender nose each time he brought his gums together on the cud.

"Don't what I am saying make sense to you?" The postman asked.

"You mean the same creatures that plagued settlers in the Salt Lake Valley?"

"Exactly. They'll eat every glade of green showing above the ground," he remarked ominously moving a hand in a sweeping gesture embracing the fertile farms.

"We've got to stop them; but how?"

"Well, if the cheat grass were dry, you could burn it; it's nice and green, though."

"What about the gulls? They saved the crops of the settlers the first time."

"That they did; but here there are more crickets than the gulls can get rid of in all of the summer; there are so many that the ground seems to be flowing like hot tar."

"God…"

"Maybe," the mailman said hopefully, "you could plow a furrow and fill it with dried brush and straw and keep fire going in it to stop them. I doubt if there are enough men in the community to keep a fire going that far around the settlement." He scratched his lean chin, shook his head thoughtfully; clucked to his horse, "Let me know how you come out," he called and drove away, taking hope with him and leaving despair in its place.

John watched the buggy until it blurred and swam from sight through the heat waves on the road. He shrugged his shoulders; then turned to stare at gulls wheeling aloft, their strident cries sounding mockingly in his ears. He looked at the grass growing in a sweeping green sea from moist ground about the house, shaded by indolent shadows of poplar trees.

"Something has to be done," he pondered. "I just can't stand here swearing and praying." He walked hurriedly to the barn and saddled the horse. Mounting, he rode to the kitchen door. "Ma, oh Ma."

"What is it?" Engrid appeared at the opening, her hands heavy with dough.

John told her. "In some way we have to figure out a way to stop them."

Heavy of heart, Engrid stood in the doorway, watching until her man disappeared behind the house of their nearest neighbor; then she went into the house and continued to knead her dough. Crickets or not, men have to eat.

"Hello, Ed," John called with easy familiarity, pulling his mount to a halt at the door of a shed where a raw-boned, red-faced farmer plucked a horseshoe in a pair of tongs from a bed of coals. Satisfied that it needed more heat on one side, Ed shoved it in deeper, heaped more coal on the pile; then pumped the handle of the bellows.

"Did you see the mailman today?" John asked, trying to sound casual.

"Can't say that I did; been busy in my shop, why?"

"He just told me that the Mormon crickets are only a couple of miles from here; right along that line of foothills skirting the lake to the north and moving this way."

"What?"

"That's right."

"God, man, we can't just stand here. Let's get moving and see if there isn't something we can do to stop them." He jerked the shoe from the fire and dropped it on the dirt floor; then he ran out of the door to saddle a horse belonging to his boy. Jumping astride, he dashed off with John following, down the road at a fast lope which took him to the foothills in a matter of minutes, where both men stopped their horses as Ed said, "There they are!"

"So that's the Mormon cricket?" John sounded awed as he stared at the black, shining swarm moving by hops across the ground, and at other times crawling along and pausing only to chew hungrily at a blade of tender grass. He saw at a glance that the individual crickets averaged an inch in length, and resembled grasshoppers without wings, as he dropped the reins to walk forward through the swarm. As the invaders progressed, they spied the man, and with queer squeaks swarmed aside, sounding like the closing of myriads of rusted tiny doors on dry hinges.

Picking up a long piece of cedar, John smashed at the swarm of tiny ones averaging a quarter-inch in length where they swarmed over a dried piece of cow dung. The survivors scattered in every direction. He struck at larger ones; then stepped back curiously to appraise his handiwork. Others came forward to fall on their wounded and struggling brethren whom they proceeded to devour with the same relish that they had shown the grass.

"Good lord," John cried, "they're worse than wolves; with plenty of grass to eat, they eat their own kind!" Horror sounded in his voice as he watched the crawling, struggling, creaking creatures that tore at bodies of comrades, leaving nothing when they moved on. "You dirty, black bastards; I'll give you something to eat!" John stomped crickets underfoot until he was panting for breath.

"You kin smash 'em forever; but they'll still make it to our farms." Ed Talbot's dry voice sounded in his ears.

His sanity restored, John walked to his horse and heaved himself aboard. From his point of view he stared down on the crawling army, and watched in fascination when tall blades of grass shook violently for a moment, then tumbled to the ground and disappeared. "This is what will happen to my crops." John thought.

"Let's ride on and see how far they go," Ed suggested; and wheeling his horse he started through the brush and glistening scavengers.

"The gulls are helping a little," Ed remarked as John drew abreast and looked to birds rising from sage-covered ground at their approach. John drew his horse to a halt and watched as gulls landed and began to gorge and disgorge the crickets. After disgorging they continued to eat.

"Look at that, Ed," he remarked with a wave of his hand, "someone said that man is the only animal that makes a hog of himself; he's crazy as hell. Those birds take two bites of a cricket; then vomit them up again. No wonder they can do away with so many."

For ten miles the men rode along through an army of destruction moving inexorably toward their homes and farms. "Where in hell do they all come from?" John asked in an exasperated voice as they finally circled toward home after failing to find an end to the pests.

"As far as I know, they are always here, and the only way they reproduce enough to menace our crops is if there is an unusually dry cycle of weather for several years. Did you ever examine one closely?"

Ed climbed from his horse to grasp a large one which frantically strove to wriggle out of his clutching hand. It vented frantic sounds while spewing out a secretion from its working jaws. Ed touched a pointed black tail about an inch long with one finger. "After they breed, this thing here is thrust in the ground or in a cake of dung, and the eggs are laid through it. If the weather is right, they hatch in a couple of weeks and begin to eat their homes up. Dad told me about this; he was one of the original pioneers who almost starved at their appearance, that first year in Salt Lake Valley. Since that time, I've heard of the damn things covering half of Utah; they have even got as far as Colorado before disappearing."

"What can we do?" John asked as the man tossed the creature to the ground. "The mailman says that they stretch right to the lake."

"I don't know," Ed said dourly.

"They stop at the lake," John pondered thoughtfully fingering his chin. "Water stops them. Hey, the ditches; they'll wash them into the lake! If both pumps are run at the same time, will they throw enough water out to wash them away when they reach the main ditches?"

"You old son, you!" Ed pounded his companion on the back. "You've hit the nail on the head! Let's get everybody to irrigate their land with both pumps running until the crickets reach the ditches; then we'll cut the water off the land and just let it run back into the lake. In that way, none of the crickets will be washed onto the farms. Let's go tell the pump man!"

The pair rode at a gallop to the pump house where John immediately made the pump man aware of their peril.

"It's lucky for you that the other pump is in working shape," the operator told them; "I just finished taking up the bearings. I'll get some oil and give her a try."

He filled the housing surrounding the bearings with oil to the desired level. He checked the oil in the motor and make certain that everything was in the clear. Satisfied that things were right, he opened pet-cocks on the head of the pump, and water spurted from the vents as he threw a switch. An indicator told him that the pump was operating smoothly as the pressure reached the normal level on the discharge side. His keen eye spied a breath of smoke rising from the packing around the shaft. Grasping a wrench, he loosened two nuts until a trickle of water ran from an orifice at the base of the gland. The smoking ceased and the operator placed a hand on the gland.

"It's alright," he remarked laconically, and a load of worry slid from John's mind as he listened to water surging through the iron pipe which had been cast especially for the job.

The crickets reached the canals two days later and a barricade was placed on the bridges. Those of the horde entertaining notions of walking on water were promptly washed into the lake where a moderate west wind, made them easy prey for circling gulls and schools of carp and catfish. The black tide moved sluggishly on beyond the settlement, its crest marked by wheeling gulls who before the summer was over, were forced to make a round trip daily of eighty miles for their feasts and Louise wrote to Engrid, informing her that the gulls appeared over Tintic daily, using the pass over the mountain range.

"Craziest thing I ever saw," the mailman told John one day as he drove up to the gate in front of the house.

"What is?"

"Those gulls; they eat their fill of crickets, puke them back up; then they do it over and over again. It's lucky for the farmers that they don't eat grain."

"They eat fruit," John commented; "they riddled my cherries; I had to shoot one and hang it from a tree in the orchard. That stopped them, but they still do more good than harm."

"Thank God for that."

The weather continued unendurably hot. Miniature whirlwinds swept through the valley, causing dust-devils to dance across the valley floor. Springs in the mountains ceased flowing; cattlemen were forced to bring their charges to the shrinking lake for water, and feed them costly hay.

"I haven't seen the likes of this in forty-five years," Ed Talbot remarked one spring day. "Of course, I didn't take much interest in the weather when I was a kid; I just accepted it and played in it, cold or hot, wet or dry, weather was weather and to be enjoyed."

The seventh winter after the farming community was established was so warm that inhabitants of Tintic went about in their shirt sleeves and dresses, reveling in warmth which cut down fuel bills and gave them more money to spend for talking machines and beer. However, papers were filled with ominous reports and predictions, stressing the need for conservation of water. That year, eighty-four percent of the farms across the lake from Garden City went into the hands of receivers.

"We're luckier than the folks across the lake who depend on the river water from the mountains; there isn't any. At least we can keep on using what we need," John said thankfully one morning scanning his green fields, and mentally chalking up the value of his harvest in the coming fall, given hot weather and ample water.

"Another five years at this rate and we'll have everything paid for," he told Engrid as he sat contentedly enjoying an after-breakfast smoke when a buggy rolled into the yard. From it a man whom John recognized as the County Sheriff from Lehi, walked up to the door.

"Well, well, a long time no see; have a seat," John said jovially. He stood erect and extended a hand. "Had you breakfast?"

"Thanks, John; that I have." He sank to the porch beside John and pulled out his pipe. John observed his action in silence; wondering why the visitor had come.

"It's hot as the hinges of hell," John remarked; "although I like the heat, my crops really grow. How are things your way?"

"Bad, John, that's what I came to see you about." His tone was terse and visage dour as he wiped with a bandana of faded red. "Most of the farmers are losing out to the banks. They haven't made enough in the last four years to meet their debts, and the banks are just letting them live on land that used to be theirs, hoping that the weather will swing to another wet spell before too long. Your crops are doing alright, I see. Nice to see green stuff as pretty as that alfalfa again."

"I'm going to have a better hay and potato crop then I have ever had," John remarked proudly. He flipped his cigarette into green grass. "This soil is rich; it hasn't been farmed to death. Of course the lake is way down compared to what it used to be; but there is still plenty of water. Maybe it will snow next winter."

Clearing his throat, the officer came straight to the point. "John," he said in a brusque voice, "the only reason I made this long ride out in this heat was to bring you some bad news, and it is bad for every farmer here. You're being forced to stop using water; here is the court order." He stood up and brushed his trousers and adjusted his hat after sweeping back his iron-gray hair with a sinewy hand. "I've got to notify everyone in Garden City, and it hurts like hell. Damn my soul for ever taking this job."

He handed John a legal-appearing document, and returning to his buggy, he drove out of the yard.

John experienced fear and futility so intense as to be almost tangible when he perused the document. He read and reread to assure himself that he was seeing right.

"My God," he half whispered, half moaned. His eyes rose from the paper and apparently that was too much of an effort, so shaken was he, for they dropped on a pair of brown chickens busily helping themselves to scraps from a swill bucket swarming with flies. A brood of yellow chicks dashed hither and yon in pursuit of hoppers. He laid the paper on the porch and stared over the farm through rising heat waves heavy with the moisture of growing crops. Beyond, the sage shimmered in the distance, and his eyes were blurred as hot tears squeezing between the lids dropped to the steps in ragged splotches. Wiping his eyes on the sleeve of his shirt, he steeled himself for the ordeal of informing his wife. Swiftly he concluded that he had better stress the fact that it meant all of the people in the community. Perhaps that might soften the blow. Taking a firm grip on his emotions, he called his wife to the door.

"What is it, John? What have you there?" Engrid crossed the porch and picked up the paper. "Who brought this?" She struggled with the legal phraseology, understanding some words, and stumbling helplessly over others. "But I don't understand, John, you mean…" she looked at him wide-eyed and her lips quivered, "oh, no, John, it can't be!"

"It is an order from the court denying us the use of water after twelve o'clock tonight. We're finished here, Engrid. We can't raise the crops to maturity without water. The people, in Salt Lake Valley, who filed on the water coming from the lake before we started buying surplus water, are using water from the Jordan River at the over-flow end. The lake has reached what is called compromise point, and below this, the contract maintains that we cannot draw water, or the farmers in Salt Lake Valley will be faced with the same situation that we are. They won't be able to get any water. It is a choice of doing without water themselves; or allowing us to continue buying it; and I can't picture them doing that."

Dropping the paper, Engrid's hands went listlessly to her face. This land she had learned to love. What could they do? She stared at trees in front of the house, their shadows dappling the grass. Soon these would dry up and the grass would become sere. She stared with a clarity that astonished her at her vegetable garden; so lovely did it look in its green raiment. These plants are to whither and die. Bees from a dozen hives droned busily about the house during their flights to and from the fields of brave green alfalfa. They would starve to death. She stared about her, picturing how the valley had appeared when they had first moved here, so long ago, it was, and she had wakened the first morning to gaze over sage-covered wastes, visualizing as best as she could green crops that would someday grow with the addition of water to fertile soil. Utter dejection spoke in the droop of her shoulders when she lowered her glance to the porch.

"I guess we shall have to leave what we have," she said in a lifeless voice which was barely a whisper as she withdrew from the porch and moved dispiritedly into the house where she slumped into a chair at the kitchen table and poured forth bitterness in a flood of tears. Only this morning she had been thinking about a new bedroom set and a repaint job on the house.

"Don't take it so," John murmured coming in and laying hands on her shoulders; "we're still young and we've got our health. Yes, we're still young. We're not the only ones in the same boat," he told himself as well as his wife. "The others, too, will have to leave. We've made a decent living here, and we have known the meaning of independence. All Louise and Emil have to show for their years in the mining camp is a living." He looked about him trying desperately to formulate some reason for the catastrophe which would take a livelihood away from every person in the community. There had to be some explanation. He knew with a lucid practicality that several dry years had lowered the contents of the lake to the point where a further lowering would wreck harm on people who had legal and ethical rights to use it. That was explanation enough. Of course the weather might change for the better. Just how did the weather run over a long period of years? People hadn't lived here long enough to find out. That was that.

He looked out of the window to where the pump house stood, and faint to his ears he could hear the motors whine. Two pumps going, pumping water that would be useless; they might as well be shut down right now, for all the good that they would do. He looked farther and perceived that his neighbors were continuing to irrigate. He peered toward Lehi and perceived that the sheriff had finished serving a restraining notice on all of the farmers, and then had taken his leave. Queer creatures are human beings. There the neighbors continued to irrigate and plow as though a bombshell had not been thrown into their midst. Maybe by working as they did, and pondering about their sorrowful situation, they could fully accept it when their minds and bodies tired.

"When we first moved here, the kids could swim in ten feet of water. Now they have to wade out for a mile to get wet up to their bellies. The lake is about dry, by the looks of it," he said aloud to no one in particular.

A tired sob from his wife was his answer. She rose and bathed her face in tepid water. Finally she turned to face her husband where he stood at the window.

"The bank will take everything?"

"Yes."

"We can't just sit here watching things dry up and die by inches. Let's go to Tintic, John, and come back next fall. If there is anything to harvest, we can harvest it then."

"It's only March; there won't be anything to harvest."

"Oh…"

"We have to eat," he stated in a flat voice.

"We have to eat," she echoed sadly. "Can't we do anything? Can't we get any of our money back?"

"We bought the land for fifty-dollars an acre; we can't give it away," he said soberly. "People have no use for this land without water."

"What about the house?"

"The bank will take that, also; we can't pay for it. How much money have we got?"

"I have a little over fifty-dollars in my box. I counted it this morning."

"It's lucky for us that we didn't have it in the bank, or the banker would demand that as partial payment on next month's…"

"John," Her voice came timidly.

"What?"

"Do you think that there is anything dishonest about the whole setup?"

"No, dear; I read the contract that we signed when we began farming here. It states simply that the Salt Lake Water Users Association would sell us surplus water which was running into the Salt Lake and being wasted."

"Oh."

"Still," he mused, "I've got a good notion to see the banker. I might be able to get some of my investment back."

John spoke with two of his neighbors, Ed Talbot and Carl Johnson and they all decided to see Mr. Reynolds the banker the following day.

"I suppose you know what we are here for," John stated firmly as he eyed the banker.

Mr. Reynolds regarded the three men thoughtfully; then he nodded. "I take it that you want to know what you are to do about water."

"That's right. If we don't get water, we won't even be able to harvest the first crop of hay; what there is of it. Our potatoes won't be any bigger than the end of a man's little finger. As for the wheat, there won't be any."

Mr. Reynolds reached into his pocket and pulled out a pearl handled knife and began to pare fingernails which were already pared. His hands, John noticed, were immaculate and soft. He looked at his own hard ones and clenched them into fists, then forced himself to relax them. The banker reached into his desk and found a key; then he went to a safe and inserted the key into a lock. He swung a drawer open and brought forth a sheaf of papers. After a brief search he found the paper he was looking for. He glanced at the paper's contents, dropped the paper to the desk as he seated himself and extended soft hands with palms upward in a gesture of resignation and finality.

"This is a copy of the contract you men all signed. It states simply that if the time ever comes, through an act of God, when the lake drops to what is called the compromise point, and there should be a reduction of water from the overflow, the Salt Lake Valley water users could and would refuse to sell more water to the holders of those contracts."

"But," John protested, "You have also been selling land to settlers in the Salt Lake Valley who use water from the Jordan River."

"True, true; but even the last forty or fifty farmers there will be cut off, if need be, to protect the prior rights of others."

"We'll turn the pumps on if you cut the water off," John said heatedly. "There's something that smells about this whole deal, and it's stronger than rotten carp on the mud banks out from the pump house. You sell us land for fifty-dollars an acre, and now it isn't worth five cents. They, including you, sell us water long enough to build up some damned nice farms, and then serve us with a notice that we can't have any more water. Most of these men, including myself, have the places mortgaged to you, and without water, we won't be able to pay off."

"I'm sorry, but that is the way it is. You can still live in your houses; I'm not evicting you," the banker said in a placating manner.

"What the hell! We can't live on cheat grass and carp." Ed Talbot interjected his voice into the discussion to say heatedly. "And as for the houses; what are you going to do with them when we can't pay them off?"

"I can leave them where they are in charge of a caretaker until the weather changes and the water comes back. I can't hazard a guess as to when that will be; but you fellows can continue to stay where you are, or leave; it's entirely up to you."

"It seems as if we lose everything. You never lost a damn thing on those two-thousand dollars I paid you for the land."

"Certainly not, John, and if you were in my business, neither would you. It's true that I made a small profit after paying for the development of the land; but that is business. I am entitled to a profit for my efforts. The greatest share of the money went into the pumps and irrigation system. I spent a lot for that hotel, thinking the state might run a main highway down through here to do away with the necessity of going around through towns to the east of the lake. Gentlemen, allow me to inform you that I haven't made a small fortune on what you have paid in, although you might think so. Now that you can't have any water, the papers that you signed to borrow on for livestock, farm machinery, houses and barns, isn't worth a cent to me. The only way that I can realize a profit is by you men continuing your payments. If the water doesn't come back, I'm ruined. I plunged on this deal, and what I can get out of those houses won't net me ten-cents on the dollar."

Silently the men accepted the man's statement; soberly they took their leave, and despondently climbed into John's buggy.

John smiled grimly. "A lifetime of work has come to nothing."

"I'm busted flat," Ed Talbot said as they rolled from town in the depressing heat.

John raised his eyes from the road as the animal set off at a slow trot. His glance rested on Packard Peak towering well above the others on the west range.

"I'm going to Tintic and get out of this damn heat. It's cooler up there and a man can feel good. If I have to sit home and watch my crops dry up, I'll end up in the crazy house. I've got a claim and with a little perseverance, I can make something out of it." He clucked to the horse and it quickened its gait. "It's there; I know it's there," he said in an impassioned voice.

"Oh, how do you know?" the taciturn Ed drawled. He pulled out a plug of tobacco and bit off a man-sized chuck. He mauled it for a moment then spat over the dashboard.

"How do I know?" John's eyes followed a swirling, erratic funnel of dust which was born in the sage off to the side of the road. It danced toward them, gathering dry twigs and leaves until it moved on them with a whooshing, heat-laden sound. John closed his eyes until the wind subsided. "I know it is there in the same way that I now there is a God, regardless of what he looks like, and in the same manner that I know that I love this country, and my wife and children. I know it in the manner that I know that they love me."

One can't argue with convictions; so for a time the men rode in silence, each occupied with personal implications of the tragedy that had broken into the regular tone of communal affairs. Clouds of alkali dust rose behind the buggy; and flies swarmed over the sweating horses. Heat waves seemingly caused the mountains to dance and jump in the manner of a reflected object in a gently disturbed pool of clear water. The rank odor of sage came to the men's nostrils on oppressive gusts of furnace-hot air. The sun beat down relentlessly, causing the men to regard this monotonous waste through squinting eyes.

"What are you going to do?" John asked of Ed Talbot as he stopped the buggy and the man descended to the ground before his house. Ed kicked dejectedly at a clump of sere, bunch-grass before answering.

"The first thing I am going to do is get that quart of whiskey I've had cached away in the potato cellar for the celebration of my birthday, and get completely drunk. After I sober up, I can think of the future."

"I'll see you again," John said. He shook his head after declining a drink, and Carl Johnson remained with Ed, glad to help the man consume his liquor. When John reached his house; he drank a quart of water from the bag hanging in the depths of the well. He spat distastefully and walked into the kitchen.

"Remember how good the water in the hills was, mother?"

Engrid looked up from the table where she and her children were eating bread and milk. Unconsciously she brushed back a strand of hair which always persisted in detaching itself from her tightly coiled tresses when she worked. She made no comment, however.

"No more calloused hands and sore back for you, little mother."

"What do you mean? Why?"

"We're going to Tintic and rent a house. I am going to see C.L. Beck about the loan of some rails, a mine cart and some supplies from the warehouse. When and if I have to, I can work for wages in the mines."

"What did you find out about the farm?"

"The same as everybody else found out. We're broke and the banker holds the pot of gold." He grinned wryly. The despondency that had gripped him for the last few hours had loosened its grip. Determination sounded in his voice. "Let's start packing."

"Now?" she gasped in amazement.

"Certainly; we can't sit around here all summer, folding our hands and watching the crops die. It's cool up in the mountains during the nights, and there's work to be done there. Of course, if you'd rather, you can stay here, waiting for the lake to rise again, smelling dead carp on the mud banks and fighting mosquitoes."

"Merciful heavens, no. What could I do here? Nothing."

She stared about at a room which had somehow lost its character. She glanced out of the window at trees drooping dispiritedly, and swaying gently at times as a funnel of dust washed through them to spatter the house with sand. She couldn't remain here. This would be a place of desolation in thirty days. Weeds would replace growing grain, and trees would lose their luster.

"Come, Johnny, we're moving to Tintic. But what if there are no houses for rent?"

"There are plenty of them. They're building on that plot of ground where they had the first graveyard. The City Council had the bodies removed to the one west of town. The dead make way for the living; that is the way that it should be," he said as she objected to the sacrilege of disinterring the bodies.

"Did they dig them all up?" asked wide-eyed Johnny.

"Yes, son, every last one of them."

"What about the ghosts? Will they still be there?"

"And who has been filling your head with nonsense?" Engrid demanded angrily. "There aren't any ghosts, only stories."

"But I like ghost stores," the boy protested.

"I asked you a question," his mother reminded him.

"Jack Nelson who helped paw put the hay up last fall, he said there are too ghosts, he…"

"The fool!" Engrid's tone was embittered. "He'd have you growing up to believe all of that nonsense that they used to stuff into our heads in the old country. When the nights were long and all people had to do was sit about the fireplace, drinking coffee and outdoing each other with lies they told."

"But I like ghost stories."

Engrid smiled. "So do I; I suppose it is alright."

With mouth agape, "How you can change!" Johnny gasped to his unpredictable mother.

Engrid's gloom was dissipated in peals of merry laughter as she went at the job of packing their household goods. After the wagon was loaded, John placed the big bows into the strap- iron holders on the sides, forming a canopy over which he spread the top canvas. He then piled the heavier pieces of furniture in and placed lighter articles on top of these.

"Can I go with you, paw?" Johnny asked.

"If your mother says so."

Engrid assured him that he might accompany his father. John kissed his wife, and climbing to the seat of the wagon, he said, "We'll see you tomorrow."

"Goodbye, ma," Johnny called importantly as he climbed to the seat with a full water-bag.

"Goodbye, son."

The heavily laden wagon pulled out of the yard, the rack on the back heavy with hay and oats.

"Tell Louise I'll see her in a few days, and make certain that Johnny stays out of mischief; and don't get drunk, John."

"I will. I will. I won't."

Engrid watched from the roadside until the wagon became a jumping white dot in the heat; then she went into the house where she began sorting the remaining household articles, and packing them into apple boxes for the next load. She worked hard until she noticed that darkness had come. She cared for the stock by lantern light; then she sat down to supper made cheerful by the presence of her two daughters. At length she retired with her daughters on either side of her. She said a prayer, asking for guidance for her family and all of the other settlers; and with the familiar sounds of night more noticeable than ordinary, she fell asleep after a period of weeping.

Coming back from the Tintic the following day, John met another wagon moving slowly in the pitiless heat, with two refractory cows tied at its rear.

"So you decided to move to Tintic, after all," he remarked as the wagons rumbled to a halt opposite each other. He descended to the ground and stretching his legs, he eyed Ed Talbot who perched in a dejected heap on his wagon seat. His wife sat beside him, peering from squinting eyes below the faded blue of her sunbonnet.

"Hell and damnation, John," the neighbor exploded, "like you said, a man can't sit around and watch his place go to hell, and die inside while it happens. I'm going to get me a job in the mines, a much as I hate to."

"Howdy, Mrs. Talbot," John said raising his hat in greeting to the woman who suckled a babe. Six other children peered curiously from under the canvas tap of the wagon, clamoring for a drink of water.

Ed reached for one of five water bags and passed it around to the children after first taking a swallow. "Damned alkali," he spat wrathfully as he passed the bag with quivering hands. He regarded John with wide, red-rimmed eyes. "Godfrey, I feel tough." He licked his lips nervously. "I'd give a million dollars for a shot of whiskey, or even a glass of warm beer. My nerves are shaking so bad that I find it hard to sit still, and it is too hot to walk."

"If that is all you want, here you are," John said reaching into his coat pocket extracting one of two pints he had purchased. He grinned at his neighbor who stared at the bottle and licked his lips fitfully. Ed tilted the bottle with shaking hands and the liquid made gurgling sounds. The bottle was half-emptied when he passed it to John who took a short swallow. Ed belched and shook his head, and his face wreathed in a smile of relief.

"You're a visitation from heaven," he breathed. "If I'd only had one when I opened my eyes this morning."

"So you could have been too sloppy drunk to move," his hungry looking wife snapped as she buttoned her dress and passed her baby to the oldest daughter.

"Drink?" John asked with a kindly smile. She shook her head disapprovingly. "Some good cold water as soothing as rain in your face from Hommansville springs?" he suggested.

"Have you got water from the hills?" Melba gasped.

"A whole barrel full, wrapped in wet burlap. I stopped at the springs as I came down the canyon." He climbed inside of his wagon, opened a spigot and began passing out dipperfuls of water to the woman and children who scampered from their conveyance, pushing and shoving to be the first in line.

Ed took another long drink of whiskey and chased it down with approximately a half-gallon of icy spring water, and after herding his brood, whose bellies were distended, to their seats in the wagon, he turned to John, meaning to express his gratitude; but John was already on his way with a cheery wave of a hand, feeling glad that he had made the journey lighter for his homeless friends.

"How does it happen that Ed took his family with him?" John asked of Engrid as he drove into the yard and she came to meet him with a kiss.

"He's taking them up to his sister's place. Melba said they have everything packed, and all he and his oldest son have to do is throw it in the wagon."

"Why didn't we do it that way?"
"Because I could trust you not to get drunk," Engrid replied, "and his wife couldn't trust him."

John considered the compliment appropriate and told her so. Then he pulled out the remaining full flask and told his wife how he had given Ed a drink.

"That's alright, dear; I don't mind you having a bottle occasionally, but to make a habit of it is more than I can stand. That is why Melba hated to move back to the mining camp. Her husband can't leave it alone."

John went to see the banker in Lehi, after first making the necessary trips to move his furniture. He disposed of the house, barn, two cows and his farming implements; and with a little over one-hundred dollars in his pocket, he moved to Tintic with one cow trailing dejectedly behind the buggy. He stabled the cow and horse at Emil's place.

Chapter 28

The road ending at the residence of C.L. Beck skirted a swimming pool which, during normal winters, was used for ice skating. The ground sloping from the house toward town was colorful with growing plants. The gardener was a handyman whose underground usefulness was at an end due to a back injury. Rose bushes of every shade of red, white, pink and yellow lined the bridle path and various flowers of every description released their fragrance on the dry air. Here and there under transplanted aspen and coniferous trees, tables and chairs were sheltered.

After tethering his horse at a hitching rack, John glanced around at the ivy-covered side of the house. He breathed deeply as he walked to the door on the cobblestone walk rising above the level of the grass-covered yard. He nodded to a mild-appearing Swede who was clipping flowers; then he tipped his hat a trifle self-consciously at a stately-appearing girl of twenty whom he recognized as C.L.'s daughter who had matured during John's years away from town.

He eyed the white ornately carved door with its lion-head knocker, and striving to overlook the fact that his heart was threatening to burst out of his chest from suppressed excitement; knocked firmly then stepped back a pace as footsteps sounded inside. The door opened and John glued his eyes on a white fluff of lace tied over the comely maid's hair as she curtsied in the approved manner.

"What is it, sir?"

John told her; then waited.

Sounds of activity from mines and town blended cheerfully together, so unlike the peaceful silence embracing Garden City. From the Little Chief mine came the ring of an anvil as a smithy sharpened picks; a familiar sound, long since thrust aside when he had turned his back on the booming camp.

Wagons rumbled by on the outside of a green lattice-work fence, placed to break the violence of winter winds sweeping around the bulk of the Blue Bell mine dump. Vines in places had climbed to the top and spilled over in swaying clusters and single tendrils.

A robin, fluttering to the ground, pulled a worm loose and chopped it into pieces; then it flew to a tree, bearing a segment in its mouth, and reappearing shortly for another morsel.

John was startled from his absorption of the bird's antics by the reappearance of the maid, who said, "Mr. Beck agreed to see you. May I take your hat?"

John handed her his hat and she placed it on a rack. He followed her through a long, carpet-covered hallway into the cool interior of the huge front room with its stained furniture. Here was a room which John had heard about from shifters at the mine. Oil paintings hung here and there, depicting work underground and on the surface of the mine. A huge fireplace at each end of the room suggested comfort during the chill of winters. Several shelves of books gave a scholarly air to one corner.

From behind a huge desk, a man arose from his chair. He waved John to a seat after shaking his had warmly. "Sit down, John; I was just going over a few reports."

"Perhaps I am intruding?" John suggested striving to find an ease in conversation which he scarcely felt. He was the cock at the bottom of the dung heap, feebly attempting to crow; and the well-fed, keen-eyed man facing him over the desk had been using his spurs many years.

"Not at all; sit down and have your say. I'm rather lazy today and perhaps a bit of conversation will prove stimulating."

He surveyed John with eyes which were a cold gray and a warm gray by turns, reflecting the devious workings of his mind. This man, John knew, had worked in the Michigan iron mines and had followed the people who had flocked to these hills in the seventies. He had bought claims from disgruntled prospectors who had tired of their work because a few days of digging had failed to reveal gold nuggets in ground which contained no placer mines.

"Is it true that you purchased the claim in which you first found ore, for a flask of whisky?" John asked in an attempt to break tension which had him feeling as though he were at the end of a long rope.

C.L. grinned disarmingly; the ice was broken, and John relaxing responded with a smile of his own.

"Mr. Semell, what you say has more than a grain of truth. I had to go east and use some high-powered persuasion to raise capital necessary for the buying and developing of most of these claims." He pointed to a map in various colors hanging on the wall behind him. "That, in itself, was no easy matter; but fortunately I contacted several men who were willing to gamble a few thousand on the venture in exchange for shares of stock in my newly-organized company." He turned to look at the map for a time, his thoughts far from the room. A clock ticked noisily, and chiming three times, recalled the man to the present. He went on, "One claim that formed the nucleus of the vast ore bodies of the mine, I bought from a man who was ready to leave town for Nevada. He had a shaft down seventy-five feet and wanted to go on a drunk before leaving. 'My claim for a pint of whiskey,' he called as he entered the saloon where I sat playing poker. Many laughed and shouted him down, and while refusing to accept his claim, several gave him a drink. On a hunch, I walked over to the man and offered him a quart of the best whiskey; naturally he was happy that he had found a buyer."

John mulled over the good fortune which had directed the man's actions, and the ill-luck which had ridden the man who had accepted the whiskey. "God," he breathed, visualizing the dramatic scene which a few well-chosen words had called into being; the crowded saloon, the discouraged miner longing for a drunken orgy before departing, and C.L. accepting the claim while others in the room laughed their derision.

"Would you care for a drink?' Mr. Beck asked, and without waiting for an affirmative nod from his guest, pulled a cord; and from the vicinity of the kitchen, the maid came to receive her instructions. "Whiskey for me and my guest."

The maid curtsied and soon reappeared with a tray on which reposed a bottle of scotch. Accepting a glass after his host had poured a drink, John smacked his lips approvingly and disposed of the liquor a sip at a time tasting and testing its flavor.

"That is the finest whiskey I have ever tasted," he said truthfully.

"I have a relative in the old country that sends it to me by the case; have another?"

John, accepting, drank the second. The gracious host extended his own blend of tobacco, and two pipes fogged the air.

"Now for the business that you wished to see me about."

His eyes glowing, John went right to the point. He informed his host of the years that he had put in developing his claim. He told him, also, of years wasted on his farm, and of his resolve to procure backing to further prospect the ground.

"What I need is someone to furnish me with a dump car, a flat car, some rails and equipment enough to keep going ahead on a streak which I have in my tunnel. I need credit for food, powder, timber and incidentals to continue because a hungry man can't work, and I hate the thoughts of going down into any mine for wages. If I can get enough to continue working my wife will be satisfied just to live and have a roof over her head; because she feels as I do about the prospect."

John ceased speaking and looked at the mine owner. He could feel blood pounding in his ears, and a flush of excitement gripped him as he observed his host regarding him with an amused grin. John felt his face flush even deeper as no remarks were forthcoming from the man. He raised himself on an impulse from the chair, still under the amused glance of the wealthy man.

"I guess I have stated my case clearly; but perhaps it sounds too much like begging to you," he admitted starting toward the door and his hat.

"Just a minute," Mr. Beck barked, causing John to stop in his stride. "You damn Finns are too hot-headed. Your dad was the same way, no wonder you're always in hot water. Sit down, man and calm yourself. You're not the first man that has come to me with a story like that; and I'm not above being amused when I see in you the same eagerness that characterized my actions when I felt that I had something to sell in the world. There isn't much that amuses me anymore, because my mind is always on business. Mind you, John," he said with a pointed finger for emphasis, "I'm not above giving a little help if I feel that it is justified. In fact, that is how I have made most of my money." He leaned backward and spread his fingers fanwise, then brought the tips of them together. He peered out of windows and over the fence to his mine. Finally, he rose and paced up and down the room. He stopped and stared out of another window to the west, overlooking the west Tintic valley.

"Where is this property, John?"

John sprang erect and pointed out a line of hills several miles away, explaining as he did how they could get there.

"How would it be if I should pick you up at say, ten in the morning?"

"That would be fine! I'll meet you in front of Garrity's barber shop."

He received the handshake of his host, noticing with a shade of envy that the man's hand was smooth and soft; although the grip firm and warm. C.L. summoned the maid and then bowed his head over his papers as she showed John to the door.

Stepping into the sunshine, he felt light of heart; a distinct contrast to his emotions when he had received the order preventing him from using more water, and years of work had lain there drying in the sun. He climbed into his buggy, noticing that birds' voices had acquired an extra sweetness and flowers fairly poured perfume into the air. The commonplace sounds of iron wheels of ore cars on the high trestle of the Blue Bell mine took on a new meaning. John paused momentarily and watched while the trammer tripped the latch and the glittering ore showered into the bin. He watched the figure of the man until it disappeared into a shed, accompanied by the rumbling sound of wheels on the wooden trestle; then he rode lightheartedly downhill, going through a pack of dogs whose clamor sounded like music to his ears.

The following day, C.L. descended from his surrey and the horses were fettered to the same tree where John had tied his horse that winter day so many years ago when Engrid had accompanied him. Eagerness gripped John which he could hardly control; and he was forced to restrain himself as the mine owner, impressive appearing in white tie, black shirt, high-tops and whip-cord trousers, topped off by a cream-colored Stetson, puffed up the hill behind him. How eager John had been when he had accompanied Engrid up the slopes leading to the tunnel and had acquainted her with his dreams! Necessity had forced their temporary dismissal; but now he could uncover them, dust them off and polish them holding them aloft for this man to examine with a critical eye. He would decide whether John should bury them again in the hill where they were hidden.

The cabin brooded in an aura of desolation; although it had been but a short year since John had come along to spend the time necessary in doing his annual assessment work. Yet a look inside assured him the place was a shambles.

"Some of those roughneck kids from Tintic have been raising hell with the cabin", he commented unnecessarily as he looked at the stove whose lids were scattered helter-skelter. From a nest made of stick, bark and dried cow-dung, a pack rat jumped out through a broken window. The single-spring bed had been torn half off as though someone had maliciously jumped up and down on it. The revolting rat odor caused John to wrinkle his nose and spit distastefully. An empty coffee bag and a litter of papers, yellow and faded, reposed in a corner where wind had blown them. Spider webs festooned the corners and rafters, hanging in sticky, dust-coated strands.

The window through which the gray animal had made its exit, bared jagged teeth in an ugly snarl.

"Things sure go to hell when there is no one to look after them. I had a man living here until I couldn't pay wages any longer," John informed his companion. "I don't know where he has gone to now; probably out on a prospect of his own."

Leaving the cabin and using the same trail which Engrid traversed with John, the men started up the hillside. Fields of sunflowers nodded brazenly through the cheat grass. The sunflower odor was heavy and sickly in their nostrils. Yellow buttercups waved invitingly, and sage was heavy with round, gray, fuzzy-coated seed-pods. Here and there, Indian red-shawls blushed in vivid patches of scarlet, and bluebells bobbed a greeting under the shade of cedars gay with clusters of new needles of lighter green than those forming the body of the parent trees. Bluebirds chirruping their plaintive lament sounded a note of sadness over the hillside. Gray chipmunks saucily whisked about, and magpies, their white and black feathers contrasting, discussed the men's presence in ribald voices.

At the mouth of the tunnel, John fumbled overhead until his exploring hands found a pair of candles; and lighting them he passed one to his companion; then he led the way into the gloom of the tunnel. The rat smell was strong here, also and John caught a glimpse of a gray form as it scurried out of sight behind lagging where heavy ground had necessitated the erection off tunnel sets. At intervals, along the length of the drift, slabs of rock and gravel had sloughed out of the back where seepage had loosened talc confining it. These, the men stepped over with an air of apprehension bred of caution which had become an integral part of their natures as a result of familiarity with the underground.

"It looks as if this tunnel could stand a few sets, in spots," John heard Mr. Beck say, and John echoed approval, knowing that his visitor was noting everything with critical eyes.

"Here is the cross-break," John ventured stepping over a wheelbarrow which for long had not been used. "And there is the streak of ore I have followed."

C.L. held his candle aloft; he scratched at the streak of quartzite with a sample pick from a leather holster on his belt. He examined several fragments in the light from both candles.

"Quartzite intruded into the dolomite," he commented. "What values?"

Reaching into his coat pocket, John extracted a number of sample sheets and passed them to the man. "It's not pay rock," he stated.

"Uh-huh, let's go to the face of the drift," C.L. answered.

John trailed him and watched while the man surveyed the streak which ran a little off perpendicular. C.L. said, "Uh-huh," then pulling out a compass, he noted the direction with extreme care that the streak of ore and tunnel were running. He wrote the dip and strike on the fools-cap, then retracing his steps, carefully paced the distance to the point where the ore had been found. He wrote that down, and after taking a bearing on the direction which the drift ran from this position, he stepped it off while John, without comment, trailed him. They replaced their candles and stepped into the light. At first, the outside air seemed pleasantly warm, but soon became unbearably hot, causing the men to perspire.

"Let's go up the hill and see what this looks like from the surface."

"Alright," John replied, and he followed the engineer who, while climbing the slope, carefully observed formations of rock protruding through the weathered surface. Just a short distance below the summit of the peak, Mr. Beck chipped at several outcroppings.

"I don't seem to be able to find a thing on the surface indicting the location of that streak of ore below, John," he said a puzzled expression altering his features.

"Neither did I; but here I ran my tunnel, as long as my funds held out."

"Tell me, then," C.L. said, shrewdly appraising his guide, "how did you come to run a prospect tunnel here and not ten miles east, west, or just any old place?"

"Well," answered John, pulling out his pipe when his companion touched a match to a cigar, "your mine, you know, is located in exactly the same formation of ground as this streak of ore. I drove my tunnel here, because, well, allow me to show you from the very top of this ridge, if you will?"

They climbed higher, C.L. groaning his protest. After the pair's breathing returned to normal, John wiped sweat from his forehead and pointed toward town. "It is true that there is a fault cutting that valley. On the south of it, you have ore; and on the north side, there is barren porphyry rock."

"That is right."

"Now, Mr. Beck, as you know the porphyry rock forming the north side of the valley is just an intrusion, shoved in there when the mountains were elevated. It is my theory that the lime rock and dolomite were laid on top of the porphyry in horizontal layers until it was several thousand feet deep. That happened before the land rose from the ocean floor, forming these mountains." He placed one hand on the palm of the other to clarify his explanation. "This right hand represents lime rock and dolomite. My left is porphyry. Now, when the stress came causing the porphyry to tilt almost vertically, the lime masses were also shoved into a vertical position, and being softer, fractured in countless places, and through these fractures, whether in gaseous or molten state, ore was forced in under pressure. It was able to penetrate dolomite and lime, but was unable to go into the porphyry to any appreciable extent. I don't believe that nature confined that particular action to only one place; where your properties are located, but in more than one. Down below are ore bodies comparable to yours; but I haven't the funds to sink the shaft; therefore, all I can do is to follow that streak in a horizontal position, hoping that the ore actually made it this close to the surface. You can see for yourself how the two different kinds of rock come up here, all these miles away from where your fault produced ore. Between here and there," John explained earnestly, "there is nothing but a huge block of porphyry, but here," he pointed to the east, "the lime and dikes of iron outcroppings go through here that strongly resemble dikes going through your mine, and also coming to the surface of Packard Peak where the Blue Bell found its vast ore bodies."

C.L. while listening to the enthusiastic man, whose emotions were fanned to a white heat by his recent failure, and his desire to make this second dream into a reality, looked about him. Sweat trickled down John's spine and beaded his brow, and he vaguely sensed that it was not all due to the sun's heat.

"If you could only stake me to enough to continue running this tunnel into the mountain to where the dikes come through to the surface, we might find what I think is here. It is a gamble, of course; but I am willing to do the work for the grub-stake, and cut you in as a partner if I find anything. If we find what I think we will, you will be a rich man beyond your wildest dreams.

"I am that already."

"God, if you weren't so self-assured and smug; and I weren't so enthusiastic," John thought. Aloud he said, "That is as it may be, but do you follow me?"

"Follow you? I'm way ahead of you. Over there is the fill similar to the one in which my major ore bodies made, and going the-lord-only-knows how deep down. We have found it on the twenty-five hundred foot level. If what you think is so, we are now standing off to one side of the duplicate channel in which my major ore bodies were formed. How did you figure it all out, anyway?"

"I like mining and geology. I spent summers before marriage, prospecting all around the district, when I took time off to get fresh air and sunshine. I finally came to the conclusion that, 'this is the place', as the Mormon leader once said."

"I hope you're right, man. How many claims have you? Let us file some more," he said after John told him. "I'll send engineers out to stake what I think we need, and men to do the development work necessary to make the claims valid. If it becomes known hereabouts that I am interested in your property, all of the country adjacent will be taken by someone else, and all we'll get for our work and expenses is an opportunity to take some other man's ore out for a royalty. Let's tie this thing up properly."

'You mean…" John said, standing for a moment, mouth agape. "You'll furnish me with a car, rails, powder as well as grub for me and the family?" A lump rose in his throat and he swallowed convulsively.

"Wait a minute, wait a minute, John," C.L. said, raising his hand, "We're not going to have you continue with a measly prospect tunnel that will take forever and a day to run in order to find out what is in this mountain; we're going to sink a shaft and run tunnels from the vertical shaft, and prospect different levels."

"You'll do that?" John gasped. He lapsed into silence and C.L. laughed uproariously at the vacant expression which came over his companion's features as John sank to the ground and began to pull aimlessly at sere cheat grass.

"Let's go back to town and see my lawyer. Do you think that you can supervise the project from scratch?"

"It's a little hot, isn't it?" John asked rising unsteadily to his feet and running his bandana across his brow.

"Hey, what goes on here?" C.L. sounded concerned. "Don't you feel good?" reaching into his pocket, he produced a bottle and passed it to his companion. "Take a swig."

John complied, and in a moment, muscles and nerves knotted by excitement, and the out-and-out shock of the counter proposal submitted by his companion, loosened, and feelings gradually returned to normal.

"You looked just like a fellow did when I hit him instead of a tree when we were timbering," C.L. chuckled. "I was just asking if you could supervise the work."

"Hell, man, you furnish the money and material, and I know a bunch of tough Swede-Finns who can sink a shaft to China!" John answered with the pride of race in his voice. He thrust out a firm hand, and C.L. grasped it. "You've got yourself a partner."

As John released the man's firm grip, he turned away to conceal emotions leaving him weak-kneed. The realization of his hopes; help far greater than his own conservative speculations, left him spent and shaking as he found his way back down from the hills. When they reached a bluff directly over the draw where the surrey rested, and after seating himself, C.L. uncorked the flask once again.

"If there is anything I like better than a drink, occasionally, it is to drink with one whom I like and admire. Here, John," he said, thrusting the flask toward his consort who surveyed it with a wry smile, "as you Finns and Swedes say, 'Skoal!'"

"To the mine!" John cried joyfully.

Chapter 29

In Mr. Beck's study and office, John discussed the contemplated project with his host who explained exactly what he had in mind. After two hours of discussion, C.L. told John, "Of course, you understand, John, before we sign any papers, that if we strike pay-dirt, all expenses incurred for the development must be refunded to me as fast as is practicable, outside of your own salary. That you will earn for instigating the project, and in a small way, for years of thankless work. I believe that it would be best for you to move out there and oversee the project from the beginning. I am going to send someone to run a survey for a road to the site of the shaft. We won't attempt to follow that streak down because it will be on an incline, and we'd have to keep after it, no matter where it goes; we'll have a good shaft with vertical walls, and in good ground the engineers will see to that."

"That's a good idea, C.L.; your shaft ran into ore and made operation of the mine more costly, did it not?"

"True, just bad luck on my part." He said with a wave of a hand.

"Then let's have some of that bad luck on our place," John said prayerfully.

C.L. smiled and went on, "I'll get in touch with the boss-carpenter at the Little Chief and have him rush construction of the gallows-frame and the necessary surface structures, including a boarding house for the men, and a house for you and your family; I think…"

"You mean a house other than the one there?"

"Certainly, man; you can't expect your wife to live in a rat's nest, can you? We'll put the house on a hillside overlooking the whole shebang. Oh, by the way, there is the matter of water."

"We can pipe it in from Hannifer Springs," John assured him, "and erect a couple of tanks on top of the hill overlooking the mine shaft and house!"

"You see to that, John. Tell the engineers what you want, and they'll lay the proposed route out. Let's get the line at least three feet underground to eliminate danger of freezing. The weather won't last like it is forever."

"That's right," John agreed; "but it lasted long enough to break me."

"And how about teamsters and teams for the road, ditch and hauling of supplies?" C.L. asked. "Will that be a problem?"

"Not at all; those fellows who are being forced to abandon their homes in Garden City will be willing to do the work, and then continue with the shaft under some sort of bonus setup."

By the time the afternoon had spent itself, the pair had clarified details and planned what had to be done to get the work underway, and he took leave of C.L., secure in the knowledge that the surveyors were already staking additional claims.

With heart overflowing, John burst in on Engrid and grabbed her to dance jubilantly about the room.

"I've done it, I've done it!" he exclaimed through tears of happiness as he squeezed her in a bear-like hug. Then he went on to explain in detail how the mine owner had more than accepted his proposal. "I am the superintendent at a salary, and we're going to have a brand-new home built to live in, right on the job!"

"Don't bellow so," she protested, "the whole town will hear you."

"I want them to hear me," he crowed grasping her and kissing her forcibly.

"Let me have supper, ma; I'm going to ride down to the lake and see those heart-broken farmers. There'll be a job for every man, and also their teams. Hell, I'm so happy that I could sing; I will sing!" Out of his throat came one prolonged roar of elation as he paced up and down the floor, clapping his hands together. He was man triumphant again, and filled with an underlying faith in the goodness and rightness of his existence!

John's welcoming news burst in on the dying community with the excitement attendant on finding of ore. There was a hiatus in the pall of hopelessness and lethargy into which the inhabitants of Garden City had quickly fallen. He drove into Erick Peterson's yard and dispatched the man to inform settlers to meet at Erick's' house; while he rested from the cross-country ride and drank coffee.

When the throng of despairing men had all gathered expectantly around, John informed them that there was work for every last son and their teams.

"It's not hot as hell, there; so you can suit yourselves as to what you're going to do in regards to your women folks and children. I believe that most of you can sleep in tents until we get the boardinghouse erected, if you will leave your families here. How many of you want to work?" He counted hands, and satisfied that all were agreeable, he went on, "I'll expect to see you in Tintic no later than day after tomorrow."

With the exultant shouts of his late neighbors ringing in his ears, John rode into the night at a slow pace, and long before reaching home, he was asleep in the saddle while the horse chose its own route to the stable.

Emil jubilantly agreed to accept the job as foreman for the undertaking when the actual sinking would get underway.

The road was finished and a house and boarding house were built. Engrid moved into a six room structure after a pipeline was run from a spring two miles up-country and two wooden tanks erected to hold surplus water. A changing room for the men was constructed, and a gang of men under the boss-carpenter's supervision erected a head-frame of huge timbers with the aid of several teams of horses, blocks and tackle. When these timbers were set in cement with their bases deep in the ground, braces were run to hold them stead and to compensate for the pull of the cables which would hoist the buckets with their loads of debris.

Finally came the day when the miners began drilling into the solid rock of the hillside. As the noise of the hammers burst on the air, Engrid stood by her husband and watched a man who rested his weight on the bucking machine drilling the first hole in the solid rock.

Turning away, she gazed at the flats below where already tents were being folded away in favor of frame houses which an enterprising contractor had built, knowing that if ore was found, house rent would pay for the houses, time and again.

Where sage and cedar had stood, stores, a livery stable, a church and a dance hall had been thrown together on each side of the road leading to Tintic. Interspersed with these places, were several saloons.

Over the road winding through the sage and cedars hung a haze of dust, heavier where team after team pulled huge burdened wagons of supplies along this same road which Engrid had traveled with her future husband when the mine was but a dream nurtured in the heart of her youthful admirer.

From below at night came sounds of revelry; the music of pianos, sounding tinny in the distance. There the town paused, as if holding its breath while waiting for the word that ore had been struck. All of the ground surrounding the mine for a distance of several miles had been filed on and the claim owners, devoid of cash as John had been, waited expectantly for developments.

Every hundred feet that the shaft was sunk, a station was hollowed out and drifts run to explore the ground adjacent to the shaft.

One night, shortly after the graveyard shift had disappeared into the shaft, and John had settled himself in troubled slumber, a pounding on the door startled him; and wondering if some hapless miner had been caved in on, or had picked into a missed hole of which there had been many, John lighted a lamp then strode to the door. Admitted the shift boss, Erick Peterson, who was in a profound agitation so at variance to his usual calm cried, "We've found it, John!"

John was forced to back away lest the lamp be swept from his grasp by the agitated man. He forced himself to remain calm as he placed the lamp on the front room table.

"Where is it?"

"Here!" Eric deployed a sample sack and fumbled at the string tied about its top.

"I mean; what level?"

"In the west drift on the eight-hundred foot level; come and look at it, man, where shall I dump this sack?"

"On the table."

John grasped a handful of rock. He sniffed at it and weighed each piece in the palm of a calloused hand. He went into the bedroom where Engrid lay wide-eyed and expectant. "Is someone hurt?" she asked with a troubled look toward the closed door.

"We've got ore on the eight-hundred in the west drift," he assured her with a smile, as he pulled on his flannel shirt and laced his boots.

"No!"

"Yes."

"Where are you going, John?"

"Down to inspect the strike", he replied.

Lying there, Engrid looked at her man who kissed her and started for the door. As he stepped across the threshold, she rose and placed the coffee pot on the stove, as she was in the habit of doing whenever her husband was called from the house at night.

Other calls had spelled trouble; once a bucket had gone too low in the shaft, breaking the back of a man and John had aged visibly in a few short days until a doctor in Salt Lake had assured him that with proper care, the man would be well again. Right now the man had a job of running the hoist while someone else had taken his place in the bottom of the shaft. Another time it had been a cave-in when three men had been trapped on the bottom, and John had worked side-by-side with his men until the men had been removed; one with a broken leg and another with two broken ribs. They, too, had been given easier jobs about the mine. John took good care of his men.

Although this should cause her to feel different, Engrid paced the floor, glancing from the window toward the gallows-frame until the skip came to the surface and John again walked toward the house, his face pale in the cleared patches where the moon shone full through the gigantic cedars. He opened the door and sniffed with a grin of delight as he tore off his cap and threw it in a corner by the stove.

"Pour me a cup of coffee, mom. The ore is there, covering the whole end of the tunnel, and going up and down. After the men get the round cleaned up, the drift timbered in a place or two and the sinking-buckets replaced with a cage, I want you to come down with me and look at it. You aren't afraid, are you?" His heavy brows lifted perceptibly.

Engrid's face blanched as her hand went to her throat, and her voice sounded faint and shaken. "I am afraid," she gasped.

"Come now, little mother," he said jovially; "you promised me that sometime you would take a trip down the mine with me. Why not make it now, in your own mine to see your own fortune staring you in the face?"

Engrid fought down the horror she felt as she contemplated the descent into the gloomy depths of the shaft. What if the cable should break? What if a rock should fall and crush her? What if the shaft should cave in and she couldn't get out? Suppose that the hoisting engine should breakdown, and she couldn't get to the surface without climbing up hundreds of feet of ladder where it was slippery, odorous with the powder gas and dead air of the underground, where sunlight could never penetrate?

The following morning, before the men were to shoot lime, Engrid appeared with John at the hoist room where a cheerful Swede stood at the controls, and two perspiring firemen mopped at brows with dirty rags.

"Where are you hoisting from? The wife and I wish to go down and inspect the strike."

"No place ret now, Yohn," the engineer assured him after discharging a stream of snuff through an open window behind him. "Dar all cleaned oop and vaiting to spit their rounds. We have a half-hour yet to go."

"Drop us to the eight-hundred, and take it kind of easy because it's the wife's first trip."

"She'll float like a feather," the engineer said reassuringly as Engrid left the room and walked with her husband to the cage. The top-man nonchalantly closed the doors in her face and asked, "Ready?"

John nodded his head, and before Engrid could no more than blink her eyes once, the cage dropped and Engrid grasped John's massive arm tightly. He chucked and assured her that everything was going to be alright.

Engrid's feelings at the beginning of the descent were comparable to those experienced repeatedly in her dreams when she had found herself falling off a high cliff. A sinking and tugging at her stomach, of part pain and pleasure, gripped her momentarily. Quickly this disappeared as she found herself dropping through a void. Daring a look upward, she beheld a tiny pinpoint of light shining through the protective bonnet of sheet steel which came together leaving only room for the cable fastened to the cage by several clamps. Fear left and excitement replaced it as the cage drew to a shuddering halt. At the floor of the level, a cage-rider waited for them with lighted candle. John procured two from his coat pocket and broke the points off, exposing a half-inch wick. He touched these to the station-tenders candle and handing one to his wife he cautioned her to take care lest the grease drip onto her coat.

Engrid following after her man and gazing apprehensively at black surroundings, shivered at the damp, cold air. Soon she discerned candle lights ahead, bobbing about. As she drew closer she made out six separate flames held by as many begrimed men to whom she gave a cheerful, "Hello!"

"There she is, Engrid, wide as the drift, and the devil alone knows how deep or how far ahead, by the looks of her. She's going to be as big as the Little Chief ever was!"

The men moved ahead, holding their candles aloft so that Engrid could gaze in awe on the solid body of ore showing. All the colors of a rainbow she could distinguish in the light from the candles. Shining steel galena winked brilliantly as her light moved about and she placed her hand on the smooth surface, gasping her admiration.

"We had better go on top so that they can have the cage," John commented after a time. At the station, the cage-rider pulled on a hanging wire. The cage dropped as if by magic and hung suspended a foot above the floor.

"Come on," John directed his wife as he stepped aboard and reached a hand to pull her up. "Give it hell!" he said buoyantly, and the man grinned as he tugged three times on the wire.

The guides slithered as man and wife rose swiftly through the stygian darkness, their candles extinguished lest one of them suffer a burn, and attempting to pull away from the flame, have their heads torn off by the timbered sides of the shaft.

John gleefully told Engrid of the life and wealth which would be theirs. However, Engrid listened to his excited account with but a small part of her being; her nerves, mind, spirit and body strained frantically toward the light and clean air in the hills far above. Right at this moment, the sun should be rising and the cool breeze of morning wafting up from the valley. Her head ached of powder fumes.

"We'll have the world at our feet!" John gloated.

"It's over my head," shrilled a disturbing voice inside of her.

"A trip to the old country to see your brother and friends."

"I'd give this mine and its wealth if I could only stand on the surface of this country", her spirit cried.

"A new city will spring from those shacks at the foot of the hill; and when it does, we'll get electricity," John crowed.

"Those shacks are above somewhere," the inner-woman cried despairingly, when the cage trembled violently, and water splashing in her face, caused her to gasp.

"We can have a stable of horses for the use of our guests, just as C.L. has. You can buy clothes that you've dreamed of buying. Your children can have a college education; and all of our past heartaches will be a troubled dream."

"This is the troubled dream," the frightened woman thought.

"Oh, sweetheart;" John went on giving her a squeeze, "are you listening?" He kissed her wet face as the cage safely and miraculously rose above the surface of the ground and the grinning top-man unhooked the door.

"I'm listening," she answered weakly, and stepping thankfully from the cage to the firm ground, she breathed deeply and turned her eyes to where a carpet of light was unrolling over the dark mountains. Her heart ceased its fluttering and she signed pensively, John placed an arm about her and squeezed her reassuringly. "But look, John," she exclaimed, "it's the sun!"

The End